S0-BVZ-478

*From springtime
to harvest,
true love takes
time to grow...*

❋ ❋ ❋

By the Light of the Moon

"Couldn't sleep?" Caleb asked low.

She nodded. "I suppose the fact that you're out here means you couldn't, either."

"Right. I, uh . . ." He looked off into the velvet sky and the vast expanse of darkness that was the prairie. "I don't often admit to a mistake. Sorry about rushing off like that earlier. I'm still trying to get used to—"

"The fact that I am who I am?"

Silence. Then, "It's a bit hard to swallow, that's all."

"Just like the fact that you hate my pa is hard for me to swallow."

Their eyes seemed to touch. Laura felt her breath quicken. He moved, took a step toward her. Every nerve in her body sparked. She stepped back, knowing what—who—the danger was now.

"The best thing for us to do, Mr. Main, is—I think—perhaps I should get a message to my fiancé," she managed breathlessly.

He cocked his head. "You didn't tell me you had a fiancé."

"There was never any need to."

"Until now."

"Until now," she said.

He grasped her arm as she stepped toward the door. His breath was hot on her hair as he pulled her back against him . . .

Prairie Dreams

Teresa Warfield

DIAMOND BOOKS, NEW YORK

This book is a Diamond original edition, and has never been previously published.

PRAIRIE DREAMS

A Diamond Book / published by arrangement with the author

PRINTING HISTORY
Diamond edition / October 1992

ISBN: 1-55773-798-3

Diamond Books are published by The Berkley Publishing Group, 200 Madison Avenue, New York, New York 10016. The name "DIAMOND" and its logo are trademarks belonging to Charter Communications, Inc.

PRINTED IN THE UNITED STATES OF AMERICA

10 9 8 7 6 5 4 3 2 1

For Missy, for saying, "I'm going to win that spelling bee today, Mom," and winning. By bringing home that medal, Miss, you showed me that with determination and faith anything can happen.

And especially for Tanya, my Amanda. There is love in the world, Babe.

Acknowledgment

A very special thanks to Mr. Harvey Teets of the Minot Historical Society, for listening to the woman who called one
day and said she wanted to set a book around Minot, North
Dakota. Mr. Teets took time to read to me from various
books in the Minot Historical Society collection and to de-
scribe Plum Valley. Without his assistance, I could not have
drawn the setting for this book.

✼ ✼ ✼
Prologue

Bismarck, Dakota Territory
Spring 1887

FINGERING THE LOCKET dangling from her neck, Laura
Kent reined the gelding before her father's small clapboard
office, separated from the elegant main house by a long dirt
path. Four steps led to the small porch and the door Laura
expected to swing wide any second. She trembled with excitement. Soon Pa would greet her with a wide smile and
merry blue eyes. She just knew.

No.

She shut her eyes and forced herself to recall Adrian's
words. *"He's dead, Laura. He's been dead for four months.
It's time you went on with your life."*

Adrian was right, but her grief was still raw, sometimes
swelling painfully in her chest. God, how she missed Pa.
She'd thought he was immortal, that any man exuding the
love and warmth he did couldn't die.

But he was dead, she kept telling herself. Stricken down
by a massive heart attack, the doctor had said.

That seemed impossible. He had been the healthiest person she had ever known, sometimes riding hundreds of miles
during cattle drives. He'd had a hand in huge land specula-
tions, too, and had often ridden out to inspect the crops on
his various farms. Just hours before she had found him dead
in the office, he had been laughing and joking with her.

She opened her eyes and stared at the door, a door she
hadn't braved since Pa's death. Lately she had forced herself
to get this close. Somehow she must convince herself that he
would never again walk through that door, that she would

never again open it and find him smiling at her from behind his huge desk. She would never again sit on one corner of the desk and laugh and joke with him. She would never again embrace him.

Tears slipped from her eyes. Grief choked her. "I miss you, Pa," she whispered. "If I could only talk to you again. I want to—"

The door creaked open.

Laura gasped. Pa. No . . . she was dreaming . . . had to be . . . he was dead . . . had been in the ground for four excruciating months.

Adrian Montgomery stepped into the doorway. A thin beam of morning sunlight enhanced the gold in his curly blond hair. His clothes were elegant—tan trousers, a white silk shirt with billowing sleeves, and a waistcoat trimmed in gold thread. A gold watch chain dangled from one pocket. He raised a brow in surprise. "Laura. Good morning."

"W-what are you doing here?" she managed, struggling to catch her breath.

"Going through records, as you asked me to do."

"Thank you. I couldn't seem to get to it." Her heart still pounded painfully. How foolish of her to think, even for a split second, that the person coming through the door could have been Pa! When would she stop wanting him to appear at her side? When would the terrible hurt end?

Adrian inclined his head, his eyes assessing her. She had never been one to cry in front of people. She had Pa's pride. She wiped away the wetness and drew deep breaths to compose herself.

"Want to come inside?" Adrian asked.

"No."

A cool breeze touched Laura's face and rustled the leaves of the huge elm Pa had loved so. Its branches overhung one edge of the office roof, its huge trunk flared near the bottom. How many afternoons had she shared a picnic with her father beneath those branches and near that huge trunk? *Many.* Laura battled more tears.

"Come inside, Laura," Adrian urged. "It's quiet and cool. I had breakfast brought from the kitchen."

Laura shifted in the saddle. "I'm not ready to go inside his office, Adrian. I don't know if I ever will be."

He studied her for a time. How could she possibly expect him to understand the pain she felt just looking at the office door and the elm? She'd feel worse if she ventured inside. All the memories of finding him that horrible morning would rise up and swallow her. She couldn't go inside. She just couldn't. Adrian had known Pa all of his life, but no one had shared the times and the love with Pa that she had.

"Laura."

She forced a smile. "I'll be all right. Don't worry about me."

"I do worry, you know. I just never know what to say."

"There is nothing to say. Nothing that will help."

"I love you."

Laura looked down at her gloved hands clutching the reins. He loved her. She loved him, too, she supposed, though she couldn't remember the last time she had told him that. Something always held her back, something she didn't understand. They had known each other virtually their entire lives. Their fathers had both started as land speculators, then raised cattle years later. She had always assumed she would marry Adrian, and so had everyone they knew. The announcement of their engagement six months ago, after her return from an eastern school, had certainly surprised no one.

Grief, she told herself. Perhaps that's what kept her from feeling the familiar girlish thrill when Adrian took her in his arms. Grief was doing strange things to her. She was changing inside. She had no control over that, but her feelings for Adrian had changed shortly after her return from the school, not necessarily after Pa's death, hadn't they? Adrian had insisted on a rushed engagement, and when she objected, he had been angry. The rumors that Adrian's insurance firm was having financial difficulty had reached her ears. She had hated suspecting he wanted to hurry things because she was the daughter of a rich man and he needed funds. But that was exactly what his behavior suggested.

"I love you, Laura," he repeated, as if expecting her to respond in kind. He seemed so sincere when he said the words, and she felt a twinge of guilt for suspecting him of wanting to marry her so he could save his business. Perhaps he did need money, but his declarations of love seemed genuine.

She glanced up. "I know. You'll have to excuse the way I've been acting. I'm caught up in something I don't understand. I never expected Pa to die."

"I am willing to wait."

His warmth touched her. She gave him a weak smile. "I had planned to see you about something this afternoon," she said, knowing he would not like what she was about to tell him. "I received a letter from Aunt Rebecca in Kenmare. That's up north, near Canada."

Alarm flickered in his eyes. "I know where it is. Laura, you're not thinking of—"

"She invited me to spend the summer with her."

"The summer, Laura! Months," he said, spinning away. He spun back just as quickly, anger twisting his boyish features. "What do you hope to find there? You have everything here. Your father was a rich man. You don't need to go anywhere. Get the notion out of your head. I've been more patient than most men. But this . . ."

"It will be good for me," she said hurriedly, not meaning to give him an opportunity to talk her out of it. "I need to go away. You can't imagine the pain I go through just walking into Pa's favorite rooms, just looking at his things. Coming here, seeing the office ... that tree."

Adrian swore softly and gripped the doorframe. "Stay and marry me soon, Laura. I want you to be my wife."

She tensed, twisting the reins around her hand. "Why must it always be what *you* want, Adrian? You insisted on becoming engaged as soon as I returned from school. Now you're demanding that I marry you soon. That is not what *I* want, Adrian. Not this time. Not yet. Try to understand."

He stared at her. "All I understand is that I've waited years to marry you. Years! Now I feel like I'm losing you. If you go, you might not come back."

"That's a crazy notion," she said, giving a sharp laugh of

disbelief. "I will be back. This is my home. Nothing could keep me away."

Adrian stared at her for a moment longer. Then, without another word, he turned and disappeared into the office, closing the door behind him.

❋ ❋ ❋
Chapter One

STORMS HAD dumped rain on northern Dakota Territory. The soil was muddy, the prairie grass vivid green. Twice the coach bearing Laura and her traveling companions—Mr. and Mrs. Trumball—had become stuck. Each time Laura and Mrs. Trumball had to climb out and wait while Mr. Trumball and the driver used wooden beams under the back wheels to push the coach out of thick mud.

Now Mr. Trumball sat beside his wife on the seat opposite Laura, looking as haggard as a man could possibly look. His green eyes, normally so alight, were dull. His hair, neatly combed when they began the journey hours ago, was in disarray. His hands gripped his knees until his knuckles turned white.

"I refuse to climb out and wait in the mud anymore," Mrs. Trumball said, tapping one foot impatiently. A huge woman with cheeks stained the color of ripe cherries, she had been whining and complaining for the last hour. She busied herself arranging her fashionable skirt around her, then leveled a sharp look at Laura. "Don't you agree, Miss Kent, that it will be a long ride if we must keep enduring this nonsense?"

You could have taken the stage, Laura nearly snapped. "Oh, quite," she said instead, forcing a light tone she didn't feel. The woman was grating her nerves raw.

She could have taken the stage, too, and avoided Amelia Trumball. But she had not wanted to ride in a coach filled with talkative traveling companions. Sometimes, as soon as people heard her name and realized she was Matthew Kent's daughter, they had too many questions and wanted to talk as if they had known her her entire life. Weeks ago Laura mentioned to Mr. Trumball, who had been her father's attorney, that she was going to Kenmare to visit her aunt. He'd said he and Mrs. Trumball would be embarking for Kenmare soon, too, and she was welcome to the extra space in their private coach. Laura had snatched the opportunity. Now she regretted her hasty decision.

A year had passed since Mr. Trumball had married Amelia in New York and brought her to Dakota, but Laura still didn't care for the woman. Even the most annoying person usually grew on her after a time. Not Mrs. Trumball. Her endless gossip and various ailments always whittled at Laura's nerves. Despite all that, she'd never thought the woman was this bad.

My mistake, she thought grimly, watching Mrs. Trumball inspect the hem of her mud-splashed skirt. Mrs. Trumball gasped at the sight, and Laura fought a twinge of pity for the senseless woman. Everyone knew a coach journey was anything but comfortable. Why had the woman dressed in a gown of lavender silk and worn a hat decorated with delicate feathers? And to complain about having to wait in the mud! Mr. Trumball and the driver had made certain she and Mrs. Trumball were well removed from the possibility of flying mud each time they'd had to free the coach wheels! Mrs. Trumball should be delighted the men hadn't requested her assistance. She was certainly large enough to pack a lot of weight behind just one of those levers, Laura thought, feeling a twitch of wicked amusement.

"What have you found to smile about?" Mrs. Trumball demanded of her.

"The thought of going to sleep for a time," Laura lied.

Thick silence. A scowl. "I don't know how you dare to smile or think of going to sleep at a time like this!"

"It seems the perfect time to me," Laura replied sweetly. "What else is there to do?"

The coach lumbered along. Mr. Trumball shifted uncomfortably on the seat. Laura watched him level a heated gaze on his beloved wife as Mrs. Trumball fluttered a silk handkerchief in front of her face and whined something about the dreadful heat and how she should have stayed in Bismarck. No doubt Mr. Trumball was thinking she should have stayed behind, too, so he might peacefully conduct his business in Kenmare. He sighed deeply and said, "Dear, I thought the time away together would be—"

"Oh, you!" Mrs. Trumball spat. "Time away! I wish I'd never left New York! Where were my senses? It's so dreadfully hot in this godforsaken land. If it's not hot, it's cold or windy or—or something. Grasshoppers or hail. Sometimes there's rain, sometimes there's only dust! Dreadful, I tell you."

Mr. Trumball lifted a folded newspaper to fan her. She batted it from his hand. His eyes widening in shock, he sat back on the seat. He cast a glance at Laura, offering a silent apology for his wife's behavior. But there was more in his green eyes. There was anger. The man had nearly had his fill of his spoiled wife. Laura gave him a look she hoped revealed the fact that she'd lost patience with Mrs. Trumball an hour ago. She had said nothing that might shut Mrs. Trumball up because she'd been invited along, after all. Besides, she had not wanted to offend Mr. Trumball. But there was little danger of that now. And he obviously couldn't do the task himself. He might be relieved if she did.

"And you!" Mrs. Trumball said to Laura. "How can you sit there during all this bouncing and bumping, looking so—so—fresh?"

Laura's last taut nerve snapped. If she and Mr. Trumball were going to have to spend two entire days in the confines of a coach with this woman . . . well, things would have to be different. "The bouncing and bumping doesn't disturb me nearly as much as your incessant complaining, Mrs. Trumball."

Gasping, Mrs. Trumball put a hand to her throat. "Don't you dare speak to me that way, young woman. Harold, tell her!"

Mr. Trumball narrowed his eyes at his wife. "Amelia, either you shut your mouth, or I gag you with that handkerchief you're waving around. Miss Kent is quite right. *You* are the disturbance."

Laura fought laughter. Apparently Mr. Trumball had just

needed an ally. Mrs. Trumball stared at him in utter shock for a moment, then shrank back in the seat.

For the next five miles or so, she didn't say a word.

Peace at last. Laura gazed out the window at the brush prairie unrolling like a huge brown and green carpet. White cumulus clouds filled the sky. Up ahead she saw hills, their graceful curves outlined in the late afternoon sun.

"Should be a smoother ride from here," Mr. Trumball said, trying to make conversation. "Hasn't been much rain in these parts. Amazing how one area of Dakota's so different from the next."

"It's beautiful," Laura agreed. "Aunt Rebecca says there are mountains near Kenmare."

"Northeast of Kenmare. Turtle Mountains, she probably means. And Canada beyond that."

Smiling, Laura closed her eyes and gave in to the sleepiness that had plagued her for the last hour. Turtle Mountains, Canada . . . Aunt Rebecca. Surely she would not have time to dwell on the loss of Pa once she reached Kenmare. Just thinking of him now brought pain to her chest. She tried to turn her thoughts to the last time she had seen Aunt Rebecca, her mother's sister. Laura had been sixteen. She was nineteen now. Three years. Of course, they had corresponded during that time and remained close through words.

Suddenly the coach wheels ground over something. The conveyance jolted to a stop. Laura pitched forward. Only Mr. Trumball's restraining hand prevented her from landing in his lap or tumbling to the floor.

"Not again," Mrs. Trumball whined. Mr. Trumball glared at her. She clamped her mouth shut.

"I'll go see what's happened," he said, flinging the door open.

Laura climbed out behind him, more to escape Mrs. Trumball for a time than to satisfy her curiosity. They weren't stuck again, she was sure of that.

"Damaged wheel," said the driver, his clothes caked with dried mud. "Rocks fall from the hills in weathered places, you know." He jumped from the seat, wiped his sweat-beaded brow, and bent to inspect one of the front wheels.

Mr. Trumball hunched beside the man. "Doesn't look too bad. Just a small crack."

"I don't like traveling on something like that, no matter how small the crack is. Now, it's a lot farther to Kenmare than back to Bismarck—"

"Damn Bismarck!" Mr. Trumball blurted. "It's only a crack. I have a schedule to keep, people waiting in Kenmare. We'll stop somewhere along the way and have it repaired."

The driver wiped his brow again. "You're not paying me to risk my life, Mr. Trumball. Have to turn back."

"No. Minot's some distance up ahead. A little off our course, but we'll waste less time stopping there to have it repaired than we would going all the way back to Bismarck."

"Why are you in such an all-fire rush anyway?"

Mr. Trumball huffed up his stout chest. "You work for me, Mr. Ames. I'll double your pay if you take this thing on to Minot. If I don't get to Kenmare soon, I'll lose out on a business proposition I've worked months to acquire."

"Double my pay, eh?"

Mr. Trumball nodded. Greed lit the driver's eyes. Laura watched him slowly run his tongue across his lower lip and knew he would continue the journey, no matter how long he took to consider the offer. She walked back to the coach door, lifted the hem of her dark blue skirt, and climbed inside.

"Well, what is holding things up now?" Mrs. Trumball demanded.

"Minor damage to one of the wheels. But we are going on. We'll have it repaired when we reach Minot."

"Damaged wheel? That's horrible. We cannot possibly go on. What if we get stranded out here? Indians, you know or—or thieves! We'll be easy prey."

"The Indians live on reservations now, Mrs. Trumball. Nothing will happen. Stop fretting."

"Oh, merciful heavens! This is not going well. No, not at all," Mrs. Trumball said.

Sighing, Laura closed her eyes.

Soon Mr. Trumball climbed back inside and settled himself; then the coach started off again. Laura finally succeeded in drifting off to sleep.

Shouts from the driver woke her. The coach lurched, then tipped precariously. Horses screeched, Mr. Trumball cursed, and Mrs. Trumball gasped a prayer.

Laura grappled for the strap above her head and glanced out her window just as the coach tumbled over and began rolling down a hill.

Caleb Main jerked the reins tight, bringing his horse to an abrupt stop. The animal whinnied, and Caleb soothed him by leaning over and stroking his sleek black neck. "Quiet, Soldier. I heard something. Might be that bear we've been tracking." His dog, Sam, barked excitedly. Caleb ordered him to be quiet, too. Then the sounds came again.

Crash. Crash. Crash!

Caleb's blood ran cold. Had a wagon taken a plunge down the side of one of those hills? A pretty bad plunge, if he judged right. And he reckoned he did. He'd spent years in Dakota Territory before finally settling on a wheat farm near the Souris River. Hell, he'd hunted nearly every inch of land between here and Canada and always relied on his instincts. He'd damn sure rely on them now.

He scanned the land, a mixture of prairie and hills. The sounds had come from the east, in the hills. He snapped the reins in that direction. "Let's go see what it's about, Soldier."

The faithful horse obeyed, trotting off. Sam followed. Caleb knew that if a wagon had taken a plunge, it was at the bottom of one of those hills by now. The sun was a huge reddish-orange ball against a clear blue sky, but that ball would melt soon in a fiery Dakota sunset as dusk claimed the land. When darkness settled in, finding anything out here would be impossible. He had to work fast.

Guiding Soldier through the many hills, Caleb looked for evidence of an accident. Sam ran off, probably on the scent of an animal. In some places the land was smooth and rolling. In other places pebbles and rocks coated the ground, and huge boulders sprang up. When Sam's barks echoed, sharp and crisp, from up ahead, Caleb knew the dog had found something. And he didn't think it was just a rabbit or a prairie dog. He kicked Soldier into a trot.

Sam stood at the top of a hill, his body stiff. He barked at Caleb, then at the bottom of the hill. Caleb slid off Soldier's back, whistling low at what he saw.

Lying at the bottom of the small, boulder-ridden hill was a coach, splintered and broken. No human could have survived. Three horses lay dead. Another struggled, whinnying softly, its eyes darting.

"Damn," Caleb swore softly, yanking his rifle from Soldier's saddle. He had to put the animal out of its misery. Sliding down from his horse, he let the reins dangle.

Through rocks and loose pebbles he descended, Sam at his side, Soldier waiting at the top of the hill. When he was a distance of a few feet from the struggling horse, he lifted his rifle, aimed, and fired. His gut churned as he watched the horse go limp. But he'd had two choices: shoot the animal or let it suffer a slow death. He knew he'd done the right thing.

He glanced to the coach wreck, not expecting to find a sign of life. The driver lay some distance away, his body twisted and mangled. Another man lay lifeless near the bottom of the hill, the side of his head stained with blood.

Figuring there was nothing more he could do but resume his hunt for the grizzly, then go tell the Minot sheriff about the coach wreck, Caleb started to climb the hill. Then, from the side of his eye, he spotted the movement of a delicate hand extending from beneath a piece of jagged wreckage.

Whoever was under there was still alive.

He marched over and tossed away pieces of wood, uncovering the body of a woman. She was clad in a dark, tattered traveling outfit. Caleb's attention shifted to her face, and he whistled low.

She was a beauty. Golden hair fell loose, but the pins were still there, tangled in the silken mass. Long feathery lashes splayed against her cheeks. Her skin was as white as the snow that coated these hills during winter, except where a long red slash cut across her forehead and smaller slashes marked her face. She'd taken a hell of a beating.

He lifted her. She was light in his arms and more shapely

than any woman he'd ever held. He fought to ignore that as he carried her a short distance away and placed her near several boulders, cradling her head and lowering it onto the grass. Her breathing was regular, he noticed, and that relieved him. She'd live, but he sure wouldn't travel with her till she improved. Damn grizzly got lucky, he thought grimly. Tracking the beast after a few days of sitting here would be impossible.

He went back to the wreckage to see if anyone else had lived through the plunge. He found one other woman, a big woman, but her skin was already cold with death.

Caleb gave a sharp whistle, and Soldier took the rocky hill carefully, meeting Caleb and Sam at the bottom. Caleb reached into a saddlebag and pulled out a bundle of biscuits wrapped in a checkered cloth. He unwrapped the biscuits, dropped them in the pack, and held on to the cloth. Grabbing the canteen, he headed over to the woman.

He wet one corner of the cloth and used it to wipe away the blood on her forehead. The gash was deep. She'd be left with a scar, but she could arrange her hair some way to cover it. Next he examined her to see if any bones had been broken. He didn't think any had. Then he unfastened a few jacket buttons near her waist, unrolled the blanket from the saddle to make a pallet, and placed her on it.

While he fussed over her, washing her many cuts, Sam wandered off. Caleb set the cloth and canteen aside and searched the area for twigs and branches so he could start a fire when the coolness of night stretched over the land. Already the sky was turning bloodred, casting a fiery haze on the land.

Some time later, when sunset began to fade, Sam returned, clutching a rabbit between his teeth and wagging his tail. Chuckling, Caleb rubbed his coarse beard, then took flint and steel from a saddlebag. "Now, why do I need a rifle to hunt when I have you, Sam?"

Sam dropped the rabbit at Caleb's feet, barked once, and trotted away to lay on the ground beside the woman. Caleb produced a spark from the flint and steel and put it to the twigs and branches.

Then he slid a knife from its leather sheath at his waist and set to work on the rabbit.

Pain ravaged Laura until she felt certain her head would burst. She cried out and tried to escape, but a gentle hand pushed her back down. She smelled leather, tobacco, and the muskiness of perspiration. Something wet touched her brow, something cool, then soft words were whispered near her ear by a deep rumbling voice.

"Sleep now, pretty one. You're safe."

"Cold," she whispered through dry lips, not having the strength to even open her eyes. A blanket was drawn up and tucked around her shoulders by big hands. More words were whispered.

She must be drifting on the edge of unconsciousness, drifting toward heaven. She remembered the accident, remembered screaming as she slammed against the walls of the coach. Yes, she must be approaching heaven, for she couldn't have lived through that ordeal. An angel was sheltering her, nursing her even now.

She slipped into blackness again.

Some time later she awoke and forced her eyes open a little this time. She was alive, she realized. There was a fire, the flames flickering and jumping, and a horse, she thought. A large shape was bent near the fire. It straightened and approached her. Laura saw that it was a man.

He was tall with thick limbs and a wide chest. His hair was as black as the velvet sky, and his eyes were also dark, with small flickering stars. His face was peppered with whiskers, and he wore a white shirt and dark homespun trousers. Laura wondered if this rugged man had emerged from some cave.

He lifted her head and pressed something cold to her dry lips. The mouth of a canteen. Not until she smelled the fresh scent of the water did she realize how thirsty she was. She took several gulps before he snatched the canteen away.

"Slow now. I made some broth. I'll get it," he said. "It'll give you strength."

She wanted to ask who he was, but she was too relieved to

be alive and too weary to press him for answers. Still, there was one question she must have answered now.

"The others?"

She watched his expression harden and didn't need to hear words. She knew.

"Sorry," he mumbled. "Hope none were kin to you."

"No. Mr. and Mrs. Trumball . . . friends."

He nodded at that, then moved away, slipping into the shadows.

Laura shut her eyes. So weary . . . so weak . . . as weak as a newborn pup. Sleep claimed her again.

After a time she awoke, shivering violently now, although the blanket still covered her.

Strong, warm hands lifted her head. A deep voice urged her to drink again, and this time she tasted a flavorful broth that warmed her throat and stomach momentarily. Still she trembled with cold.

Caleb had built the fire close to her and kept the flames going by piling more twigs and branches on now and then. He'd wrapped her in the blanket. Now he did the only other thing he knew would help her.

He pulled up one end of the blanket, climbed under, and drew her into his arms, hoping to warm her with his body. She stiffened and started to object, but Caleb put a finger to her lips. "Quiet now. Sleep."

Soon he felt her relax. Her breathing deepened. She snuggled close, her head on his shoulder, a hand on his chest. When he'd touched her face while bathing her wounds, he had discovered her skin was as soft as a babe's.

He closed his eyes and tried to sleep.

Seemed like only minutes till the sun stole up over the hills and roused him. When he moved from the blanket, the woman groaned. She was still asleep, though, and he was glad. She was a temptation of feminine curves. More than once he'd been awakened by her silky hair tickling his nose. He needed a few minutes to get himself together after spending the night with her so close.

He rolled up his sleeves and splashed water from the canteen on his hands and face. Sam sat nearby, panting and wagging his tail as if he couldn't wait to get started for the day.

"You're staying here," Caleb said. Sam whined. Caleb turned away, shrugging. "Someone's got to watch her. Don't let anything happen to her."

With that, he set off in search of breakfast.

Shortly after he left, Laura cracked one eye open. She was still weak, pain still ran circles inside her head, and every muscle and bone in her body still ached. There was a dull pain in her left ankle. She needed to have a look at it.

When she moved, trying to ease herself up, her head spun and sharpness raced up her leg. God, she hoped the ankle wasn't broken. She wouldn't like spending weeks here while she healed. She glanced around at the rocks, hills, and prairie grass in the distance and felt the cold hard ground beneath her. Right now just a simple room with a bed in it would do. Not a lot was needed to improve the living conditions here. She supposed she should be more grateful; she'd been more fortunate than Mr. and Mrs. Trumball.

Mrs. Trumball. She had whined and complained for hours. She had grated on Laura's nerves, and Laura had snapped at her. Remembering, Laura felt a touch of guilt. Now Mrs. Trumball lay dead not two hundred feet away. Laura shuddered and fought tears.

A dog whined. Laura spotted it lying nearby, its face resting on extended front paws while it gazed at her with pleading eyes. When she shifted, the dog shifted and growled low, those eyes never leaving her. Obviously it had been set to guard her. Why? Had she gone from near-death inside a plunging coach to being held hostage by a strange man?

She quickly discarded the notion when she recalled the gentle touches and words of the stranger who had nursed her. No . . . perhaps the dog had been put on duty to make sure she didn't hurt herself by trying to get up.

With considerable effort and pain she managed to sit up and plant her back against a boulder. She shut her eyes, fighting ripples of nausea.

No good. The sensation wouldn't go away. Gulping air, Laura eased back down. Only when she was lying again did the ripples cease. She was *worse* than a newborn pup! She couldn't even wriggle her way around without nearly blacking out.

The dog approached and stopped a few inches from her face, seeming to inspect her. Finally it wagged its tail, turned around, and resumed its original position.

Laura closed here eyes, knowing she would feel better if she did.

She didn't hear her rescuer return. When she opened her eyes and saw him hunched near the place where the fire had been, she gasped in surprise. She must have been asleep for a while.

He glanced at her over his shoulder, his wavy hair and intense eyes as black as midnight. He was sturdily built, as muscled beneath his clothing as any of the men who worked Pa's ranch, she guessed, perhaps more so. His skin was browned by the sun. He watched her watch him for a long, awkward moment.

"Morning," he said finally, unmoving.

She still didn't know what to think of him. He had been gentle and caring, yes, but she had spent the night in his arms—a stranger's arms—if she hadn't dreamed what she felt last night. The memory of his strong chest beneath her hand and the sound of his harsh breathing was too real in her mind, clouded though it was from the blow she'd suffered. She drew the blanket more securely around her and issued a soft "Good morning."

"Breakfast'll be ready in a bit. How do you feel?"

"Sore. I think my ankle might be broken."

"Let's see." He strode over to her, hunched, and carefully pushed up the hem of her skirt. His rough fingers touched her ankle and a shiver raced through her. Then he lifted his dark eyes, capturing her gaze.

Laura drew a swift breath in response to his gaze. "What do you think? Is it broken?"

"Twisted. Sprained. Won't take long to heal," he said, withdrawing his hand. He turned and went back to building a fire.

Laura was curious about him. So far he was merely her

mysterious rescuer. There must be more to him. "Do you live up here?" she couldn't restrain herself from asking. "In these hills, I mean."

He grunted a response, and Laura knew no more than she had before she had asked the question. She was determined to get him talking.

"What is your dog's name?"

"Sam."

She nodded. Pain stabbed her head and sent sharp slivers through her body. She caught her breath and saw the man twist around in concern. "I'm all right," she said breathlessly. "Or will be if I don't laugh or move. Every inch of me must be bruised."

"You're lucky, coming out of that mess as good as you did."

"That is precisely what I've been thinking. I'm amazed I came out of it at all," she said in disbelief. "I have you to thank for that."

An odd expression lurked in his eyes, suggesting he would enjoy crawling back under the blanket beside her and taking her in his arms. A ripple of fear shot through Laura. In reality, he could do whatever he wanted to do with her, and there was no one to stop him. She clutched the blanket a bit tighter.

His gaze slid to her hands, then back to her face. "Don't worry, I'm not a barbarian. I plan to help you, not hurt you," he said softly.

Laura looked down at her hands, decidedly uncomfortable with his open admiration, and suddenly ashamed that she had been thinking he might plan to ravish her. "Thank you for that assurance. Please understand . . . a woman does not often find herself stranded and at the mercy of a stranger."

He gave a nod of understanding, then busied himself with the pile of twigs and branches.

Moments passed. "So you live in these hills and have a dog named Sam," she said, again trying to make conversation.

"Never said I lived out here."

"Where do you live, then?"

"Near Minot, by the Souris River. Have a wheat farm."

"What are you doing here?"

He chuckled, finally coaxing flames to life. "You have a passel of questions for a lady who could hardly lift a finger just yesterday."

Laura smiled. "I suppose I do. You must have put something magical in that broth you fed me."

"Made it from rabbit, some leaves, and a few flowers. Nothing magical about it."

He took a pan from a saddlebag tossed across the horse's back and busied himself preparing breakfast. Within moments the smell of frying eggs made Laura's stomach growl. "Where did you find eggs out here?" she asked. He shot her a humorous look, his eyes glittering with amusement. She smiled. "I know, I know . . . another question. Well, if you would volunteer information, I would not need to ask so many questions, Mister . . ."

"Main," he supplied. "Caleb Main. Found the eggs in a nest."

"I see. A nest robber. That must be a crime."

She saw a smile twitch the corners of his full mouth. "Didn't stay long enough to ask permission."

Laura watched as he swirled the pan with a few wrist movements, then stood and brought it over to her, heat still rising from it. "I'll help you sit up to eat," he said.

"Oh, no. No, don't do that. I tried to sit up. It didn't work."

"Must be that place on your head. Got hit there once myself. Took a couple of days before the headache went away. Longer than that before I could walk around for long."

He offered her water from the canteen so she could wash her face and hands. Then he fed her the eggs. Laura marveled at the gentleness she sensed in him. His black hair hung in thick waves just beyond his shoulders, the dark shadow of a beard, and mustache, and his dark eyes added to his untamed look. Without his assurance that he was not a barbarian, she might still be frightened of him. He was a large man, must stand over six feet. The smells that clung to him were smells of the land—the sweetness of the eggs he had just fried, the smokiness of the fire he had bent over, a slight scent of horses and leather.

"We'll stay here for a few days till you gain some strength. After that I'll take you to the farm, where you can heal, and we can get a message to your family."

"*Your* farm?" she asked. She had to consider her reputation, after all. If anyone ever learned she'd spent so much time alone with him, there would be questions and unpleasant assumptions. If she slept within the walls of his house . . . well, if Adrian ever learned of it, he might not be very understanding—what fiancé would? She sincerely hoped no one would ever discover she had spent the night in Caleb Main's arms. The fact that she was the daughter of one of Dakota's wealthiest speculators would matter little.

"My mother and sister live with me," Caleb Main said, as if reading her mind again.

"Oh, I'm sorry. It's just that . . ." Laura wondered if her relief showed.

"No need to explain. Judging by your clothes, you're a lady. Wouldn't do for you to stay alone with me."

"No, it wouldn't. But I am quite alone with you now. That is"—she glanced to the ever watchful Sam—"if we only count people."

He chuckled, then mumbled something about washing the pan in a stream some distance away. Walking off to do it, he left Sam at her side again.

After a few moments of fighting to keep her eyes open, Laura surrendered to sleep.

When she awoke, Caleb Main was moving around, near the coach wreckage, she realized. He had tied his hair back with a strip of leather. She watched him easily lift and toss pieces of the wreckage aside. He stepped off to one side and grabbed hold of something. What Laura saw chilled her.

She had a direct view of Mr. Trumball's white face, his eyes still wide with fear.

She cried out, and Caleb Main twisted to look at her, following her gaze. Swallowing hard, she again fought nausea as she turned her head to the other side. Dear God. She had spent the last five months trying to cope with the fact that Pa was dead. Now here was death staring at her again. Dear Mr. Trumball. She had always liked him. And the others . . .

Presently Caleb Main wandered over and dropped something near her. "This yours?"

Laura opened her eyes and stared at her carpetbag. "Yes. Thank you."

"And this?" he asked, hunching down and dangling her open gold locket in front of her. One side bore a miniature of her, the other of Pa. It was her most treasured possession. Pa had given it to her just last year.

She cried out in happiness. "The chain must have broken. I never realized it was gone!"

"Matt Kent," Caleb Main said in a low voice. "Never thought I'd see that face again. Damn sure *hoped* I'd never see it again."

Laura's gaze flew to his face. She saw the torment in his dark eyes, the undisguised hatred, as he stared at the miniature of Pa in the locket. Why would anyone look at Pa that way? Why would anyone say such things about him?

Laura grabbed the locket and clutched it to her breast. "Matthew Kent is my father," she said, and for a long moment they stared angrily at each other.

Then Caleb Main cursed, stood, and walked away.

✳✳✳
Chapter Two

MATT KENT.

Damn it all to hell anyway. The last thing Caleb wanted was to be linked up with Matt Kent again.

But he was. He'd taken on the responsibility of Kent's injured daughter, and that alone would lead him to Kent or Kent to him sooner or later.

The day passed slowly. He wasn't prepared to talk much with Kent's daughter, pretty though she was. He made sure she had plenty to eat and drink. Later Sam brought another rabbit, and Caleb dipped water from the stream. He took beans from one of the saddlebags and boiled them over a low fire. He fed Kent's daughter first, giving her a few biscuits alongside beans and rabbit. Her eyes were on him some, but he wasn't about to look up and have her start asking questions.

Dusk settled over the hills. In the distance the mounds gave way to prairie grass that swayed in a sudden wind. That was the unpredictability of Dakota. As fast as that wind had kicked up, a storm could also kick up. Caleb gave Sam what was left of the beans and rabbit. Soldier fed on a patch of green grass. And Kent's daughter started talking as Caleb had feared she would eventually.

"Ever since you learned Matthew Kent is my father you haven't said a word to me," she said from the blanket.

"Matt Kent and me didn't get along well. I'd just as soon not talk about him." Caleb positioned his head on the saddle blanket he'd taken from Soldier and stared up at the slivered moon that had just become visible in the dark sky.

"So the time we must be together will be spent in silence?"

23

"Seems the best way."

She grew quiet again, as if considering that. Then, "I would be most appreciative if you would simply take me to Bismarck and—"

"You're injured, and Bismarck's nearly fifty miles away. My farm's closer."

"I *live* in Bismarck, Mr. Main," she argued. "You could at least—"

"I already told you I'm taking you to the farm. Decided a long time ago I'd never go near Bismarck and Matt Kent again."

Laura inhaled deeply, her patience with the man shortening. She thought about telling him he wouldn't run into Matthew Kent because Pa was dead. But Caleb Main's attitude infuriated her. For some reason he hated Pa, and she would not give him the satisfaction of knowing Pa was dead.

"Fine," she snapped. "Is there someone in this remote little farming area you live in who will at least deliver a message to Bismarck? I'll pay someone. I have money, plenty of money."

She thought she heard him draw a sharp breath. "I'm aware of that," he said. "My farm's close to Minot. For the right price, someone there'll take the message."

"Of course," she said dryly. "For the right price."

"You offered, lady. You can even telegraph yourself."

Laura watched him roll over and turn his back on her. His blatant way of letting her know the conversation was over, no doubt. "Telegraph. Why didn't you say right away that I could telegraph from Minot, Mr. Main?"

Silence.

"Since you hate my father so much, I'm terribly sorry to have imposed upon you like this. I'll be happy to pay you for the trouble you've gone to so far. I have—"

Cursing, Caleb Main shot up from the ground with one agile move and leveled a dark glare at her, his huge fists clenched at his sides. Laura flinched, wondering if he had gone mad and meant to attack her. Apparently she had pushed him beyond his limit.

"Don't offer me Kent money," he growled. "If one of the

others was alive and had a chance, I'd take care of him just like I've taken care of you. I didn't expect money when I found you and don't expect it now. Damn sure don't offer me Kent money!"

Laura stared at him. He stared back. "Kent money is as good or better than any," she finally found the sense to retort.

"No, it's not." He paced a patch of ground for a few minutes, then stopped short and sighed wearily. "Listen, I don't hate you for what your pa did. But I don't want anything to do with Matt Kent, Bismarck, or Kent money. I got rid of those problems a long time ago, woman."

"Matthew Kent was a wonderful man, Mr. Main. Bismarck is a pleasant city, and Kent money is . . . well, just money."

Caleb Main shook his head. "I don't see it that way."

He grabbed his rifle and stalked off. Laura listened to him settle himself some distance away, as if she might contaminate him because she was a Kent. Never in her life had anyone ever treated her this way. Most everyone had liked Pa. His only enemies had been those who resented his wealth and position in Dakota Territory, but she'd never had one of those people take his hatred for Pa out on her. Still . . . would mere resentment cause Caleb Main to hate Pa so? Laura didn't think so. Something far beyond resentment was swirling inside Caleb Main's head, something long forgotten and stirred to life again by the picture of Pa in the locket and the fact that she was Matthew Kent's daughter. Something Caleb Main didn't want to talk about.

She was curious. But on the other hand she wasn't sure she would believe his story, whatever it entailed. Pa had always been kind and gentle—a good man. And he wasn't here to defend himself against accusations Caleb Main might make.

No. Mr. Main was right. They shouldn't talk about it. If they did, they would argue. She would go with him to his farm near Minot and telegraph a message to Adrian. When Adrian came after her, she would return to Bismarck and forget Caleb Main and the hatred he had for Pa.

It would be as simple as that.

* * *

"You plan to leave them there?" Laura demanded from the bed of soft grass where she sat. She had finally managed to sit up without feeling dizzy or nauseous. She stared wide-eyed at the bodies scattered near the stage wreckage.

"For now."

She shifted her gaze to him, pleading silently. Poor Mr. Trumball, Mrs. Trumball . . . the driver.

"Ah, hell!" Caleb Main said, pacing. "What the hell do you expect me to do, woman? Build something to haul them on? We've got a day's travel ahead of us, it isn't getting cooler, and there are already flies around those bodies and buzzards overhead that'll follow. Coyotes and other animals will track the rotten scent, too. By tomorrow afternoon the smell will be—"

Fighting nausea at the thoughts he conjured, Laura covered her ears. "All right, all right! You've made your point, Mr. Main."

"Well, I hope so, Miss Kent. I do hope so, because I'm the one who knows how things are done out here. You're not in Bismarck, inside a fancy house where things can be done the way you think they ought to be done."

Laura pursed her lips, anger and a great sadness rising within her. Pa was dead . . . now these people were dead. "I am quite aware of that. It's just that . . . well, Mr. Trumball was so kind. Mrs. Trumball bothered me—a lot—but no one deserves to be left out here to be eaten by coyotes and buzzards," she said, tears stinging her eyes.

Memories of the horrible coach accident hit her with nearly unbearable force, and she buried her face in her hands and turned away, refusing to allow Caleb Main to watch her cry. Mrs. Trumball had been a nuisance. Still, she had been a living, breathing, *feeling* person. And Laura had always liked Mr. Trumball. She couldn't help but wonder if things would have turned out differently if she had taken the driver's side and urged Mr. Trumball to turn back toward Bismarck.

She sobbed softly, remembering how short she had been with Mrs. Trumball and how she had shared a smile or two with Mr. Trumball when they had first set out. Why did these horrible things happen? Why?

A big warm hand touched her shoulder. "Miss Kent."

"The wheel . . . Mr. Trumball told the driver to go on. He wanted . . . he wanted to turn back. Mr. Trumball said no. I said nothing. If we had turned back . . ."

"Don't blame yourself now," Caleb Main said gently. "Accidents happen all the time out here on the prairie and in the hills." He sat down next to her, hesitated a moment, then enfolded her in his huge arms.

Comforting arms. Ah, yes, she had needed to be enclosed in arms like this for months. She had needed to be held by someone. Simply held.

Laura rested her head against his strong chest. The warmth of his gesture snapped what little restraint she had on her tenuous emotions, and she cried unashamedly. She forgot that his manner toward her had turned cool after he'd discovered she was Matthew Kent's daughter. She forgot that he had made brutally plain what would happen to the bodies of Mr. and Mrs. Trumball and the driver. She forgot that he was still a stranger to her—she knew nothing about him. What she *did* know was that she needed to hear his heartbeat and draw strength from it.

She buried her face in his shirt, felt the corded muscles beneath, and inhaled his wild scent. She clung to him and released tension she had not been aware of harboring.

Caleb stroked her silken hair—strands more golden and lush than ripe wheat. Matt Kent's daughter she might be, but she was hurting, and he knew a need to comfort her. He'd never felt such a strong emotion. He took part of her pain—it seized his heart. And he knew that if there was a way, he'd haul those bodies with them. For her.

He silently cursed himself now for blurting those things about flies, buzzards, and coyotes; that had been cruel. She was more delicate than prairie women—mostly farmers' wives. She hadn't seen the things they'd seen. Yet from the minute he'd learned she was Kent's daughter, he'd spoken harshly to her. What had happened between himself and

Matt Kent had not involved the woman in his arms. Caleb felt deeply ashamed for the way he'd been treating her.

"I'm sorry," he murmured. That didn't seem to be enough. So he held her, sensing that was what she needed more than anything.

Presently her sobs died down, and she lifted her head to gaze up at him with eyes the color of a cloudless blue sky. Her thick lashes were wet feathers clumped together; her cheeks and lips were flushed. She was the most beautiful creature he'd ever seen.

As he stared down at her, Caleb grew aware of her soft yet firm breasts pressed against his hard chest. Her heart pounded with his. Her hands had wandered to his upper arms, and now they slid up and over his shoulders, her fingertips exploring the muscles beneath his shirt.

She reached up and touched his jaw, traced one side of it from his ear to his chin. Then she smiled, murmuring, "Caleb Main . . ." as if he were a mystery.

Caleb felt his breath quicken and his heart leap. If he didn't get away from her, he'd be kissing her in a minute. What the hell was she doing, touching him like that? He lowered his arms and scooted back, putting space between her and him. But he couldn't seem to take his eyes off her.

"Thank you for enduring my weakness," she said, wiping her face with her hands. She sniffed. "It won't happen again, I assure you. We were about to move out, you said. Let's go now before my ankle begins throbbing again."

Caleb nodded in silence.

Letting the front door snap shut behind her, Ruth Main put her hands on her wide hips and shook her head at the sight before her. A woman was propped in front of Caleb in the saddle, loose golden hair splayed about her shoulders. By the strained looks on their faces, the ride had been pleasant for neither.

"Well, that's sure no grizzly you're packing there, Caleb," Ruth said aloud to herself, although she meant to question him later. The way she asked him about things sometimes annoyed him, she knew, but she was nearing sixty and didn't intend to change her ways. When she had questions, she got answers. And right now a bushel of questions was overflowing in her head.

First the two of them had to be tended to, of course. They looked tired, were probably hungry, and could use baths. Ruth wiped her hands on her apron and walked down the porch steps to meet them.

"I was starting to worry, Caleb," she said as he slid down and reached for the woman. "It's been nearly a week since you left."

"Tracked that bear clear to the hills southeast of here," he said, lowering the woman. "Shot at it once and missed. Maybe it won't come back."

Ruth met the woman's apprehensive blue gaze and smiled reassuringly. "I'm Ruth, Caleb's mother. I'll get a bath together for you in no time at all. After that, there'll be stewed chicken and corn bread. I was just fixing to put it on."

The woman nodded and extended her hand. "Laura Kent."

A jolt went through Ruth, and she glanced at Caleb as she took the hand in greeting. Caleb's jaw was set. "Kent," Ruth repeated.

"Yes." The response was curt, as if Laura Kent and Caleb had already had a discussion about the name and what it meant to him.

"Well, I'll call you Laura if that's all right," Ruth said, putting an arm around the young woman's shoulders and drawing her toward the house.

Despite Ruth Main's outward warmth, Laura wondered if the woman disliked her, too, because she was a Kent. She had witnessed the uneasy look that had passed between Caleb and his mother. She couldn't wait to telegraph Adrian and go home.

The big farmhouse was built of logs. A long wooden porch ran along the front of the house. Ruth Main smelled faintly of bacon and some sort of strong soap. Laura spotted a big wooden tub and a scrub board to one side of the house where the gray-haired woman had obviously been doing laundry a short time ago. A line of clothes extended from one corner of the house to a large red barn. In between, hens and roosters clucked and scratched noisily at the ground. A cow mooed. Laura spotted it beyond the barn. Farther out black specks dotted the prairie. Probably cattle. And to the left was wheat, swaying like a green ocean. Laura caught her breath. The scene before her was magnificent.

"Good thing that grizzly started its trouble long after Caleb put the crop in," Ruth Main said as they entered the house. "Otherwise, Caleb couldn't have left. Wheat's the money crop in this part of Dakota. It's sure how Caleb makes his profit, though he'd like to raise more cattle. Can't see that, not with some of the winters we have out here. Cattle die of cold just like people. You just have a seat, Laura. I'll get some water heating for a bath."

The house smelled of wood, long ago cut and dried, and was full of plain carved furniture. The main room was large, and a narrow staircase to the right led upstairs. One corner contained a rocking chair, a small table piled with scraps of material, and a half-finished calico dress hanging from a hook. Several slat-back chairs and a long wooden settee, the seat lined with red cushions, stood before the large hearth.

A few rugs woven from rags decorated the floor, and tied-back checkered curtains adorned the windows. A basket filled with eggs sat on a large table. Small cabinets were situated along the walls. In the center of the room stood a large iron stove, its pipe stretching upward and disappearing through the roof, its top cluttered with iron pans and skillets.

The entire room exuded a feeling of warmth to Laura, who had been cold for so long, it seemed. But she refused to allow herself to be fooled. In truth, she wasn't welcome here—she was Matthew Kent's daughter, after all, and she would do well to remember that whenever she thought of making herself comfortable in the Main home.

She sat on the settee near the hearth. Pulling aside a brown curtain draped over a rope before an alcove, Ruth revealed a tub. She reached for a bucket that sat nearby. "Back in a minute," she assured Laura as she moved to the door.

Laura forced a smile. Ruth went outside.

When Ruth returned, she poured water from the bucket

into a huge pan on the stove and stirred heat from coals inside the stove. After a time the water boiled. Then she poured it in the tub and went for cool water to add to it.

Once the tub was prepared, Laura moved to the alcove and drew the curtain. She stripped off her tattered traveling dress and stepped into the coaxing water. There was little of it, but it soothed her bruised body. She closed her eyes, certain she had gone to heaven.

She heard Ruth busy herself in the big room beyond the curtain. By the time Laura had scrubbed her hair and body with the soap and cloth Ruth had left, the delectable smell of chicken stewed with carrots and onions filled the house.

"Caleb gave me your bag," Ruth called. "I put some of your things on the back of the chair by the tub."

Laura found fresh underthings. She hadn't packed many clothes, since she had thought to have a few gowns made once she reached Kenmare, so now she had to choose between a gown of blue silk or one of green satin decorated with flounces and embroidered roses. Both seemed inappropriate here. In the end she slid the blue silk over her head, took a silver-back brush from her carpetbag, and drew the curtain aside.

As soon as Ma took Kent's daughter to the house, Caleb led Soldier to the barn. There he dumped a bucket of oats in a feeding trough and began brushing dust from the horse. Sam had run off, but Caleb knew he'd be back by nightfall to sleep on the porch and guard the house.

So her name was Laura, Caleb thought as he ran the brush down Soldier's neck. He hadn't bothered to ask when he rescued her.

Laura.

A pretty name. It suited her, a young woman with golden hair and clear eyes. At least something good had come from Matt Kent—the man had fathered a daughter prettier than any female Caleb had ever laid eyes on.

Course, he hadn't known Laura Kent long enough to say if Kent had instilled his crooked nature and bad temper in her. He hoped he *wouldn't* know her long enough to find out.

Once she got a message to Kent, the man would probably show up here and whisk her away. That would be just as well for everyone concerned. Ma had a passel of questions— Caleb had seen them in her eyes when Laura had stated her name. Having a few bad feelings toward Matt Kent herself, Ma was probably wondering what the devil had led him to bring Laura Kent to their home.

"I don't see a bearskin anywhere."

The light female voice drew Caleb from his unpleasant thoughts and made him smile. "He got lucky."

"Or did he just outsmart you?"

"Stacey Ann, you know how to irritate me."

Stacey drew close to the stall, folded her arms on the top rail, and propped her chin on her hands. Her sleek black hair was pushed back and bound by a ribbon at her nape. From there it hung down her back. She was pretty, with dark eyes and fair skin. "I saw Sam and knew you were back, brother. He's out chasing the cattle."

"Already? Mutt. We'll find him stomped into the ground one day," Caleb said, moving the brush across Soldier's back.

"So what did you bring back? Anything?"

Caleb shook his head, hoping Stacey would keep her opinions to herself when she met Laura Kent. She knew all about the business with Kent, although she'd been pretty young when it had happened. She was too talkative sometimes, and things tended to spill out of her before she even realized what she was saying sometimes, too. Other times he knew she said exactly what was on her mind and didn't give a damn who objected or who she offended. "Something," he responded uncomfortably. "That's right. I brought back something."

Something I damn sure wasn't counting on. Set out to get a grizzly, brought back Matt Kent's daughter.

"Well, what? What did you bring?" she pressed.

"A woman."

Silence. Caleb brushed. Stacey stared. He felt the sharpness of her brown eyes. As much as he loved his sister, he was in no mood for her questions. "Look, Stacey, why don't you go off and—"

"A *woman*?" she blurted. "What do you mean—a woman?"

Irritation prickled the back of Caleb's neck. He turned and shook the brush at Stacey. "Exactly what I said. Now go off and leave me alone," he growled, turning back.

More silence. Presently Stacey asked, "A wife?"

"No, Stace. There was a coach accident in the hills. She was the only survivor. She lives in Bismarck—a long way away—so I brought her here until she gets better," he said wearily.

"Then you're going to take her to Bismarck?"

Caleb tensed. "I'll get someone else to take her. She'll be telegraphing her pa. Maybe he'll come after her."

"You're still scared of that man in Bismarck, aren't you?"

She meant Matt Kent. "I'm not scared of him, I just don't care to ever see him again."

"What does she look like?"

"Stace, you have more questions than she does! She has golden hair and blue eyes. Fair skin and cherry-colored . . ." Caleb stopped himself and leaned his head against Soldier. He'd been about to say "cherry-colored lips." He looked up and found Stacey smiling knowingly at him. "Hell. Why don't you go see for yourself?"

"Why don't you finish telling me?" she shot back softly. "Things were just getting interesting."

"Go on, Stace. I'm busy." Heat crept up his neck to engulf his face. She'd be seventeen soon. She'd figured out certain things about males and females a long time ago, and she'd spent the last year bothering him about when he was going to get married.

" 'Go on, I'm busy,' " she mocked, giving him a sly look from the corner of her eye. "Sounds like you're trying to avoid talking about her. You make her sound pretty. Thought about marrying her, brother?"

"Stace—it's not your business, but no, I haven't. How are the new calves? You said you'd keep an eye on them while I was gone."

She laughed. "I can't wait to meet her. You don't even like talking about her. You changed the subject! Well, for your information, the new calves are just fine. Healthy as can be. I'm just fine, and Ma's just fine. But you're not. Something's happened, something to do with that woman. It's about time, if you ask me."

"I didn't ask you, Miss Nosy. And it's not what you think," he said. *And never will if I can help it.* Involving himself with Matt Kent's daughter would be like throwing himself into the fire after he'd managed to escape.

"Maybe it is, maybe it isn't. I'll help you finish here. Then we'll go look at those calves. *Then* we'll go look at that woman," Stacey said excitedly, grabbing another brush from a nail. She marched into the stall and started brushing Soldier's other side.

Shaking his head, Caleb narrowed his eyes at her. "Get any foolish notions out of your head, Stace. I just pulled her from that wreck, that's all. Pretty soon she's going home."

Stacey's eyes twinkled. Caleb inhaled deeply, knowing those twinkles meant trouble. "Notions?" she said innocently. "What notions, Caleb?"

He groaned.

Working together, they finished quickly and walked out to look at the brown-and-white-spotted calves. Weeks old, they were a lot sturdier than they'd been when they were born. One nursed eagerly. The other hovered near its mother.

"See? I told you. Just fine," Stacey said.

"Great," Caleb answered softly. Every new healthy calf helped build his stock. He'd started two years ago with five cows and three bulls. After buying, trading, selling, and breeding them, and after the grizzly attacks, he still had at least thirty head.

He wandered off to the wheat fields, Stacey at his side. So far summer hadn't brought much rain, but the wheat didn't look bad. Last year he and a number of other neighbors had lost entire crops to drought.

They walked to the house and went inside. Ma was busy stirring something on the stove. Caleb's gaze found Laura seated on the settee brushing her long wet hair, her thick lashes lowered as she stroked. The dark blue of her dress contrasted with the white of her skin. Caleb felt his body respond to the sight of her beauty. Silently cursing, he turned away to hang his rifle on hooks above the door. He'd never been one to drool over a woman, and he damn sure wouldn't start now.

Stacey had never been a shy one. From the time she'd been old enough to walk, she'd always greeted strangers who happened to stop on the way west. Caleb watched from the corner of his eye as she walked over to Laura and stuck her hand out in greeting. "I'm Stacey, Caleb's sister. He told me what happened. I'm real sorry."

Glancing up, Laura found a kindness in Stacey Main's face as she had in Ruth's. She wondered if Stacey knew that Matthew Kent was her father and about Caleb's trouble with him. She lowered the brush and took Stacey's hand.

"I'm Laura," she said, choosing to leave *Kent* out for the moment. She had grown weary of hostile looks whenever she mentioned her last name. Ruth's troubled expression had gone away quickly, but Laura suspected that was because Ruth Main would take in a needy person no matter who she was. Except for Pa if he were still alive, Laura thought. He was an enemy here. The fingers of her other hand went instinctively to the precious locket lying a few inches below her throat. She had managed to repair the chain after Caleb had dropped the locket on the ground near her. No matter what these people thought of Pa, she would always cherish her memories of him.

"Hi, Laura," Stacey said. Laura had the uncanny suspicion that Stacey was inspecting her, looking for faults, making sure she was good enough for . . . for what?

"You're pretty, just like Caleb said."

Laura glanced at him as he leaned over a basin of water resting on one of the cabinets near the table. He had said she was pretty? Well, why should she care whether or not Caleb Main thought she was pretty? He shot her a glance, his eyes sweeping coolly over her, and he inclined his head in acknowledgment.

"Your dress is—is silk!" Stacey said incredulously.

"It was all I had in my bag," Laura explained, shifting her gaze to Stacey. At least if she couldn't get along with Caleb Main, she might find a friend in Stacey.

"Oh, there's nothing wrong with it. You must come from a wealthy family, that's all." Stacey giggled. "That's all? Listen to me! That's enough. Oh, this is incredible. You must know how to dance, I mean really dance, not like the country steps we do. I mean waltz and all that. And I bet you've been to some real schools, not little one-room things like you find out here."

Ruth laughed. "Stacey, you're overwhelming Miss Kent. Come on and help me."

Stacey's smile faded. Her jaw dropped open, and she stared at Laura. "Kent?" she whispered, her entire attitude changing in the space of seconds. "Matt Kent? Are you kin to him?"

"Yes," Laura responded proudly, lifting her chin. Her eyes turned toward Caleb, who was slowly drying his hands with a cloth, then to Ruth, who paused to grip the edge of her apron. Then she turned back to Stacey, who shrank back as if struck. Laura rose. "Yes, I am Matthew Kent's daughter. And if all of you have such a problem with that, perhaps you know of somewhere else I could stay for a few days."

❋❋❋
Chapter Three

LAURA LAY STARING at the ceiling, a feather tick cushioning her. Moonlight spilled into the room and dripped silver over the sparse but comfortable furnishings—the bed, a chest of drawers, and a few chairs. The night was hot with hardly a breeze to billow the curtain on the one window. Laura thrust a sheet away, preferring to rest uncovered in just her cotton shift. More than the heat and the slight pain in her ankle kept her awake.

The Mains had stared at her in disbelief when she had suggested staying somewhere else. She had stood her ground, staring back, daring them to say anything bad about Pa. Stacey had been the first to sincerely apologize, then Ruth, both saying they wanted her to stay. Caleb had mumbled an apology that sounded like a forced one, but he had said nothing about wanting her to stay. Then he told Ruth he wasn't hungry, and he'd gone out the door, not giving Laura so much as another glance.

That was just as well, Laura thought now. He might have given her another cool glance, and she'd had quite enough of those from him. With his dark, intense eyes and ruggedness, Caleb Main could level a look that would surely send chills up the bravest man's spine.

She heard him come inside finally—hours after he'd left. She heard the thudding of his boots on the wooden stairs, then sounds that indicated movement in his room down the short hall—a chair scraping across the floor, a drawer creaking open. She listened until the sounds grew fainter, then stopped altogether. He was settled for the night, she hoped; who could sleep with him clomping all over the place and pulling chairs across the floor? She was still angry that he

37

had mumbled that apology, then turned right around and insulted her by refusing to eat with her.

Maybe she was just being tormented by paranoia. He hadn't actually said he didn't want to eat with her, but his actions had spoken for him. He had washed for supper. When the subject of Matthew Kent came up again, he'd decided he wasn't hungry. So paranoia had nothing to do with how she perceived his behavior; thoughts of her and Matthew Kent had obviously made the man lose his appetite.

Even worse, he had ridden on the same horse with her for an entire day, had spoken little, but at least had been pleasant. Now she suspected he had sat behind her counting the minutes until he could put her from his horse and not have to be near her again.

"Well, Caleb Main," she muttered into the night, "if you prefer to avoid me, that's fine. I'll certainly do my best to avoid you. With all this open prairie surrounding us, that should not be difficult to accomplish." Tomorrow she would ask if Ruth and Stacey would take her to Minot so she could telegraph Adrian. Yes, the house exuded warmth, but Caleb Main did not. The sooner she left, the better.

She flipped on her side and stared out the window at the moon beyond. There were night sounds—locusts singing, cows lowing, an owl hooting. Far off a coyote sang. A peaceful night, but there was not one breath of air, it seemed. She wiped perspiration from her forehead and sat up, licking her dry lips. She needed a drink of water.

Her cotton shift was thin, but she was so hot she took one look at the blue robe tossed across the foot of the bedstead and frowned. She wasn't about to put that robe on. The well was probably close to the house. She would find it, get a drink, then come right back in. No one would ever know she had been out.

The house was quiet and dark, but she remembered where the furnishings were, and her eyes were adjusted to darkness, so she found her way easily to the front door.

Once outside she located the well to the right of the house. There she lowered and raised the bucket, found the dipper, and drank. Cool . . . refreshing . . . wonderful. She splashed water on her face and on the back of her neck, wincing when pain shot through her neck. Another sore place. She really was lucky to have lived through the coach accident.

As she started to lower the dipper, she heard a click behind her and froze.

"Hot night," Caleb Main remarked, his voice drawled.

Laura spun around, the dipper still in her hand, her heart pounding an unsteady rhythm. She could barely see his form sprawled on a chair in the porch shadows. He had both legs extended and propped on the porch rail. She couldn't see his face but could see the definite glint of a rifle barrel. He must have watched her come out the door and sat staring at her.

She dropped the dipper and pulled the fullness of her white cotton shift around her waist to better cover herself. She wished she had that robe now. "You might have let me know you were there, Mr. Main."

"*You* might've been eaten by something, wandering out alone with no protection, Miss Kent. We lose a chicken or two sometimes. Lately, whole cattle."

"Oh? Well, I merely came for a drink of water. I was going right back in. The night is so peaceful—what is there to be afraid of?"

"Don't come out alone."

His gruff command irritated her even more than the fact that he hadn't let her know he was there when she first came out. Laura found herself in the uncomfortable position of having to stand her ground again. "I don't like being ordered about, Mr. Main. I'll be gone soon enough, then you won't have to trouble yourself about me anymore." She waited, expecting a harsh reply.

She received silence. Seconds passed, minutes.

When he moved, she jumped and silently berated herself for doing so. Why on earth was she allowing the man to unnerve her? She didn't like nearly jumping out of her skin whenever he did something as simple as move an arm or a leg or look at her.

He moved from the shadowed chair to the porch rail on her right and braced both hands on it, leaning forward slightly over the edge. In that instant Laura could do no more than gape at his form, silvered by moonlight.

His shirt was unbuttoned, and the two sides dangled freely. Thank God his chest was hidden in shadow. The shirtsleeves were rolled up beyond his elbows, and the way he had braced his hands on the rail emphasized his forearm muscles. He was a strong man, hardened by the outdoors, and she didn't doubt that his chest beneath the open shirt was every bit as magnificent as his arms. She swallowed hard.

"What is there to be afraid of?" He repeated her question, mocking her softly.

She couldn't deny that his deep voice sent ripples of excitement through her. "Yes, that was my question, Mr. Main."

"Come here."

Despite the refusal that touched her lips, Laura's feet moved her toward the porch . . . and Caleb.

He was propped near one side of the steps. She stayed on the other and folded her arms. Moonlight glittered in his eyes as he studied her.

"Couldn't sleep?" he asked low.

She nodded. "I suppose the fact that you're out here means you couldn't, either."

"Right. I, uh . . ." He looked off into the distance, at the velvet sky and the vast expanse of darkness that was the prairie. "I don't often admit to a mistake. Sorry about rushing off like that earlier. I'm still trying to get used to—"

"The fact that I am who I am?"

Silence. Then, "It's a bit hard to swallow, that's all."

"Just like the fact that you hate my pa is hard for me to swallow."

Their eyes seemed to touch. Laura felt her breath quicken. He moved, took a step toward her. Every nerve in her body sparked. She stepped back around the railing, just out of his grasp, knowing what—who—the danger was now. She was entirely too vulnerable to him. What would happen if he reached for her? Would she fight him? *Could* she fight him, as weak as she felt?

"The best thing for us to do, Mr. Main, is—I think—

perhaps I should get a message to my fiancé in Bismarck," she managed breathlessly.

He cocked his head. "Fiancé? You didn't tell me you had a fiancé."

"There was never any need to."

"Until now."

"Until now," she said, then turned and stepped toward the door.

He grasped her arm before she could complete her first step. His breath was hot on her hair as he pulled her back against him. His body was lean and hard. "Don't wander out alone again, Laura. There are bears . . . coyotes . . . wolves, most definitely wolves," he said slowly. "Understand?"

She nodded. "Oh, yes. I understand more than I want to, Mr. Main. Much more."

Then he released her arm, and she fled inside.

The next day Stacey sat in the rocking chair in the big room and held up a patchwork quilt for Laura's inspection, her eyes bright.

"I finished it. I can't believe it. My first one," Stacey said, then looked meek. "Of course, you must think that's so simple. What I mean is, you're used to doing more important things than sitting around and watching someone stitch a quilt."

Laura smiled. "No one forced me to sit here, Stacey. The quilt is lovely, and it's more artistic than anything I've ever done. I bet it took months to finish."

"It has. Tell me again about that welcome-home ball, the one where you danced until you could hardly stand up anymore."

"Well, everyone, including several long-forgotten cousins came, and—"

"The milk, Stacey," Ruth reminded gently. "I asked you two hours ago to milk that last cow. Caleb didn't have time. He went to the town meeting about getting a new schoolteacher and to see if he could find anyone to go back to those hills and . . . Well, maybe Miss Kent can tell you about the ball while you're milking the cow."

"While I'm milking the cow?" Stacey blurted. "She's probably never seen a cow be milked. Ma, that's so simple."

"So she'll have a new experience to tell folks about when she goes home."

"She won't want to tell anyone about that, Ma. Besides I don't want her to ruin her silk dress in the barn."

"I'll tell you about the ball again, Stacey, if you'll make me a dress more suitable for wearing around here. A dress like yours," Laura suggested.

Stacey's eyes widened. "Really?"

Laura nodded. "Really."

"I can't believe you'd want to wear anything like this," Stacey said, fingering the blue-and-white gingham.

"To tell the truth, I feel rather out of place in this," Laura said, indicating her silk gown. "And it's all I brought. I just want something to wear until I leave."

"All right, all right. We'll get Caleb to take us into Minot tomorrow to buy the material. Oh, this will be fun."

"But only if you milk that cow," Ruth said sternly. "And don't you forget we're going to Mrs. Dahl's later to take her some food. Poor woman's hardly been able to climb out of bed this past week, what with her cold and all."

"I'm going, Ma. Right now," Stacey said. With that she and Laura went to the barn, Laura hobbling on the ankle that still tightened in pain now and then. She wondered if Caleb was trying to get someone to go for the bodies still lying at the bottom of that hill. She had been certain that was what Ruth had been about to say. She also wondered if Caleb would telegraph Bismarck for her while he was in Minot this afternoon. Surely he would, if for no other reason than to speed her departure from his house and life as quickly as possible.

Over supper that evening Caleb avoided Laura's gaze. She told herself she didn't care. He agreed to take her and Stacey to Minot the following day, and that was all that mattered. Caleb Main could keep his hatred inside of him. She wanted no part of it. The episode between them last night had shown her how vulnerable she was to him, and she had resolved never to be caught in such a position again. She did ask if he had telegraphed. He mumbled something about forgetting.

After supper she climbed aboard a wagon with Ruth and Stacey to go visit Mrs. Dahl, who had apparently been suffering with a summer cold. Laura had never just sat and done nothing. Her ankle felt slightly better, her head felt completely better, and she liked Ruth and Stacey more than she had thought she would yesterday evening. She felt relieved to be away from Bismarck and all the painful memories of Pa, even if she had not reached Kenmare to visit Aunt Rebecca. She made a mental note to telegraph Kenmare when she telegraphed Bismarck.

During the ride, there were a few bumps along the way that reminded her of her bruised body, but she kept the aches and pains to herself. Stacey chatted about people in Minot and wanted to hear more about balls and supper parties. When a lull came in the conversation, Laura drew a deep breath of the Dakota evening air, watched the sun as it began its red descent, and smiled at Stacey across the wagon.

They stopped near a sod house that was the same rich green as the prairie. Wild vines scaled the sides, and a burst of blue flowers with white necks gathered around the door. Laura had heard of sod houses but had never seen one. The sod had been cut from the prairie and pieced together over strong boughs, Stacey explained. The first Dakota settlers had built sod houses, and many still remained.

Ruth knocked on the door. When a small voice answered, she entered, waving Stacey and Laura in. The earthen walls were whitewashed, the dirt floor solid beneath their feet. A stovepipe hole had been cut in the ceiling, and a little stove sat in the middle of the house to warm it during winter. There were several greased-paper windows and rickety chairs. Tin dishes sat on a little cupboard alongside a washbasin. To the left, a white-haired, wrinkled woman smiled from the middle of a narrow tick.

"Sit down, sit down," she urged. Stacey carried a plum pie to a small block table, and Laura carried a dish of boiled squash. Ruth placed a crock of beef between the pie and squash, then went to sit beside Mrs. Dahl on the bed.

Stacey tried one chair while Laura tried the other. The chairs creaked and groaned. She and Stacey glanced at each other, wide-eyed as if expecting the chairs to give out any second. If they did, she and Stacey would land on the floor in the middle of a bunch of splintered wood. Laura smiled at the thought. The way Stacey lifted her brows up and down in a clownish way made her want to giggle, but out of respect for Mrs. Dahl, she restrained herself.

She was having a wonderful time. She hadn't felt so mischievous since her childhood. Why . . . since Pa's death, she hadn't smiled genuinely and experienced a moment's happiness until now.

"Why don't you come and stay with us, Mrs. Dahl?" Ruth pleaded with the old woman. "We'll take care of you until you're well, then bring you back, I promise."

The woman had sat up on the side of the bed. Now she shook her head angrily and let loose a string of words Laura didn't understand. Some foreign language, Laura thought, but felt that asking Stacey about it right now would be rude. So she sat very still on the chair and waited patiently while Ruth tried to soothe the woman.

"All right, all right, Mrs. Dahl. I won't ask again. Now . . . we brought food."

Mrs. Dahl ate very little. Ruth convinced her to let them move the cupboard and table closer to her bed so she could reach the food if she became hungry. Soon Mrs. Dahl fell asleep. Ruth, Stacey, and Laura left.

As they rode through the darkness, Ruth explained, "She's Norwegian and more set in her ways than anybody I know. Came to the states forty years ago with her husband. Twenty years ago, after her husband died, she came to Dakota Territory with her daughter and her daughter's family. They built that house and fought off the Indians for a while until everyone but Mrs. Dahl was killed one day. She refuses to leave the house, as you saw. She'll die there."

"But she'll die happy," Stacey added.

It was the most heart-wrenching story Laura had ever heard. But she agreed with Stacey. As old as Mrs. Dahl was, she deserved to at least die happily in the sod house.

For a time they rode in silence. Somewhere close a wolf howled. Another responded. Stacey picked up something that had been lying beneath a blanket in the wagon bed where she and Laura sat. Laura saw the outline of the rifle and gasped. "Why did you bring that?"

"Because I hate wolves," Stacey responded. "I sure don't want to get eaten by any." She rubbed the barrel, checked to make sure the gun was loaded, then hoisted it to her shoulder to practice her aim.

Laura watched. "You handle that thing like a—a—"

"Man?" Stacey asked, her white teeth gleaming in the dark.

"Yes."

"On the prairie, man or woman—you learn to survive."

The wolves howled again as if to stress Stacey's point. Either Laura's imagination was playing games with her, or she really did see a pair of glistening eyes a short distance to the left, the animal keeping step with the wagon. She shivered and was suddenly glad Stacey held the rifle. She had always felt safe and snug within the walls of Pa's huge house or at the various schools she had attended. She had not realized how Pa had sheltered her until now. This was a different way of life. This was the Dakota prairie. Sod houses, coyotes, wolves . . .

"Yes, I suppose you must . . . survive," she commented, swallowing hard. She crossed her arms to hug herself.

Minutes later Stacey fired the rifle. The shot split the air and made Laura jump. Ruth didn't flinch. The horses weren't troubled in the least, either. The glistening eyes disappeared, and the wagon rambled on. Laura shook her head in disbelief. This certainly *was* a different way of life. The simplicity she could learn to like, but dealing with such harsh realities as having to carry a rifle to ward off wolves was difficult to accept.

When they reached the farmhouse, Laura went straight up to bed. Unlike last night, a breeze cooled her room now, and she fell asleep easily.

She awoke to sunlight shining through the window, creating a lazy morning haze. She stretched and smiled. She looked forward to another day with Stacey and Ruth.

Caleb lurked in the back of her mind—another wolf, a dark brooding figure that made her heart pound and her breath catch. While she dressed, she remembered what being curled up intimately against him under that blanket in the hills had felt like. She had barely been conscious—it had occurred after he had pulled her from the coach wreck—but she remembered the steely length of his body, his earthy smell, and his bristly whiskers on her face.

She had been certain he was going to reach for her when he'd told her to "come here" the other night and she had approached the porch. He hadn't. She had been certain he was going to turn her to him and kiss her when he'd grabbed her arm to stop her from going inside the house and pulled her back against him. He hadn't.

Of all the men she had ever met, Caleb Main was, by far, the most difficult to predict.

Once dressed and downstairs, Laura found Ruth covered with flour to her elbows and rolling biscuit dough on a small tabletop near the stove. The patchwork quilt Stacey had finished yesterday had been tossed across the back of the rocking chair. A broom, its bristles bound to a stick with twine, nestled in a corner of the fireplace. The settee looked cozy and inviting. Windows on either side of the fireplace were open to allow a breeze to flutter through the room. The table was set with pottery, and the rich smell of coffee filled the place. Laura smiled, the warmth of the room again washing over her.

Bismarck and the haunting memories of Pa seemed far away.

"Good morning. May I help?" Laura asked Ruth brightly, eager to start the day.

Ruth looked up from her work, a brow lifted in surprise. "Well, I suppose you can if you want."

"I do. I know nothing about cooking, though, so don't just set me to a task. But I can do simple things."

"Dressed in silk and wanting to do kitchen work," Ruth said, chuckling.

Laura laughed with her. "We'll soon have that remedied. Do you know when Caleb will be taking us to Minot?"

"Around noon, I reckon. Here, put on an apron and you can cut the biscuits, like this." Ruth demonstrated with a little tin cup. She pressed gently, lifted the cup, then held up a perfect circle of biscuit dough.

"That looks easy," Laura said.

"It is."

Laura tied on a white apron. She took the cup and cut several biscuits, placing them on the pan Ruth had set out. Ruth showed her how to roll out the remaining dough, then Ruth moved to the big table and grabbed a basket. "Stacey went to help Caleb take the cattle to water. They'll be in for breakfast soon. I'll go for eggs while you're doing that."

When the door snapped shut behind Ruth, Laura cut three more biscuits, rolled the soft, floury dough, and cut more. After she had cut nine biscuits, her nose itched, and she reached up to rub it with the back of her hand. Then she remembered she had flour all over her hands. Oh, well. She probably had flour all over her nose now, too. She laughed. She would wash it off later.

She placed the tin cup on the dough again and pressed down. Flour wooshed up in a puff of white smoke. Laura jumped back and blinked, trying to wipe specks of flour from her eyes. She must look a sight: flour in her hair, flour on her face, flour on her hands.

She heard the door swing open but couldn't see a thing. Blinking more, she finally glimpsed Caleb shutting the door. She didn't want him to see her looking so horrid. But before she could even make a move to turn around and race upstairs, he turned, stopped abruptly, and burst into loud laughter that bounced off the walls.

Her humiliation was great.

Bad enough he disliked her because she was Matthew Kent's daughter. Bad enough she would not have had the willpower to stop him if he had tried to kiss her on the porch that night. Bad enough they were alone together again and he had shut the door.

He was laughing at her!

"Stop it," she said, brushing flour from her eyes.

"Oh, don't be so all-fire indignant, Laura," he said between waves of laughter. "You're a sight. I haven't seen anything as funny since Stacey came screeching up to the house four years ago with a badger hanging on the hem of her skirt."

"It's in my eyes," she told him. "And it hurts."

He crossed to her and took her by one elbow. "Come on. To the washbasin. We'll wash it out."

She wrestled her arm free. "I can get there by myself, Mr. Main. Allow me to retain at least a little of my pride."

He tipped his head and made a sweeping motion with one arm, indicating she should go ahead. Half-blind, she walked slowly to the basin, sensing Caleb right behind her. She bent over the water, meaning to splash some gently in her eyes.

Caleb reached around her with both powerful arms, cupped handfuls of water, and tossed them up at her face. The sudden onslaught took Laura's breath away. Water soaked her hair, her skin, her jacket bodice. She gasped and tried to wipe water from her eyes, but her hands came away smeared white. To add to her embarrassment, Caleb's body was pressed against her back in a most intimate way. If she wriggled, the situation would only become worse.

All the sensations of the night she had gone to the well came back. Her heart pounded. Her breath quickened. Her body tensed. She knew she should find a way to escape him. But within . . . deep within . . . she was thrilled to be this close to him.

"There. That must feel better. You're not complaining about your eyes hurting anymore. Turn around and let me wash your face." His deep voice was near her ear; his warm breath made her tingle all over.

Laura turned.

Her vision was clearer. Perhaps an inch separated them. She couldn't be sure, and it didn't matter. A huge room separating them wouldn't have made a difference in the way her body responded to him.

Stepping to one side, he dipped a cloth in the water, wrung it, and stepped back.

He started near her eyes, dabbing gently. His chin, jaw, and upper lip were covered with the black stubble of a beard, and his wavy black hair hung to his shoulders. His dark eyes were sharp and intense, and, as always, Laura felt as if they touched her as he looked at her.

He told her to close her eyes. She did. He washed her lids, her brows, her forehead. She heard him dip and wring the cloth again. He washed her nose, her cheeks, and the sides of her face.

Then he touched her lips.

She opened her eyes to find him staring at her, his gaze as black as a midnight sky. Slowly . . . so slowly, his head lowered, his lips hovered just above hers. She breathed his name, watching his nostrils flare. His eyes searched hers and measured her reaction, flickering in uncertainty one second, settling with lazy confidence on her mouth the next.

The kiss was tentative. His lips were soft yet firm and tasted slightly salty. He smelled like the Dakota morning— fresh, a scent of dew-damp grass clinging to his homespun clothes, his hair, his skin. She parted her lips, inviting him.

Footsteps on the porch shattered the intimacy. Caleb calmly stepped back, putting a few inches between them while he washed her chin. Ruth came into the house. Still breathless and trembling inside, Laura wondered if Ruth would suspect anything.

"Beautiful day, beautiful day," Ruth sang, placing the basket filled with eggs on the table and stealing a glance at Caleb and Laura. Her brows lifted at the sight of Laura, and she smiled. "Pressed that cup a bit hard, did you?"

"She had flour all over her when I came in," Caleb said. "Even in her eyes. But we washed it out. Except for the dress, she's fine."

Fine?

A sharp laugh of disbelief nearly tore loose from Laura's throat. His kiss had left her weak, confused, hungry for more. Adrian's kisses had never made her feel this way.

Oh, no—she was anything *but* fine.

❄❄❄

Chapter Four

As the wagon began descending into the valley toward Minot and the river and bridges below, Laura was amazed at the sight before her. Behind her she saw the open prairie with tall, sometimes golden grass; up ahead were trees—oaks, elms, and ashes. Branches waved in a light breeze. And plum trees were everywhere, dangling luscious fruit and dotting the green land with reddish-purple splendor. Laura's mouth watered.

She had awakened to rain this morning and had been greatly disappointed by the thought that they might not take the short trip. But an hour after breakfast sunlight had peeked through the clouds. A short time later, deciding it liked the world below, the sun had burst through in full force, pushing the clouds away until not one hovered in the sky.

Breathing the musty scent of foliage after a shower, Laura admired the town nestled deep in the valley, houses and buildings like miniatures in the distance. A rail platform and station were situated at one end of the town. But the surrounding land was what held Laura's attention. So lush, so green, curving, rolling, dipping. Breathtaking. A river sliced unevenly through the valley, and sunlight danced on its surface, creating the illusion of a million glittering stars. A huge rail trestle cut through the river.

"The Indians called this place Plum Valley when they were here," Stacey said, noticing the awe on Laura's face. She and Laura sat across from each other on blankets in the wagon bed. She liked Laura a lot, no matter that Laura's last name was Kent. She loved Caleb, too, and knew he hated Matt Kent. That was why she'd been shocked when she'd

first learned Laura was Matt's daughter. But she'd known
that first night that Laura didn't have evil in her. She didn't
think Caleb trusted Laura, though, because of her last name.
Maybe that was the reason he'd gotten in some bad tempers
during the past two days whenever she mentioned Laura's
name. She'd heard everything from "Go off and mind your
own business, Stace" to "Get out of here. I have work to do."

Well, she had a piece of work to do, too, she figured. Caleb might fly off in those dark moods, but he couldn't fool
her. During the last few days, she'd seen him looking at
Laura a few times, and those looks hadn't been the looks a
man gave a woman he wanted to go away. She knew. Caleb
didn't want her to grow up—to him she would always be a
little girl—but she *was* growing up, and she had figured certain things out. From time to time during church service,
she'd seen Charles Duncan give her the same look Caleb
gave Laura lately. She knew what it meant. Something had
sparked between Caleb and Laura, and she was going to do
what she could to encourage it.

Laura smiled. "Plum Valley. Very fitting. It's certainly a
beautiful place. The plums look delicious."

"They are," Caleb said from the wagon seat where he sat
gripping the reins. "Want to stop and pick some?"

"Could we?" Laura asked eagerly. Glancing over his
shoulder at her, Caleb laughed, a rich sound that touched her
inside and made her laugh, too. She smoothed her skirt.
"What I mean is . . . that would be lovely."

Caleb nodded. Amusement sparkled in his dark eyes. A
smile twitched the corners of his full mouth. Laura felt a
thrill of excitement. He turned to watch the path ahead, his
black hair waving freely to brush against his wide shoulders.
Laura glanced around at the land again and the town below.
But soon her attention was fully on Caleb's back. She just
couldn't seem to help herself.

He wore dark trousers and a white shirt that was damp
with perspiration in places. His every movement made the
cloth cling to flexing muscles. How tall he sat on the wagon
seat, controlling the horses. He exuded strength and mascu-
linity, from the gentleness of his smile and a touch she re-

membered well, to the firm line of his jaw and the power of those shoulder and back muscles. Her heart quickened. She had never encountered a man who had affected her more.

Soon the wagon halted near a little grove of plum trees. Caleb lifted Stacey from the wagon. She immediately grabbed a woven basket and wandered off. Laura called for her to wait, but she didn't seem to hear. She was whistling.

When Caleb reached for Laura, their eyes met and held during the brief moment it took for him to plant his large warm hands on her waist and lift her down to stand before him. Thoughts of Adrian and the pledge she had made to him to become his wife lurked in the back of Laura's mind. Odd how that pledge always seemed a hundred years in the past lately—whenever she was this close to Caleb Main. She resented his hatred of Pa. Still, she could not deny that she wanted to continue what had been started this morning. If Caleb ever drew her fully into his arms, she suspected she would receive more than just a brush of a kiss. The thought made her breathless.

"The sun brightens your hair. It's pure gold," he said softly, his dark eyes sweeping appreciatively over her hair, then resting on her lips. His hands were still on her waist, his fingertips searing the flesh beneath her skirt.

Laura stiffened. "Mr. Main. Stacey . . ."

"Took a basket and wandered off, in case you didn't notice. And my name is Caleb."

Calling him by his first name seemed too familiar, so she ignored the statement. "She couldn't have gone far."

"Far enough, if I know Stacey." He leaned close, so close she felt his warm breath on her cheek. "Why did you let me kiss you this morning?"

Her eyes widened. Her pride refused to allow her to admit how deeply he affected her as a woman. "Don't be so arrogant, Mr. Main. I did not *let* you kiss me."

A grin twitched the corners of his mouth. "No?"

"No. You have a way of just doing and saying things with no regard for my feelings. Now, if you would be so kind as to move—"

"You said you have a fiancé in Bismarck."

"I don't see that that is any of your business. Now—"

"It it when you tell me you have a fiancé, yet want me to kiss you."

"I never said I wanted you to kiss me, Mr. Main."

"You didn't have to say anything. Some feelings aren't given in words. Like right now—you're angry and a bit uneasy because Stacey went off and left us alone, but you're wishing I'd kiss you again."

Laura inhaled a sharp breath, angry and excited at the same time. The man was brash! Mustering strength, she planted both hands on his chest and attempted to push him away. He chuckled, and she felt the vibration of the laughter rush through her fingertips to every prickling nerve in her body. It stole her breath. She jerked her hands back. "I-I don't understand you. I'm Matthew Kent's daughter. Because of that, *you* hate me. Yet—"

"No. You don't know how wrong you are. I don't hate you, Laura," he murmured.

She stared at him, knowing she must join Stacey soon if she wished to avoid questions. "Then you are playing a game with me, Mr. Main. Perhaps trying to use me to exact revenge on my pa?"

The muscles in his jaw tightened. Something flickered in his gaze, some deeply embedded, unreadable emotion. His intense eyes roamed openly to her nose, then to her lips. They rested briefly on her bosom, then shifted back to her face. Without further delay he moved aside to let her pass. "Maybe that's it. Revenge," he said gruffly, gripping the edge of the wagon bed with one hand. "Go on. Get out of here."

His words hit Laura like a bolt of lightning. She had made the accusation, not really believing it, not really *wanting* to believe it. But it was true—he *was* trying to use her as a weapon of revenge! He had intended to seduce her, then dangle the knowledge before the enemy he didn't know was dead. Twice now she might have played into his hands.

"Stay away from me, Mr. Main," she said evenly as she stalked off. "Stay far away from me."

Caleb clenched his jaw and watched Laura walk away.

She was wrong, but he wouldn't tell her that. Let her believe he really wanted revenge. That might keep her out of his arms. After all, she belonged to someone in Bismarck, not him. He hadn't set out to get revenge. In fact, if she knew how much she and hardly anything else occupied his mind lately, she'd laugh at her accusation. Matt Kent hadn't entered his thoughts today until Laura had mentioned her pa. The image of her beautiful face and smile filled his head.

He couldn't seem to hang on to clear thought whenever he was close to her. He had only meant to lift her from the wagon, put her on her feet, then step back so she could be on her way. Unfortunately her crystal-blue eyes always revealed more of what was going on in that pretty head of hers than she probably wanted to show. He knew she desired him nearly as much as he desired her. On the porch that night he'd nearly given in to the urge to press her to him. He'd wanted to feel her soft curves and inhale her sweet scent. Just touching the silken skin of her arm had nearly destroyed his control. So he'd given her the warning about the wolves.

And this morning . . . what the hell had happened this morning? One second he'd been washing her face, the next he'd been touching her tempting pink lips and leaning over to kiss them.

And why did he ask about her fiancé minutes ago? Her private life in Bismarck was none of his business. Did he have a subconscious urge to claim Laura Kent for himself? No. Never. He'd best remember who she was. Laura Kent would lead a straight path to Matt Kent. And embroiling himself with Matt Kent in any matter was the last thing he wanted to do.

Laura and Stacey soon drifted back to the wagon, their basket filled with ripe plums. Carefully avoiding Laura's gaze, Caleb lifted her and Stacey into the wagon, then climbed up on the seat. They moved toward Minot again, an afternoon breeze cooling him.

As they entered Minot, Laura glanced around. Just last year, when the Manitoba Railroad had come to Minot, the town had been the end of the rail line, Stacey said. But the line had quickly been extended west; and right now it was probably headed into Montana. The railroad had brought not only the telegraph but an awful lot of newcomers to Minot as well. Main Street was flanked by covered wooden walkways and wooden storefronts. People went about the day's business, stopping to talk now and then beneath signs hung high above walkways. Horses were tethered to hitching posts in front of a number of saloons and gaming houses. Music and laughter drifted on the breeze. Horses nickered, and wagons creaked.

Warner's Mercantile and Harvey Alman's Dry Goods stood between two gaming houses on one side of the street. On the opposite side, next to three saloons, a sign dangled from a post near a door. It read HARLEY FRANKLIN, M.D. At the far end of the street stood the rail station and platform. Beyond the Main Street buildings there were houses.

Caleb maneuvered the wagon around horses and vehicles in the slightly muddy, rutted street. Soon the wagon stopped near the mercantile and the dry goods store.

"We'll do our shopping, then go meet some people if you want," Stacey said. Laura nodded her agreement.

Caleb jumped down and lowered Stacey. Then he reached for Laura, again avoiding her gaze. She had certainly been careful, after they had all climbed back into the wagon in the plum grove, to keep her gaze off of Caleb's back. She wondered what he meant to do all afternoon. Surely he didn't wish to follow behind them. "Are you coming with us, Mr. Main?" she asked as he planted her on her feet.

He turned away. "Meet me back here in a few hours," he said.

Her jaw dropped open. This was the second time he had turned his back on her! The first time had been shortly after learning that Matthew Kent was her father. He had not wanted to talk about the past. Now he didn't want to talk to *her*, probably because he was still angry that she had ruined his plan for revenge. But she was angry, too, because she had been an instrument of that plan. When the man didn't want to talk about something or to someone, he simply turned away.

"Mr. Main, I would appreciate being addressed face to face," she said.

Stacey stood to Caleb's and Laura's left. She snickered. Laura flashed her a confident yet stiff smile. Caleb turned and gave Laura a hard stare, but Laura continued to smile. She had won a small victory, after all—he no longer had his back to her.

"Get your shopping done," he grumbled.

"You sure are cranky today, ordering us about and all. Still sore about losing track of that grizzly?" Stacey taunted.

"Something like that."

Stacey marched over and took Laura by the arm. Together they walked toward the store. " 'Get your shopping done,' " Stacey mocked under her breath. "He's cranky, real cranky."

Laura fought to keep a straight face. "I seem to have that effect on him."

"You sure handled him good."

They put their heads together and laughed as they entered Harvey Alman's Dry Goods store. Numerous shelves were cluttered with tin pans and pots, lamps and lanterns. Plows, stoves, and stovepipes proudly occupied one whole wall. Nearby rolls of wire and kegs of nails nestled together. Saws, hatchets, knives, and hammers hung on an opposite wall, and in front of a long wooden counter stood a keg of mouth-watering pickles and a barrel of dark molasses. Several tall wooden pails nearly overflowing with candy sat on the countertop, and a crate of crackers rested an inch away. Shelves behind the counter were lined with bolts of cloth—yellow-and-white-checked gingham and blue in several shades; pretty calico decorated with black-eyed Susans and spiked goldenrod; lavender and yellow challis.

As Laura and Stacey drew close to the counter, a dark curtain hung in a doorway near the shelves was pushed aside, and a tall, lanky man with silver hair and merry blue-green eyes appeared. "Miss Stacey, Miss Stacey. Always good to see you. And you brought a friend this time."

"Mr. Alman, meet Laura Kent," Stacey said.

Laura gripped the long-fingered hand that extended across the counter, and she searched the man's eyes for any sign of hostility. Stacey had included her last name in the introduction, which made her uneasy. After the way Ruth, Stacey, and Caleb had reacted to the name, she couldn't be sure how others in this town might.

The merriment stayed in Mr. Alman's eyes. If he knew the name and hated her father, too, he hid his feelings well. But she sensed that he hid nothing. The breath of relief she released surprised her; she hadn't realized she was so tense. "I'm pleased to meet you, Mr. Alman," she said sincerely.

"Likewise, Miss Kent. Did you see we started the new school, Stacey?"

Stacey's eyes widened in surprise. "You did? Already? Why didn't anyone let us know? Caleb would have come to help. Me and Ma would've brought food."

"Didn't want to trouble you," Mr. Alman said, propping his lean form against the countertop with the aid of an elbow. "Knew Caleb went off to hunt that bear, and you and Miss Ruth was mindin' the place alone. Still work to be done. Only got the frame up, but everybody's real excited. Was some day, that first day. Some brought boards, some brought nails, some just brought theirselves." He and Stacey laughed together. A smile touched Laura's lips. She liked Mr. Alman. His excitement about the new schoolhouse was childlike and charming.

"When will everyone be working on it again?" Stacey asked.

"Tomorrow morning, bright an' early."

"I'll let Caleb know."

"Caleb's back?"

Stacey nodded, eyeing one of the pails of hard candy. She ran her tongue over her bottom lip.

"Totin' a bearskin, if I know Caleb," Mr. Alman said, chuckling. "Man gets what he goes after."

"Not this time. This time he came back with Laura."

Mr. Alman squinted one eye at Laura. She felt heat engulf her face. She would like to believe he was merely examining the bruises on her face but suspected that wasn't the case; his thoughts were tying her and Caleb together romantically. Stacey obviously did not realize what he must be thinking.

"You don't say?" he drawled. "What'd Caleb go hunting for anyway? He didn't get himself married, did he?"

Stacey shifted her gaze from the candy to Laura, a flicker of devilment in her eyes. Laura nearly groaned aloud. Stacey was matchmaking! That certainly explained why Stacey had wandered off in the plum grove, leaving her and Caleb alone. Stacey had probably heard her calling and chose to ignore her!

"As much as I'd like to have Laura as my sister-in-law, I have to tell the truth—Caleb dug her out from under a coach wreck."

"Well, that's good . . . that's good he was there."

Laura shifted uncomfortably. Mr. Alman was still studying her through one eye, still not quite believing there wasn't more involved than just a rescue. "I'll be contacting my fiancé by telegraph and going back to Bismarck soon," she said, wanting to assure both him and Stacey that she had no romantic interest in Caleb Main. She also wanted to squelch any rumors they might start. She liked Mr. Alman, but if Minot was anything like Bismarck, rumors spread as fast as fire. She didn't want Adrian to show up and be confronted with ugly rumors about her and Caleb.

"Fiancé?" Stacey blurted. "That ruins everything."

"There was nothing to ruin, Stacey," Laura said dryly.

"Well, there might have been!"

Mr. Alman chuckled again and straightened. "Guess that's wrapped up tight. Now . . . why'd you ladies wander in here? Wasn't to spend some time with an old man like me, was it?"

"No," Stacey said, disappointment obvious in her voice. "Ma sent me for a half pound of sugar, a pint of molasses, and a half pound of coffee. You can add, oh, six yards each of that yellow-checked gingham and the calico with the black-eyed Susans. And some white thread, too."

"And a few pieces of that candy you've been scooping from those pails since you were eight years old?" he teased.

Stacey nodded her head. "Yes, a few pieces of candy, too. Make that four."

"Two for Miss Laura and two for you, is it?"

Laughing, Stacey turned away. "We'll pick those things up in a while."

Outside the sun had dipped behind a lone cloud. Wagons rattled by, leaving more ruts in the muddied street. Horses whinnied. A mother halted just beyond the wooden walkway to scold her young son. Stacey stopped to talk with an old man seated on a settee just outside the store. Rowdy laughter drifting from a nearby saloon drew Laura's attention. Over the top of the swinging doors she glimpsed a blond woman leaning against a tall staircase, her breasts swelling slightly above a glittering gown of ruby satin. The woman's lips and cheeks were painted red. She smiled and leaned provocatively against the man with whom she was conversing. Laura stared. The sight of the woman didn't shock her; Bismarck contained a number of saloons that employed women to entertain men, so she knew about these things. Her gaze settled on the man.

Caleb. Laughing and talking with that woman. Looking down at . . .

Something rippled through Laura, an emotion she didn't quite understand and didn't care to explore. What Caleb Main did was entirely his business.

Laura started to avert her gaze, but Caleb shifted, and his eyes met hers. His expression did not change. He merely inclined his head in acknowledgment, then turned back to his afternoon entertainment.

Another dismissal.

Why did his action bother her? He had left her to do her business. He had gone to do his. She should be glad he hadn't decided to accompany her and Stacey.

He preferred that woman's company to hers.

And just what did she expect him to do? Look at her, rush out of the saloon, and sweep her into his arms? She wrinkled her brow. Nothing could be further from her mind. She wanted him to keep his distance.

She refused to allow the incident to trouble her further. Putting Caleb from her mind, she joined Stacey at the settee, and they started down the walkway together.

"Do you know what happened between Caleb and my father?" Laura asked suddenly. She was immediately surprised and exasperated with herself. She had only *thought* to put Caleb Main from her mind. The truth was, he was still there, always lurking in the shadows. She might try to erase thoughts of him and questions about him, but they never completely went away. She had been curious about his past ever since he had stared at the picture of Pa with such hatred. Learning that he had planned to use her to avenge that mysterious past had made her more curious.

Stacey glanced at her, nervousness in her pretty brown gaze, then looked away. "Why ask me? Why not ask Caleb?"

"I did. All he said was that he didn't want to go near Bismarck or Matthew Kent ever again. I also asked him to take me home. He refused."

"Home . . . to Bismarck?" Stacey asked. Laura nodded. Stacey grew quiet. They passed Warner's Mercantile, where several dusty-looking men were seated in chairs on either side of the door. They tipped their hats to Laura and Stacey. The young women inclined their heads and walked on.

"Stacey—"

"Listen, Laura, I was young. I don't know all that happened. All I was told is that Caleb spent some time in Bismarck. Then some land deals went bad. Real bad. The only thing Caleb ever said to me was that your pa was the crookedest man he'd ever known."

Irritation crept up Laura's spine. Pa was the crookedest man . . . ? Caleb Main was so perfect, was he? To sit in judgment of others while he had been plotting to use her in a game of revenge? "Do you believe what Caleb said about my pa?" she asked cautiously, suspecting Stacey would be loyal to her brother.

Stacey was silent for a long minute. "What else do I have to believe? Besides, Caleb's never lied to me. He wouldn't. He's an honest man. He believes in hard work and just wants to live in peace."

"Believe me, I did not intend to bother him."

"Oh . . . you bother him, just not in the way you think," Stacey said, the hint of a smile playing on her mouth.

"Sometimes I wish I knew what he was thinking."

"It's hard to know what goes on in his head. Caleb gets real wrapped up in his thoughts sometimes. He's always been like that."

"His head is full of hatred," Laura said without hesitation. "I know that much."

"It's not aimed at you, Laura. You don't know . . . I've seen the way he looks at you sometimes. He's trying to untangle things, you know—separate you from your pa. I think he likes you a lot."

Laura managed a stiff smile. Stacey didn't know Caleb as well as she thought she did. She didn't know the ruthlessness of which he was capable, didn't know of his little plan for revenge. Laura did, and she meant to stay on guard during the remainder of her stay beneath his roof.

Children were playing up ahead in an open grassy area opposite a gaming house. They scurried about, tossing a ball back and forth, laughing and singing. Some girls turned a rope while others skipped through it, giggling. Their gaiety was refreshing.

"That must be the schoolyard," Laura remarked.

Stacey nodded. "The new school will be farther out, away from all this . . ." she said, indicating the saloons and gaming house with the motion of one hand. "A whole lot of these places went up this past year when the railroad came. Decent folk want to drive them out but haven't figured out how yet. You don't happen to teach, do you? We're looking for a teacher. Old Mr. Wilkes died a few months ago. Mrs. Statum's been teaching since but doesn't want to continue. We haven't found anyone else we want teaching our children."

"*Our* children?" Laura said, smiling at the reference.

"Well, Minot might appear rough—you know, with all the saloons and other places. There are plenty of fights from what I hear. But for some of us, it's like a big family. We live in separate houses but group together on important things, like building a new schoolhouse. We care a whole lot about our children. Come on. You can meet Mrs. Statum."

The schoolhouse was a one-room, white clapboard struc-

ture, weathered with age. Inside there were two rows of
benches, empty at the moment. Behind a small desk in the
front of the room sat a small dark-haired woman, gray sprinkled at her temples and a crop of gray curls resting on her
forehead. Doubtless her little green eyes, chiseled features,
and sharp chin earned the utmost respect from her students,
Laura thought, recalling a few of her own severe-looking
teachers.

"Hello, Mrs. Statum," Stacey greeted. "Recess?"

Mrs. Statum smiled, her features smoothing, almost as if
she had one face for teaching children and another for greeting adults. "Stacey Main, you should take this job," Mrs.
Statum said. "I am too old for this. Simply too old."

Laughing, Stacey hurried to the desk and bent to plant a
kiss on Mrs. Statum's cheek. "You're doing a wonderful job
and you know it. Don't know why you ever quit."

"Because I wanted a rest. I have five grandchildren now,
you know, grandchildren I like to go enjoy sometimes."

"No, I didn't know."

"Mmh. In Fargo."

Stacey waved Laura over and introduced her to Mrs.
Statum. Then Laura and Stacey perched in chairs near the
desk. Stacey asked about the grandchildren, and Mrs. Statum
described them all, as well as each of their cute little habits.
Laura and Stacey smiled and laughed, sharing in the woman's obvious love. Then Stacey told Mrs. Statum how Caleb
had saved Laura from the coach wreck and that Laura was
staying with them until she could reach her family in Bismarck. Mrs. Statum didn't flinch at the mention of Laura's
last name, either, so Laura decided the Kent name must only
be hated in the Main household, not by the entire town of
Minot. Mrs. Statum sincerely wished Laura well and asked
to see her in her new dresses once they were made.

"Bring her to church, Stacey. There'll be a picnic after this
week's service. Now it's long past time for me to ring the
bell and bring my pupils in," she said, standing.

Stacey and Laura said goodbye and went to wander along
Main Street again, something that wasn't always a good
idea, Stacey said. "Too many rough sorts. I've only been

troubled once, however. Caleb plowed through the man—
and I do mean plowed through. Since then I haven't been
troubled at all. Caleb doesn't drink much or put his money
on the tables in those places, but he gets respect."

He goes into "those places" for other reasons, Laura
thought, but immediately chastised herself. Why was the
matter still bothering her? She cared little where Caleb Main
went or what he did while he was there. She recalled her
first, fearful impression of him—a giant of a man, an un-
shaven man who looked like he'd been living in the hills
with that grizzly he had been hunting. She was still fearful of
him at times, yet at other times—when he had rescued her
and this morning when he had so tenderly washed her face—
she thought Caleb Main was the gentlest man she had ever
known. He certainly was complex. Kind one minute, a threat
the next . . .

As she and Stacey started back up the street, Laura sighed,
not understanding why she even cared to sort through his
complexities. She would be gone soon, and understanding
him wouldn't matter anyway.

Laura and Stacey encountered Dr. Franklin in front of his
house and office and engaged in light conversation with him
as well as with two town women who stopped. One was Mrs.
Belcourt, the other Mrs. Green. Mrs. Green invited them into
her home for lemonade and talked about the new schoolhouse and the upcoming church picnic.

By the time Laura and Stacey returned to the store, Laura
was tired but felt warm inside. Her injured ankle ached a little from all the walking, and her body still hurt whenever she
turned a certain way, but she didn't care. Minot might have
its share of bad sorts, but most of the people she had encountered today were genuine and sincere, full of loyalty and
value . . . Unlike many of the people with whom Pa had sur-
rounded himself.

The thought struck Laura hard. She had never taken the
time to try and understand why she had never felt quite at
ease with many of Pa's acquaintances. He had been a sociable person, a man who liked fancy gatherings and enjoyed
impressing people. But he had had a tendency to attract the

wrong sort of people, those who had enjoyed only the company of his wealth, not him. Pa with his booming laughter and open arms . . . Laura smiled sadly. She would always miss him, but being away from his acquaintances and being in the company of honest people like Ruth and Stacey, and the others she had met today, was refreshing.

❅❅❅
Chapter Five

As Laura and Stacey settled across from each other in the wagon bed for the five-mile trip back to the farm, Stacey smiled at her friend. "Well, what did you think of Minot?"

Laura thought, then said, "There are a lot of saloons."

They laughed together. "Twenty-seven was the last count," Stacey said. "They're everywhere. It can be a rough place. I wouldn't stay in town at night, that's for sure."

Laura feigned seriousness. "Probably a sensible idea, Miss Main." They laughed again, then Laura leaned forward and squeezed Stacey's hand. "I'm glad we are becoming very close friends."

Stacey's eyes twinkled. "So am I."

Caleb took the wagon seat, grabbed the reins, and they were off. The ride lulled Laura. Her eyelids grew heavy. Shortly after the wagon departed Minot, she was jolted awake several times when her head drooped to one side. Laughing, Stacey told her she should lie down on top of the blankets and go to sleep among the supplies and fabric. The ride wasn't a long one, but at least she'd be comfortable. Too sleepy to sit up, Laura decided that was a good idea.

Some time later Stacey nudged her awake.

The sweet smell of roasting ham wafted to Laura. Her stomach growled. Sitting up, she rubbed her sleepy eyes and brushed strands of loose hair from her face. Stacey had already been lifted from the wagon. She had an armful of supplies. "We're home, sleepyhead," she teased.

Laura smiled and stretched. Then she felt Caleb's dark eyes on her.

Turning, she found him staring at her from where he stood beside the horses. His look contained none of the resentment and bitterness it had when he had first realized whose daughter she was. It was different from the passionate look he had given her this morning in front of the washbasin. His eyes were alight and filled with gentleness now. Again his rugged look was softened. "Have a good rest?" he asked.

Nodding, she tried to blink the sleep from her eyes. "It wasn't long."

"You should go up to bed early. Your head's probably still healing."

"It hasn't bothered me since that first day, when I had such a headache."

He drew near the wagon bed as Stacey carried supplies into the house. "Let me help you down," he said.

Laura frowned. Stacey was beginning to make a habit of leaving her and Caleb alone together. In mere minutes Caleb could play havoc with her senses. She studied him, not trusting him. His hair was unruly, and his clothes were splattered with mud. Despite his unkempt appearance, there was still something about him that sent a thrill ripping through her whenever he looked at her in a tender way or drew near her. "You are the most puzzling man I know, Mr. Main. One minute you don't like me, the next you like me too much, the next—"

"I'm offering to help you get out of the wagon, Laura. That's all."

"You have also become quite familiar with my name," she pointed out softly. "One day it was Miss Kent, the next it became Laura. I'm not at all certain I like that." But she did, and that was the truth. She liked the deep tones he used when he said her name, was thrilled every time it rolled off his tongue.

He shrugged. "Just the way we do things out here."

"While I'm certain I need help out of this wagon, I'm not certain you should be the one to lift me down." *Considering what happened this morning and this afternoon*, she thought. The day had been entirely too eventful where he was concerned.

A grin played at the corners of his mouth. "There's no one else here who can help you."

"Then I'll manage alone, Mr. Main. After the incident at the washbasin this morning, and considering what happened this afternoon, you should keep your distance."

"When I'm close, you're as nervous as a new colt."

She lifted her chin. He raised an eyebrow. She raised her skirt, preparing to climb over the wagon edge without assistance. He propped wide-stretched hands on the rail, effectively blocking her.

"Mr. Main . . ."

"Seems we have a passel of stubbornness between the two of us, *Miss Kent*," he drawled, stressing her name, his eyes sparkling.

"A passel of stubbornness? Exactly what is a passel?" she asked, irritated.

"A whole lot."

"Get out of my way, Mr. Main."

"Woman . . . you're the most stubborn—"

She shot to the other side of the wagon, lifted her skirt, and put one leg over the rail. She wasn't entirely sure how she would accomplish this, but accomplish she would. She didn't intend to allow Caleb Main to put so much as a hand on her waist again. Surely if she got one leg over, she could swing the other over and slip off the edge. Simple. And wouldn't Caleb be furious at the ease with which she did it? She fixed a smug look on her face, confident she had already won another small battle. Then she swung the other leg over, her bottom resting on the wagon rail, and started to ease down the side. "I think—"

The back of her silk skirt snagged on something and rode up her silk-encased legs. Gasping, Laura reached frantically around to try to free the skirt before she either toppled head first onto the ground or was forced to climb back into the wagon bed somehow. Her palms perspired. Her heart thudded. She lost her hold on the rail and slipped . . . right into Caleb Main's waiting arms.

He grinned, his heated gaze fixed on her legs. The back of her skirt was bunched up around the curve of her bottom, the front dangling just below her knees. "I've had my share of beautiful women," he said thickly, "but none has fallen into my arms like this. Just thought I'd come around to this side to help. Seems I was just in time."

"Put me down," she demanded. His body was too hard and too lean. She was aware of his corded shoulder muscles beneath her hands, of every little crease around his mouth and eyes, of the way his black hair curved to just below his shoulders. He was having quite a time ogling her. "I-if you have an ounce of decency in you, you'll look the other way, Mr. Main. You were with that woman all afternoon. Didn't you get your fill . . ." Gasping, Laura clamped a hand over her mouth.

His grin widened, if that was possible. "Never claimed to be decent. And a man never gets enough."

"Mr. Main!"

"Patience, Laura," he said, laughing. "If I just put you down, you'll walk away from this with no skirt. I'll enjoy that, but you won't."

She swallowed a retort to that. She just wanted to get out of this predicament. One big hand held her firmly against him while the other eased around her to work on freeing the skirt. They were thigh against thigh, stomach to stomach. She felt his length pressing against her and swallowed hard, more aware of him as a man than ever. He smelled slightly of perspiration. His strong jaw was covered with the black, coarse whiskers of his beard. The first few buttons of his shirt were unbuttoned, and Laura's gaze fastened on the dark curls just below the hollow of his throat. Her heart leapt. She tried to muster what little dignity she had left, and even that failed her. How easy slipping her arms up and around his neck would be! How easy pressing her fingertips to the back of his head and urging his head down—

"Do you realize," he murmured, his warm breath smelling of rich molasses, "that you forgot to telegraph Bismarck?"

She had. In the midst of her body's heated response to him, the realization hit her with the force of a flying stone. Her jaw dropped open, then clamped shut. She had spent hours in Minot and had not even bothered to ask where the telegraph office was located! She shot him a look of annoyance. "You sound as if you remembered all afternoon and *hoped* I wouldn't remember."

He stirred against her. She gasped, not knowing how much more of this bodily contact she could endure without making a fool of herself. A light flickered in his glazed eyes. Amusement? Satisfaction? Both, she thought angrily. He said, "A body might think that, yes. . . ."

"Why didn't you remind me, Mr. Main?" she managed.

Now his eyes narrowed. He had managed to free the skirt, but still he held her against him. His gaze dipped to her breasts, rising and falling with the rapid force of her breath. Finally he released her and stepped away. Laura breathed deeply, as if she'd not had fresh air in days. She clung to the side of the wagon for support.

Caleb turned away and walked to the wagon seat, where he gathered some tools he had bought in Minot. "I'd rather not have Matt Kent showing up here any sooner than he has to."

Laura squared her shoulders. The man had just put her through a humiliating ordeal. Now this! She put her hands on her hips and stomped to the front of the wagon. "You refused to take me to Bismarck because my pa's there. You couldn't remind me to telegraph because you don't want him *here*. . . ."

"I'm not your keeper, woman."

"No, you are not. But if my name was anything but Kent, you would have reminded me to telegraph, isn't that right, Mr. Main?"

"Maybe."

Spinning away, Laura gave a cry of frustration. She gathered the edge of her skirt and stomped to the house. "I am sick of this business about my pa, Caleb Main!" she shot over her shoulder.

By the time she reached the porch, her feet were flying and she was nearly in tears. Infuriated, all she could think of was getting as far away from this man as possible.

Ruth appeared in the doorway. Mumbling an apology, Laura brushed by her, then swept past Stacey near the stove and hurried to the little staircase. She didn't stop until she was safely upstairs in her room. She plopped on the edge of the bed, but bounced right back up and paced, unable to sit still. Damn him!

Downstairs, Ruth and Stacey shared a look of confusion and shock. Stacey started for the stairs. Ruth shook her head and said, "No. She'll come down when she's ready, girl."

Nodding, Stacey pushed the cloth bag of coffee back on the cupboard shelf and shut the door. She smiled to herself. Just like she'd figured might happen, the more she left Laura and Caleb alone, the more things heated up. "I'll get the material from the wagon, then," she said. She couldn't help but wonder aloud, "What do you suppose happened?"

Ruth stared at the door. "I'm not sure. But I think it's time I had a talk with Caleb." With that, she followed Stacey outside.

Stacey went to the wagon to gather more things. Ruth went to the shed near the house and found Caleb hanging a new saw on a hook over an iron plow.

"Guess you have a passel of questions," he said without looking at her. "I thought you would the day I brought Laura Kent here."

Ruth put both hands on her hips. "I only want to know why she's up in her room crying right now, Caleb."

His head jerked around. "She's crying?"

"I imagine. She had tears in her eyes when she flew past me and Stacey and charged upstairs. Next thing I heard her door shut."

Caleb swore under his breath. "She had some trouble getting out of the wagon. And she forgot to telegraph Bismarck while we were in Minot. I remembered and didn't remind her," he said, looking stunned and a little sheepish. "She's crying?"

"Yes. Why didn't you remind her if you remembered?"

He leaned against the plow, the line of his jaw hardening as he studied the dirt floor. "Why the hell do I do a lot of the things I do when I'm around her? I told her I didn't want Matt Kent coming around here any sooner than he had to."

Ruth's temper flared. She moved to stand near him. "Now, I raised you different, Caleb. Hate the man all you want, but Laura Kent's done nothing wrong. If you didn't telegraph for her, you'd best saddle a horse, ride back to Minot, and let her kin know where she is. The girl must feel terrible! She lived through that accident. Now she's staying with strange people in a strange place. She had nothing to do with the things that happened between you and her pa when she was younger. Remember the manners you were taught and treat her right!"

Caleb turned back to reposition the saw. "I telegraphed Bismarck, just didn't get the chance to let her know I had. The telegraph said something about the three bodies Harlan and James went after—I paid them to take the bodies on to Bismarck. I didn't say exactly where Laura was, just that she's near Minot. I don't want Matt Kent on my land, Ma, and you know it. He'll go to Minot and ask questions. I told some friends there to let me know when he shows up. I'll take Laura to him then. If Kent doesn't show up by the time Harlan and James come back, I'll think of something else."

"You could take Laura to Bismarck yourself."

"You know I'm not going anywhere near that place."

"Don't growl at me, Caleb. Remember who I am."

"Ma . . . I have the evening chores to do."

"You have a lot of thinking to do, too, and you'd darn well better do it." She turned away and quickly walked back to the house.

As Caleb drove the cattle to water at a small creek that cut through his land, his thoughts centered on Laura. She was in the house crying, Ma had said. Damn.

Laura . . .

The woman stirred him like no woman ever had. This afternoon, when she and Stacey had returned to the wagon, her blue eyes had shimmered with contentment. Just this morning, when he'd kissed her, he'd seen those same eyes slit with passion. She'd tasted as sweet as molasses candy and had smelled like morning freshness. He'd wanted to pull the pins from her hair and watch the spun gold fall around her face and shoulders. He'd wanted to push his fingers into the cornsilk.

He'd hardly had an hour's sleep since Laura had been under his roof. Every time he laid back on his bed, he thought of her—beautiful Laura, who lay in another bed just down the hall outside his door. He wanted her in his arms, wanted to press his lips against her soft, creamy neck.

Laura. A woman he wanted to gather in his arms. Not like some saloon girl. Like a woman he wanted to keep in his life. His thoughts seemed to go off in that direction a lot lately.

This afternoon in Minot he had stood staring at the telegraph building for a long time, wondering if he should even go inside and give the message that would bring Matt Kent to Minot to collect Laura. Then he'd thought of Laura, knowing she hadn't planned to be stranded. She was caught up in circumstances beyond her control. She'd endured the coach accident and the deaths of those people only to find herself right in the middle of his old feud with her pa, a feud she hadn't known anything about. She would be glad to go home, he assumed, if only to escape his hatred of her father.

But he wouldn't be glad when she left.

Three times today he'd been painfully close to her. Three times now he'd somehow managed to put her from him. What he wanted didn't matter. Laura was what mattered. For her, he'd paid Harlan and James to go after the bodies and take them to Bismarck. For her he'd sent the message that would bring Matt Kent to Minot.

In the plum grove Caleb had said he was using her for revenge, which wasn't true. Still, letting her think that would force distance between them, he'd *thought*. But his plan hadn't accomplished a thing, and he doubted if any force in the world would keep them away from each other if Laura stayed much longer. She was burning for him just as much as he was burning for her.

The cattle came back peacefully. Caleb went to the barn and pitched hay into a pile while the dog, Sam, plopped down in a far corner and watched. Presently Caleb and Sam went outside to watch the sunset on the endless prairie. Miles away the land blended with the sky, and the sun hovered, a blazing red ball on the horizon. Squatting, Caleb rubbed Sam behind the ears.

"I meant to tell her I'd telegraphed," Caleb said to the dog, his thoughts still centered on Laura. "Other things got in the way. She fell asleep. Then she had that mule-headed attitude about not letting me help her down from the wagon. I thought I'd tease her a bit and . . . damn."

Sam barked, his eyes fastened on the horizon. A small shape moved some distance away, and Caleb followed the trail of tall, parting grass with his eyes. Sam twitched, itching to go after whatever it was. Caleb chuckled. "Go on, mutt. I need a friend and all you want to do is chase prairie dogs. Get out of here. Chase it but don't kill it."

Sam barked again, then tore off through the prairie grass. Caleb watched him run straight, curve, run circles, then plow a path to the east.

Sam disappeared. Birds flew overhead. There was Sam's distant barking and the sound of the breeze sweeping, rippling through the grass. Sunflowers waved like open yellow hands. Caleb breathed deeply of the summer-scented evening air.

He thought again of Laura's golden hair and clear blue eyes. He thought of the way she'd responded to him this morning, opening her mouth in sweet offering. He thought of the way she'd looked waking up in that wagon bed, stretching her beautiful, slender arms. His body tightened, wanting her.

Things couldn't go on this way. They were both miserable.

He'd kissed her, but that didn't give him a right to her. She was engaged, probably to a rich man, if Kent had had anything to do with the matter. Only the best for a Kent—that had always been Matt Kent's motto. The best and all. Caleb doubted if that had changed.

Fiancé aside, hooking up with Laura Kent, as much as he wanted her, would mean clashing with Matt Kent again. And Kent would remember him. Caleb wanted no part of that.

Early the next morning Caleb was in the shed mending a yoke. The door stood open. He watched Laura come from the house and move toward the privy. She saw him and inclined her head to him as she passed. Returning the gesture, Caleb continued his work. Then, knowing he owed her an apology, he strode to the door and waited.

She soon emerged from the privy, avoiding his gaze. Her hair was pulled back and braided. The long beautiful golden plait slithered down the back of her green dress to her waist, where it tapered off. Her eyes were slightly puffy with sleep, and her skin glowed with morning freshness. Caleb spoke her name low. She gave him a slight nod and continued toward the house.

"Laura," he said louder. "We need to talk."

She stopped but didn't turn around. Crossing her arms, she hugged herself. "There is nothing more to say, Mr. Main," she said wearily. "You've made your feelings toward me very apparent."

You don't know a thing about my feelings for you, Caleb thought. *You don't know I want you so much these hands ache just to touch you.*

Then he felt guilty again.

She had people back in Bismarck, family, friends . . . a fiancé, he reminded himself. But she looked so soft and pretty right now, he could easily say to hell with Bismarck and everything waiting for her there. He could easily say to hell with that fiancé, whoever the man was.

But he wouldn't. Laura's life belonged to her. He had no claim on it.

"Just wanted to say sorry about that telegraph business. I did telegraph Bismarck. Even sent someone after the bodies."

Slowly she turned around, her eyes as clear as the morning sky and sparkling with surprise. "Did you?"

He nodded. "They're on their way to Bismarck to be buried."

"Thank you. I'm certain Mr. Trumball's sister in Bismarck will thank you, too."

"No one there'll know I'm responsible. I'd rather not have my name mentioned. I wanted to say sorry. I didn't remind you to telegraph because I'd already done it. I have a passel of fun teasing you sometimes, something I shouldn't do because things get away from us. Soon we're arguing."

She smiled weakly—an act that touched him inside—and thanked him again. "I don't expect you to be 'my keeper,' as you put it. I never have. Our meeting was sheer accident. I do need someone to take me to Minot again soon, however, so I can telegraph my Aunt Rebecca in Kenmare. That's where I was going when the accident happened."

Caleb nodded. "I didn't mean what I said. We both have tempers, I guess. There's something else I need to say—using you for revenge was never in my head. Hope you believe that. I'll even take you to Kenmare if you want."

She paused, as if giving his admission some thought. "No. You already telegraphed Bismarck. My fiancé will be coming. And no more explanations are necessary. Ruth and Stacey and I enjoy each other's company. If you will permit me to stay here until my—"

"Stay as long as you want."

Nodding, she murmured yet another thank you, then turned away. She took several steps in the direction of the house. Caleb watched her—her high shoulders, sleek braid, and thin waist and arms. Someday she would walk away from this place for good, he knew. His gut tightened at the thought.

Suddenly she turned back, not looking at all surprised that he was watching her. "I suppose since you've made an attempt to mend certain things between us, I should be completely honest with you, too. I thought a lot last night, about you and my pa mostly. I'm not sure what happened between the two of you, Mr. Main, and perhaps I'll never know. I'm not sure I want to know. He was a loving father. Ma died when I was three, and Pa raised me. I remember mornings when he would scoop me up, toss me over his shoulder—me still in my nightdress—and take me for a ride on his favorite horse."

She crossed her arms again and hugged her shoulders, looking up at the sky. Caleb thought he saw tears glisten in her eyes. She was a beautiful vision, her head tilted back that way, her neck smooth, her lips pink. Caleb wondered why she was telling him this. Her childhood experiences with Matt Kent changed nothing between him and Kent.

"Sometimes . . ." She swallowed and smiled weakly. "Sometimes when I was scared of the dark, something that still happens occasionally, Pa would hold me and rock me for hours. He sang songs and . . . well, those are just some of my memories." She brought her gaze down to rest on him again. "To me, Pa was a good man. I'm not trying to say you are wrong, Mr. Main. I'm just saying this is how I saw him. In any case, since we are having a few moments of honesty, and since you hate Pa so and do not want him here, you should know he will not be coming at all. He died in February."

Caleb stood in stunned silence, as if he'd just hit a stone wall. He'd been preparing to come face to face again with the man he hated more than anything, and she was telling him Matt Kent was dead? The man had stood well over six feet and had been as packed as a mountain. Caleb still had an image in his mind. Kent's hair was lightened by the sun and his skin was bronzed. A hell of a physical man. Word was, he rode from town to town doing his own business. He slept under the stars and helped drive his own cattle. He wasn't a man to hide behind a pile of papers in that fancy Bismarck house of his.

Caleb remembered the scuffle he and Kent had had the day of their last encounter. Kent had robbed him of everything and Caleb had gone to try and pound some sense into him. He'd taken a beating he almost hadn't lived through.

Matt Kent dead? Impossible. The man seemed as solid to him now as he had then. Caleb rubbed his jaw and swore under his breath.

"I thought you should know, Mr. Main," Laura said in a choked voice. "When the coach went over that hill, I was trying to escape Bismarck for a time. All I wanted to do was heal inside."

With that, she turned, still hugging herself, and walked to the house.

Caleb stood in the doorway for a long time. He damn sure hadn't helped her heal. She was a woman who had just lost a father she'd loved. He'd been feeling sorry for himself because her appearance in his life had stirred up things he didn't want stirred up. He knew how bad Matt Kent could be, but all she had were good memories of the man. Memories that ought to be left alone. He had hurt her.

Cursing himself, he shrank back inside the shed.

✳ ✳ ✳
Chapter Six

FOR THE NEXT several nights after everyone went to bed, Stacey stayed up late in her room to sew one of Laura's dresses, using the calico patterned with black-eyed Susans and goldenrods. Ma knew. During the daytime Stacey would be doing her chores, turn around, and there would be Ma to help. Laura volunteered to gather eggs, saying Stacey looked tired. At first Stacey didn't want her to help, but the disappointment on Laura's face made Stacey agree. Besides, Laura said, if Stacey didn't have help, how would she ever find the time to teach Laura how to make the dresses? Stacey smiled, guarding her secret, and handed Laura the egg-gathering basket.

From that point Stacey let Laura help in various ways. She and Laura talked a lot while they picked tomatoes, corn, and spinach from the kitchen garden. Twice they took meals to Mrs. Dahl and cleaned the Norwegian woman's sod house. Laura Kent wasn't snooty as Stacey had always thought the daughter of a rich man like Matt Kent would be.

One afternoon they took eggs and butter to a family that lived in a rickety tar-paper shack between the Main farm and Minot. The small home had two windows, a door, and several stovepipes. Laura sat quietly as Stacey reined the horses to one side of the shack, and Stacey realized her friend was shocked by the sight of the shack. "Sorry," Stacey whispered. "Should've explained. I forget you've never seen some of the things you're seeing out here."

Laura smiled weakly, picked up the basket of eggs, and followed Stacey to the door.

The Kincaids were happy to get the eggs and butter. They greeted Laura, then asked about Caleb and Ruth. Stacey talked with Paula Kincaid, while Paula's husband, Blake, sat by one of the stoves, spreading some of the butter on a slice of bread. Laura sat on a stool and sang softly to the smallest child—a little blond girl. The other child, a boy of eight, retreated to a corner to spin a wooden top on a table. Presently Laura wandered over to talk to him, too, but he shied away. She couldn't help but notice how shabbily dressed this family was.

Soon Stacey and Laura said goodbye, went outside, and climbed back up on the wagon seat. Stacey spotted a small figure dash around one corner of the house and knew it was Amanda, the middle child, the strange one people stayed away from. Amanda was violent, some said. She'd attacked her ma and her brother, which was why she wasn't even too welcome around her own house. Her thin blond hair was always tangled, and her limbs were like twigs. She limped, and one arm just hung at her side—the effect of an illness she'd had as a baby, Ma had once said. Amanda wandered about alone, sometimes out here on the prairie, sometimes in town. Stacey had seen her many times by the river after church service, staring curiously at the church as though she wanted to go inside. She felt sorry for Amanda, but like most everyone else, she just didn't know what to do to help the child. Word was some folks had tried to befriend Amanda once, but Blake hadn't taken too kindly to the gesture. The Kincaids preferred that Amanda be left to herself. The situation was bad, but with Blake having such a hot temper and all, the subject of Amanda was better off not mentioned.

Stacey took the reins and shook them to prompt the horses into action. The wagon jolted forward. Miles of prairie lay ahead, and this afternoon not one breeze stirred the tall grass or cooled her and Laura. The sun blazed down.

Stacey wiped sweat from her brow with the back of her hand and stole a glance at Laura, who hadn't said a word since they'd set out. "You're pretty quiet. And pale."

"There was hardly room for one person to be comfortable in that place, let alone four, Stacey," Laura said softly, her shock evident in her voice. "How do they even stay warm during the winter?"

"Blake cuts sod from out here and stacks it against the place. Keeps out the cold and wind. Thanks to Caleb's good luck, we have the house we do. Most don't."

"Another cold fact about life on the prairie?"

Stacey nodded. If anything came of those looks Caleb and Laura sent back and forth, could Laura accept life out here? It was probably a big change from what she was used to, but if she fell in love with Caleb . . . Stacey figured she'd just try to teach Laura as much as she could. That was all she could do. Laura would have to do the rest—if she ever wanted to. At least now Laura's face had more color than when she'd first seen the shack.

"Life on the prairie," Laura said softly, gazing across the land.

Early Sunday morning Stacey came downstairs with Laura's finished calico dress and bonnet tossed over a forearm. Laura was seated across from Caleb at the table. Spotting Stacey and the dress, she leapt up and flew across the room to hug Stacey.

"No wonder you've looked tired!" Laura scolded. "You stitched this dress in two days in between all the other things we've been doing."

"I wanted you to have it for today," Stacey said, laughing in delight at Laura's pleased reaction. "Now, let me get some breakfast."

Later when Laura was dressed in the calico, Caleb stole glimpses of her. The goldenrods on the material enhanced the gold strands in her hair. She had braided it again, only this time the braid was coiled and pinned to her nape. The bonnet framed her pretty ivory face. Her cheeks and lips were flushed with excitement.

As he lifted her into the wagon so they could ride to church, Laura met his gaze, her eyes sparkling with excitement. Caleb laughed at her. "You might look all grown up, Laura Kent, but there's a little girl in you."

"Always," she teased. "Always."

The air between them was better. They'd reached a silent understanding, Caleb thought. She understood that he hated

Matt Kent, and he understood that she loved her pa. Simple as that.

Once Ruth and Stacey were settled, Caleb took the reins and shook them gently. The horses pawed, dipped their heads, and started off. The wagon eased forward.

As they entered the valley of plum trees again, Laura smiled. She was glad things were less tense between her and Caleb. During the past few days, he had been polite, a perfect gentleman. The man really was not such a bear after all, unless he was—what was that word Stacey often used? Riled. An adequate word. The business about Pa was fading, or at least it had been put aside. Laura was glad. As she had tried to point out to Caleb Main, he had his memories of Matthew Kent, and she had hers. There was nothing to argue about.

The church, a small white structure that resembled the schoolhouse, was set apart from the town, which amused Laura. She supposed if the church weren't set apart, religious music and saloon music might clash, annoying people in all establishments.

Rows of benches filled the inside of the church. Up front a wooden stand held an open Bible. Four open windows allowed a cool breeze to drift through the little church. Off to one side people were gathered around a man Laura assumed was the preacher. He wore an immaculate white shirt, a dark waistcoat, and dark trousers. His brown hair was neatly combed. His eyes were sharp, and his smile and body movements revealed his sincerity as he talked with people. Laura caught a glimpse of Mrs. Statum, the schoolteacher, who waved. Laura smiled as the warmth of the people and the surroundings enveloped her.

When Mr. Alman, the storekeeper, appeared to talk to Caleb, Laura realized Stacey had somehow managed to cleverly maneuver her way around so that Laura would end up sitting next to Caleb. When they filed between benches, Stacey and Ruth sat to Laura's left. Caleb would have to sit on Laura's right when he finished talking to Mr. Alman. When they had first walked in, the order had been Ruth, herself, Stacey, and Caleb—Stacey should have ended up be-

tween her and Caleb on the bench. At some point, possibly
during the time Laura had been inspecting the preacher,
Stacey had eased in front of her. Glancing at Stacey in
amusement, Laura shook her head in a knowing way. Stacey
lifted her brows, pretending not to know why Laura was giving her such a look.

The members of the congregation took their seats. Mrs.
Green, with whom Laura and Stacey had visited on Laura's
first trip to Minot, sang an opening song. She was a stout
woman with a thick brown braid twirled and pinned to the
crown of her head. Her powerful voice filled the church and
held the attention of most everyone, save a few restless children. Mrs. Green finished, a few amens were murmured,
then Preacher Jacobs took the stand. More people had entered the church—every bench was filled, and several people stood near a wall. Caleb moved closer to Laura to make
room for a bonneted woman cradling an infant.

His thigh pressed against Laura's, and suddenly she was
no longer enjoying the quaintness of the church, the people,
or the service. Caleb Main was entirely too close for her
peace of mind . . . and body. She tried to subtly ease closer to
Stacey but found no room there. Of course not, she thought
dryly. The situation was exactly as Stacey wanted it. Laura
frowned at Stacey, but she stared straight ahead at Preacher
Jacobs, pretending she didn't feel Laura's glare.

Caleb sat straight and rigid, his thigh muscled and firm
against hers, his hard upper arm pressing against her shoulder. His big hands were clasped in his lap, and he was rubbing his thumbs together. His squared, whiskered jaw was
clenched and his hair a bit ruffled from the ride. His clean
white shirt smelled slightly of the strong lye soap Ruth used,
but beneath that smell was another, a smell that taunted Laura's senses and made her want to squirm on the bench: the
musky masculine scent of Caleb.

Despite the breeze from the windows, the inside of the
church became stifling. Laura could hardly breathe. Her
pulse raced, and her body tingled. She wondered if Caleb
was as uncomfortable as she. Through the corner of her eye,
as she pretended to keep her gaze on Preacher Jacobs, she

saw that Caleb stared straight ahead, stone-faced and somber, his breathing even and steady. She wanted to throttle Stacey.

As uncomfortable as she was, Laura did manage to hear part of the sermon. The preacher spoke about the evils of gossip. Just in case anyone had noticed her awkward reaction to being this close to Caleb, Laura certainly hoped people would take the message to heart and seal their lips. Unfortunately such noble behavior wasn't true to human nature. Mouths might stay shut for a time; at least until this evening, when Preacher Jacobs's message began to fade. For some, the sermon would be lost as soon as they departed the church.

During Preacher Jacobs's closing words, Laura felt Caleb's dark eyes on her. She turned her head, and their eyes locked, his affectionate expression making her feel desired. She was seized with a sudden longing to reach out for one of his big hands, still clasped in his lap, as if . . . well, if he didn't keep them there, they might stray. She subdued her longing, aware of the many people surrounding them. Still, just to take his hand in hers, to trace the fingers and touch the palm she knew was probably callused from years of hard work . . .

Adrian. What about Adrian? His name pulsed in her mind. She could hardly believe she was having such intimate thoughts about Caleb while she was engaged to Adrian. Looking at Caleb with obvious want in her eyes was surely unfair to him, too, since she had every intention of marrying Adrian when she returned to Bismarck.

Despite her and Caleb's harsh words to each other from time to time since she had met him, they had settled into a kind of understanding. Laura suspected there was more to their relationship but refused to put a name to it. It was something she must leave right here in Minot when she left for Bismarck anyway, so why dwell on it? Dwelling on it would only permit it to grow.

She tore her eyes from Caleb's, sensing that with a mere glance she had just revealed a lot of what she was thinking.

As he had once told her, sometimes words were not needed to express oneself.

Preacher Jacobs said the final prayer, ending it with "Amen." People immediately lifted their heads, and the little church filled with conversation and laughter. Children scampered about. Some raced outside, where Laura knew wagons and picnic baskets awaited. She followed Caleb outside.

At the church steps they parted, Caleb going off to talk with a group of men, Laura going with Ruth and Stacey to talk with a group of women. Quilts and picnic baskets began appearing on the grass. Nearby the Souris River stirred, rippling and glittering under bright afternoon sunshine. Tall willows waved from the riverbank, and little plum trees called to Laura. She meant to pluck a few of their sweet offerings before leaving later.

She was introduced to a number of people and finally settled into a conversation with Mrs. Statum, who spoke again of her grandchildren. During Laura's last year at school in Chicago, she had tutored children for a time and had grown to love them. With much interest she listened to Mrs. Statum.

Presently someone called to Mrs. Statum. She squeezed Laura's hand affectionately, then wandered off. Laura drifted to the other side of the church, where she knew Caleb had left the wagon. There she found Ruth just spreading their quilt. Caleb and his group of friends were nearby.

Caleb was dressed in dark brown trousers, a white shirt, and suspenders. The trousers fit him wonderfully, molding to his thighs and buttocks, Laura noticed as he stood with his back to her. She silently scolded herself for letting her gaze take such a path, particularly so soon after she had decided nothing could ever come of the desire they felt for each other. Caleb hadn't noticed she was watching him, thank goodness. A short time later she saw him walking toward town.

"He said he's going to telegraph your aunt in Kenmare," Ruth said from behind her.

Turning, Laura smiled and took one side of the quilt Ruth

had just unfolded to spread on the ground. Stacey appeared, her face flushed. She took Laura's hand, and they wandered off, Stacey introducing Laura to more people. After a time they returned to the quilt.

Soon Caleb joined them, stretching out on the quilt and propping himself on an elbow. He told Laura there was no telegraph in Kenmare, but if she wanted to write her aunt a letter, he'd be glad to send it to Kenmare with a riverboat captain. He explained that the Souris River connected with the Des Lacs to the northeast, and Kenmare sat on the banks of the Des Lacs. Laura nodded. Ruth handed him a plate. He passed it to Laura. She smiled and thanked him.

"He's never so mannered to me," Stacey teased.

Laura felt heat spread across her face. Caleb narrowed his eyes at his sister. "Stace . . ."

"Well, really. You never are, Caleb."

He tossed an empty tin cup at her. "You look pretty all pink like that. I noticed your Charles Duncan saw fit to come to church for the first time in weeks."

"You devil!" Laughing, Stacey tossed the cup back at him. It hit him on the head. Caleb growled an objection, but playfulness showed on his face. He lunged for Stacey, scattering other tin cups Ruth had just removed from the basket. Stacey screeched and jumped up.

"You two just get yourselves away from here if you're going to be doing that," Ruth scolded.

"He couldn't catch me even if there weren't people and plates in the way," Stacey taunted.

Muscles twitched in Caleb's cheek. His eyes were on Ruth, but Laura could tell that he was actually watching Stacey from the corner of his eye, fighting a grin and the urge to go after her.

"Sit down, Stace," he said. "You're too old to be racing around the churchyard."

" 'Sit down, Stace,' " she mocked. "You just can't catch me and you know it."

The taunt proved too much to swallow. Caleb jumped up. Stacey raced off with Caleb at her heels. Laura laughed, watching them tear through the maze of quilts. Ruth shook her head and said, "*She's* too old? Pshaw! Look at *him*."

Stacey was right. He never caught her. Some time later he came back to the quilt, breathing hard. A smile teased the corners of Laura's mouth. Caleb shot her a playful glare. "Say anything and I'll turn you over my knee. And wouldn't that be downright embarrassing?"

"Caleb!" Ruth gasped.

Laura turned away to hide her smile. Soon she turned back, composed, a stern expression set on her face.

But Caleb saw the twinkles in Laura's blue eyes and wasn't fooled . . . wasn't fooled at all. He snatched up a plate and filled it with food. The beef was moist, the bread thick and crusty. The dried plums were chewy and sweet. When he finished eating, he put the plate down and wandered off to visit more people. He spotted Stacey when she returned and sat on the quilt beside Laura. He vowed to catch his sister before the end of the afternoon—sometime when she least expected it.

Laura and Stacey finished eating and went to turn a rope for a group of young girls. The girls skipped through it, singing in cadence with the snap of the rope on the grass. During the fourth song, Laura spotted a small child huddled beneath a tree on the riverbank.

Possibly five or six years old, the girl had tangled honey-colored hair. She was dirty, and her patterned dress was torn in places. Her thumb was firmly set in her mouth as she stared at the river. Laura couldn't fathom why anyone would bring such a child to church looking so disheveled.

Stacey soon tired of turning the rope and said she was going to rest on the quilt. A tall blond girl took Stacey's place. Laura swept the rope around a few more times, then handed her end to one of the other girls.

As she approached the child near the riverbank, Laura thought she would take the girl's hand and bring her over to play. She lowered herself to the girl's level. There was no movement, no acknowledgment of Laura's presence. Dark blue eyes continued to stare at glittering water.

"Hello. My name is Laura. Want to come and jump rope?"

Silence. Birds fluttered and chirped overhead. The picnic sounds were distant—laughter, conversations, shouts.

"When I was a girl, I loved jumping rope," Laura said. "Would you like to come and try?"

Nothing.

"Please?"

Suddenly the girl jumped up and limped away, one arm dangling at her side. Laura's first thought was that the girl was injured, but the child wasn't screaming or crying or doubling over with pain. Something was very odd here, and Laura meant to find out what. She feared that if the girl wandered too far from the churchyard, her parents might worry. The girl might get hurt, and no one would know. Laura started to follow.

A strong hand suddenly gripped her arm, halting her. She glanced over her shoulder to find Caleb solemnly shaking his head. "Leave her be, Laura."

She stared at him. He did not understand the situation, that was all. Once she explained it to him, he would agree that she should go after the girl. "She could get lost or hurt. I cannot simply 'leave her be.'"

"She won't get lost. She does this all the time. She's different. Everyone knows that and treats her different, too. She deals with it by staying in her own world," Caleb responded, his dark eyes soft. "Leave her be."

Laura's chest constricted at his words. *Everyone knows that and treats her different?* She remembered a deformed child she had tutored once in Chicago. Benjamin. Benjamin, who had been born without fingers on one hand. When she and Benjamin had done something as simple as walk up and down the street, enjoying a nice afternoon, other children and even adults had been cruel, whispering and giggling within hearing distance. One day Laura had arrived to instruct Benjamin and had found him huddled in a closet with tears streaming down his cheeks. She had drawn him against her breast and had held him until his sobs ceased. Then he had told her how cruel his own father had been, ridiculing him about his deformed hand and telling him how he would never amount to anything. Laura would never forget the day she had taught Benjamin to play a beautiful piece on the piano. He had played the treble clef, and she had played bass. They had ended the lively piece perfectly and were laughing together when a round of applause from behind interrupted. There stood Benjamin's father, repentance shining in his eyes.

Now a little girl was being forced to live in "her own world." The thought pained Laura. "She limps, and something seems to be wrong with one of her arms. But how is she 'different,' Mr. Main?" Laura asked tightly.

He studied her, as if not wanting to tell her more. Finally he sighed and offered his arm. "You don't understand, Laura. Walk with me. I'll tell you about her. Believe me, she'll be fine. She'll get home. Her family didn't bring her here, that's for sure. They leave her to herself, and that's the way she prefers it. Amanda's always by that tree when service lets out."

Because of the many things that had passed between them, Laura was fearful of taking Caleb's arm. She didn't relish walking off and finding herself alone with him. Her reluctance must have revealed itself in her eyes.

"Laura, I won't bite you," Caleb said.

She smiled weakly and took his arm; she wanted to know more about Amanda. Caleb led her along the riverbank in the opposite direction from which Amanda had fled.

The grass was mossy here. Rushes, sleek and jointed, sprang up in places. Dragonflies flew in and out of the rushes, their wings blurry. The air smelled of sweet foliage and fresh water.

"Amanda was sick as a babe. No one knows what her illness was, but it left her with a leg and an arm that don't work right," Caleb said.

Laura flinched. " 'Don't work right?' You have a crude way of putting things, Mr. Main."

"It's the truth."

"All right, Amanda is different, but she is still just a little girl. A little girl who looks as though she has never been bathed. Her dress is too small and—"

"She's an angry girl, Laura. She won't let anyone touch

her, not even people in her family. Not that they want to help her. She's better off left to herself. That's the way they prefer it."

"Because of an illness she has a limp arm and leg, but surely she has a heart that needs love as the heart of any child does. She's a human being, not an animal," Laura said in disbelief.

"Not if you ask some people of Minot. Not if you ask her pa."

"What a horrible thing to say!"

He sighed in exasperation. "That's the way it is. You can't change it."

"I can try," Laura said, feeling an overwhelming urge to find Amanda and cradle the girl against her. What a wretched story! A story that stirred her emotions. Amanda was a child wounded by circumstances, just as Benjamin had been.

"All right. Try. Then what, Laura? You'll leave for Bismarck, and things will be the same for Amanda after you're gone. Do yourself *and* her a favor and don't stir things up during the little bit of time you'll be here. Some folks won't appreciate your meddling."

Laura stopped walking and withdrew her hand from his arm to stare at him incredulously. "Is that what you will think if I try and help Amanda? That I am meddling?"

Caleb was silent for a few seconds. "Yes, Laura. Yes, I will."

Caleb watched her, knowing her temper. He expected her to explode like dynamite any second and rail at him with words. Her eyes turned the color of leaping blue flames. Twisting in the direction Amanda had gone, she stomped off.

Caleb shook his head and muttered under his breath, "Stubborn woman. *Damn* stubborn woman."

Laura lifted the hem of her skirt and followed the river, hoping to catch up with Amanda. Reeds brushed against her skirt, and a willow branch scratched her face, but she kept going. Past the huge willow, its top roots gnarling and twisting. Past a crop of tall grass that swayed in the afternoon breeze. Past a little log house that faced the Souris. In places the grass gave way to dirt and pebbles, and Laura's boots slipped, but she regained her footing and kept going. She walked for what seemed a mile, scanning the riverbank and the sparse trees and brush to her left. Finally she stopped, knowing when to face defeat. Amanda was nowhere to be found.

Turning back, she suddenly decided this wasn't really defeat. Later she would ask Caleb more about Amanda. She would also ask about Amanda's ma—Caleb had said Amanda's family preferred to let her run wild like an animal. Laura wanted to talk with Amanda's parents and berate them for not taking care of their child. Perhaps that could be called "meddling," but she didn't care. Amanda should be treated as well as any child, maybe even more tenderly.

Caleb had said, "Folks won't appreciate your meddling." Well, there must be someone, somewhere in Minot, who cared about what happened to Amanda. What about the people she had met at church today? Surely they would care— she would simply bring the matter to their attention. But Caleb said Amanda was always beneath that tree after church service. Wouldn't someone else have noticed Amanda by now?

No one had, Laura decided. That was the only logical explanation for why no one had acted to remedy Amanda's situation. Well, Laura would visit Preacher Jacobs soon and tell him about Amanda. He would help. She would also enlist Stacey's aid. Obviously Caleb wanted no part of helping the girl, so she wouldn't trouble him about the matter. Ruth would help. There was Mr. Alman. And Mrs. Statum. As Laura started back toward the church, she thought of others she had met today who would help, too.

Laura returned to the picnic and saw that now was not a good time to wander around enlisting aid. People were gathering quilts and picnic baskets. Ruth tucked her quilt away in the wagon and was just reaching for the white cloth-covered picnic basket Stacey held when Caleb crept up behind Stacey and grabbed her by the waist. Lifting her, he spun her around. She screeched and struggled to free herself. Ruth grabbed the basket just as it slipped from Stacey's hands.

"Told you I'd catch you, Stace," Caleb said playfully. "Now, what should I do with you?"

"Put me down?"

"Oh, no. That would be too easy for you and too hard for me. You wounded my pride, Sis."

Stacey kicked at him, but Caleb managed to dodge her boots. Laura drew near the wagon, half smiling as she watched them. She was still annoyed that Caleb wanted no part of helping Amanda but couldn't help but admire the love that so obviously existed between him and his sister.

"Put me down, Caleb. Or I'll—I'll . . ." Stacey warned desperately.

"You'll what?"

"Caleb!" Ruth blurted, laughing. "Put the girl down."

Caleb gave his mother a boyish grin and Stacey a shake for good measure, then put her on her feet. Stacey spun around to face him. He narrowed his eyes to halt her. "Any retaliation and I'll dunk you in the river."

"Don't you dare do such a thing, Caleb Main!" Ruth said, gasping.

"To such a darling like my little sister, you mean?" Caleb's voice was filled with sarcasm.

"That's not it. I'm trying to get her to be something of a lady, and here you are chasing her around the churchyard and threatening to dunk her in the river."

"She needs a good dunk now and then. As for being a lady, well . . . that may never happen. She's got too much spice in her."

Stacey put her hands on her hips, mischief apparent in her eyes. Laura lifted a brow, not knowing what to expect next. "Watch out, mister," Stacey said.

Chuckling, Caleb skimmed a hand across the top of her head. "You've been threatening me since you were two feet tall and haven't carried through with one threat yet." He hoisted Stacey up and plopped her ungracefully in the wagon bed. She grumbled something but made no more moves that might be read as retaliation.

As Caleb lifted Laura up to the wagon bed, his hands big and warm on her waist, she frowned at him to let him know she was still annoyed with him about his attitude toward Amanda. He said nothing. Seconds later he strode to the front of the wagon and climbed up to sit beside Ruth, who waved goodbye to friends. Then Caleb snapped the reins, and the wagon jolted forward.

Away from the little church and through the valley of plums trees they rode. Elms mingled with ashes, and the late afternoon sun hung in the sky above a line of oaks. Through tree branches sunshine decorated the ground in places. As the wagon rambled on, a skunk paused to watch them, wriggling its nose, then disappearing into a crop of bushes. Some distance further, a yellow flickertail raced between several elms to find sanctuary.

"Do you know about Amanda?" Laura asked Stacey, whose eyes flared in response. "I see. You do. I had only to say the name."

Stacey shrugged. "I know her."

"You know *about* her."

"I know about her," Stacey said, nodding. Her answers were short and clipped. She glanced past Laura's shoulder, at the land beyond. She obviously didn't want to talk about Amanda, either.

Laura folded her arms stubbornly. "Tell me about Amanda. Tell me where she lives. Who is her mother? Was Amanda at the school the day we visited? Is she even *allowed* to go to school?"

"Is who allowed to go to school?" Ruth inquired, twisting around to look at Laura and Stacey.

Stacey took a deep breath and released the child's name. "Amanda."

"Oh."

Everyone remained quiet.

"Amanda . . ." Laura reminded them.

"Her family's real poor and just don't know what to do with her," Ruth said. "They live in a tar-paper shack. Have two other children. Have a hard enough time taking care of them. Amanda gets passed over."

The information hit Laura like a huge flying stone. Tar-paper shack? Two other children? She could be wrong, but seeing the way Stacey hung her head and the way Caleb stared straight ahead, his face stony, she didn't think so. Laura took a deep breath, trying to control her anger. "Amanda *Kincaid*?"

"Now, Laura," Caleb said, as if expecting her to explode. He would have good reason to think that.

"Beside the river today, Mr. Main," Laura said icily as she stared at his back. She was furious, and sometimes when her temper flared, she stumbled over her words, something she feared might happen now. "Beside the river you neglected to tell me who Amanda was, that I had already visited her family once. You said . . . well, instead you chose to go on about how I would be meddling by asking questions about Amanda. And you, Stacey . . . you should have told me just moments ago that I had already met Amanda's family, too. What in the world . . . ? What is wrong with everyone? She's a little girl, for heaven's sake!"

Ruth sighed. "Laura, some people would just as soon not bother with a child like Amanda. The kindness in your heart is a good thing, but, just like with Mrs. Dahl, a body can only do so much. Beyond that, people start thinking you're poking your nose in where it doesn't belong. We take food to the Kincaids and try to see that Amanda gets some now and then."

" 'A child like Amanda?' " Laura echoed, shaking her head, watching Ruth's stiff back.

"She can't be taught and—"

"You think she cannot be taught just because there is something wrong with one of her arms and legs?"

"Laura, you don't understand," Stacey said.

Laura drew yet another deep breath and exhaled slowly to try to catch her racing temper. "I'm trying. I am trying. But you're right. I don't. I've learned to care about all of you during the time I have been with you. You are decent people. But this . . . I don't understand . . . I can't believe what I'm hearing!"

Caleb gripped the reins. Ruth stared straight ahead. Stacey

twisted her lips and said softly, "It's just the way things are, Laura."

"Another fact about life on the prairie?"

Stacey was silent, guilty.

"Well, this is one thing I cannot accept," Laura told them all.

❋ ❋ ❋
Chapter Seven

"I WANT TO help Amanda," Laura told Ruth.

They were seated at the table, shelling peas. Stacey had gone out to help Caleb with evening chores. Sunset spilled into the big room through the windows, casting everything in a reddish-orange glow.

The peapods felt slightly coarse. Laura popped the end of one, the way Ruth had shown her to do, and pulled the string down, opening the pod and spilling the little peas into the bowl resting beneath her forearms. Laura glanced up, thinking Ruth had not heard what she said. Ruth had. Her usually relaxed features were drawn tight.

Laura pressed on. "She's a child, Ruth. A child who needs love and nurturing. She is obviously not getting that."

"You can't just snatch the child away from her family," Ruth said gently. "Think about it, Laura."

Laura set her jaw. "I have. All I care to. Something must be done."

"You can't change the situation. It's best left alone."

"Left alone, Amanda will wither and die."

Sighing, Ruth shelled more peas. Her experienced hands worked fast at this sort of work. The bowl set in front of her was half full. Laura's contained about a third less. She supposed she would get better at the task.

"How do you think you can help?" Ruth asked softly.

Laura felt a surge of surprise. At least Ruth was agreeing to listen. Laura had thought there would be much more of an argument. "I thought I would ask you and Caleb if I could bring Amanda here. I'll tell her stories, hold her, teach her. She needs something. She needs . . . affection and love."

"Don't know if her pa will let you take her."

99

"I'll talk to him. I'll convince him. He seemed nice enough."

"He thinks Amanda's better off left alone."

"I'll get Preacher Jacobs to go with me—someone Mr. Kincaid trusts. I'll—I'll take blankets and food, even clothes. I'll buy whatever they need. I brought some money. I can get more. All I need do is say my name in any bank in Dakota Territory and—"

"Don't be throwing the Kent name or Kent money around as long as you're here," Ruth warned, her eyes fixed on Laura.

That stopped Laura cold. She hadn't thought before she blurted out her ideas, but she so desperately wanted to help Amanda. She had been trying to convince Ruth and think aloud of a way to convince Blake Kincaid, too. She had watched Pa use his money so often that she had naturally tried to do the same thing. She was shocked at herself. These people lived plain and simple lives. As she had learned shortly after meeting Caleb, honesty and sincerity meant more to them than flashing money before their faces, particularly Kent money. Deeply ashamed, Laura stared down at the peas in her bowl. "I'm sorry, Ruth. I suppose I became so accustomed to Pa doing that sort of thing that I simply didn't think before I spoke or I never would have said those things. I meant no harm. Please believe me. I'll go see Mr. Kincaid by myself if all of you are so uncomfortable with my idea."

Ruth reached for another peapod from the pile in the middle of the table. "You're a stubborn one. If I let you venture out of here alone, Caleb'll have my head and yours."

"I just want to help."

"Oh, Laura."

"Ruth . . . please. I know Caleb already sent a telegraph to Bismarck. I'll send another and tell Adrian not to come yet, that I need to stay longer. I want to help Amanda. I know that will take time. I know that asking you to let me bring her here is asking a lot, but I won't expect you to take care of her."

Ruth glanced up sharply. "What makes you think you can help her?"

"I won't know for sure if I can unless I try. I tutored children for a time. I helped a little boy. He was deformed."

"All right, Laura. Speak with Caleb, but convincing him won't be near as easy as convincing me."

One victory. Laura gave a little cry of delight and clapped her hands together. The bowl of shelled peas tipped, then steadied itself. Ruth laughed and shook her head. "Life got more interesting the day you came here, Laura Kent," she said. "A whole lot more interesting."

"I believe Caleb's word is *passel*," Laura said, laughing.

"You're right. You've changed our lives in a passel of interesting ways."

They shelled more peas. There were shouts outside from Caleb and Stacey. At first Laura thought something was wrong, but Ruth smiled and continued her work. Then Laura heard the rich sound of Caleb's laughter and the high pitch of Stacey's screech.

Boots thudded on the porch. The door flew open. Stacey raced into the house, her eyes wild. "Ma, stop him! Now he's threatening to dunk me in the watering trough."

Shaking her head solemnly, Ruth stood, preparing to meet and scold Caleb, Laura thought. Then Caleb thundered through the doorway. Laura clamped a hand over her mouth to keep from laughing at the sight of him.

He was drenched. His normally wavy hair hung straight down, drops of water glistened on his beard, and his clothes clung to his skin. Wet, his white shirt became almost transparent, revealing the mass of darkness on his chest. With his fists clenched at his sides, he narrowed his dark eyes at Stacey, trying to look furious. But Laura noticed the smile twitching at the corners of his mouth.

Ruth took one look at Caleb's condition and lifted a brow at Stacey. Would the girl never learn? She supposed Stacey didn't want to, really. Caleb might catch up with Stacey now and then, but mostly she got the better of him. This time, though, she had a feeling Caleb would be hell-bent on revenge. With good reason. "I don't think so, Stacey Ann. This time you can't hide behind my skirt."

Stacey's eyes widened. Caleb chuckled. "Ma!" Stacey objected.

"Back outside and finish your business, both of you," Ruth said.

"But, Ma—!"

"Go on, Stacey."

Stacey had put the table between her and Caleb. Laura watched, her eyes flitting between them. Caleb hunched his shoulders slightly, like a predator, and started around Ruth's side of the table. Stacey eased around Laura's. Laura thought for certain Caleb might come lunging over the top of the table at any moment, so she braced herself for that storm. Stacey eased past her. Laura decided to take her bowl of peas and move to a safer place somewhere in the house, perhaps by the fireplace, where two tornadoes weren't threatening each other.

Just as she pushed her chair back to rise, Caleb rammed into her. Laura and the chair toppled over. Caleb grappled for them but was too late. Laura found herself in a most undignified position—in a disorderly pile on the floor with peas scattered all around her.

Caleb drew himself up and waited, knowing that as soon as Laura caught her breath, she'd be snapping at him.

She laughed.

Caleb stared at her. He knew Laura's explosive temper, and this wasn't like her.

"Are you going to continue gaping or help me up, Mr. Main?" she asked.

Ruth chuckled. Stacey giggled, then raced back outside. Laura's words and the sounds of humor snapped Caleb into action. He reached down, grabbed Laura by the shoulders and put her on her feet. Then he righted the chair. "Sorry. Sorry about that," he mumbled, bending down to pick up the tiny peas.

Laura bent to help him. Their eyes met, and she smiled. "I suppose this means Stacey has a few steps on you."

He grinned a sheepish sideways grin. His eyes drifted to and lingered on the lower part of her neck, where she had unfastened at least three of her numerous buttons to cool herself and where her pulse beat. He sobered, his body tingling with the need to touch her. "Suppose so . . . Laura."

Caleb watched her eyes flare in reaction to the low way he spoke her name. Flushing, she tore her gaze away and scooped up a handful of peas. Ma was seated at the table, but he and Laura were on the other side, down beneath the edge of the table where she most likely couldn't see them. Reaching out, Caleb put the first two fingers of one hand under Laura's small silky chin and lifted it, forcing her to look at him again. She gazed at him, her eyes wide. He loved looking into those blue pools, loved seeing her react to things he said or did. She had a way of staring at him that made him need her in his arms. He ran his thumb across her soft lower lip, heard the swift breath she inhaled, then withdrew his hand.

He picked up more peas. He knew touching and looking at her changed nothing about the reality of the situation. She still had a fiancé in Bismarck, a man who might appear here any day, gather her in his arms, and ride away with her. He'd keep reminding himself of that so when that day came, his heart wouldn't be in a million pieces at Laura Kent's feet.

Try as he might to avoid that, however, he strongly suspected he wouldn't be able to.

Once the peas were all gathered, Laura thanked Caleb, then resumed her position at the table, helping Ruth shell the peas. Caleb went upstairs. Stacey wandered back inside, cautiously glancing around the room. Laura smiled. "He went upstairs."

Stacey looked relieved, but her eyes still sparkled with mischief. "He really would have drowned me, Ma."

Ruth just smiled.

"You seem to have made a pretty good effort to drown *him*," Laura said.

"Just one bucket of water . . ."

"One?"

"Well . . . maybe two."

Stacey sat down to help with the peas. Soon Caleb came downstairs. He scowled at Stacey. She giggled. A newspaper in hand, Caleb settled himself in a chair by the fireplace.

Once the peas were all shelled, Ruth, Stacey, and Laura went outside to sit on the porch. Carrying a lantern, Laura sat with Stacey on the steps while Ruth sat in a chair on the porch. A coyote howled, and Laura was reminded of the night she, Ruth, and Stacey had taken food to Mrs. Dahl. Stacey had produced a gun from beneath a blanket in the wagon bed and scared the wolves away with a single shot.

"Would you teach me how to shoot, Stacey?" Laura asked.

Stacey's eyes glittered. "A city girl like you?"

Laura smiled. "Since I might be here for a while until my fiancé comes for me, I should learn to handle a rifle the way you do. Surely a city girl could learn to do that?"

"Could."

Laura decided to broach to Stacey the subject of Amanda. She'd been wondering how Stacey would feel about Amanda staying at the farm, too. "I've been thinking," she said, watching Stacey carefully, "about bringing Amanda here—"

"Amanda? Laura, you're not serious!"

"I am. I've already talked to your mother about it," Laura said, glancing at Ruth. "Now I'll talk to Caleb."

"He'll never agree. Amanda is a cripple."

"Stacey," Ruth said in the sharpest tone Laura had ever heard her use. It drew a sheepish look from Stacey. She glanced at Ruth, then at her folded hands.

Laura's gaze darted between Ruth and Stacey. "Yes, Amanda is a cripple. But if you never talk about her, people will never know how to help her. Amanda will never know how to help herself."

Stacey's attention went to the flickering lantern flame. "You won't talk Caleb into it, Laura."

Drawing her shoulders erect, Laura said, "Yes, I will. What about you, Stacey? If I bring Amanda here, will you treat her decently?"

"You shouldn't bring her here, Laura. She doesn't belong here. Her pa is sometimes vio—"

"Stacey," Ruth said again in that admonishing tone.

Laura studied Ruth, who gazed out into the darkness.

Surely Ruth could feel her gaze, yet she didn't look her way. She rocked back and forth. Stacey still stared at the lantern.

Caleb came out and sat near Ruth. Stars glittered out over the dark prairie. The moon was a silver crescent nestled in a black velvet sky. Laura heard movement near the steps and realized Sam, the dog, was settling himself there. Ruth asked Caleb if he would fix the roof of Mrs. Dahl's sod house soon. It was leaking again. Caleb agreed but shook his head. "I'd rather build the woman a better house, Ma."

"She's content, Caleb."

"I know. I'll go tomorrow afternoon."

Soon Ruth yawned and said she was going inside to bed. After she was gone, Stacey yawned—a fake yawn. Laura smiled. Stacey, the matchmaker who left her alone with Caleb every time she could get away with it, would not be far behind Ruth. Stacey entertained unrealistic notions about her and Caleb, and nothing but disappointment could come from such thoughts.

Stacey went inside. Laura turned to Caleb.

Sprawled on a chair, he was barely discernible in the darkness, his arms folded as he gazed out at the prairie evening. Laura's heart quickened as she recalled the way he had, just hours ago, so tenderly lifted her chin with two fingers and ran his thumb across her lower lip. She was aware of just how alone with him she was right now out here in the darkness, and that mere thought made her breath quicken. She remembered his threat about wolves. She no longer regarded him as a danger, though. She was more afraid of herself now, afraid of the things she felt whenever he neared her, afraid of her inability to push his hands aside during moments of weakness.

She opened her mouth to ask him about letting her bring Amanda here, but he spoke first. "How did he die?"

She wrinkled her brow, not at all certain of what he was talking about. Her mind was on Amanda, and him. "Who?"

"Your pa. How did he die?"

She wondered if he really cared. Did he want assurance that Pa was dead? If Pa wasn't dead, Caleb would undoubtedly wish he were, and that thought chilled Laura. The subject of Pa had not come between them in three days—since she had told him her father had died in February.

Laura crossed her arms and hugged herself, though the night was anything but cool. She had shared some of her memories of Pa with Caleb Main—those she had felt she needed to share to stress her point. She wasn't sure if she wanted to share Pa's death with a man who hated him.

An owl hooted. Crickets chirped. Caleb Main stirred, the chair creaking under his weight. "Sorry. I shouldn't have asked," he said. "But I'm curious. Matt Kent was always one I thought would get around death."

Laura's chest constricted. "I wish he had been. No, Mr. Main, Pa was as human as you or I. And I miss him a great deal."

She remembered Pa's strength and his warmth. She remembered his way of squeezing her hand when something excited him. She remembered the countless times she had lain in bed listening to his footsteps in the hall. One day she had felt happy and secure, wrapped in his love and devotion; the next she had felt desolate, trying to convince herself that he was really gone.

"I still can't believe it," she said softly, staring out across the dark prairie. During the five months since Pa's death, she had told no one about the agony she had experienced upon finding him. She knew she had no reason to tell Caleb, but she felt a tremendous need to empty herself of the pain.

So she talked.

"His office is a small building set apart from the main house. When I wasn't away at school, I often woke early and couldn't wait to run down the little path leading to the office to hug him and say good morning. He always heard me coming. He would fling open the door and catch me up in his arms. Then we would go inside and have coffee together and talk for a time. He would sit on one corner of his desk. Sometimes when I close my eyes, I still see him sitting there.

"That morning I knew something was terribly wrong. He didn't fling the door open. He wasn't there to catch me up in his arms. I–I touched the knob and it was terribly cold. Then I turned it. I didn't want to—I knew something was wrong—

but I did. I pushed the door open, only a little at first because my heart was pounding with fear, and I was trembling."

Her pain gripped her. Tears burned her eyes. Laura fell silent and faced the scene as she had tried to force herself to do so many times. Running down the path. Stopping near the porch. Staring at the door. Feeling the awful sense of dread. Forcing her feet to carry her forward. Touching the cold knob. Turning it. Pushing the door open. Seeing him.

Laura put her hand over her mouth to smother a cry.

"Laura," she heard Caleb say softly from nearby. "Laura . . . don't. No more. Don't put yourself through this. I'm sorry I asked about him—"

"He lay crumpled in front of the desk," she continued, unable to stop. She needed to pour out the grief, the pain she had held within for months. "He had tried to reach the door—his arm was still outstretched. His face was gray, his eyes wide and blank. I knew he was dead. I gripped the knob, crying . . . then eased over to cradle his head in my lap. I whispered to him, told him how much I loved him. I don't know how much time passed. An hour, half a day . . . Finally I went to tell someone he was dead. A heart attack, the doctor said later."

Laura wiped at tears that had fallen onto her cheeks. So much grief for one person to bear. Even months after the horrible ordeal she wanted to kick and scream at God. It was unfair! She wanted Pa back. Sometimes she wanted to pretend he wasn't dead, that she could return home anytime, and there would be Pa to greet her. She had spent many months angrily denying his death. Pouring the facts of that morning out—acknowledging he was dead—soothed her in an odd way. She didn't understand grief, but she knew she must not suppress it in order to feel alive again.

She realized Caleb had moved to sit on the step beside her where Stacey had sat earlier. He reached for her. She went into his arms, needing them around her, sensing his sincerity in wanting to comfort her. He leaned one shoulder against a porch support, and she nestled her head on that shoulder. He stroked her hair. She reveled in his warmth.

"Until now I've never told anyone how I found him. I

walked to the house, told the housekeeper Pa was dead and would she please send for the doctor."

"God, Laura," Caleb whispered. He planted a kiss on the top of her head. He wanted to take her pain, ease her grief, hold her forever if that would help. He hadn't meant to put her through such pain, which she'd probably relived a million times already. Ever since she had told him her pa had died in February, he'd wondered what had killed Matt Kent. Now he silently cursed himself for asking.

He seemed to cause her an awful lot of pain, seemed to apologize to her a lot. First she'd had to face the fact that he hated her pa—a man she loved beyond everything, a man she thought had few faults. Now look what he'd done to her.

He held her. She clung to him. Together they watched the stars and stared at the moon. Together they listened to the owl, the coyotes, the crickets, and the lowing of cattle. She cried softly into his shirt, whispering Pa's name over and over. He stroked her back and her hair. He murmured her name and soothed her.

The night deepened. The moon climbed higher. Laura's sobs faded. Caleb felt her relax and realized she'd fallen asleep. Scooping her up, he stood and walked into the house.

Holding her this way felt wonderful. She was light and soft and beautiful. As he walked up the staircase, her head lolled back, and his heart stopped beating for a minute at the sight of her angelic face. Her brown lashes were feathered against her smooth, unmarked skin. Her nose was little and perfect, curving at the end. And her lips . . . pink, parted, and tempting. He longed to dip his head and taste them. Her neck was an enticing white column, offering a feast he wanted to devour.

But in truth, she offered nothing. She was a sleeping innocent. And, despite the cry of his body, that was exactly the way he intended to leave her when he put her on her bed.

When Laura started downstairs for breakfast the next morning, she wondered if the air between her and Caleb would be thick and awkward. She had fallen asleep nestled against him last night and had awakened in her bed this morning. She assumed Caleb must have carried her into the house and up to bed.

The thought made her cheeks burn. Caleb . . . lowering her onto the bed, hovering over her, perhaps stroking her hair again? She had slept in her dress. The only thing missing had been her boots. But had he thought of undressing her? Had he lingered to watch her sleep? She found the mere thought of him alone in a bedroom with her nearly overwhelming.

Downstairs, Stacey sat in the chair in the sewing corner, stitching diligently. She glanced up and smiled at Laura. Ruth was working over the stove, filling the room with the delicious smells of frying bacon and eggs.

"Good morning," Laura said, approaching the stove.

Ruth returned the greeting. Then, "There's biscuits on the table."

"Where is Caleb?"

"Mending the henhouse. A coyote dug its way underneath sometime last night and had half a chicken eaten by the time Caleb got out there with his rifle."

"Oh," Laura said. "I think I'll go talk to him."

Ruth nodded. "Might tell him breakfast is ready. I got a late start this morning."

The henhouse was a little gray building huddled close to the barn. Caleb kneeled near one side, using a hammer to pound some boards into the ground near one wall.

"I heard you had coyote trouble last night," Laura said, halting at his side.

He stopped hammering and stood up, wiping sweat from his brow. He nodded. "He would have had a feast, too, if I hadn't tore out here and stopped him."

"Ruth told me."

His gaze wavered between her and his boots. He was obviously uncomfortable. Because of last night? She felt uncomfortable, too. She was embarrassed that she had burdened him with her grief. She shifted from one boot to the other, crossed her arms to hug herself, and glanced around. Nearby, hens scratched at the ground. Roosters strutted. In the distance cattle grazed on prairie grass.

Laura and Caleb both spoke at once: "Mr. Main, I—"
"Laura, just wanted—"

They laughed, then waited for each other to speak. Caleb shifted the hammer to the other hand. Laura clutched her calico skirt. Finally Caleb grinned. "We'll never get anywhere like this. Look, I'm sorry I asked about your pa's death last night."

"Don't apologize, Mr. Main. You merely forced me to talk about what I've avoided for months. I'm sorry you were forced to listen. For the second time since I've known you, I cried in front of you. I don't usually do that."

He studied her. "You didn't do anything wrong, Laura."

"I should have simply said, 'Pa died of a heart attack,' and left it at that. I started talking, and the whole story poured out. It—it must have been difficult for you to sit and listen to—"

"Laura, stop." Caleb touched her forearm. "I didn't mind. It helped you. I'd listen to it all over again, a million times, if that would help you."

Laura searched his eyes. She saw sincerity, gentleness, devotion. And beneath all those things . . . something else. She wasn't sure what. But she did know they still didn't quite trust each other. She was still Matthew Kent's daughter after all. Whatever had happened between Caleb and Pa had deeply wounded the man before her. Questions ran circles in her head, questions about him and Pa and things he hadn't shared with her. But she couldn't speak the questions. She wasn't prepared to deal with Caleb's answers. She was just beginning to face the fact that Pa was truly dead—she couldn't face someone tearing her father's character apart during this emotional time.

Caleb gently caressed her cheek. "So you want to learn to shoot, Stacey tells me," he said softly.

Laura nodded. Caleb chuckled and withdrew his hand. "You're the damnedest woman I've ever met."

"Mr. Main," she admonished playfully, arching a brow.

"Breakfast ready?"

"Yes, but I—"

"My stomach's growling. If you want to talk more, you'll

have to do it after I eat," he said, plopping the hammer on the ground. He took her arm and turned her toward the house, giving her a little push in that direction.

"Mr. Main!"

"One of these days you're going to call me Caleb, and I'm going to fall over dead from shock."

Laura laughed.

After breakfast Caleb went back to finish filling the hole beneath the henhouse, more to keep the hens in at night than coyotes out. About all he could do where the coyotes were concerned was hope no more of them dug under, and if they did, that he'd catch them before they ate much.

He paused in his work when Laura emerged from the house and strode over to the well. She lowered and raised the bucket. When she reached for it and pulled it over to the side of the well, she splashed a good amount of water down the front of her dress. Caleb chuckled. She amazed him. No other refined lady in the world would smile right after splashing water down the front of her dress. Laura turned to glare playfully. He put on a straight face and got back to work.

A few minutes later he went to the barn to reshoe Soldier. After finishing two shoes he looked up, and there was Laura, watching him from the seat she'd taken on a little milking stool. Caleb straightened. "Well, now . . . aren't you learning to creep up on a person."

She smiled. "I hope I'm not bothering you, Mr. Main. There's something I've been wanting to talk to you about, but every time I try, we go off on another subject."

Caleb wiped sweat from his brow and shook his head in amusement. This infernal business of her calling him Mr. Main all the time had to stop. They'd sure spent enough time together and knew each other well enough now that she could call him Caleb. He approached her, waving a forefinger and trying to keep a stern expression. "Seems what we need to talk about is what you should call me. I told you to call me Caleb."

Laura eased off the stool, her brow wrinkled. "If this is a bad time . . ."

"I'll tell you what's bad, Laura. What's bad is the way you keep calling me Mr. Main," he said, closing the distance between them. He nearly laughed aloud at the way her eyes widened. She began backing up, edging around the stool as if he were a predator or some frightening animal.

"It's not bad. It's proper!"

"Not out here. On the prairie we call each other by our first names."

"The choice should be mine," she objected.

Caleb saw the pile of hay behind her and couldn't resist temptation. He kept stalking her. She kept backing up—right where he wanted her. The door was behind him. She couldn't reach it without getting around him, and he wasn't going to let that happen. He'd grab her.

"Proper," he said, tasting the tart word. "The ever proper Miss Laura Kent. I'll just bet you know all kinds of things about being proper. Things like who to put by who at a fancy dinner party. Just how far to lift the hem of your skirt when you're dancing. All kinds of things."

"What do you think you're doing? Mr. Main . . ." She glanced over her shoulder at the haystack just as he gave her a slight push. She toppled ungracefully onto the hay, sank down, and sat there gaping at him, too stunned to speak. Caleb chuckled.

"Why did you do that?" she finally managed.

"To take some of the proper out of you, Laura. You don't look so full of dignity sunk down in the hay like that."

She glared, her eyes glittering. "You're a beast!"

"Maybe I am." He chuckled, then started to turn away. "Believe I'll finish shoeing my horse—"

Caleb tripped over something and went sprawling onto the earth floor. Laura had stuck her leg out and tripped him.

She giggled. "Neither do *you* look so full of dignity now, Mr. Main."

Caleb growled playfully. She scrambled to get out of the haystack. He lunged for her, catching her by the waist.

"Woman, you called me a beast. Maybe I should act like one."

He tossed her back in the hay, then joined her, tickling her waist until she squirmed and begged him to stop. Laughing, he rolled over onto his back and lay there looking up at the rafters. Laura lay at his side, trying to catch her breath.

"No—fair. You're stronger," she managed. "You're—also a—bully."

"No more names, Laura. Haven't you learned your lesson yet?"

"Beast! Bully!"

She struggled to get up. Knowing she meant to call him the names, then run off, Caleb twisted his body and grabbed at her waist again. He wrapped his arms around her and pulled her back against him. She wriggled, trying to break his solid hold. When that didn't work, she eased down to try and duck under his arms. Laughing again, he held her. Then realization hit them, and they both stopped moving.

His arms were no longer wrapped around her waist. After all Laura's wriggling and his struggle to hold her, his arms were now beneath her breasts.

Caleb felt the mounds of tempting softness pressing against his forearms. Suddenly he was painfully aware that her bottom was pressed against his groin. He felt the first tingle of his response to touching her like this, and he shut his eyes, trying to fight his ever-growing desire. Yet he didn't want to release her.

His hands slid around, rubbed the undersides of her breasts, then cupped them fully. Laura gasped but no longer struggled to free herself. Caleb waited to see if she would. If she did, he'd help her up . . . walk with her to the barn door, keep his hands at his sides. He wouldn't touch her again, God help him.

He gently massaged her breasts, felt them swell in his hands. Through the material of her dress and her undergarments, he found her nipples and teased them to tautness. Laura moaned and tossed her head back, offering the side of her neck. Caleb feasted on it, nipping at the white column, licking the hollows and gentle curves, trailing kisses up to her beautiful jawline.

His hands found her bodice buttons and began unfastening them. Over her shoulder he watched his hands work. "Tell me if you want me to stop, Laura," he murmured.

He slid his hand inside the open bodice and beneath a silk camisole. Growling low in his throat, he felt the flesh of a breast, then took its hardened nipple between his thumb and forefinger.

There Laura stopped him. She placed her hand over his and whispered breathlessly, "No. I can't do this. Adrian . . ."

Caleb shut his eyes and somehow mustered the strength to withdraw his hand. Then he withdrew his arms, rolled onto his back, and stared at the rafters again, one arm draped across his forehead. "That his name? Adrian?"

"Yes. Please understand," she said. "I wanted you to touch me. I still do. But how could I face Adrian if I allow you to continue? How could I live with myself?"

Caleb nodded in understanding. She sat up and buttoned her bodice. He couldn't help himself—he reached up and plucked straw from her silky hair. "You're beautiful, Laura Kent. Adrian's a lucky man."

She turned her head to look at him with her big blue eyes that threatened to swallow him, lure him, entice him. He wanted to pull her back down on the hay and ravish her.

But he wouldn't.

"Ever change your mind about marrying him, let me know," he said. Laura nodded. Caleb got to his feet, brushed himself off, and went back to finish shoeing Soldier.

Laura squeezed her eyes shut. She had been a wanton, reveling in the hay, letting Caleb touch her so intimately. A wanton, yes, but she didn't fully regret what she had done; there was nothing more exquisite than his touch. She watched Caleb lift the horse's hoof and work on it again. She watched his back, the flexing muscles visible through the thin white shirt. Her neck still burned from his kisses, and her breasts were still swollen and aching for his touch. She wondered if any other man would have stopped at the point Caleb had, with just a few words from her. She wondered if any other man would have been so respectful. Adrian certainly never considered her feelings; numerous times she had been forced to fight off his more heated advances.

Her heart still pulsed for Caleb. Her body still yearned for his touch. But lying with him, making love with him, would be improper and outright disloyal to Adrian. Still, coveting Caleb in her heart, wanting him with a flaming need she had never experienced until now . . . wasn't that also disloyal?

She had loved Adrian since their childhood, a childhood spent romping around the grounds outside the house in Bismarck. She had missed him when she had been away at school. She had written him a hundred letters, it seemed. She remembered how she had trembled with anticipation at the mere thought of seeing him again.

After her return from school Adrian had been brusque and demanding, insistent about a hurried engagement. People might assume she had gotten herself in trouble and he was marrying her to save her reputation, she had told him. He had laughed, then said, "Impossible, Laura. You're as cold as a winter wind." His comment had wounded her and left her wondering why he wanted to marry her if he felt she would be so indifferent in bed. In truth, if she was cold, it was because he had changed; his kisses and touches no longer excited her.

Now one question burned in her mind: If she didn't love Adrian and they married anyway, wouldn't she soon be terribly unhappy?

On the other hand, Pa's wish had been that she marry Adrian.

She fastened the last bodice button. She was such a mess of emotions and confusion. She had to cope with Pa's death, wonder why and when her feelings toward Adrian had changed, wonder if Pa would turn in his grave if she didn't marry Adrian, and deal with new feelings stirred to life by Caleb Main.

Standing, she brushed hay from her dress and moved toward Caleb, who had lifted one of the horse's hooves up to work on it. She had originally come to the barn to talk to him about Amanda and didn't intend to leave until she'd done just that. She also didn't intend to irritate him into giving her another lesson in how to be less proper.

"Caleb . . ."

He stopped working to turn and look at her. A grin frolicked at the corners of his mouth, and his dark eyes sparkled triumphantly.

She put her hands on her hips. "Would you please try to look a little less smug? I came here some time ago to talk to you. So far, I've accomplished nothing."

"I'm waiting," he said, lowering the hoof. "Stand still, Soldier. I'll finish those shoes later."

"I want to bring Amanda here for a while," Laura said.

Eyes narrowing, he cocked his head. "Laura . . . you know how I feel."

"You don't want me to meddle. I believe that was the word you used. Caleb, she needs a home and decent clothing. She needs love. I hear she gets none of that from her family."

Caleb looked to the horse and waved his arms. "The woman's going to drive me crazy, Soldier. Crazy!" Then he looked at Laura again. "So you bring her here. You burden Ma and Stacey and—"

"I'll burden no one. I'll care for Amanda. I'll go talk to the Kincaids, and I'll go alone if someone doesn't agree to take me."

"No, you won't!" Caleb thundered.

Laura lifted her chin. "I will."

"Laura—"

"If you don't want Amanda here, I'll take her to Minot and stay there until Adrian arrives. Surely I can find an establishment there that rents rooms."

Caleb muttered three quick oaths, each louder than the last. Laura gave him a reproving look. He paced in front of Soldier—four times back and forth.

"My," she teased. "I've never seen you act so nervous. A man who hunts grizzlies and coyotes is afraid of a little girl?"

He stopped pacing and leveled a black glare on her.

"You're not staying in Minot. Too many saloons and gaming houses. And I'm not afraid of her."

"Then what are you afraid of?"

"Nothing."

"Then let me bring her here. If, after she arrives, everyone does feel burdened, I'll arrange to take her to Bismarck with me."

"Laura, you're the most stubborn female I've ever met."

"Take me to see the Kincaids tomorrow."

"Laura, I'll tell you a little secret. Some ladies in town tried to help Amanda once, and Blake Kincaid leveled a rifle at them and told them to get off his land."

Laura gaped. "Just because they wanted to take care of Amanda?"

"That's right."

"That's horrible."

"That's why no one gets involved."

"No one getting involved is cowardly."

"That may be the case, depending on who you're calling cowardly. Myself . . . I call it sensible." Turning away, Caleb leaned over and lifted one of Soldier's back hooves again.

Laura felt as though he'd dismissed her again and the entire idea of Amanda coming here, too. Determined to make him listen to her, she leaned down to his eye level. "Mr. Main . . ."

He froze. Then he cursed again. "I'll go talk to Blake. Now, go on and let me work."

She smiled. Another victory. But not quite. "I'll go along, too, to talk to Amanda's ma. Paula, I think her name is," she said pleasantly.

"No, Laura. If Kincaid decides to start shooting, I don't want you anywhere around."

"Nonsense. Stacey and I went—"

"That's different. Stacey never mentions Amanda when she takes food to them."

"Surely the man doesn't hate his daughter that much?"

"It's not a matter of hate. It's a matter of Amanda being his own—something he's not proud to admit. But he doesn't want people meddling in his family business, either. And

you, woman, are meddling," Caleb said bluntly, dropping
the hoof again. "Damn, you bother me!"

Laura inhaled a sharp breath. "That word again—
meddling. Well, no matter what you think about me,
Amanda's life matters more. You said you would talk to
Blake—"

"And I will. But right now I have a horse to shoe."

"I'm going with you."

Caleb cocked his head. "Laura . . ."

"What if he shoots you, Caleb?"

"Someone from Minot'll hear the shot. It's close. Besides,
Blake won't shoot at me. It'll be man to man."

"I remember how to get there. If you don't take me with
you, I'll saddle one of these horses and ride alone."

"Dammit it to hell anyway," Caleb muttered. He lifted the
hoof again, placed a shoe on the bottom of it, and began
hammering. The noise echoed off the walls.

What an annoying little gesture, Laura thought. He was
trying to make so much noise that he couldn't hear her. She
fought a smile, already tasting another victory, then tipped
forward to speak loudly right into his ear. "What was that,
Mr. Main? More expletives? No, words of agreement, I
think. Wonderful! I'll pack us a lunch for tomorrow, then.
We'll share a pleasant ride, take care of matters, then share a
pleasant ride back. I'm so glad I convinced you."

He stopped hammering to slowly turn and give her a hard
stare. She spun around and fled the barn before he could grab
one of those shoes and throw it at her, as she assumed he was
angry enough to do. She hoped his temper would cool before
he came in for supper.

❄ ❄ ❄
Chapter Eight

STACEY GAVE LAURA her first shooting lesson. They went to the open field behind the house, where Stacey had placed a small tin bucket on a wooden crate some distance away. Stacey taught Laura how to clean and load the rifle, then how to aim. The rifle was so heavy that Laura could hardly hoist it. She aimed, fired, and missed the bucket by a distance of several feet. The next two shots were no closer. Sighing, she glanced at Stacey.

"Practice," Stacey said. "You won't hit that bucket for a while. Learn to handle the rifle. Right now it feels big and awkward, and you won't hit anything."

"You're right about that," Laura said.

She practiced more. An hour later she was firing no nearer to the bucket than she had with the first shot. She twisted her lips and kept working, raising and lowering the rifle, loading and shooting.

Finally a bullet pinged off the edge of the bucket, upsetting it. Laura squealed with glee. "At least if I encounter a coyote now, I can clip off the end of his tail."

Laughing, Stacey took the rifle. "Supper. I'm starved. You're amazing. When you make up your mind to do something, you do it," she said in wonderment.

Laura shook her head, hardly believing she had actually hit the bucket. "Tomorrow I'll get more than the edge."

At supper Caleb didn't speak to Laura. Stacey teased him, remarking that he was in a foul mood on such a nice evening. He grumbled something about being tired and getting to bed early since he had to go somewhere tomorrow. He was going alone, too, he said, whether or not a certain person liked the

119

idea. Laura smiled smugly. She was going with him whether or not *he* liked the idea.

After supper she and Stacey washed dishes in the basin on top of one of the cabinets, then went outside to sit on the porch and talk again.

Presently Stacey asked, "Now, just how do you plan to get around Caleb?"

Laura smiled. "Tomorrow, you mean?"

Stacey nodded.

"I haven't decided yet. But I will. Caleb can talk all he wants, but the fact remains—I'm going."

"Should be interesting," Stacey said, chuckling.

Laura didn't know how to shoot very well, but she knew how to saddle a horse. After dinner the following afternoon that's exactly what she had in mind to do when she left the house.

In the barn she found a saddlebag hanging from a long nail. She took the food she had gathered—slices of bread wrapped in cloth and chunks of cheese—and put them in one of the saddlebags. Then she saddled one of the horses.

She was just tightening the cinch when Caleb walked into the barn and stopped cold in his tracks. "What the hell do you think you're doing, woman?"

"Why, I'm going to see the Kincaids, Mr. Main. And I do wish you would stop using such expletives in my presence. Save that sort of talk for the saloons you sometimes frequent." Little did it matter that she had used profanity at least once since meeting him and had thought profanity countless other times when he had angered her. She didn't want him talking to her like that.

"Uh-huh. You're going to the Kincaids. A woman traveling alone. Easy prey for any—"

"Save your breath. I can shoot now, and Stacey let me borrow a rifle."

He leaned casually against a stall rail. "That so?"

"Yes. That's so. I practiced all morning. While I may not be an expert shot, my aim is decent."

"Takes more than decent aim to kill some of the things a

body could run into on the open prairie. Especially a woman. Hungry wolves. Sometimes a grizzly. Lonely man now and then."

She stared at him, feeling a prickle of apprehension she wasn't about to acknowledge aloud. "You're trying to frighten me, Mr. Main, and it will not work."

He edged toward her. She stood her ground, refusing to allow him to back her up into the haystack again, or some other place. He would not sway her. Her mind was set. She was going to talk to the Kincaids this afternoon, with or without him. She had borrowed the rifle but had not asked Stacey to go with her because doing so would have put Stacey in a bad position with Caleb.

His expression had changed. His eyes had narrowed, and he glared at her with barely restrained anger. "You're not going anywhere, Laura," he said. There was a hard edge to his voice.

She lifted her chin and shot back: "I am. I am going to see Amanda's family. You would have to tie me up to keep me here."

He took another step, then stopped and tilted his head as if considering something. He moved to one wall of the barn, and Laura released a rush of air, thinking he had given up. Caleb reached for something hanging from the wall, then turned. What Laura saw chilled her.

His eyes were the color of black storm clouds now, and draped over one arm was a rolled-up length of rope. She gasped.

He shrugged. "You thought of it."

She backed up toward the horse's head. Caleb eased toward her. "Mr. Main, you stay away from me!" she warned, panic clenching her stomach. He wouldn't really do it . . . or would he?

"And just when did you decide to start calling me Mr. Main again?" he demanded.

"When I decided I was angry with you." She had to think of a plan fast. If she fled through the open barn doors, he would simply unsaddle the horse, unpack the saddlebag, and

she would be right back where she had started a half hour
ago. "I know. Why don't we—"

He grabbed her. He was so fast that she didn't have a
chance even to think about bolting. One second she had been
talking, the next he had her by the wrist. He forced her down
to the ground, pulled her arms behind her back, and wrapped
the rope around her wrists. She screamed. She kicked. She
spit out dirt. He straightened and laughed, like some trium-
phant king. Then he tossed her over his shoulder, carried her
to a stall, and dumped her on a small pile of hay.

"Beast! Brute. Untie me—now!" Laura cried incredulously.

He clicked his tongue. "Laura, Laura. You're calling me
names again."

She breathed deeply to try to calm her sizzling temper.
She couldn't believe he had tied her up like—like an animal. But she would get nowhere fuming at him, she knew
that. She would only make things worse. "Caleb . . ."

He laughed. "Oh, it's Caleb now, is it?"

She ignored the taunt. Though he was standing nearby,
she had to muster every ounce of self-discipline in her body
to resist kicking him directly in the shin. "Caleb, this is ridic-
ulous. Untie me. Now."

Caleb tied the other end of the rope around a stall rail and
pulled it tight. He checked the rope around her wrists to
make sure it wasn't too tight—he didn't want her to have
rope burns. When Ma heard of this, there was going to be
hell enough to pay. But it seemed the only way to keep Laura
from riding off either before or after him, and he'd just have
to think of the hell to pay later.

He stepped back and brushed off his hands. Laura glared
at him, her fury evident in those stormy blue eyes. Good
thing she hadn't learned to shoot well yet. If she wasn't tied
up and could reach a rifle, she might just shoot at him.

"Why not gag me, too, Mr. Main? Let's do this correctly,
after all."

"Careful there, Laura. You suggested being tied up, and I
obliged. Now you're suggesting a gag. I could find something to use, I'm sure. I told you yesterday you weren't go-

ing. I meant it. I'll be back in a few hours and tell you what Blake said."

She kicked at a bucket of oats hanging on a nail just above her legs. "I wouldn't—" Caleb tried to warn her, but he was too late.

Oats showered down on her. She shook most of the flakes off, but some still clung to her hair and her clothes. She breathed rapidly, indignantly, angrily.

Caleb left the stall. He didn't want to aggravate the situation further. He went to see what she'd put in the saddlebags. Satisfied, he lifted them, took them outside to the side of the house where he'd left Soldier waiting, and slung them over Soldier's saddle. Then he mounted and rode away.

Inside the stall Laura cursed Caleb one minute and praised him the next. He was a beast for tying her up, but at least he'd done so in a gentleman's fashion, with regard for her comfort. Later he might regret that. She maneuvered her hands this way and that, felt the rope loosen, then finally slip. She pulled one hand out, then the other. An easy task, thanks to Caleb.

She didn't even pause to brush oats from her hair and clothes. She darted to the horse she had already saddled. "All right, Caleb Main," she muttered as she mounted and jerked the reins around in the direction of the doors. "I'm right behind you."

For Caleb the ride to the Kincaids' shack was long and filled with guilt. He hadn't really tied her up, had he? He winced. He had. The hell was starting now, it seemed, and Ma was nowhere in sight. Maybe he hadn't loosened the rope enough. She was struggling, if he knew Laura. He just hoped she didn't end up with raw places around her wrists. She was just healing from all the bruises and cuts she'd gotten from the coach accident. Damn the woman anyway. He shouldn't have tied her up, but at the time he hadn't been able to think of any other way to keep her from following him. He should have known she'd make trouble, that he couldn't just tell her no and have her mind him. Laura wasn't that kind of woman. He was fast learning that when she set her mind to something, she meant to follow through until her task was completed.

He'd tied her to that stall. Damn. What if she got thirsty? Or hungry? Or needed to use the privy? He couldn't leave her there.

He'd just gripped the reins to turn back when the Kincaids' tar-paper shack came into view. Blake Kincaid stood in front of the place, looking tired and dusty but waving in a friendly way. He was a tall, lanky man, his cheeks drawn and hollow. Four years ago, when Blake had first turned up here, Caleb wondered about his health. But Blake looked the same today as he had then. He turned his head and spit to one side. Then, gripping a limp prairie dog in one hand, he wandered over to several stools placed near one corner of the shack and sat down.

Caleb realized he'd be a fool to turn back now. Besides, he'd have to think of some excuse to give Blake about why he'd ridden out here. Maybe he could just ride up, talk to Blake, settle the business, then be on his way. Laura wouldn't be tied in the stall for long.

Caleb rode forward.

"Afternoon, Blake," he said, sliding from Soldier. He noticed the small field of wheat to the east of the shack. In the past Blake Kincaid had had the reputation of being a lazy sort. But he'd tried last year to plant a crop, and the same drought that had killed Caleb's wheat had also killed Blake's. Two years in a row now, Blake had planted. He was trying, and Caleb respected him for that. "Got a healthy crop this year, I see," Caleb said, taking the stool next to Blake.

"Yep. Need some rain, though. Sun'll kill it if we don't get none."

"It'll rain soon. We're having a good year."

Blake reached down, picked up a knife from the ground, and set to work on the prairie dog. "What're you doing out this way?"

Caleb breathed deeply. He heard the sounds of children playing inside the shack behind them. "Came to talk to you, Blake, friendly-like. About Amanda."

Blake didn't hesitate. "Reckon you heard I scared off that

last group of folks asking about Amanda," he said, still working on the prairie dog.

"I heard. But I reckon you know if you point a rifle at me, I'll twist it right out of your hands," Caleb said. Blake paused in his work to glance up, one eye squinted at Caleb. Caleb gave him a level stare. "I didn't come to fight, Blake. I came to talk and try to work something out peaceably."

"What's there to work out? She's my daughter."

"I know a woman who wants to take care of Amanda. She's Stacey's friend," Caleb said, so he wouldn't have to do a lot of explaining about where Laura came from and why she was staying at his farm. "She's staying with Stacey. She wants to take Amanda to the farm and try to help her."

"Amanda cain't be helped, Caleb. She ain't normal."

"She was sick as a babe, that's all. She needs help. It's time you stop treating her like an animal and let someone help."

"Go on and get outa here, Caleb, if that's all you came for. Amanda ain't going nowhere. She gets food in her belly and clothes on her back," Blake said, a dangerous glint to his eyes. "I can take care of my own. I'm pretty good at using this here knife on this prairie dog. Reckon I'd be just as good at using it on you."

Caleb studied Blake. Then, in one swift move, he snatched the knife from Blake's hand, took the tip between the forefinger and thumb, and hurled the knife into the field of wheat. Blake started up from the stool.

"Sit down," Caleb said coolly. "No man turns a rifle on a group of women. And no man makes threats he can't make good. I came to talk peaceably. I told you that. Now . . . let's start over. I know a woman who wants to care for Amanda. She wants to teach her—"

"Amanda cain't be taught."

Caleb shook his head. Hadn't he said the same thing to Laura just a few days ago when they were walking along the riverbank? It shamed him now. Countless times he'd seen Amanda huddled beneath that tree near the church and other than . . . well . . . he'd tried to help her some. But he hadn't done as much as he could have. "We won't know that until we try. Maybe what she needs is some love and attention so she feels like a person," he heard himself say now. And damn if his words didn't sound like Laura's.

"Don't suppose you're meanin' to leave the matter alone," Blake said.

"No, I'm not. Even if I do, there's a lady who won't," Caleb returned, thinking of Laura. "I want some promises from you, too, Blake."

"Don't reckon I have a choice."

"I don't want you turning up at my doorstep, demanding to take Amanda home. I'll bring her back when the time's right."

"If you decide to bring her back."

Caleb studied him. Did the man even care? Caleb sensed that he did. Beneath the threats and gruffness was a father, and while Caleb had never been a father, he remembered the closeness he and his pa had shared. A hard-shelled man like Blake Kincaid was difficult to read, but Caleb thought he saw a flicker of sadness in the man's eyes. "Do you want her back someday?" Caleb asked.

Blake turned his head and stared at his crop. "Amanda's been a hard one. We ain't never known what to do with her. She only started to walk at three years old, kids always teased her, not just ours. Others, too. She started gettin' real mad about then. She'd throw things in the house, break things. Hurt the baby once."

Caleb felt for the man. He just hoped Amanda wouldn't be too much for Laura. "Where's Amanda now?"

"Don't know. She runs."

"Not inside?"

"Nope."

"She's always by the church on Sundays when service lets out. I'll find her then."

Blake nodded. Caleb stood to leave. He remembered that he'd thrown Blake's knife out in the wheat field, and he strode over to Soldier, slipped a knife from its sheath by his rifle, and took it over to Blake.

"Thanks," Blake mumbled, taking the knife.

"Sure." Caleb moved back to Soldier's side and mounted.

"Blake, I think I told you once before—a long time ago—I have a lot of work at my farm. If you're interested, I could use a hand. Wouldn't make you less of a man to work for someone till you get a good crop in. Sometimes . . . well, sometimes we just have to do things we wouldn't normally choose to do."

That was damn sure right, he thought as he turned Soldier away and headed back toward the farm. Before Laura came, he damn sure would never have thought of coming here today and confronting Blake as he had. Not that he was scared of Blake, but he just hadn't thought that putting his nose in Blake's business was right. Laura had made him see that Blake's business was really Amanda's business.

Remembering that Laura was still tied up in the stall, he kicked Soldier into a trot across the prairie. He didn't look forward to having her glare at him again.

But he damn sure wanted to see her smile when he told her he'd convinced Blake.

After riding for a few minutes Laura decided to first go to Preacher Jacobs and ask if he would ride with her to the Kincaids'. Surely Blake Kincaid would not point a rifle at a preacher.

She cut through the green and gold prairie, riding toward Minot. She passed the point where, if she turned north, she would reach the Kincaids' tar-paper shack, but she kept going. She might have squared her shoulders and pretended courage to Caleb's face, but she really was just a little fearful of facing Blake Kincaid alone.

She entered Plum Valley, the beautiful, lush green valley splashed with purple. Her braid fell loose from its pins and slithered down her back. The sun beat down, but a cool breeze tempered it. She realized she'd acted rashly after freeing herself in the stall—leaping on her horse and flying out of there. Caleb had taken her canteen and saddlebags, and she hadn't bothered to take the time to look for others. Now she was thirsty. And hungry. And tired.

She reined the horse near a plum tree, jumped down, and plucked a piece of fruit. It was juicy and sweet, and she de-

voured several plums within the space of only a few minutes. She wiped the juice from her mouth, thankful no one
could see her. She really had been schooled in manners; she
just didn't seem to remember them at the moment.

A little stream splashed and gurgled nearby. The water
looked clear. Laura kneeled down, cupped some water, and
drank. It was so cool . . . so refreshing. She drank more, then
returned to the tree to pluck another plum to eat on the way
to Minot. She could see the buildings and the bridge from
here, and if she listened closely, she could hear the faint
sound of saloon music. Or was that her imagination? She remembered what Stacey had said about bad sorts in Minot.
She wondered about her sanity in coming here alone. There
were nice people in Minot—she had met many at church—
but there were too many saloons and too many rowdies who
hung around the saloons for her peace of mind.

She didn't dwell on her worry for long, though; she forced
it from her mind. She was here now, and she might as well
march forward and talk to Preacher Jacobs exactly as she
had planned to do. Besides, if there was trouble, she had the
rifle Stacey had loaned her. Caleb hadn't taken it. And only
she and the Mains knew she couldn't shoot very well.

She settled herself on her horse and guided the animal
deeper into the valley and across the bridge. Fortunately the
church was on this side of town, so she wouldn't be forced to
pass through Minot. Beside the river near the church she
reined the horse and slid down, tethering the animal to a
fallen log. Then she approached the church.

The churchyard was quiet now, empty of people. The little
white building with the creaking front steps seemed lonely
somehow. The clapboard was weathered in places, rough
and gray, but there was still a serene beauty to it. The
branches of a nearby willow dipped down over one front
corner of the church in an almost protective way, and a slight
breeze rustled the leaves.

The door creaked open with a small push. Someone spoke
from within. "Yes? May I help you?"

Laura recognized Preacher Jacobs's strong, even speaking
voice and peered around the door. "I'm Laura Kent. I was

here with the Mains last Sunday for the service." She didn't know if he would remember her, but she had to try. If he didn't, she would merely explain who she was, then move on with her request that he go with her to talk to the Kincaids.

"Miss Kent," he said, coming up the aisle between benches. "Of course I remember you. Fortunately you caught me here. I was just closing up to go home." He took her arm and led her to a back bench, concern etched in the lines of his face.

"What is it? Is something wrong at the Main farm?"

"No . . . I . . . well, I don't know how much you know about how I came to be staying with the Mains," she began, pleased at the kindness she found in his aged eyes. Probably she had only to say what she wanted, and he would go with her. But she wanted to make things clear for him.

"Ruth told me about the accident."

"Oh, good," she said. "Then you know I had hoped to leave soon. Well, last Sunday afternoon I changed my mind. I saw a little girl by the river. Amanda Kincaid. Caleb said most everyone in Minot knows about Amanda and—"

"Everyone does," Preacher Jacobs said, shaking his head sadly.

"Ruth and Caleb have given me permission to take Amanda to their farm and care for her. But I understand her pa does not like people meddling in his business."

"That's the truth of it."

"I thought that I would go talk to him, but . . . well, I thought I would come here first and ask if you would go with me. I don't want trouble, you see."

Smiling gently, Preacher Jacobs stood. "I see. You think Blake Kincaid would never dare lift a rifle to a minister of God."

Laura looked up at him, studying the bleak expression of reluctance on his face. Her hopes slid clear to her feet and melted in a puddle there. "He didn't."

"I'm afraid he did. I went to speak with him soon after our brave group of women went."

Laura sighed heavily. Then she frowned. If Blake Kincaid had dared point a rifle at Preacher Jacobs, surely he wouldn't think twice about pointing one at Caleb, who might already be lying dead somewhere near that shack. Oh, damn him for his stubbornness! But was he any less stubborn than she? He had insisted on riding to the Kincaids' alone; she had ridden here alone.

"Thank you, Preacher Jacobs," she said, rising.

"You're not thinking of going there alone, are you?" he asked in alarm.

"I have to find Caleb," she said, more to herself than him. "And I pray he's safe."

With that she raced outside and to her horse, trying to force from her mind the horrible image of Caleb lying dead beside the tar-paper shack. She might have been furious with him for tying her up the way he had, but right now all she wanted to do was wrap her arms around him and make sure he was safe.

Caleb kicked at the stall door and spun around, raking a hand through his hair. The stall was empty except for the rope and the pile of hay scattered on the floor. Laura was gone, and he couldn't believe what he'd just heard. It wasn't possible.

Ma stood near the barn doors, wringing her apron, her eyes wide. Stacey paced in the middle of the big barn, and Caleb could almost see the steam rising from her. "I can't believe you tied her up! Of all things! That's a pretty stinking thing to do to someone."

"If I hadn't tied her up, she would have ridden off with me!" Caleb thundered. "After what Blake's tried in the past, I sure didn't want her going along. I tried to tell her that."

Stacey stopped pacing to glare at him. "Wouldn't riding with you have been better than riding off by herself? She barely knows how to shoot!"

Caleb flinched. She was right. If he'd let Laura ride with him, she'd be with him now.

"All right now. Stop going at each other," Ruth soothed, although her brow was drawn and she still tugged nervously on her apron. "She didn't go to the Kincaids'. We know that.

Stacey watched her tear out of here pretty soon after you left."

"Oh, God!" Stacey said, pacing again. "I would have gone after her, but I thought she was going after Caleb— straight to the Kincaids."

Caleb leaned against the stall rail. "Never mind, Stacey. You're right. I should have let her go with me. If you had gone after me, we might have two lost women wandering around out there right now."

"I don't get lost on the prairie, and you know it," Stacey said indignantly.

Caleb nodded. "Well, that's true."

"I should have gone."

"She mentioned Preacher Jacobs," Ruth blurted. "She said if she couldn't get you to go with her, Caleb, she'd get Preacher Jacobs."

That news gave him hope and somewhere to look. The prairie was such a huge place when he thought of Laura wondering around lost on it. If she'd ridden all the way to Minot, he'd be angry. But when he found her . . . Damn. When he found her, if she was alive and healthy, fiancé or no fiancé, he'd take her in his arms. He'd give her a million apologies for tying her up like that. He'd kiss her.

"She wouldn't have rode to Minot alone," Stacey said. "She knows there's a lot of bad sorts there."

Caleb shook his head. "You don't know her as well as you think," he said, then sprang into action. He grabbed the saddlebags from Soldier's back and the half-empty canteen.

Stacey took the canteen from him. Their eyes met. Caleb saw tears sparkle in hers. "I'll fill it. I'm sorry," she said. "Just find her. Please."

Caleb could find no words to express what he was feeling. A huge knot had formed in his chest. He'd grown to care for Laura, and so had Stacey and Ma. He wouldn't even allow himself to dwell on all the dangers Laura might face out on the prairie or alone in Minot. He just had to find her. He nodded to acknowledge Stacey's words, then tossed the saddlebags over his shoulder and headed for the house to fill them with food. Earlier, he'd taken the saddlebags Laura had packed, and her canteen, too. He cursed himself for that now. Unless she'd bothered to pack others, she'd had no food or drink for hours.

Once the canteen was filled and the saddlebags packed with biscuits and dried beef and tossed over Soldier's back again, Caleb mounted and rode off.

Laura was tired, hungry, and thirsty. She thought of Caleb and prayed again that he was safe; but the little spring beside the plum tree where she had stopped earlier beckoned, and she stopped again. She reined her horse, slid off, and eased to her stomach on the mossy grass, reaching out to scoop fresh spring water into her hands. It was cool, wet, refreshing. She couldn't seem to get enough.

Finally she stood and reached to pluck plums from the tree. She made a little pile on the ground where she planned to sit in a moment and eat. Soon she would have the strength to ride more.

She was eating her third plum when she heard horse's hooves pounding the ground behind her. She froze, fearing she was probably about to encounter one of those bad sorts wandering a little off course from Minot. She wasn't that far from the town, after all. Two miles, perhaps. But, dear God, her horse—and rifle—were at least a distance of five feet away downstream, and the five feet seemed much more significant at the moment than the two miles. She would never be able to reach her horse and rifle if someone suddenly pounced on her.

Mustering strength, she jumped up and ran for the horse. There was a low chuckle behind her, then strong hands gripped her waist and pulled her back. She went tumbling to the ground with her attacker. She kicked, screamed, elbowed, and tried clawing. She couldn't get away.

"Ouch!" the man cried. Then, "Stop kicking! I swore I'd never tie you up again, Laura, but I'm about to change my mind."

Laura froze again. "Caleb?" she said in a tiny voice.

"It's about damn time you realized who had you."

"Caleb!" Laura twisted in his arms, relief showering

down on her from heaven. "You beast! Why do you always insist on not letting me know you're near?"

He laughed, and what a wonderful sound that was, deep and rich. It touched chords inside her, thrilling her. "It's fun," he teased. "Besides, I figured if you had that rifle anywhere close, you just might shoot me rather than talk to me again."

She cupped his bearded face and stared into his dark, merry eyes. She felt his hands on her hips and loved the feel of his body pressed against hers. Then she kissed him. Impulsively, lovingly, happily. She showered kisses on his lips, his cheek, his nose, his scratchy neck. He laughed again, and his hands went to her hair to stroke and soothe.

"How do you know I still don't plan to shoot you?" she asked.

"You're too glad to see me."

Laura playfully pushed him away and sat up, pouting. "You're conceited, Mr. Main."

"Uh-oh," Caleb said, sitting up beside her. "She's angry again."

"I never stopped being angry. I was just a bit worried, that's all." In truth, she wanted to fling herself back into his arms and bury her face against his neck again.

He ran a forefinger over the pink places circling one wrist. "Sorry, Laura."

"Fortunately you don't tie a very good knot," she said on a softer note, touched by his apology. "You shouldn't have tied me up."

He lifted her hand, brought it to his lips, and sprinkled light kisses on the back of her wrist. Laura watched him. His head still hovering over her hand, he glanced up to measure her reaction. His eyes had darkened, and the intense look he gave her, a look filled with desire, made her heart quicken. He slowly turned her hand so that the inside of her wrist was bared. His tongue flitted lightly over the rope marks there, as if to wash them away. Her entire body tingled now, and her heart pounded. Her wrist was so exquisitely sensitive, that she gasped and shut her eyes.

"Now do you believe I'm sorry?" he asked.

"I never . . . said I didn't."

"I brought food. You must be hungry. I am."

She opened her eyes and met his gaze again. They stared at each other, wanting each other in a forbidden way. The real meaning of his words was clear to her. She smiled. "Has anyone ever told you you have a way with double entendres, Mr. Main?"

His brows shot up. "Double what?"

"Entrendres. Double entendres. Words or expressions that sometimes have two interpretations."

"I wouldn't have known if you hadn't told me."

Laura laughed now. He might not have known the meaning of double entendres, but his words *had* contained two meanings. "Yes, I am hungry," she admitted. "Very."

❄❄❄
Chapter Nine

ORDINARILY LAURA HATED the taste and texture of dried beef, but she was so hungry right now she would have eaten almost anything. When Caleb opened the saddlebags and pulled out the beef and bread, Laura cried out gratefully. The plums she had eaten had not filled her stomach for long. She folded her legs beneath her, the length of her calico skirt tossed to one side, and began chewing on a strip of beef. Caleb settled beside her, his legs bent, and his arms resting on his knees.

"How did you find me?" Laura asked.

"Pure luck. I was riding to Minot. Ma remembered you'd said something about asking Preacher Jacobs to go with you to the Kincaids'."

Laura sighed in frustration. "I didn't know at the time that Preacher Jacobs had already been to see Mr. Kincaid and had already had a rifle pointed at him. He's frightened of Blake, Caleb."

"What?"

"You didn't know, either?"

"Course not. Blake threatened the preacher? If I'd known, I would have skinned Blake like a rabbit."

Laura nearly choked on a bite of beef. "Caleb Main, you would have done no such thing! Despite your rugged look, you have a huge heart. I can't imagine you ever hurting anyone. Tying them up, yes, but not shooting them or skinning them."

"Well, I might have thought about skinning Blake. Preacher Jacobs . . ." Caleb shook his head in disbelief. "Let's hope Blake remembers the things I said this afternoon."

"What exactly *did* you say? What about Amanda? Did he threaten you?" Laura pressed, her heart racing again when she thought of how terrified she had been that Blake had done something awful to Caleb. "When Preacher Jacobs told me Blake had pointed a rifle at him, all I could think of was how dangerous he is and that I had forced you to go talk to him. He could have shot you, too. I jumped on my horse and raced off, thinking I had to reach the Kincaids' before Blake went mad and—"

"Laura," Caleb said, chuckling, his hand on her arm.

She stared at him in exasperation. "Why are you laughing? I really was frightened for you!"

"Woman, I can't imagine you being too frightened. You meet things head-on."

"I'm very frightened sometimes. I just don't like to admit it. I really thought you might be dead when I reached you."

His eyes glittered. "Most likely you were *wishing* I was dead."

"Caleb! I was not."

"Don't pretend with me. I saw that murderous look in your eyes when I tied you to the stall."

"All right. I admit—I thought about killing you after you did that, but when I realized you hadn't told me those things about Blake simply to frighten me into not going with you, I really feared for your life," she said.

"No. What you feared was that Blake might kill me before you could."

She gave him a playful shove. Laughing again, he grabbed her hand and held it in his. His palm was rough from years of toil and damp with nervousness. Laura smiled, and for the first time since meeting him, she wondered how she was ever going to forget him once she returned to Bismarck.

Bismarck . . . the city seemed so far away. Laura was glad. She realized how easily she had made the decision to stay here for a while and care for Amanda. In the back of her mind, had she been trying to escape returning to Bismarck so soon? So many memories of Pa were there, memories she was afraid to confront. And yet, with her hand in Caleb's like this, his so big and hers so small in comparison, she wondered if there was any troublesome thing in the world they couldn't face together.

His grin had faded. He turned her hand over and began stroking the sensitive palm with his rough thumb. His dark eyes were filled with caring and smoked with need. "You scared me, Laura Kent. My head was filled with bad things that could have happened to you while you were alone on the prairie."

"So you were racing to rescue me?" she teased lightly.

He narrowed his eyes. "Weren't you racing to rescue me?"

"I was, but . . ." She laughed at herself now. What could she have done to save him? She could barely hit her mark with a rifle, and she'd had no water or food to sustain her. "My actions seem foolish now," she said, looking out at the gurgling spring. She felt guilty that she hadn't heeded his words and warnings as she should have. She had coerced him into going to talk to Blake Kincaid and might have gotten him killed by doing so. He hadn't said anything about his talk with Blake or if he had even had one, and she wouldn't ask. She wanted to help Amanda, but she wouldn't involve Caleb in the matter anymore. She would think about renting a room in Minot.

Caleb put a forefinger under her delicate chin and turned her face back to him. Her feathery lashes came up, and he was immediately lost in the beautiful blue of her eyes. "You're actions were courageous, not foolish," he said in a husky voice. Then he scowled for good measure. "But don't ever go running off from the farm like that anymore. I want a promise from you."

Laura hesitated. "Caleb, I don't want to endanger you again. I'll convince Blake to let me take Amanda, and I'll rent a room in Minot. You won't even be involved, because I'll be taking Amanda away from here."

Caleb tensed. Rent a room in Minot? She was off and running again, all sorts of things going around inside her head. "Laura," he said sternly, "until someone from Bismarck comes for you, you're staying at the farm. If you think I'm going to let you rent a room in Minot . . . Blake's already been convinced. Besides, nearly every room for rent in Minot is above a saloon. You're not going anywhere."

"You convinced Blake?" Laura asked in surprise.

Caleb nodded. "Now we just have to find Amanda."

"Oh, Caleb!" Laura wrapped her arms around his neck and hugged him tight. He groaned, pretending that she was hurting him. She laughed.

There hadn't been a minute since he'd met her that he hadn't been aware of her as a woman, and now was no different. Her full breasts were pressed against his chest; strands of her silky hair teased his face. Riding by and seeing her sitting beside the spring, a little pile of plums in front of her, had brought him more relief than rain after a long drought. He held her, and every second he did so his body responded more. He breathed her scent—a mingling of fresh air, the lye soap Ma used to wash clothes, and the perfume Stacey made by boiling the petals of various prairie wildflowers.

He couldn't help himself—he lifted a hand and pulled the ribbon from the end of her braid. Laura lowered her arms and pulled back, surprise brightening her eyes. They had both grown serious. If the glaze in her eyes was any indication, he was sure the same want that made his heart thump in his chest did the same to hers. He knew he should say something like, "We ought to get going now. Ma and Stacey are worried." But the words couldn't seem to find their way to his mouth. And he really didn't want to get going.

He watched her reach back, draw her braid around, and begin separating it. Her hair was crinkled. Sunlight shimmered down and touched it with gold. She glanced at her hands as they worked, and her brown lashes touched her ivory cheeks. Caleb shifted his position; his trousers had grown tight and uncomfortable. He wanted Laura. He sensed she wanted him. Nothing else seemed to matter.

He caressed her cheek, and she pressed her face into his palm and closed her eyes, her pink lips parted and inviting. Caleb touched them, skimming his fingertips over the softness. Leaning over, he licked at their sweet moistness and drank Laura's sigh of contentment as she melded against him. He knew there would be no hurrying home. He guessed they would spend the remainder of the evening right here, under the plum tree, beside the trickling spring, in each other's arms.

"Laura," he whispered against her lips. Her hands finished their work. Her hair was free, hanging in golden crinkles to her waist. Caleb withdrew slightly to gaze at it and touch it, the strands like cornsilk in his hands.

Her fingers inched their way to the back of his neck and pressed his head down to hers again. One hand slid around to caress his jaw, her hand rubbing against the coarseness of his beard. She beckoned him with her parted lips, shimmering blue eyes, and the rapid rise and fall of her breasts.

He lowered her onto the mossy grass.

Laura could think of nothing but needing Caleb. Passion blazed throughout her body. The promise of pleasure she saw in his eyes and her own thoughts of the pleasure she might give by offering herself pulsed in her mind. They were man and woman, needing each other, caught in the forces of nature. The rest of the world slipped away.

His hand slid over her breast, and she cried out, a sound forced from her by the sheer delight his touch sent rippling through her. He worked at her bodice buttons, and this time she knew she wouldn't stop him when he pushed the material aside and sought to touch her bare breasts. She felt a throbbing begin in her most feminine place and knew it cried for fulfillment only Caleb could give. She instinctively arched to his touch, needing his hands on her flesh as badly as a starving person needs food.

He captured her mouth with his. His tongue sought hers and tasted, tentatively at first, then dived deep. Laura received him, caressing his jaw, pressing his head ever closer. His hands parted her unbuttoned bodice and untied the ribbons on her camisole.

The first touch of his rough hand on her bare flesh made Laura cry out in pleasure. He gently kneaded one swollen breast, lifting his head to look at it. He touched the peaked tip, and she caught her lower lip between her teeth. "Beautiful," he whispered, then dipped his head to taste it.

His mouth was hot, his beard slightly scratchy. He twirled his tongue around the peak, then drew it fully into his mouth as his hand continued massaging the flesh surrounding it. Pleasure shot to every tiny nerve in Laura's body. She buried her hands in Caleb's hair, pressing his head closer. She arched to offer more and Caleb growled low in response. He slid an arm beneath her hips, lifting them to him. Laura felt his hardened length through his trousers and her skirt and knew a sudden urge to feel their bare bodies pressed together.

"My dress," she said softly. "Let me take it off."

He showered kisses up her neck to her lips, then stared intently down into her eyes. "Is this what you want, Laura? What about—?"

She pressed her fingertips to his lips to silence him. "Don't ruin our time together. This is what I want now, Caleb. Help me with my dress."

She sat up and pulled the skirt from beneath her. She unfastened several more buttons at her waist, then Caleb lifted the dress over her head, slid it off her extended arms, and tossed it aside. She wore only her drawers and open camisole now. His eyes, hot as smoldering coals, raked over her. She laid back beside him. One big hand traveled the length of her body, lingering again on the swell of a breast, dipping to her flat stomach and following the flare of one hip to her thigh. At her calves Caleb gently removed her boots, then returned to her stomach, where he put several fingers beneath the waistband of her drawers. Laura inhaled a sharp breath, knowing that within moments she would be unclothed beneath him.

Their eyes met and held. "Stop me now, Laura, if you want to stop me at all."

She couldn't deny that she was fearful. Her first time with a man . . . She knew some pain awaited her; she'd heard the whispers and giggles of the girls at the last school she had attended. She wasn't entirely naive. But her body yearned for Caleb, and she wouldn't stop him. She covered his hand with hers and helped him untie and part the drawers. Then she discarded the loose camisole.

His gaze burned with the fury of boiling passion as he looked at her now naked body, hunger flaring his eyes. A thrill went through Laura when she saw that he found her so desirable. The spring gurgled, and the plum tree branches brushed together in excitement. Even the mossy grass beneath Laura seemed alive, cradling her, providing a soft bed for her and her lover. Through the plum branches, clouds mingled joyously in the sky, and the sun shone down.

Laura boldly skimmed her hands over Caleb's muscled shoulders, his hard chest, and lean stomach. He shut his eyes, his hands pressing her hips to his. She reached for the buttons on his shirt, shakily undid them, then pushed the shirt over and off his shoulders. Her breath caught in her throat as she gazed at the magnificence of him—the sculptured muscles that became even more defined with his every movement, the thick crop of black curls on his chest and the pink nipples that hid beneath. She exhaled slowly, running her hands along the outsides of his strong arms, interlacing her fingers with his. He dipped his head to feast at her breast again, and Laura moaned in sheer pleasure, every fiber of her body tense and aching for release.

She buried her hands in his hair, pressed his head ever closer, grappled at his shoulders and arms. His hands caressed her, finding every sensitive point, teasing her other nipple to tautness, toying with her neck and earlobe, fluttering over her breast again to her stomach. He slid his hand beneath her and cupped her buttocks, then let his hand wander down the back of her thigh and around. Laura gasped when he touched the throbbing feminine flesh between her thighs. But instinctively her legs parted for him, and she offered a woman's most sacred possession, her eyes linking with his as she did.

Caleb touched her, finding her tiny, swollen bud beneath light curls. His fingers slid along the hot, wet flesh, exploring. He slipped a finger inside her, making her more ready for him. She cried out, gripping his shoulders and burying her face in his chest. He slid his finger in and out of her until she instinctively thrust her hips up to meet his every movement. Now . . . and she'd feel only brief pain.

He withdrew from her. Laura lay waiting for him. He removed his boots, then his trousers. Laura's eyes widened at the sight of him naked.

"Don't be scared, Laura," he said, his voice low and raspy. "I'll be gentle."

"I know," she whispered.

He eased between her thighs, his hands clasping her silken hips. Then he gave a thrust and buried himself within her. Tensing, Laura whimpered. When Caleb lifted his head, he saw the tears in her eyes. Sheathed in her velvety warmth, feeling her pulse throb around him, waiting was difficult, but wait he did. He kissed her breasts, tenderly suckled each sweet nipple and ran his hands up and down her back. Only when Laura moved her hips against him did he begin movements in and out of her.

They set a pace, slow at first, then the tempo increased. Laura's soft cries and gasps as he filled her again and again excited Caleb until he felt he would explode—journey to satisfaction without her. His senses were more alert than they'd ever been. The wet sounds of their joining enveloped him, and the smell of their mixed scents filled his head in a primitive way. He moaned and slowed the pace, knowing if he didn't, their loving would be over almost as soon as it had begun.

Laura drew him within her, feeling she couldn't get enough of him. The sensation of fullness he created made her cry out and arch for more. Breathing was difficult, but she welcomed even that sensation. She touched him, his shoulders, his back, his sinewy buttocks. And she marveled at their exquisite joining. He was powerful, beautiful, gentle, and tender—everything she had sensed he would be. She caught his head between her hands and kissed him, whimpering her pleasure into his mouth. She felt their storm rising, swirling, sweeping her along on a powerful wind. She raced with it to meet the crest, hearing her cries of ecstasy even as the storm roared in her ears and ripped through her body with incredible force.

Caleb felt her spasm around him and clasped her to him, diving deep to seek his own release. Something gripped him, a raging storm more powerful than any he'd ever experienced. He swelled within her, tensed, then spilled his seed.

Heaven couldn't possibly be a more glorious place. Laura rested her head on his chest, her fingers playing in the mass of black curls. The land around them was cast in red; the Dakota sun had begun its fiery descent, painting the sky in various breathtaking shades and spilling color over the tops of trees. Even the springwater appeared red. Caleb's breathing beneath Laura's hand was heavy and even. One arm was tossed back beneath his head; the other was under her shoulder. Laura wanted to lie with him like this forever—in the valley of plums, beside the whispering spring, with the setting sun painting beauty everywhere. Surely this was paradise.

Caleb stared up at the sunset, not wanting to move. This dreamy scene would change if he moved. Right now he had the only woman he wanted in his arms. But if he moved . . . if he released her . . . where would they be then? She'd remember her life waiting in Bismarck and her fiancé there . . . a man he'd never met and didn't care to meet. He'd faced prairie wolves, coyotes, bears, even a gun or two in his life so far. But nothing had ever scared him as much as thoughts of losing Laura did. When they left the valley, when she was thinking clearly again, would she still talk about returning to Bismarck? He wouldn't ask her to stay and marry him right now. There were too many problems in her head that she still needed to sort through. And when she sorted through them, depending on what she decided, maybe then he'd speak the words that itched to spill from his mouth. Laura wasn't the only woman he'd ever had; he'd bedded a number over the years. But making love to her had been different than with any other woman. He knew he loved her.

"Better be getting back," he said, forcing the words as the golden silk of her hair slipped through his fingers. "Stacey and Ma were worried when I left. I've been gone so long, they're probably out looking for us by now."

He felt her eyes on him and wondered what she was thinking. Did she already regret giving herself to him? Had guilt crept into her mind? Would it haunt her dreams? Would it drive her back to Adrian?

"What happens when we go back, Caleb?" she asked softly.

He drew her closer to him. She was scared, too, for her own reasons. She had decisions to make, difficult decisions no one could make for her, not even him. And he wouldn't try. "We find Amanda and start taking care of her," he said.

She nodded, then withdrew from him and reached for her clothes.

Caleb's arms had never felt so empty.

✹✹✹
Chapter Ten

As soon as Laura dismounted in front of the barn, Stacey nearly plowed her down. Stacey grabbed and embraced Laura, hugging her as if she had been away for years, as if she thought her friend might not have come back.

"I was so worried," Stacey said, drawing back, her face tight with concern. "I was having terrible thoughts. Ma just kept telling me to stop fretting, that Caleb would find you. I still worried."

Laura smiled. "I'm fine, really. Stop worrying."

"You must be tired."

"I am."

"Come on. Ma made soup," Stacey said, leading her toward the house.

From inside the barn, Caleb heard them talking. Then their voices faded, and he was left with just the soft nickering of the horses as he unsaddled them. He tossed the saddles over stall rails, then began feeding and brushing the horses.

His mind wandered, as it had all during the ride home. Laura's hair had been like silk in his hands. Her skin had been smooth except for the almost-healed places where she'd been injured in the coach wreck. Despite the fading cuts and bruises, she was beautiful. He remembered the time they'd spent locked together, whispering words, her soft cries of pleasure filling his ears.

He wanted her to stay here and marry him. He didn't want her to go back to Bismarck. But he reckoned she had a lot more waiting for her in Bismarck than she had here—money, friends, the home she'd been raised in, her memories of her pa. She'd never meant to end up here.

He finished with the horses, then went to the house to

wash up. Stacey and Laura were sitting on the red-cushioned
settee by the fireplace, talking softly. Ma was just coming
downstairs. Caleb locked eyes with her. She spotted something in his gaze; her eyes narrowed slightly as if she'd been
suspecting something. One look at him told her she was
right. He hoped he didn't give away too much, but Ma knew
him. Stacey knew him, too, and just as Ma had probably already guessed he was in love with Laura Kent, Stacey would
know soon, too. He might hide things from other people, but
hiding anything from his sister and mother was pretty damn
hard, if not impossible.

Caleb hung his rifle above the door, then propped the one
Stacey had loaned Laura in a corner near the fireplace. At the
washbasin he washed his hands and arms. Ruth busied herself near the stove. Laura and Stacey moved to help her, filling wooden bowls and putting them on the table. Ruth put a
plate of sliced bread in the middle of the table, then everyone
sat down to eat.

"I'm sorry for causing everyone so much worry," Laura
said.

Stacey smiled. "It's over."

"Did you see Preacher Jacobs?" Ruth asked.

Laura nodded, then explained how Preacher Jacobs had
gone to see Blake and had been threatened the same way the
group of woman had been. Ruth shook her head and sighed.
Caleb told her and Stacey that he'd gone to the Kincaids'
shack and what had happened there. Laura suggested she
take Amanda and stay in Minot so Caleb, Ruth, and Stacey
could resume their normal lives.

Caleb tensed. Did that mean she'd already thought about
whether or not she should stay and had decided she
shouldn't? Well, she was dead wrong if she thought he was
going to stand for her staying in Minot. Ruth and Stacey
stared at her, then objected. Caleb clenched his jaw and fixed
an angry gaze on Laura.

Laura felt it and wondered if he would say something
now, in front of Ruth and Stacey, or catch her alone later.

"You're not staying in Minot, Laura," he said, choosing to

air the argument now. "Get the notion out of your head. You're staying here until the day Adrian comes for you."

"Who's Adrian?" Stacey asked innocently.

"Laura's fiancé," Caleb said.

"Oh."

Laura shifted uncomfortably and lowered her gaze. She could still feel Caleb's eyes penetrating her, searing to her very soul. Was he thinking that after what they had shared, she wanted to leave? If he was, he was wrong. She simply didn't want to trouble them further where Amanda was concerned. Yes, she wanted to take care of Amanda and make sure the girl was fed and clothed right, and Caleb and Ruth had agreed to let her bring Amanda here. But she had had to talk them into it, and that had not been easy. She couldn't help but feel that she would be burdening them if she brought Amanda here. Staying in Minot and taking care of Amanda there seemed a better solution to the dilemma.

In front of Ruth and Stacey, she couldn't very well tell Caleb that her plan to stay in Minot had nothing to do with her and him. She couldn't tell him that from the moment she had urged him to make love to her, thoughts of staying and marrying him had been in the back of her mind. During the ride from the plum tree to here, she had certainly thought about telling him, but Caleb had been quiet. He had seemed immersed in his own thoughts, and the time had not seemed right. He had once told her that if she ever decided to change her mind about marrying Adrian, she should let him know. Well, she intended to, as soon as possible.

"Adrian Montgomery?" Ruth asked.

Laura, Caleb, and Stacey fixed their eyes on her. "Yes," Laura managed. "How do you know his last name?"

Ruth stood and walked over to a cupboard. She reached up to one of the shelves, then returned to the table, carrying a small piece of paper, and stopped beside Laura. "Mr. Cecil, who runs the telegraph office, sent his boy out here while Stacey was taking the cattle to water. He'd heard about your accident and thought you'd be real happy to have this. Said it was from an Adrian Montgomery in Bismarck," she said, pressing the paper into Laura's hand.

Laura hesitated, feeling three sets of eyes on her. Then she unfolded the note and read:

LAURA KENT STOP I WILL ARRIVE NEXT WEEK STOP HAVE BUSI-
NESS TO CLEAR UP STOP I LOVE YOU STOP
                                          ADRIAN MONTGOMERY

Laura shifted in her chair. "He . . . he says he'll be arriving next week. I'll need to telegraph back and tell him not to come yet," Laura said.

"Won't he wonder why you want to stay longer with people you just met?" Stacey asked, a touch of sadness in her eyes.

"I'll try to explain. I might have known everyone here for only a week, but it seems like a lot longer."

"But I'm sure you're wanting to get back, too," Ruth said.

"I want to take care of Amanda," Laura responded, glancing at Caleb. His eyes were fixed on his soup. He ate slowly, calmly, and she saw no indication that the message in the telegraph disturbed him. He had put on an indifferent facade, one she found intolerable. She wanted a tender look, something from him to indicate he cared and wanted her to telegraph Adrian back and tell him not to come at all. She sensed that he cared, but Caleb was an expert at shutting out things he didn't want to deal with. Wasn't that exactly what he had done with the business between him and Pa? She didn't know the entire story; she could only assume what took place. But she knew that until he had found her after the coach wreck and realized who she was, he had shoved the bad business between him and Pa to some dark, remote corner of his mind that he never approached.

Silence fell over the room for a time. Everyone ate the soup and bread. Laura told Ruth supper was delicious.

"Me and Stacey started your new dress today, Laura," Ruth said. "Come on, we'll show you."

Laura smiled at their thoughtfulness. "All right. But after tonight, leave the rest of it to me. I was taught how to stitch in school. I never expected Stacey to make the dress I'm wearing. I simply wanted you two to show me how to pattern it. I'm not skilled at that."

Laura, Stacey, and Ruth went to the sewing corner, where pieces of yellow-checked gingham were tossed across the back of the rocking chair. Stacey held up the pieces while Ruth explained how they'd been cut. While Laura listened to them, she watched Caleb from the corner of her eye. He stole around the table and glanced at the telegraph message. Laura's heart almost stopped. Why had she foolishly left the paper there? Caleb scanned it quickly, then moved away to put his bowl beside the washbasin. His arms widespread, he gripped the edge of the cabinet, letting his shoulders and head slump. A moment passed. Laura ached to go to him.

Finally Caleb straightened, breathed deeply, and strode to the door. "Going to do some chores, Ma," he mumbled.

Then he was gone. The creak of the shutting door vibrated through Laura's body and touched her soul. Had he given up on them ever sharing a life together? She prayed not. She would find him later and talk to him.

Stacey held out a piece of shaped gingham, and Laura feigned a smile and took it, nodding her head in response to something Ruth said about fitting this piece to that piece.

Presently she settled with Stacey on the settee, and they stitched the pieces of material that would eventually be Laura's dress.

"I always wanted a sister," Stacey said softly. "At least, someone near my age I could do things like this with."

Laura smiled and said, "I'm glad I'm here."

And that was the truth. She had never planned to come to this place or meet these people, but her life had changed for the better since she had. She had faced Pa's death and, in facing it, was also beginning to face the fact that she must take charge of her life. Pa had always been subtly domineering. She had never minded or even given it a second thought until his death, when she had had to start making some of her own decisions. Her life with Pa was all she had ever known, and she had loved him tremendously. He had chosen her schools and which social functions she should or shouldn't attend. On occasion he had even picked her gowns.

Pa had once told her he had known from the time she and Adrian were toddling around that they were right for each other and that he had arranged for them to spend more and more time together. She realized now that she had not even been given a say in the matter of choosing her husband. Pa had arranged it all. She remembered evenings right after she had returned from school when Adrian had called, and instead of spending the usual time with her walking or riding or engaging in some sort of game, he had gone to Pa's sitting room and spent a great deal of time in hushed conversation with Pa. Laura had peeked into the room more than a few times. Adrian had spied her finally and had laughed, then said something about how he and her father were discussing a business proposal. Pa's blue eyes had twinkled, and his head had bobbed in agreement. Adrian's family owned cattle and Montgomery Insurance and had done business with Pa a number of times, so Laura had had no reason to suspect that Adrian—or Pa—was deceiving her. But had they been? Had the subject of their business been her and Adrian's engagement and marriage?

She didn't find that thought particularly disturbing. Pa had hinted a number of times that now that her schooling was finished, she needed to marry and give him some grandsons. It was just like Pa to plan her marriage the way he would a business arrangement. But she knew Montgomery Insurance had had a number of financial problems during the past few years, and remembering how eager Adrian had been that day *did* disturb her. Aside from the usual dowry arrangement, had he and Pa discussed money? Had Pa not seen that Adrian only wanted to marry her to get his hands on the money? And if Pa had, yet had continued the arrangement despite that, what would he say to her now if he were alive and she told him she couldn't marry Adrian?

She smiled sadly to herself. She still cared so much about what Pa thought of her. She always would. Despite that, marrying Adrian was one thing she simply could not do. Pa was dead, and she had to seek her happiness.

She felt that Minot and the Mains farm were the beginning

of a new journey in her life, a journey she knew she wanted to take.

Caleb stayed busy during the next few days, which helped keep his mind off of Laura. Several times he caught her looking at him as though she wanted to talk to him. He'd just go on with his work, thinking if she did, she'd be typical Laura and walk right up and start talking. The fact that he'd been doing chores the day she'd wanted to talk about bringing Amanda here hadn't stopped her then. Why would his work stop her now? He reckoned she was still sorting things out in her head.

He drove some cattle to Minot one day and sold them there. The next day he spent traveling to a ranch south of his farm to look at other cattle and driving back head he bought. When not buying and selling cattle, he did chores. And when not doing chores, he searched the prairie for Amanda.

He didn't find her. He searched near the Kincaids' tar-paper shack and near the church and in town, but he always came home carrying only his rifle. Usually if Amanda couldn't be found on the prairie, she could be found by the church. Caleb caught himself hoping something hadn't happened to her. Something bad. He made sure the worry was erased from his face whenever he met Laura's gaze. But the truth was, he *was* worried.

Where the hell was Amanda?

When Caleb didn't find Amanda after the first day, Laura began to worry. Two evenings later there was still no sign of Amanda, and Laura felt panicky inside. She and Stacey were sitting on the settee, stitching her new dress. Caleb sat across from them in a chair with a newspaper in his hands. Ruth sat in the sewing corner, knitting a sock. Laura watched Caleb for a while, wondering how he could appear so calm when Amanda could not be found. Her needle slipped, pricking her finger. Instead of crying out in pain, she blurted, "Do you think she might have gone off somewhere and—"

"Don't even think it, Laura," he said, his eyes remaining on the paper.

Laura stared at him. Finally he glanced up, and she searched his eyes for some sign of fear that something terrible might have happened to Amanda. But she saw only the same cool darkness that had edged into his eyes shortly after they had returned from making love under the plum tree. No emotion, only fathomless darkness. During the last three days he had kept himself so busy that there had never been even a moment to talk to him. She could have told him while he was doing chores that she had decided not to marry Adrian, but she had not known how to interpret the cool looks he had been giving her.

What frustrated her the most was the way those cool, indifferent looks carried into the search for Amanda. She wanted to snap at him for acting this way. They were dealing with a little girl's life, after all, a life worth being concerned about.

"Sunday's two days away," he said. "She'll be by the church after the service."

"I hope so," Laura responded.

Stacey paused in her stitching to glance up. "She's always there after church, Laura."

Laura nodded, although she still felt uncertain.

"We'll go to Minot again tomorrow so you can telegraph Adrian if you want," Caleb said. "While we're there, I'll search some more."

Laura began stitching again. When she thought of Amanda wandering around out on the prairie, or even in the valley alone, she trembled. Coyotes, wolves, bears, buzzards, snakes . . . she was sure there were other dangers. She must find Amanda and make sure she didn't run away from her, too. How would she even get Amanda to come with her without a fight? Perhaps she could coax the girl somehow. But how?

She slipped the needle into the yellow-checked gingham again, realized she had reached the end of a seam, and was just lifting the scissors to clip the thread when a thought occurred to her. Her hands stilled, and she glanced here and there, considering the thought.

"Stacey, you have seen Amanda, haven't you?"

Stacey looked up, her brow wrinkled. "Now what's gotten into you? Of course I've seen Amanda. After church every Sunday . . ."

"Then you know what size she is. So do I. Between the two of us, we could estimate measurements and make her a dress," Laura said excitedly.

"That's a wonderful idea," Stacey said, just as excited. "Tomorrow, while we're in Minot, we'll go to the dry goods store and buy more material."

Laura cut the thread but didn't bother to tie it off. She began pulling the thread out, stitch by stitch, clipping it where she had made such tiny stitches that she couldn't simply pull them out.

"What are you doing?" Stacey cried incredulously. "You're ruining the seam. There was nothing wrong with it."

"We're not going to wait until tomorrow to start, Stacey. We already have material."

"Wha—? You don't mean—?"

"I do. Start taking out those seams you just stitched. We'll simply cut the pieces down and make Amanda a dress. We'll buy her some hair ribbons and things like that in Minot. We can make the dress tonight."

Stacey stared at her. "You've gone mad. I know you have. We can buy material for Amanda's dress tomorrow."

"If we encounter Amanda tomorrow, I want to have something to show her, something that will be hers. Something she can be proud of."

"Ma. Caleb. Help! She's gone mad. Laura, we have the bodice almost done. The sleeves . . ."

"Taking the seams out won't be nearly the work of putting them in." Laura had succeeded in taking out the one seam; now she started on another. Stacey emitted a tiny screech and turned her head, as if she couldn't bear to watch.

"Laura, are you sure you want to do that?" Ruth asked from the sewing corner.

"Of course I am. Amanda needs a dress."

"So do you."

"I already have one. From what I saw of the materials

clinging to Amanda's body last Sunday, she needs one much worse than I do."

"Caleb, do something!" Stacey cried. "Laura, stop!"

For the first time in days, Laura saw a grin twitch the corners of Caleb's mouth. The barrier that had coated his eyes slipped away, and the darkness sparkled. "Do something . . ." he said, as if considering what to do exactly, or even if he should do something to stop what Stacey obviously felt was needless destruction. "Let's see, I reckon you could tie her up."

"Caleb!" admonished Ruth.

Stacey leapt up. "Don't joke! This is terrible. She's ruining what we've already done. Tie her up if that's what it takes! Laura!"

Caleb laughed. "Oh, no. I said I reckon *you* could tie her up. You're forgetting how angry you were when you found out *I* tied her up. Besides, when the woman decides to do something, I figure the cavalry couldn't stop her."

Realizing she would get no help from Caleb or Ruth, Stacey stomped away. For a few moments the loud thud of her boots on the wooden floor echoed through the house.

"Stacey has a bit of a temper sometimes," Ruth said. "She'll cool down in a while, don't worry."

Laura looked up at Caleb. He grinned and said, "You're a hell of a woman."

"I do try," she said, smiling. She was relieved that the little episode had alleviated some of the tension between her and Caleb. She searched his eyes for more emotion, but he seemed to realize what she was doing, and his eyes quickly darkened again.

She went back to taking out seams. He went back to reading. Ruth sat quietly for a time and knitted. Soon Caleb rose and mumbled that he was going upstairs to bed.

Stacey soon drifted back downstairs, her head lowered. "Sorry. Suppose you'll be needing some help there," she said to Laura.

Laura glanced up. "I do, but only help me if you really want to, Stacey. When I asked if I could bring Amanda here for a while, I told Caleb and your mother that I wouldn't expect anyone but myself to care for her. That includes making her clothes. I know you don't like the idea of Amanda coming here, so if you really don't want to help me with her dress, please don't."

"I want to," Stacey said. She picked up the piece of the bodice she had been sewing, sat, and began pulling out the stitches.

When all the stitches were gone from the pieces of material, Laura and Stacey laid the pieces out on the table. They talked about how much they thought needed to be cut away, then began the task. Once the cutting was complete, they put the pieces together and stitched again. Ruth put her knitting away and joined them, settling herself in the chair where Caleb had sat earlier.

Laura glanced at Stacey, who looked up and smiled. "I still can't believe we're doing this."

"Neither can I, if you want to know the truth," Laura said.

They laughed together, and Ruth joined in. "Like I said—things got a whole lot more interesting around here when you came, Laura."

"*My* life became more interesting the day Caleb pulled me from that wreck," she said. She began stitching diligently, concentrating on putting the needle and thread in and pulling them out. She turned her thoughts toward Amanda and the dress. As far as she knew, Amanda had never had a moment's happiness. Life had been too difficult, a constant fight to survive. The dress might coax at least the hint of a smile to Amanda's face and brighten her life.

The hour was late when the dress was finally finished. Ruth hung it on a hook near the rocking chair in the sewing corner, then stepped back to have a look at it. She shook her head, still not believing the change that had come over their lives since Laura Kent arrived. She and Stacey wouldn't have thought to bring Amanda here and try to teach the girl. They hadn't had the courage. Slowly, through Laura's goodness, they were learning something themselves—that when someone was being mistreated, others should step in, should take risks to help. Ruth knew civilizing Amanda would be hard, but she, like Laura, wanted to at least try. For years everyone, including herself, had said Amanda was beyond help. Well, Amanda had been beyond help mostly because Blake wouldn't let anyone come to her aid. Caleb had solved that problem, something someone should have done long ago. Ruth felt ashamed that she hadn't pushed Caleb into it the way Laura had. Course, he could have thought to do it himself, too.

"Hasn't been a dress that small in this house in years, not since Stacey was little," Ruth remarked, inspecting their handiwork.

Stacey yawned. "I'm going to bed."

"So am I," Laura said, also yawning.

Ruth laughed. "I'll be along. It's pretty late."

Stacey and Laura disappeared upstairs. Ruth sat in the rocking chair for a time, wondering about the stiffness that had sprung up between Caleb and Laura. Those two had bickered ever since Caleb had brought Laura here, but since he had gone to fetch Laura from town, the tension between them had gotten worse. She figured they'd argued because Laura had gone off by herself. But earlier she'd watched Caleb smile at Laura in a way that would make most women's hearts beat fast.

He was in love. The fact hit Ruth hard when she thought of that smile. Laura Kent, of all women. Matt Kent's daughter. An engaged woman—that was what really mattered.

She wondered how Caleb was swallowing the fact that Laura's fiancé would show up to collect her one day soon. Herself . . . she didn't find that eventuality a welcome thought since she'd taken to Laura. Stacey had, too. But Laura's real life was somewhere else, in a city Caleb couldn't face because so many bad memories he'd buried a long time ago might jump out at him.

Caleb had told her how Laura had poured out the way she'd found her pa and that she'd been leaving Bismarck for a time when the coach accident happened. So Laura and Caleb both had ghosts in Bismarck. Ghosts they'd have to deal with; otherwise they'd be haunted for the rest of their lives.

Ruth rocked a little more, then rose, put out the lamps, and went up to bed.

* * *

The next day in Minot, Caleb left Ruth, Stacey, and Laura in Alman's Dry Goods and went off to find someone to take upriver a letter Laura had written to her Aunt Rebecca. After that, Caleb had business of his own to attend.

After purchasing a slate and some pencils, Laura pretended to admire several plumed hats while Ruth and Stacey conversed with Mr. Alman. When she was certain Ruth and Stacey were well occupied, she slipped away. She wanted to go to the church and see if Amanda frequented it more than people knew, and she didn't want Ruth and Stacey trying to stop her.

The church was quiet. The willow towering above it and draping its branches over one corner whispered softly. Near the river the jointed rushes brushed together, and dragonflies dived in and out, swirling one second, fluttering off rapidly the next. Sun glittered down on the river and dappled the surface. Across the river trees mingled, more rushes sprang up in places, and a little clapboard house nestled along the bank. Laura wondered briefly why she had not noticed it before. Thinking her mind had simply been filled with other things the two other times she had been here, she suddenly saw Amanda, sitting alone beneath a huge willow tree near the river. Amanda rocked back and forth, her eyes fastened on the water. Laura breathed a sigh of relief that she had finally found her.

She approached slowly, Amanda's gingham dress and the slate held tightly against her, the pencils clutched in one hand. The girl twisted around and fastened her eyes on Laura. With every step Laura took that brought her closer to Amanda, she feared the child would bolt.

"Hello, Amanda. Do you remember me? I tried to speak to you last Sunday after church. You ran away."

Amanda moved slowly as if considering running away again. But she wasn't quite certain, Laura thought. Perhaps no one had ever bothered to talk to her twice in one week and she was curious as to why Laura would. "I want to help you, Amanda. I really do. I brought you a dress, one that I helped

Stacey and Ruth Main make for you. I brought a slate and some pencils, too."

She eased closer. Amanda was on her feet now, backing up. Laura stopped, fearing she would chase Amanda away.

"I could teach you things, Amanda—how to write and read. My name is Laura, and I'm staying with the Mains at their farm for a while. We'd like you to come and stay with us. You could go there with us today—we brought a wagon."

Laura took another step. Amanda bolted, limping off through the trees and brush on the riverbank. Laura started after her. "Amanda! Amanda, please wait!"

Laura had taken three hasty steps when someone grabbed her arm to stop her. She didn't need to turn and see a face. She knew who stood behind her. She struggled to free her arm. "Damn you, Caleb. Let go!"

"Laura, if you force her, what makes you think she'll stay? While we're sleeping, she might run off."

"She was listening to me! She was. Let go! I'll go talk to her more. I'll convince her."

Caleb twisted Laura around and held her tight. "Laura, go at this slowly. All right—you got her to listen to you a little. You can't expect her to jump up and down all excited when someone tells her they want to take care of her. She's never heard that before, not even from the church people. Every Sunday people come out after service and pretend she's not there."

"There must be some reason she comes to the church. Someone must have done something for her here."

Caleb studied her for a minute, as if considering something. "Ah, hell. Come on," he said, releasing her arm. He strode toward the riverbank. Laura watched him lean down beside the huge willow tree and put his hand in a hollow someone had created by digging the ground away from the bottom of the trunk. He pulled a red handkerchief out and sat staring at it.

Laura couldn't imagine what he was doing, so she walked over. "How did you know that was there?"

"Because I've been putting it there for months," Caleb said quietly, as if he had not wanted anyone to know.

"An empty handkerchief?"

"Well, it's not empty when I put it in there," he snapped. "I fill it with food—dried beef, bread, sometimes some candy or cake. Amanda's always close. I can sense her. She takes the food soon after I leave."

Laura's jaw fell open. "*You* put it there?"

"That's what I said. She was here one day when service let out. I'd seen her in town before. I tried to get her to stay and talk to me one day, like you did just now. She wouldn't do it. She walks slowly, so I figured she hadn't gone too far. I called to her, told her who I was and that I was putting the handkerchief in the tree. That's why she comes here all the time now."

"But I don't understand. *You* tried to discourage me from helping her. You said people wouldn't like me meddling. You've been helping her for months?"

He looked ashamed, staring down at the handkerchief.

Laura knelt beside him. "You didn't want anyone to know, did you?"

He shook his head. "Look, Laura, I got caught up in a passel of bad things with your pa. Didn't want to start trouble with a neighbor here. For the last ten years I've just been minding my business and living a quiet life. Now I know it was wrong to ignore Amanda just because I wanted to get around trouble."

Laura took his face in her hands and tipped it up so he was forced to meet her gaze. Tears of gratitude stung her eyes, and she could hardly speak, she was so overcome with happiness. *Someone* had been helping Amanda. "You didn't ignore her. You helped her, in the only way you thought you could at the time. You have the biggest heart of anyone I've ever known, Caleb Main."

✳✳✳
Chapter Eleven

CALEB DIDN'T PUT his hands over hers the way he wanted to. He didn't put his arms around her the way he wanted to. And he didn't kiss her the way he wanted to. He withdrew and stood, leaving her hunched down alone, her hands empty. He reckoned that since she hadn't said anything one way or the other about the telegraph she'd gotten from Adrian, she meant to go home after she had a chance to take care of Amanda for a bit. Considering all that, he'd rather not have her all soft in his arms.

"Let's leave the dress and other things by the tree. We'll ride by later and see if she took them," he said.

Laura nodded, looking dazed for a moment. Then she folded the dress neatly, put it near the tree, and placed the slate and pencils on the dress. "What if she simply keeps taking the things we put here but never wants us to help her?"

"Then there's nothing else we can do."

Laura didn't like that answer. She stood in silence, staring at the dress and other items. There had to be a way to convince Amanda. They couldn't simply keep leaving things, hoping Amanda would take them. Amanda needed shelter and decent meals, not only morsels wrapped in a handkerchief and placed beneath a tree. Caleb's effort to make sure Amanda received food was touching, but the child needed so much more.

"Laura," Caleb said softly behind her. "You have to learn that if a person doesn't want to be helped, you can't help her. We'll do what we can."

"I can't believe Amanda doesn't want help. She's just a child! She hesitated, you saw her," Laura said, turning to face him. "She was listening to me. She wants love and attention."

Caleb took Laura's hand and, against his better judgment, cradled it in his, running a thumb over the fine bones and savoring the satiny feel of her skin. He'd stayed away from her lately because he didn't trust himself whenever he got too close to her. He figured he should stay away from her altogether but didn't know how to go about doing that, except to work himself to death at the farm. Even if he tried that, this thing with Amanda would still pull him and Laura close together again, and that was something he didn't know how to fight. He couldn't just ignore Amanda the way he'd ignored so many situations—he had a little time invested in Amanda himself. He hadn't really planned on doing anything more for her than he'd been doing these past months, but then he hadn't planned on loving Laura, either. He'd gone hunting for a grizzly and had run across a woman who was changing him in many ways, a woman with so much compassion and goodness in her she couldn't just let Amanda Kincaid go on living like an animal.

He reckoned that if Laura had been in that group of women who had called on Blake Kincaid, a leveled rifle wouldn't have stopped her. Just the thought of meddling had stopped *him*; he would have done a lot more for Amanda by now if he hadn't let his rotten past interfere. He should have helped Amanda more, and the past be damned. Ten years ago he'd thought that by leaving Bismarck and Matt Kent behind, he'd shed the effects of the bad land deals and money problems. Instead he'd carried them with him. Those experiences lurked in his mind right now, warning him against involving himself in anything that smelled even a little of potential trouble. He was beginning to see that turning his back on problems and people and closing his thoughts to them didn't make them go away.

"We'll give her what she needs, Laura, but if we force her to go with us, she'll only run off when we're not looking," he said.

Laura glanced at the tree again and the items she'd placed

there. She seemed to consider his words. "All right," she finally said.

When they started back to town together, Laura realized they were alone. And Caleb wasn't working. This was the first chance in four days she had had to broach the subject of Adrian and Bismarck.

"I've been thinking . . ." she began, and suddenly her mouth was dry. Caleb lifted a brow and regarded her in the same cool way he had regarded her so many times during the last four days. "I–I've been thinking about perhaps not going back to Bismarck even after we've helped Amanda," she managed.

What was he thinking? Had he changed his mind about wanting her to stay? Could that be the reason for all the cool looks and the way he had kept himself so busy of late?

"And just what do you want to do here if you stay?" Caleb asked, wanting her to answer for herself.

She stared at him. She had expected to hear him ask her to marry him or at least ask if she had decided not to marry Adrian. She hadn't expected him to ask her what she wanted to do.

"I'm telling you I want to stay. What do you think I want to do?" she countered impatiently. Was it really so difficult for him to guess? Could he really not imagine why she wanted to stay?

He shook his head. "We can keep shooting questions at each other, Laura, and not get anywhere."

"Yes, we can." She felt exasperated. How could she reach him? Should she blurt the fact that she wanted to stay because she wanted to marry him? That didn't seem proper. He had taken some of the proper out of her during the last few weeks, but receiving a marriage proposal the right way was important to her. Proposing to him certainly wasn't how she meant to go about this.

The telegraph office was up ahead, perhaps two hundred yards away. It was a small wooden building set near the train station. Laura knew she didn't have much more time to talk before she and Caleb would be among people again, so she hurried. "I decided that I'm not going to marry Adrian. He needs money. I think that's why he wants to marry me. I've known him all my life, and I think at one time he did love me, but not anymore. When I came home from school last year, he was different. He was attentive when he had to be, and I noticed he became much more attentive after several closed meetings with Pa. Pa wanted me to marry him. He always thought Adrian and I were right for each other. I need to return to Bismarck at some point to go through Pa's things and sell the house. There's all the money, too. I'll have it transferred to the closest bank around here. Since you refuse to go anywhere near Bismarck, perhaps I'll let Adrian come for me, and on the way to Bismarck I'll explain that I'm breaking the engagement. I don't want to simply write him a letter. It wouldn't be adequate."

She watched Caleb's jaw tighten and couldn't imagine what she had said that had made him angry. "I told you before, Laura, I don't want anything to do with Kent money. Burn it."

She inhaled a swift breath. "You have no idea how much money you're talking about burning."

"It's dirty money, that's all I know. That's all I need to know."

"Don't be foolish, Caleb. It's time to settle the past, don't you think? Pa is dead. The money is mine now. And I certainly didn't rob anyone to get it."

"Sounds like you're dead set on keeping it. If so, that's all that needs to be said."

She didn't know how to respond to that. She couldn't see burning more than a million dollars simply because Caleb couldn't settle his past with Pa. Much more was tied up in land deals and cattle at Pa's various ranches. A lot of money.

They reached the telegraph building. The cover over the walkway sloped, and a wooden crate propped open the front door. Inside a long counter extended the ten-yard width of the building. A thin spectacled man sat in a chair behind the counter, a paper spread in front of him.

"Afternoon, Mr. Cecil," Caleb said with a grin, knowing Andy couldn't see or hear him. The man's nose was buried in his reading, as usual. In the year Caleb had known Andy

Cecil, this was the way they had always greeted each other. To make matters worse, Andy's hearing was bad. His eyes stayed fixed on the page while he reached over to a small table, felt around a bit, then finally found a pinch of snuff and stuffed it in his cheek.

Chuckling, Caleb shook his head and glanced at Laura, whose brow was wrinkled. "You're thinking he should have heard our boots on the floor. Well, Andy doesn't hear too good. And he doesn't see too good, either, because his eyes are always on a paper or a book. Would never put him in charge of a bank office. Someone could walk in, take all the money, and Andy would never know till he went to check the money at the end of the day."

Laura's jaw fell open. "Caleb, that's a horrible thing to say!"

"It's the truth." Caleb walked over, picked up a big leather-bound ledger resting on the counter, and slammed it down. The crash vibrated through the little building. Grinning, Caleb watched Laura jump. Then, to prove his point, he motioned to Andy, who was still sitting undisturbed on the other side of the counter. Laura tried to give Caleb a stern setdown, but he spotted the amusement that twitched her lips as she shook her head in amazement. "See?" he said. "There could be a storm ripping things apart outside—or inside— and Andy would never know it. But watch this."

Caleb strode to one end of the counter, lifted part of it to let himself through, and approached Andy and the table. The second he put his hand on Andy's snuffbox, a sniff and muffled words came from behind the newspaper: "Got a knife in this here pocket, and I'd cut a hand off afore I'd let it take my snuff. Only one person that tries, too. Get on outa here, Caleb Main."

Grinning wider, Caleb glanced at Laura. "Take his snuffbox or his newspaper. That gets his attention."

Lowering one corner of his newspaper, Andy tipped his head back and glared at Caleb down the length of his long nose. "Yep. Had it figured right. What d'ya want, Mr. Main?"

Caleb motioned Laura, who was now smiling, to a

wooden settee on the other side of the counter. She walked over and sat. Caleb snatched a chair from nearby, turned it to face him, then straddled it and jerked his head toward Laura. "Lady there needs to telegraph Bismarck."

Andy Cecil turned his nose toward Laura. "You Miss Kent?"

Laura nodded.

"Glad to have ya in Minot. 'Cept for this fella, yer stay at the Main farm oughta be good. Ruth Main's a real decent woman."

"Thank you, I know."

Andy rose, unfolding his lean form. He folded the news-paper, then put it carefully on the table. "C'mon around here an' tell me what you wanna say. I'll write it all down and get it sent out."

Laura joined Andy and Caleb behind the counter and told Andy what she wanted the message to Adrian to say. Caleb sat quietly on the chair. But when Laura started to reach into the small evergreen reticule she had brought along, he flipped Andy a coin to pay for the telegraph. He felt Laura's stare and knew she was thinking he wouldn't even want her paying for the telegraph with Kent money, but he pretended to be looking at Andy's newspaper, scanning an article about the building of the new school. Kent money had nothing to do with why he'd paid for the telegraph.

"That'll do it," Andy said. He went to a large table near the back of the room and tapped out the message on the tele-graph.

"There was no need for you to pay for my message to Adrian," Laura told Caleb.

He turned to study her. Her blue eyes were intent on him. Strands of her hair had escaped her braid and fell around her pretty face like fine, shimmering cornsilk. Damn it all to hell, he wished she wouldn't look at him like that! All he wanted to do was pick her up, take her off someplace, and make love to her again. "Since you're telling him to stay away a bit longer, I'm glad to help."

Her eyes flared in surprise. She looked at him that way for a few more seconds, then turned away and went to stand near a small window to look outside. Caleb silently cursed himself for being so honest—and rash. She might want to get the little scene with Adrian over with as soon as possible. He wanted to put it off—in the back of his mind he couldn't help but wonder if Adrian might have just enough charm to convince Laura to change her mind.

Presently Andy returned. "It's there," he announced, then folded his frame back in the chair, picked up the newspaper, and spread it wide in front of him again. Laura moved to the door to wait for Caleb.

"Well, I guess since I've got no other reason to bother you, I'll go away, Mr. Cecil," Caleb drawled, still straddling the chair. He'd much rather stay and trouble Andy. He suspected the man liked him, but Andy would never admit it.

"You do that." Andy went back to his newspaper. Caleb eyed the snuffbox again, feeling the urge to bother Andy a bit more.

"Caleb," Laura admonished softly. When Caleb looked up, he saw Laura standing by the door waiting for him, her eyes narrowed and her lips pursed together.

Caleb sighed. His fun with Andy Cecil was over for the day, he reckoned. He swung one leg around the chair and stood, then grabbed the chair, put it back in its place, and joined Laura at the door. She smiled and took his arm. "You should be ashamed of yourself, teasing that man that way," she said as they left the telegraph office.

"Aw, Andy enjoys it. If I didn't go in there once a week to tease him, he'd miss me."

They laughed together. That was a good sound. A good feeling, too, since they hadn't relaxed in each other's company since they'd made love under the plum tree.

Minutes later they found Stacey and Ruth caught up in conversation with two other women in front of Alman's Dry Goods. Stacey spotted Laura and frowned. Caleb knew that look meant trouble was brewing.

Laura expected a scolding. This was the second time she had simply disappeared and left Stacey and Ruth worrying. But she had known Stacey and Ruth would have tried to talk her out of going to the church.

Stacey said quick goodbyes to the other women, then joined Laura and Caleb at the wagon, her sparking eyes fixed on Laura. "I can't believe you ran off like that! In the middle of Minot!"

"No one troubled me, Stacey. Settle down."

"But someone might have. Where did you go?"

"To the church."

"Laura—"

"Come on, Stace," interjected Caleb. "You know she'd do it again if she thought she had to. Our yelling doesn't do any good."

Stacey exhaled heavily, then let Caleb lift her up to the wagon. He reached for Laura next, and she wished his hands could stay on her waist for a while. She wanted him to slip his arms around her and draw her close, but she knew she was entertaining thoughts she shouldn't be entertaining right now—not in the middle of town with people passing back and forth and Stacey and Ruth nearby.

Soon they seated themselves, and the wagon creaked forward, heading out of Minot, past the saloons, gaming houses, dry goods, mercantile, and other establishments. It lumbered by the telegraph office and the train station and platform. Finally it reached the church, slowed, then stopped.

Laura peered at the willow tree, unable to see the blond head and small figure she wanted to see. Caleb jumped down from the wagon seat and walked over to the willow. Moments later he returned to the wagon, his dark eyes on Laura. "Everything's gone."

She smiled sadly. "But so is she."

He nodded. "You can't expect anything different, Laura. That's the way it's always been."

"What are you two talking about?" Stacey demanded.

"Amanda was here when I came here earlier," Laura said. "I tried to coax her into coming with me. She ran away, so I left the dress, slate, and pencils."

Ruth twisted around. "What do you mean, that's the way it's always been?" she asked sternly.

Laura had already guessed that not even Ruth and Stacey

knew Caleb had been making frequent visits to leave food in the willow tree for Amanda. Caleb had been too secretive about the matter. Laura didn't feel the information should be revealed by her, if in fact Caleb wanted it revealed at all. She looked at him, and he shifted uncomfortably from one foot to the other. Again she was touched by the fact that he had taken the time to help feed Amanda. She wanted to hug him. She might have done just that if she hadn't been in the wagon bed and he hadn't been standing near the horses.

"I smell a secret," Stacey said.

"Ah, hell. For a couple of months I've been wrapping some food in a handkerchief and putting it in a place by the bottom of that tree."

Stacey wrinkled her brow. "For Amanda?"

Laura smiled. "For Amanda."

"Why didn't you tell us, Caleb?" Ruth asked.

"Let's get going," he grumbled. "It'll be evening soon, and there'll be chores to do."

Caleb climbed up on the seat again and took the reins. Laura held on to the rail as the wagon eased forward and began climbing its way out of Plum Valley. Ahead was the lush slope, deep purple decorating green.

"Guess it doesn't matter that you didn't tell us. Fact is, you were good enough to do it, and that makes me real proud," Ruth said so softly that Laura barely heard. She didn't know if the words had been intended for her ears, but she was glad she had heard them. She smiled, watching the sun disappear behind a cloud. The branches of elms, ashes, oaks, and plums whispered together. The wagon rocked and creaked. The horses tossed their heads and trod forward. Laura watched Ruth reach over, touch Caleb's arm, and smile gently. Caleb returned the smile. The gesture was the first affectionate one Laura had witnessed between mother and son, and watching it spread warmth through her. This was a family bonded together by love and devotion—a small circle of people who depended on one another. Laura felt honored that they had opened their arms to her.

* * *

Later, during supper, Caleb asked Stacey to help him take the cattle to water afterward. Stacey made a funny face, twisting her lips and wrinkling her nose.

"Now what's gotten into you?" Caleb asked.

Stacey hesitated, dragging her fork in the gravy covering a slice of roast. "I saw Charles Duncan in Minot today. He asked if he could call after supper."

"Charles Duncan's going to ride all this way to call on you?" he asked in amazement.

"Is that so surprising?" Stacey demanded, her eyes glowing. "I'm pretty, you know."

Caleb laughed. "Course you're pretty."

That made things worse. She lifted the fork as if planning to throw it at him. "You're poking fun at me!"

"Now, Stace . . . I'm not. You are pretty. But Charles . . . he has a reputation for being lazy, that's all. Can't seem to make it to church sometimes, and I've heard he doesn't help much at the family farm. I'm just surprised a fellow like that would bother to ride five miles to come courting."

She glared at him. "Even if Charles is a bit lazy, there are other things about him I like. You might not like *anyone* who comes courting me."

"*You* might not like it too much if you end up married to Charles and his work never gets done. Better to marry someone more responsible."

"Who said anything about getting married? And I'll do my own picking and choosing, thank you! I didn't ask your opinion. I only told you he's coming because you asked me to help you take the cattle to water. I can't tonight."

Caleb held up a hand, palm out, to ward off her assault. "I'm not trying to pick and choose for you. I'll take the cattle to water later by myself. Should be interesting to sit a while with Charles and just let him know I won't put up with any funny business."

Stacey dropped her fork. It clattered against her plate. "He's not coming to talk to you. He's coming to talk to me. And how much *later* are you going to take the cattle?"

Leaning back in his chair, Caleb clasped his hands behind his head, meeting her glare head-on. "After Charles leaves."

"Ma, make him stop. He'll be listening in on every word me and Charles say. If you don't make him stop, I'll throw something at him."

"Now, Stacey, you won't, either," Ruth said.

"I will if he doesn't stop."

"Caleb, it'll probably be dark after Charles leaves. You can't take the cattle to water so late," Ruth said gently. "Don't ruin this for Stacey."

"I don't plan to ruin anything. I just plan to make sure Charles keeps his hands to himself."

"Ma!" Stacey cried.

Ruth shook her head. "Caleb . . . you go on and take the cattle. Stacey knows how to act."

"It's not Stacey I'm worried about."

Laura watched and listened in silence, realizing this evening would be the first time Stacey had ever had a man call on her. Laura thought that perhaps Caleb was merely playing the role of protective big brother and didn't realize he was severely overdoing it. The situation was obviously just as awkward for Caleb as for Stacey. Brother and sister cherished each other, but Laura could see that Stacey wouldn't stand for Caleb intruding in her business, and she didn't blame Stacey. On the other hand, Caleb was trying to play a fatherly role. Perhaps she could give him a few gentle suggestions—namely, when to intrude and when not to intrude. Not taking the cattle to water so he could lurk around and watch Charles and Stacey was definitely inappropriate.

"I'll help you take the cattle to water," she offered.

Caleb gave her an uneasy look. "You've never taken cattle to water."

"I never lifted a rifle until a week ago, either, but I learned to shoot. If there's anything I need to know about driving cattle, you can teach me," she responded sweetly. She wasn't going to let him out of this.

"Don't be foolish, Laura. I need to be here."

She gave him a hard look. "No, you don't. I'll help you take the cattle."

He unclasped his hands and straightened in the chair. "Laura—"

"You wouldn't want me trying to do it by myself, would you? I might get trampled or—or lose a calf or a cow. I might wander around the prairie and meet with terrible danger. I'll be going as soon as I've finished here and helped Ruth with the dishes. You'll be going, too, because you wouldn't want anything to happen to the cattle or to me."

"I've got Stacey to worry about, and I don't need any of your damn tricks tonight," he grumbled.

"Caleb!" Ruth gasped. "Don't talk to her like that."

Laura smiled. "Stacey can care for herself. And Ruth will be here."

"So will I!" Caleb thundered.

"I suppose I'll take the cattle by myself, then," she said, sighing.

Caleb studied her for a long minute. Perhaps to see if she was serious? Then he muttered, "Ah, hell!"

Ruth stared at him in shock. "Caleb Main."

Laura laughed and said, "Don't worry. That means he'll be going with me. I'm learning many of his annoying little ways."

Stacey clapped her hands together and smiled delightedly at Laura. Ruth smiled, too. Laura returned to eating her supper. And Caleb . . . he huffed out of his chair and stomped toward the front door, jerking it open to let himself through. Then he slammed it shut behind him.

"Just ride behind them and to the side. They'll go," Caleb said as he and Laura rode on horseback toward the cattle. He yelled something, and the cattle stirred, dipping their heads and lowing. A calf bawled as it scrambled to keep up with its mother. There were red and brown backs and white bodies with black spots. Tongues licked. Eyes rolled. The herd moved forward. Laura rode to one side, Caleb to the other.

"You bother me!" he yelled across the distance. "Just want you to know that."

Laura laughed and yelled back, "I think you told me that once before! Except then you informed me in a most uncivil way. Not that you're being too civil right now."

"Me? Uncivil? Never!"

"You can be terribly uncivil when you want to be."

They rode about a mile, the cattle plodding in front of them, the early evening sun just beginning to turn orange-red. Clouds floated by, clustered and gray in places.

"Looks like we'll be getting a storm," Caleb said, also noticing the clouds.

The creek came into view, cutting through the prairie. Tall grass sprang up around it, and several trees shaded it. The cattle tossed their heads, catching the water's scent, then surged forward to drink.

Caleb rode over and reined his horse near Laura beside one of the trees. "We'll have to watch for stragglers," he said, dismounting. He reached for Laura, and she slid down.

Their eyes met and held, his dark and narrowed. Laura thought she saw a flicker of desire in them, but it disappeared as quickly as a lamp is extinguished, and she was left wondering if her imagination was playing cruel tricks on her. Did she want him so much she was reduced to conjuring expressions on his face? She had finally told him what she had needed to tell him—that she had decided not to marry Adrian. She had left the door open for him, and he had started through it. But the subject of her money—Kent money—had made him back out. Ghosts from his past still haunted him, whether or not he acknowledged that they did.

Beside the creek she found a fallen log and sat down, wiping her brow. Caleb neared, offering a canteen. Laura thanked him and took a long drink. Finally she handed the canteen back to him and wiped her mouth with the back of her hand, something she had been taught a lady simply did not do. She smiled at the thought.

"What are you smiling about?" Caleb asked.

"Oh . . . I was just thinking that I spent so many years being taught social graces and manners, yet I just wiped my mouth with my hand."

Caleb frowned. "Seems a logical thing to do. When you don't have anything else to wipe your mouth on, you use your hand."

Laura laughed. "A lady is not supposed to do that."

"Well, when a lady's driving cattle, I'd wager she's allowed to," he said, settling himself on the log next to her.

"I don't think many ladies drive cattle, Mr. Main."

He frowned, his dark, unruly hair slipping over one brow. "What's this Mr. Main business again? I thought we agreed a long time ago that you'd call me Caleb."

"We did. But it hasn't been so long ago really. Besides, I have such fun teasing you with the proper manners you detest so." Laura reached up and affectionately tried to sweep the hair aside.

She heard Caleb draw a swift breath. Then he grabbed her hand, midstroke, gave her a hard stare, and said quietly, "Don't touch me, Laura."

His words shocked her, sent pain searing through her. She tried to read his eyes again and found them mesmerizing but empty. She spoke the first thing that came to mind: "Don't touch you? I remember a day not very long ago when you wanted me to touch you."

"It's better if you don't."

"It was merely a gesture of fondness, of—of affection."

"The more you touch me, the more I want to make love to you again."

"Then why don't you, Caleb?" she heard herself whisper as her heartbeat quickened. "Why don't you? Do you think I haven't lain awake at night thinking about you? Do you think I haven't wondered why you haven't touched me since the evening we spent beneath the plum tree? I told you I'm not going to marry Adrian. That means I want to marry you."

"Still planning on going after the money?"

She wrinkled her brow in confusion. Then realization hit her. "The money . . . Kent money. Do you realize that something that happened ten years ago is still poisoning your mind? You're allowing it to come between us, Caleb. Please don't do that."

He turned his head and stared across the creek.

"You . . . you could go to Bismarck with me. I don't mean to stay. I need to go to the house and go through Pa's things. You could go and settle your old grudge against Pa."

Muscles tightened in his jaw. Still he didn't speak.

Laura tore her eyes away from him and looked out across the creek at the scraggly bushes and foliage there, at a crooked willow tree that looked as if it might crash into the water any second. She smiled wearily, then let her hand ease over and cover the back of his. "I love you, Caleb. I want to help you end this once and for all."

Minutes passed. He sat rock still, staring across the creek. Finally he looked down at their joined hands, turned his hand over, and entwined their fingers. Laura felt a surge of excitement, of hope, of love. She fought tears of happiness.

His head turned, and his other hand caught her chin as he lowered his head and his lips brushed hers. Laura was hungry for him, hungry for the kisses she felt she had sampled a lifetime ago beneath the plum tree. She wouldn't let him simply brush her lips with his, then withdraw. She nipped at his lower lip. He groaned and kissed her fully, his tongue delving into her mouth. Their tongues met and frolicked, and they clung to each other, loving each other.

The battle cries of two bulls drew them back to reality. Caleb lifted his head and counted cattle. Laura laughed and pressed fingertips to her lips, still tasting his kisses.

Once satisfied that the cattle were all accounted for, Caleb turned to her and glared playfully. "Some cattle driver you are, distracting me and not paying attention."

"Me?" she said innocently.

His hand caught the back of her neck, and this time when he gazed into her eyes, his were filled with love and want. The emptiness, the protective barrier, had slipped away. "Damn, you're beautiful," he said.

"You certainly have an unusual way of putting things, Mr. Main," she teased.

"I love you, Laura," he whispered huskily.

She skimmed her fingertips over his bottom lip and tasted it yet again, then lifted her gaze to his. "Say it again."

"I love you—even if I do want to throttle you for dragging me away from Stacey."

Laura shook her head. "Your sister has a right to a little privacy. Don't take offense, Caleb, but you shouldn't hover over Stacey and lurk around doorways simply because men

are beginning to call on her. You'll only make Stacey angry.
Perhaps you should allow her to become better acquainted
with Charles. If he's as bad as you seem to think he is, she'll
find out by herself."

"Better acquainted?" Caleb said. He withdrew and his
brow furrowed. "She's probably doing just that right now.
She's probably getting *real* acquainted with Charles!"

"Even if I hadn't intervened, Stacey would have found a
way to see Charles. She would have been angry at you and
would have planned secret meetings."

He clenched his jaw. "And I would have—"

"What would you have done? Made more trouble?
Stomped up to her the way you do when you're angry?
Turned her over your knee and spanked her as one might do
a naughty child? Think about Stacey's side of this. She's not
as naive as you think. She's not a child. She's a young
woman, Caleb, and she deserves your respect. What she
doesn't need is you sitting there implying that she's incapa-
ble of dealing with Charles if he makes an advance."

"He lays one hand on her and I—I'll—"

"Why in the world are you so critical of Charles Duncan
trying what any man might try? Think about your own actions toward me and tell me if you are any better—or
worse—than Charles. Remember the time we shared beneath the plum tree. Think of what we might have done moments ago if not for the cattle."

That silenced him. He settled his gaze on the cattle, and
Laura knew he was considering her words.

"Because you're such a protective big brother, Stacey
should never be left alone to even watch a sunset with a
man whose company she enjoys?" Laura persisted. "Knowing Stacey, I'm sure she will deal with Charles if he offends
her in any way. And if she finds she can't deal with him, perhaps she'll come to you. *That* is when you should involve
yourself."

The cattle stirred, and a few black and white heads lifted
to gaze around. Tails swished. Something raced through the
brush on the other side of the creek. The sun had taken on a
definite red glow now and was much lower in the sky than it

had been when Laura and Caleb had first mounted their horses back at the farm.

"Guess you know about these things, being a woman and all," Caleb said.

Laura smiled gently and nodded.

"Guess I owe Stacey an apology. Sometimes it's real hard, living with two women and trying to figure out how to deal with them. Pa used to say the same thing."

Laura turned her gaze to Caleb. He had never mentioned his father. She was curious. From the moment she had met Caleb, she had wanted to know more of what was in his head, and since then he had shared little with her. He might decline to answer the questions threatening to burst from her lips, but she felt she must ask them. "What happened to your pa?"

Caleb stared at the cattle. "Battle of Little Bighorn."

Laura blinked, hardly believing her ears. She knew history and knew the battle he referred to. It hadn't occurred such a long time ago—eleven years. *In her lifetime.* She remembered hearing about it and reading about it in newspapers. "General Custer and the Sioux Indians?" she asked, her voice filled with a combination of amazement and curiosity.

Caleb nodded. "Pa was an officer under Custer. Whole damn regiment rode into a nest of Sioux. Some said Custer was supposed to meet another regiment at Little Bighorn and got there a day early. Sioux were waiting. Killed every white man in sight."

Laura put a hand to her mouth and swallowed hard. How well she remembered the accounts. The Sioux had fled, had scattered in little bands and eluded government soldiers. Sitting Bull, one of the Sioux leaders, and his followers had fled to Canada, barely surviving the brutal Canadian winters. While other bands surrendered within a few years, Sitting Bull had remained steadfast in his pride, refusing to surrender.

Caleb glanced at her. "Sorry. You asked."

She smiled weakly. "I had no idea. Truly I didn't. You must hate the Sioux. And they're on reservations right here in Dakota."

He shook his head. "Guess I have some of my pa in me—I don't hate them. They did what they thought they had to do to survive, like we do out here on the prairie. Pa always talked about how the Indian problems could be settled peacefully if the white man and the government would hold to promises they'd made the Indians. I remember the year Custer led a party through the Black Hills in the Sioux reservation, searching for gold. Pa said he was glad he wasn't part of it. He felt the white man had no business on land that belonged to the Indians. That was Pa. Fair and straight."

The cattle became restless, milling around. Laura had a few moments to digest what she had heard before Caleb said they should be getting the cattle back. Touched that he had responded to her question and shared some of his private self with her, she walked to her horse. Just as she put a boot in the stirrup, Caleb was behind her to lift her up. Then he mounted his horse and shouted at the cattle.

They turned back toward the farm and rode. The sun bled colors on the horizon; the cattle lowed and trod forward. Caleb and his horse formed a striking silhouette against the reddish background. The prairie spread as far as one could see, an infinite expanse of usually green and golden grass and yellow flowers discolored and made even more serenely beautiful by the glow of sunset. A few lone trees stood out, the glow peeking between their branches. As a flock of birds fluttered by, dark forms perfectly outlined against the red hue, Laura's breath caught in her throat. She breathed the evening air and admired the land. Was there any place more beautiful, more breathtaking than this part of Dakota? She didn't think so.

And to think she had not planned to be here.

Chapter Twelve

THE SUN WAS barely coming up when Caleb rose to go milk the cows. He slid into trousers and a shirt. Then he pulled on boots, laced and tied them, and headed out to the section of prairie where the cattle grazed. There he slipped a rope around a black and white cow's neck and led her to the barn.

Half asleep and following habit, he entered a stall and nearly stepped on a form curled up near the outer rail.

"Whoa," he told the cow, pushing her back a few steps. Twisting, he blinked and took a better look at the little form. Then he whistled softly. "You'll wait," he told the cow, pushing her back even farther and tying the rope to another stall rail.

He hurried to the house, excitement filling his head, a grin playing on his lips. The sun wasn't even all the way up yet. Sunrise was just coming together—rivers of pink, purple, red, and orange struggling to form that one huge ball that would light the sky. So the hour was early. But he didn't care. And he didn't think Laura would care about being jostled awake so early once he told her what he had found. On second thought, maybe he wouldn't tell her. Maybe he'd just bring her out here and *show* her. She had a hell of a surprise waiting for her in the barn.

Laura buried her face in the pillow and squeezed her eyes shut. She was dreaming of Caleb bending over her, gently nudging her awake. In a moment he would gather her in his arms, and his hands would skim her body. Laura smiled seductively, imagining his beard scratching against her face and words of love being whispered in her ear. Then she frowned, for he didn't gather her in his arms. His beard scratched her cheek, but the words he whispered certainly were not words of love.

"Don't know what you're smiling about, but out in the barn there's something that'll make you smile a passel more," he said. "Get up quick. If Ma catches me in your room, she'll tan my hide."

Laura squinted one eye at him. The other eye simply refused to open. "What are you talking about?"

"Come on and you'll find out. There's no time for questions, woman."

The last thing Laura wanted to do was get up. She and Stacey had sat up late. Stacey had told her how perfect the evening with Charles had gone, thanks to Laura making sure Caleb took the cattle to water. Laura closed the one eye, letting her head sink down in the feather pillow. "Go—"

"Get out of bed before I pull you out," Caleb threatened.

That forced Laura's eyes open. She flipped onto her back, pushing hair from her face and giving him the best morning glare she could muster. "Being a beast again, I see," she said, folding her arms.

Stepping back, he reached for her blue robe and tried to straighten it. Finally he simply tossed it at her. "You're cranky in the morning. Here, put this on, and let's go."

Laura grumbled more but managed to ease into the robe and wrap it around her white shift. She secured it at the waist, then slipped from the bed. Caleb was waiting to take her hand and pull her from the room.

Out in the hall he put a finger over his mouth to indicate quiet. From there they escaped downstairs.

Despite being roused in such an unpleasant way, Laura had to smile. She felt like a mischievous child, slipping out the front door, across the porch and onto the grass. It was wet with dew and chilled her feet, but she laughed, thinking this was madness. Caleb's hold on her hand was firm, and she knew she couldn't free herself even if she tried.

"What could be in an ugly barn to make me smile?" she asked, laughing as he pulled her along. His steps were so much larger than hers that she was running lightly. This was madness! Sheer madness.

"You'll see. I can't tell you. I have to show you."

They entered the barn. It smelled of horses, cows, and leather, and the earthen, straw-covered floor was cool and slightly prickly to her bare feet. A cow stood tied to one stall, looking around quite innocently. Suddenly Caleb stopped and put a hand over Laura's eyes.

"What are you doing now?" she demanded.

"When I tell you to look, look," he said. He led her another few steps, then lowered his hand. "Now."

Laura did, and what she saw made her cry out with joy.

Wearing the yellow-checked gingham dress, Amanda was curled up, sleeping soundly on a little bed of hay. She was still dirty. Her hair looked grimy. Her face, arms, and hands were smudged. But she was here. Somehow she had found them. She had understood them yesterday.

The slate and pencils rested near her head. Laura bent and lifted the slate to look at the tiny marks Amanda had scratched with the pencil. She gazed again at Amanda, whose soft breath moved her tiny chest, and marveled that she could feel such love for a child she scarcely knew. Shutting her eyes, she said a quick, silent prayer of thanks, then opened her eyes to find Caleb kneeling near her.

Laura stared at him, tears of happiness burning her eyes. "How did she find us?"

Caleb shook his head. "Don't know. Unless Blake brought her."

"But she had to have wanted to come. Otherwise she would have run away as soon as he left. If he brought her."

Caleb put a finger to his lips and jerked his head toward Amanda. She was stirring, one arm stretching, the other lying limp at her side. Her eyes fluttered open, and she stared at Caleb and Laura.

"Hello, Amanda," Laura said softly. "I don't know how you found us, but I'm glad you did."

Using her good leg and arm, Amanda lifted herself slightly and managed to scoot back into one corner of the stall. She lowered her head, strands of tangled blond hair falling over her face. Her wide blue eyes peered at them through the strands.

"I'm Laura . . . remember? You look pretty in the dress. I'm glad you're wearing it. We'll make another one if you want."

Amanda stared but made no move to run away. Laura wondered if she ever talked. But if only a few people had ever bothered to speak to Amanda, how could she have learned to talk? Laura wasn't sure how much time Amanda had spent around her family, listening to them.

"Would you like to go to the house?" Laura asked. "There are chairs. And food. You can look for yourself if you want to."

Caleb stirred near Laura. "Maybe she's not ready. Maybe we ought to leave her here for a bit and let her warm up to the place."

Laura nodded her agreement. He was right. Amanda was here, but this was all very new to her. She wasn't accustomed to having a roof over her head or people talking to her. "I'll go back to the house for a while, Amanda, and give you time to walk around and look at everything and decide if you want to stay."

Amanda was silent. Laura stood and turned away. She thought she heard a small noise from Amanda, but when she glanced over her shoulder, hoping to see Amanda coming toward her, Amanda was still in the same position, cautiously watching her.

Caleb joined her at the barn doors. "Don't worry. I'll be here. There are cows to milk and other things to do."

Laura nodded and went to the house.

Ruth was just coming downstairs, her gray hair drawn up, twisted and pinned in a bun on the top of her head. She looked curiously at Laura. "Where've you been, dressed like that?"

"Talking to Amanda."

Ruth's eyes widened. "Amanda?"

"Yes. She's in the barn. Apparently she came sometime during the night."

"Well, I'll be," Ruth said. "A strange thing. Now, how do you reckon she found us out here?"

"Caleb and I were wondering the same thing."

"Blake?"

Laura shrugged. "I don't know. Perhaps someday Amanda will provide the answer for us. I'm simply glad she's here."

"Well, let's bring her in the house," Ruth said, starting for the door.

"No. I tried to talk her into coming inside. She isn't quite that friendly yet."

Ruth went to the table and grabbed the egg-gathering basket. "I'll start breakfast so we can get something in her belly."

Laura nodded and started up the staircase. "I'll go dress and be down soon to help."

Out in the barn Caleb took the cow to the stall next to the one Amanda was in and whistled while he milked. He didn't hear movement from Amanda. Every now and then he glanced up, trying to peer through the stall rails to see if she was still there, and every time he spotted the yellow-checked gingham. Satisfied, he went back to work.

Sam, the dog, wandered in and plopped down just outside the stall that Caleb and the cow were in. When he finished milking, Caleb set the nearly full bucket aside and untied the rope. Then he took the cow out and let her go. He slipped the rope around the neck of another cow and led her toward the barn. Halfway there she balked, embedding her hooves in the ground and refusing to take another step. Caleb pulled the rope, but the cow tossed her head, rolled her eyes, and wouldn't budge.

A sharp whistle from Caleb brought Sam out of the barn. Trotting toward the cow, Sam didn't even have to open his mouth. She took one look at him and decided she'd rather go to the barn peacefully than have Sam pester her into going. Some mornings this one was more stubborn. A man newly settled in Minot was coming from town today at noon in search of a bull and some cows. "Maybe you'll be the first to go," he grumbled at the cow.

She tossed her head again as if she understood what he had said.

Once in the barn the cow settled herself in the stall. Caleb whistled again, some tune Pa had taught him, the one about Camptown ladies and doo-dah day. A lively tune. He stole another discreet peek through the stall rails to see if Amanda was still there. She was. So he settled himself on the milking stool and went to work again.

Four peeks, another stubborn cow, and about twenty rounds of the song later, he suspected he was being watched. From the corner of his eye he caught Amanda peering between stall rails. He whistled louder, and although his hands were tired, he worked harder, too. He reckoned he was about as glad as Laura that Amanda had turned up.

He took the last cow out and released her. The other two were nursing calves, so he left them. The herd was scattered, grazing here and there on the green and gold prairie grass. Two bulls were squared off, pawing the ground and dipping their horns. Sam started past Caleb, who knew the dog meant to get in the middle of things.

"Sam," Caleb said sharply.

Sam turned back, whining.

Caleb glared at him. "Get tangled up in that, you'll wish you hadn't. Get back in the barn."

Sam obeyed. Caleb followed, feeling Amanda's eyes on him again as he grabbed two buckets of milk, one in each hand. Then he carried the buckets to the house to give them to Ruth.

In the house Laura was standing to one side of the stove, flipping griddle cakes in a skillet. Ma stood on the other side, stirring eggs and frying slices of ham. The rich smell of fresh coffee filled the place and made Caleb want a mug full, but he had to get back to the barn first and finish there. Laura and Ma looked up when he kicked the door shut and started across the room to put the buckets on the table.

"How's Amanda?" Ruth asked.

"Watching me a lot."

Using a spatula, Laura lifted a griddle cake and put it on a plate. Then she set the plate on a small chopping table close to the stove, took a bowl from the table, and poured more batter in the skillet. Her hair was now brushed back from her face and braided down her back. Her dress was the one Stacey had made her, the one with black-eyed Susans and goldenrods that made her look even prettier. A white apron covered the top half of her skirt and was tied back at her waist. She looked at home.

Caleb couldn't resist teasing her: "For a city girl used to having the cooking done for her, you're getting pretty good at that."

Blushing, she smiled. "I'm enjoying myself. Has Amanda said anything to you?"

"No. She's just been watching me milk the cows."

"Perhaps she wants a drink of milk," Laura said.

Caleb lifted a brow in surprise. "Maybe you're right." He grabbed a tin cup from a cabinet and headed back outside.

In the barn he stopped midstep at the sight of Amanda bent down by the last bucket he'd left in the stall where he'd milked the cows. She dipped her finger in the milk, then licked her finger. Caleb grinned. Laura was right. During all that time he'd spent milking cows, knowing Amanda was watching him, he hadn't realized she'd wanted a drink of milk.

He crept over to her, not wanting to scare her. She sensed him just as he stepped up behind her. He saw her back go rigid, and he tensed, not wanting to scare her. Hunching down beside her, he said, "I brought a cup. Laura thought you might want a drink."

He reached around her, the tin cup in his hand, and scooped up some milk. Then he held the cup in front of her and waited. "Here you are, Amanda. It's good and sweet. Course, you already know that."

He waited. Minutes went by. She stayed frozen. Maybe she didn't want to take the cup from his hand. Maybe she wanted him to put it down and walk off. Caleb started to do just that.

Then she reached for the cup.

Her little fingers touched his big ones. Since she had only one hand that worked right, Caleb brought his other arm around and used both hands to show her how to hold the cup in her palm and grip it with her fingers and thumb. Then she put the cup to her lips and drank.

She emptied the cup, then filled it again. She emptied and filled it three more times before she decided she'd had her fill. Then she twisted slightly and took Caleb's hand. Spreading his fingers, she put the cup in his palm and pushed his fingers up the way he had done to hers. Caleb grinned. She said nothing, and he read nothing in her eyes, but the way she'd put the cup back in his hand showed she was grateful.

"All right now," he said, unsure of what he was supposed to do next. He glanced around. "You, uh—you settle yourself again, maybe on that haystack over there"—he pointed to the haystack he'd pushed Laura into some time ago— "and I'll take the rest of this milk inside and be right back to clean this stall."

She braced a hand on the edge of the bucket and used it to help her stand. Once on her feet, she limped to the haystack and sat down. At least he knew she understood him.

He took the bucket and hurried to the house. Laura and Ruth looked at him with questions in their eyes.

"She drank three cups. No, four!" he said, putting the bucket on the table with the others. "She took the cup out of my hand, and when she finished drinking, she put it back in my hand."

Laura laughed. "I believe you're enjoying yourself, Mr. Main."

Ruth laughed, too. Caleb grinned and headed back to the barn.

There he took a shovel and began whistling again while he cleaned out the stall, filling a wheelbarrow he'd take and dump near the garden later. He cleaned other stalls, too, and began laying fresh straw. He heard movement and glanced around at the haystack. Amanda had left it. She had a hand-ful of hay, scattering it around the stall next to the one he was working in.

He kept working, feeling ashamed that he'd assumed Amanda couldn't be taught. By copying what he was doing, the child was proving she could be.

Laura looked proudly at the two high stacks of griddle cakes she had cooked. Stacey came downstairs, her eyes glowing. Laura smiled, thinking Stacey must still be floating on clouds after her visit with Charles.

Last night Stacey had told her how she and Charles had walked for a time and talked. According to Stacey, perhaps Charles didn't help at the family farm as he should because he had no desire to farm. His interest was in medicines. He had been spending numerous hours learning from the doctor in Minot, who had apparently taken an interest in Charles. Stacey had told Laura she was excited for Charles and hoped he did someday open his own apothecary. He would if people like Caleb would stop trying to make a farmer of him. Then Stacey had leaned over and whispered, "He kissed me. Just a little kiss, but it was nice."

Laura smiled, recalling their conversation. She took the plate of griddle cakes to the table and found Stacey sitting there looking at her warmly. Stacey put her hand over Laura's wrist and whispered, "Thanks for listening to me for so long last night. I wish you'd never leave. I'll miss you when you go. I've never had anyone to talk to like that."

Smiling, Laura lifted the stack of pottery plates, turned, and put them on the table. Ruth emptied the skillet of eggs into a bowl and brought it to the table.

Laura was putting the last plate in its place on the table when the front door opened and Caleb and Amanda walked inside. Shock froze Laura in place. She heard Stacey's gasp and Ruth's whispered, "Well, praise be," but couldn't move. How had Caleb convinced Amanda to come inside? She was holding his hand, too! How had he managed that?

"Got a place there for Amanda?" Caleb asked, snapping them all into action. Ruth grabbed a chair from beside a cabinet. Stacey stood and moved her chair over to make room for Amanda's. Laura rounded the table to get another pottery plate from the cupboard.

Caleb took Amanda to the washbasin. He bent over and washed his face and hands while Amanda watched him. Laura watched them. When Caleb finished, he grabbed a small towel and dried himself. To Laura's amazement, Amanda repeated his actions, scooping up what water she could with one hand and splashing it on her face. But her face needed a little more washing than Caleb's had, so Caleb took a cloth, wet it, and washed her face for her.

Realizing she was staring, Laura forced herself to sit at the table, but she still watched them from the corner of her eye. Amanda lifted her limp arm up to the basin and Caleb washed it for her. The man never failed to amaze Laura. He looked so formidable, and sometimes acted so formidable, but he could still be so gentle.

Ruth began dishing out food as if this were a routine morning. Laura and Stacey heeded her example. Caleb brought Amanda to the table and helped her into a chair. Once he was seated, they began eating. Presently Laura noticed that Amanda was watching, not eating, and she began to worry. She glanced from Amanda to Caleb and met his gaze. With a slight jerk of his head, he indicated that she should eat and not worry. She didn't need to hear his thoughts; she guessed what he was thinking: "Give her time, Laura." Still, Laura brought a forkful of eggs to her mouth and worried more.

Finally Amanda picked up her fork and attempted to scoop up some eggs. She managed to get a forkful, but some fell off during the fork's journey to her mouth. Amanda concentrated hard on keeping the next forkful together from her plate to her mouth. No eggs fell off this time. Laura wanted to clap with joy.

The rest of the meal passed in a similar fashion. Amanda was an observant child, learning from example. After breakfast Caleb told Amanda he wanted her to stay inside now while he went out to do more chores. Stacey went with him to help.

Amanda began following Laura around, watching while Laura helped Ruth sweep floors and make beds. Ruth skimmed the cream from the milk, then poured the milk and cream into pottery jugs and went to store the jugs of milk in the icebox in a little room at the back of the house, away from the heat of the stove. Twice since Laura had arrived she had watched a wagon come from Minot to deliver blocks of ice for the icebox.

When Ruth returned, she took another jug of cream from a cabinet and traded it for the new one. Then she went outside to make butter, one of her daily rituals. She had once told Laura that during Caleb's trips to town she often sent butter, eggs, and milk along to be sold to Mr. Alman and other merchants.

Laura went outside to dip well water to heat for a bath, thinking that if she took a bath and Amanda watched, perhaps Amanda wouldn't object when Laura bathed her.

Amanda didn't. She unbuttoned her dress and pushed it over one shoulder, then pushed it over the other and shrugged out of it before Laura could even reach her to help. Amanda appeared thin and frail, but Laura was sure that once Amanda began eating well, she would look better. She lifted the girl into the bath, took the soap and cloth, and gently bathed Amanda. She scrubbed her hair as she had scrubbed her own, then gathered Amanda in a towel and lifted her from the tub.

Gently she dried Amanda and dressed, making note of the fact that she would have to ask Caleb to take her to town to buy Amanda underthings or at least the material to make Amanda some underthings. The girl needed other clothing, too—stockings, shoes, at least another dress. Anything Amanda needed, Laura planned to get.

Amanda had been silent during the chores and the baths, and Laura wondered again if she could talk. She settled her on the settee, brushed her own hair to a sheen, then started on Amanda's. "Can you say anything, Amanda? Can you say your name?"

Silence.

In her mind, Laura heard Caleb's voice yet again saying, "Give her time, Laura."

* * *

Caleb opened the front door, stepped inside, and closed it behind him. Stacey had stayed outside to help Ruth. Caleb started across the room, meaning to go put away the money he'd just been paid by the man from Minot who had come for the bull and cows. Then he saw Laura and couldn't help himself—he stopped and stared at her. She'd washed her hair, brushed it, and left it hanging like a thick curtain of golden silk down to her waist. He wanted to go to her, gather her hair in his hands, and rub it across his face. Hell. He wanted to gather Laura and . . .

He forced himself across the room to the cabinet and reached for the bowl Ma kept money in. He put the money away, then the bowl, and turned around.

And there was Laura, not two inches from him, smiling, her eyes bright. Her silky hair brushed his arm, and he went rigid, remembering how pleasurable pushing his hands into that mass of silk had been. Damn, he needed her. Somehow he managed to keep his desire under tight rein.

"You won't believe how easy it's been all morning," she said excitedly in a low voice. She smelled like Stacey's wildflower perfume, only it smelled so much better on her than on Stacey. He wanted to bury his face in her neck and inhale her scent. Her hair brushed his arm again, and a shiver of need rippled through him and settled in his groin.

"After breakfast Amanda followed me around while I swept floors and made beds," Laura continued. "Then we watched Ruth skim the cream off the milk. I bathed, and Amanda watched me. Then I bathed her and brushed—"

"Damn it all to hell anyway, Laura!" Caleb blurted, unable to stand having her this close to him and not being able to make love to her or even touch her. "Go braid your hair so I don't have to look at it."

Her jaw dropped open. His eyes went to her pink lips, and Caleb inhaled a sharp breath, fighting the temptation to taste those lips again right now. "And close your mouth before I kiss it in front of Amanda!"

With that, he tore himself away from her and hurried to the front door.

❄❄❄
Chapter Thirteen

CALEB DIDN'T COME in to eat dinner. Ruth wondered aloud what he'd gotten so busy with that he couldn't see fit to come in and eat what she and Laura had cooked. "Turkey's his favorite, too," Ruth remarked. "Turkey, sweet potatoes, and beans. He's just right out there in the shed." She shook her head, sighing heavily. "Can't force a grown man, I reckon. Still, he knows when dinner is, and it's downright inconsiderate not to come in and eat."

"Maybe something's bothering him," Stacey said.

Laura ate in silence, not questioning Caleb's absence or offering an excuse. She knew why he hadn't come in—he was avoiding sitting across the table from her.

She watched Amanda finish her dinner. Stacey finished, too, excused himself, and wandered off. After helping Ruth with the dishes, Laura settled Amanda near her on the settee and spent the remainder of the afternoon sewing another dress for Amanda from the ample amount of calico left after the first dress had been made. Amanda sat near Laura, watching. Laura sang verses of "Oh! Susanna" and "Pop! Goes the Weasel," then repeated the verses because Amanda watched her so closely during the first verses.

In the sewing corner Laura found a small bowl of buttons that were molded in different shapes and sizes and put it in Amanda's lap. The child slid to the floor, put the bowl to her right side, and began making rows of buttons in front of the settee. Laura thought about counting the buttons from one to ten to show Amanda how to count, but finally decided that right now she and Amanda simply needed to get to know each other. Teaching and learning could come later. Besides, so much of what Amanda needed to learn were the simple ways of living decently, like a human being, not an animal. Amanda needed to know that she was worthy, something Laura was certain the girl had never realized.

From upstairs Ruth brought some quilt blocks and a rag doll with buttons sewn on for eyes. "They were Stacey's," she said, handing the toys to Laura. "She hasn't played with them in years. Don't know why I kept them, except to be sentimental. Amanda can have them if she wants."

Laura smiled at Ruth's thoughtful gesture, then put the blocks and rag doll down beside Amanda. Ruth wandered off to start supper. Amanda stared at the rag doll for a time, then carefully picked it up and touched the hair that had been fashioned from yarn. She pulled the tiny clothes off of the doll and tried to put them back on but couldn't.

Laura set her stitching aside and reached down to gather Amanda and the doll on her lap. Amanda quickly squirmed away. Laura thought that perhaps Amanda simply didn't like to be held. She dressed the doll and handed it back to Amanda, then reached out to touch her face affectionately. Amanda dodged her hand. Had she ever had love shown to her, or merely an affectionate hand placed on her? Since Amanda didn't speak, Laura couldn't be sure. But she knew what she suspected in her heart. Perhaps after living here for a while Amanda would learn about love and affection. There was certainly enough of both in this household.

While Amanda played with the doll more, Laura's thoughts turned to Caleb and his absence at dinner. Earlier, when he had come inside and she had approached him to tell him how easily the remainder of the morning had gone with Amanda, she had not realized the turmoil he felt having her so close until she had looked into his dark, clouded eyes, saw the desire in them, and realized he wanted to be with her again. She had not realized that her hair had been brushing across his arm until he'd told her to go braid it and she had looked down and saw it tickling his arm. Suddenly aware of how close she was to him and of the sparks heating up her own body, she had swept her hair back with one hand and stepped away from him, nearly stumbling over a chair behind her. Caleb had not wasted even a moment to steady her;

he had fled the house. Breathless, she had braced herself with her hands on the back of the chair until her pulse and breathing had slowed. Then she had returned to Amanda.

When she had approached Caleb, she had not been considering the desire that was still—and always would be, she suspected—such a force between them. She had been excited and she'd wanted to share her excitement with him. Obviously Amanda could hear since the girl followed simple instructions. Laura hadn't wanted Amanda to hear them talking about her, and she had drawn close to Caleb to prevent that. She had never meant to torment him or herself. She hoped they could find a way to be together again soon and release all of this tension.

Caleb couldn't keep ignoring the rumble of his stomach, so he came inside for supper. But since he knew Ma would think he didn't have a right to touch Laura until she broke her engagement to Adrian and married *him*, he didn't enjoy sitting across the table from Laura. He listened to her soft voice as she talked to Ma and Stacey and Amanda, and all he wanted to do was drag her into his arms, take her off somewhere, and make love to her. He was trying like hell to keep from doing that. Things might be a sight better if he just did what his body was telling him to do. But if Ma ever found out, there'd be hell to pay. Besides, he respected his mother too much to go against her wishes.

So he shoveled food in, met Laura's clear blue gaze, and shoveled faster. He had to get back outside, away from the house, away from Laura. He finished supper. Mumbling an excuse, he rose. He left his plate at the washbasin, then went back outside.

The sun was dying in a red river over the prairie. Caleb gave a sharp whistle, and Sam came running toward the house from the west, plowing through the prairie grass with long strides. He nearly ran Caleb down. Caleb grumbled at him and the dog plopped down a few feet away, his chin propped on outstretched paws. The meek look in Sam's eyes made Caleb sorry for the way he'd growled at him. He walked over, hunched down, and scratched Sam's head.

They sat like that for a while, Sam wagging his tail and enjoying Caleb's scratching, Caleb watching the sunset and wondering if he could resist touching Laura until he married her.

"Hell," he said after a time. "I don't know."

Then he let himself think about her for a bit. She'd changed him, by bringing Amanda here. She'd made him face the fact that he couldn't keep turning his back on the situation. She'd done the same thing with Stacey and Ma, and he reckoned she would have taken on the whole town, too, if she'd had to. She'd come from a big house where she had servants and probably never had to do much for herself. But she was learning to live on the prairie. She was learning the dangers, learning to shoot, learning to cook, learning to take cattle to water. Caleb grinned at the last thought. He knew what might have happened if Laura hadn't forced him away from the house that evening and made him see things Stacey's way: He and Stacey would have fought stubbornly, him vowing to watch her and Charles, and her vowing to not let him.

Stacey came up behind him and offered to help him take the cattle to water. He stood and stretched. They started walking toward the barn to get the horses. She looked curiously at him, and he knew she had a passel of questions. "So what are you going to do, Caleb, miss meals every day just so you can avoid Laura for a few hours?"

"Maybe I will," he said, his strides lengthening as soon as she asked the question. She had to hurry to keep up with him.

"Don't you try and get away from me, Caleb Main. You'll get awful skinny after missing afternoon meals. I knew you were interested in her the first evening you described her to me. Maybe you should stop running from the truth."

"Ever occur to you that maybe I'm not running? I might be interested, real interested, but she's an engaged woman right now. Best thing I can do is stay away from her till she fixes that."

They entered the barn and reached for saddles to toss over their horses' backs. "What do you mean, until she fixes that?" Stacey asked as they worked, arranging the saddles and tightening cinches.

Caleb grinned. "You're not one to keep your nose out of other people's business, are you?"

Stacey's eyes narrowed. "You two are cooking something. I know it. Tell me, Caleb. Tell. Are you going to marry her?"

He worked on the saddle more. "All right. You win this one. We've been talking about it. But a lot of things still have to be settled, and I'd rather not tell Ma anything yet. Until the day Laura says her engagement to Adrian Montgomery is broken, I won't sleep well. She wants to go back to Bismarck one day and settle memories of her pa, too. I've got to do some thinking about the man myself. And right now," he said, seeing her grin, "you and me have cattle to get to water."

Ruth found a pair of Stacey's old shoes and stockings. The shoes were a little big on Amanda, and they were old and dusty, but they would serve until Laura could manage to go to Minot and buy her another pair.

Sunday morning Amanda went to church with them. People stared and not as many drifted over to talk this time. Laura suspected they would need time to get accustomed to the idea of Amanda being among them.

After service Preacher Jacobs took Laura's hand, smiled, and shook his head in disbelief. "You're very courageous," he said. "I don't know how you managed to get past Blake Kincaid, but I'm glad you did."

"Actually, Caleb accomplished that," Laura responded.

Preacher Jacobs gazed at Caleb in amazement. Caleb shrugged, looking sheepish.

Outside Ruth and Stacey were still talking to their friends. Laura watched Amanda wander over to the willow tree where Caleb had hollowed out the place for the handkerchief. Amanda reached into the hollow, but her hand came out empty. She settled herself by the tree and stared at the river. Laura gave her a few moments alone at her old familiar place, perhaps the only place where she had found comfort of any sort before she had shown up at the Main farm. The comfort she had found there had come, undoubtedly, from knowing that someone cared enough to put a handkerchief filled with food in the hollow. Laura smiled, still touched that Caleb had been doing such a compassionate thing.

She wandered over to join Amanda. "You must miss this place," she said softly. "But now you have another place. A place that will be warm during the winter. You'll always have clothes now and food that you won't need to search for. And you'll have people who love you, Amanda."

Amanda stared at the river for a while longer. Then, as if she had resolved something within herself, she struggled to her feet and stretched her hand out to Laura's. Laura was touched that the child was reaching out to her for the first time. She took Amanda's hand and let her lead the way to the wagon.

On the way home they stopped in the plum grove to gather plums. Stacey tossed one playfully at Caleb. Growling, he shot off after her. Stacey squealed and raced through the grove. Laura laughed. Ruth shook her head, smiling gently from where she still sat on the wagon seat. Amanda gripped Laura's hand tightly. One glance at Amanda's worried frown told Laura that Amanda didn't realize the others were only playing a game.

"They're playing," Laura assured her. Still, Amanda peered through the trees, her concerned expression wrinkling her nose. Laura offered her a plum, which she took and then bit into the sweet ripe fruit.

A short while later, Laura took Amanda's hand, and they wandered off together. A cool breeze whispered through the plum tree branches overhead, and the sun speckled the ground through the leaves. Laura hoped Amanda was enjoying the afternoon as much as she.

They walked for a while, Laura lifting her skirt and stepping cautiously as they ventured through a maze of fallen trees. There were more trees ahead, standing tall, and the grass thickened like an evergreen quilt in places. Wildflowers peeked at them, a myriad of blue, yellow, purple, and white. Laura began plucking them, gathering a pretty bouquet in one hand. Amanda followed her example and soon had a handful. A little farther ahead was a tree stump. Laura led Amanda to it, sat her on it, and explained that she was going to put some of the pretty flowers in Amanda's hair. This morning she had braided Amanda's hair much like she did her own, and now she untied the blue ribbon at the tapered end of the braid and separated the plaits. Then she rebraided Amanda's hair, weaving the colorful wildflowers through it by holding the stems in place and braiding over them.

Smiling, she stepped back to have a look. "You're beautiful, Amanda. Beautiful! Like the meadow. Come along. We'll walk a little more, then go back before everyone starts wondering where we are."

A little farther along elms and ashes overcame the meadow, but a few plum trees appeared as well. Laura heard water trickling and bubbling but didn't realize where she and Amanda were until she saw the spring up ahead . . . and the plum tree she and Caleb had lain beneath. Her breath caught in her throat, and her heart pounded as she stood staring at the tree.

"Let's go back, Amanda," she said, knowing the others would be searching for them. She stole another look at the tree and smiled. Once she and Caleb were married, she knew she would be everything to him, just as he would be everything to her. He was a man strongly devoted to those he loved. To Adrian she represented money. To Caleb she was much more.

She and Amanda walked back past the tree stump where Laura had sat Amanda and braided her hair, across the meadow where they paused to pluck more handfuls of wildflowers, and through the maze of fallen trees where Laura lifted her skirt again and laughed as she helped Amanda across the logs. Amanda was somber, as always. Laura wondered what this child would look like wearing a smile. Someday she would know. Amanda Kincaid would be as happy as all little girls deserved to be.

Laura and Amanda joined Stacey, Caleb, and Ruth at the

wagon. Once everyone settled in the wagon, Caleb shook the reins and the horses started off, the wagon creaking and groaning with the movement.

The sun had relinquished the sky to gray clouds that looked more threatening with each passing minute. A wind kicked up, at first whispering through the branches of trees and blowing across Laura's face. But by the time the wagon had emerged from the valley and was traveling across the prairie, the wind had strengthened, whipping the prairie grass and bending the few scattered trees on the land ahead. The wind was stronger on the prairie simply because there were so few trees and no valley to break or lessen it.

"We've had no rain in three weeks," she heard Caleb tell Ruth, "but this'll be a hell of a storm."

"Hope we make it home before the rain hits," Ruth said.

"Don't reckon we will."

Caleb was right. They traveled perhaps another mile. Suddenly the sky cracked with a loud rip, and hail hammered down. The horses screeched and lurched forward in a straight run. Laura, Stacey, and Amanda tumbled into a big heap. They managed to grab the wagon rail and sit up. Laura saw Caleb yank the reins tight. The horses still tore across the prairie. Clutching Amanda against her side, Laura shielded the girl's head with her arms. She ducked her own head so the hail wouldn't hit her in the face. Instead it pelted her arms and the back of her head and clattered steadily down on the wagon.

"Here, put this over you!" Stacey shouted.

Laura glanced up. Stacey, drenched, held a wet blanket, trying to spread it. If they could get it over their heads, it would soften the blows of the hail.

Laura grabbed one side of the blanket and pulled it over her and Amanda. Stacey climbed under, too, and they all huddled close together, Amanda in the middle, safe and snug.

Safe and snug . . . unless the horses were running away. If they were, would they even stop when they got to the farm? Would they run right past it? Or perhaps try to run through it? Laura shuddered.

Not another crash. Dear God, no, not another crash.

She was amazed that the horses were so accustomed to the shot of a rifle that they hadn't even flinched the night Stacey had fired her rifle to frighten off wolves, yet hail and thunder frightened them. Perhaps the animals had somehow sensed that Stacey and her rifle meant them no harm, that the wolves were the worse danger. But the slamming hail hurt them.

The wagon tipped, and Laura bit her lower lip to keep from crying out, wanting to be brave for Amanda. But inside she trembled. Even the horrible coach accident hadn't been this frightening. It had happened quickly, before she had had much of a chance to be frightened. But this . . . this seemed to drag on. She shut her eyes and whispered a prayer.

The horses raced on. Many more times Laura felt the wagon tip. Miraculously it always righted itself. She was just beginning to whisper another prayer when she heard Caleb's shouts.

"Jump! Get ready to jump! They're not going to stop!"

Fear clutched Laura's heart. She could jump to safety, but what about Amanda? A small, frightened child couldn't jump. She might land wrong because of her bad leg and injure herself. And Laura refused to leave her.

Stacey scrambled out from under the blanket. "Come on, Laura!"

Laura poked her head out from under the blanket. Hail pelted her again. Water poured down her face. "No! Amanda can't jump!"

Stacey stared at her for a few seconds, then scrambled back under the blanket. "Then we'll all stay together. I'm not leaving you."

They heard Caleb shouting again, thundering at them to jump, but they ignored him. If they couldn't jump together, they would stay together right here in the wagon bed.

Seconds turned into minutes as the wagon rattled, shook, and tipped in flight. Laura held her breath and waited for it to overturn. *Please, God . . .* She didn't want to be the only one to live through another crash. *Please God . . . make the horses stop.*

And then, as if her prayers were being answered, the wagon began to slow. Only a little at first, but enough for Laura to feel the break in pace. She shut her eyes, pressing Amanda to her breast. Surely Amanda felt the pounding of her heart and knew her fear. Laura's hand found Stacey, too, and pressed Stacey to her and Amanda.

Hail stopped hammering them. Rain, driving down with incredible force, took its place. The wagon slowed until, compared to the speed at which it had been tearing across the prairie, it seemed to creep along. An eternity later Laura heard Caleb commanding the horses to stop. Then the wagon wheels creaked to a halt.

Stacey pulled the blanket away. "We're home. Come on!" she shouted through the fierce rain.

But Laura was frozen in fear. She had almost been involved in another crash. Dear God. She couldn't seem to move a muscle, though she knew she needed to get Amanda inside the house.

"Come on, Laura!" Stacey shouted again.

Still frozen, Laura felt Amanda stand and tug at her hand. Laura stared at her. Amanda's wet hair hung straight down. Water dripped from her head. Her little dress clung to her body, and her eyes were wide with fright.

Stacey's voice again: "Laura, we're safe. Let's go in the house."

Still Laura couldn't move. Then a tiny voice touched her ear. "L-laura. Come!"

"Amanda?" Laura whispered. Amanda had spoken? She had!

Laura moved. What had been fear turned to joy. She grasped Amanda's outstretched hand, steadied herself by gripping the wagon rail with the other hand, and stood. Caleb came to lift everyone down. Then Laura, Amanda, and Stacey raced for the house. Ruth was waiting on the porch. She flung the front door wide, and they all poured in. Caleb had stayed behind to take the horses to the barn.

Inside the dry house Laura lowered herself to her knees in front of Amanda and stared deeply into her blue eyes. "You spoke," she managed hoarsely, for emotion was choking her.

Amanda nodded.

Laura embraced Amanda, happiness overflowing from her in tears. "You're going to be all right. I love you, Amanda. I love you."

After a few moments Laura withdrew and wiped her eyes. "Let's remove those wet clothes, shall we?"

Ruth was coaxing a fire from coals in the open stove. Stacey had disappeared, and Laura assumed she had gone upstairs to change. Laura turned Amanda in the direction of the staircase, and they, too, went upstairs. In the bedroom they had been sharing, Laura removed Amanda's clothes and wrapped her in a warm blanket. Then she peeled away her own wet clothes and replaced her calico dress with the elegant blue silk one she had brought from Bismarck. Wearing it would make her feel out of place again in this house and around the Mains, but she had no choice while she waited until the calico dress dried.

She took a towel and rubbed Amanda's head until her hair was only damp. Then she unbraided her own hair and rubbed it partially dry. She brushed her and Amanda's hair, placed the brush on the chest of drawers, and draped the wet dresses over a forearm. Then she and Amanda went downstairs.

There Caleb had taken over Ruth's place at the stove and was fanning flames from the coals inside. Ruth and Stacey were nowhere to be seen. Laura draped her and Amanda's dresses over the backs of table chairs. Caleb glanced up from his work, meeting Laura's eyes with a dark look of fury.

"You should have jumped," he said in a low voice.

Laura tensed. Her nerves had snapped long ago. She certainly didn't need him making matters worse with a lecture. "Don't tell me what I should have done. I did the only thing I could think of to do at the moment," she said, tearing her eyes from his.

"Dammit, Laura. I told everyone to jump, and no one moved! The wagon might have crashed into something. You might have been killed!"

She turned away, intending to take Amanda and sit with her on the settee. "It's better to be killed with others than live through something like that and know you're the only one who has," she said. "I know. Besides, there was Amanda. She couldn't jump." She heard the quiver in her voice and hoped Caleb didn't. She was trying to act courageous, when, in fact, inside she still felt weak and frightened.

Two steps more and she would reach the settee. Suddenly she felt Caleb's rough fingers slip around her arm just below her elbow, pressing her to stop. Then his hand slid to hers. Laura turned around. Their eyes met for a split second, then Caleb pulled her into his arms and buried his face in her shoulder. "Damn you, Laura. I was thinking about Ma and Stacey and Amanda, but most of all I was scared of losing you."

Caught by surprise, Laura sucked in a sharp breath. Her hands hovered near his head. She wasn't quite sure what she should do—free herself or soothe him. She was still angry that he had snapped at her, but she loved him, too. She felt as though he had reached inside her and now held her heart in the palm of his hand. She had to comfort him.

She felt him shudder. She entwined fingers in his wet hair, and her other hand stroked his muscled upper back. "I'm all right. We all are. And I'm here. I'm here," she said softly. Then she bent to kiss his head.

She heard the thud of boots on the steps and lifted her head. Stacey stood frozen partway down the staircase. Ruth stood behind her. Both of them were staring at her and Caleb. The fact that she was still engaged to Adrian flashed through her mind.

"Caleb," Laura whispered, though she didn't necessarily want him to release her until he had regained his composure.

He seemed to sense that they were being watched. Lifting his head, he straightened, but didn't meet her gaze. "I'll go change. Sorry I got you wet again," he mumbled, turning away.

The front of Laura's blue silk gown bore dark places left by the wetness of Caleb's hair and body, making the proximity she and Caleb had shared quite obvious. Her fingertips caught the folds of her skirt and toyed nervously with them. She struggled to gather not only her composure but her courage. What must Stacey be thinking right now? The first time

Laura, Stacey, and Caleb had gone to Minot together, Laura had made her future intentions quite clear to Stacey in Mr. Alman's store. Stacey had implied that she would like to have Laura as a sister-in-law, and Laura had informed her that she was already engaged. Perhaps Stacey was thinking that Laura was pursuing an illicit affair with Caleb, yet still planned to return to Bismarck and marry Adrian.

And what about Ruth? What must she be thinking? Laura cringed. All Ruth knew was that Laura was engaged. She had no way of knowing that Laura and Caleb planned to marry someday.

She thought about telling them she planned to break her engagement to Adrian, but, considering the awkwardness that had sprung up, now didn't seem to be an appropriate time. Caleb excused himself past Ruth and Stacey on the stairs. Laura lifted her eyes to meet Stacey's and found her friend smiling as if she knew something. Ruth's expression was one of pleasant surprise, certainly not incrimination.

Laura was shocked but relieved. Ruth and Stacey continued downstairs. Laura went to the sewing corner and gathered the pieces of calico that, when stitched together, would be Amanda's new dress. Material, scissors, and thread in hand, she then went to sit beside Amanda on the settee.

Her hands trembled, and she couldn't seem to make a straight stitch. Caleb's words echoed in her mind: "I was scared of losing you." How close they had all come to losing their lives.

She loved him. Nowhere else in the world could she find the beauty she had found in Caleb's arms. Not in Bismarck. Not in Pa's house.

And certainly not in Adrian's arms.

❄❄❄

Chapter Fourteen

LAURA WAS LYING in bed, staring at the ceiling and listening to the sounds of crickets and owls. She heard Caleb's boots in the hall and on the stairs. The hour was late. He obviously couldn't sleep. Neither could she, and she was tired of lying awake for hours every night thinking of him and how wonderful his hands had felt on her body.

So she rose and went to find him.

The night air was cool on her face as she neared the porch steps. There was a half-moon among a million stars glittering down from a black heaven. In the distance cows lowed, chickens stirred, and a coyote howled. Laura smiled to herself. She still respected the wild animals of the prairie but no longer shivered with fear every time she heard one. She realized she had not brought a rifle out here with her but decided not to turn back. She wanted to find Caleb. She would be safe in his arms.

She gathered her thin cotton shift around her and took the first porch step. She heard the familiar click of a gun and froze, smiling though her heart raced in anticipation of Caleb's touch.

"When we're old and gray, you'll still be doing whatever the hell I tell you not to do," he said from somewhere behind her with a hint of amusement in his voice. He was behind and to her left, she thought. Sitting with his boots propped on the rail again? Doubtless. She wondered how many nights he had spent sitting right there while she lay awake in her bed.

"And you'll still be sitting in the shadows, frightening females, Mr. Main," she teased. She turned and settled her bottom on the stair rail, barely discerning his form in the heavy shadows that had spread over that side of the porch. He *was* sitting with his boots propped up on the rail.

He swung them down, and the chair creaked as he stood. Laura could scarcely breathe. She wanted his touch so badly. Her body tingled and ached with desire. She knew her need was probably revealed in her eyes, but she didn't care. *Let him see it, let him want me as much as I want him.*

"Are you frightened?" he asked softly, moving into an area bathed in moonlight.

Laura drew a swift, painful breath. He wore no shirt, and he looked magnificent. Moonlight defined his muscled shoulders and arms. And his chest . . . she wanted to run her open hands over the expanse of it. "What . . ." She swallowed hard. "What makes you think I'm frightened?"

He leaned against the porch rail opposite her, his hands grasping the rail on either side. Perhaps a distance of two feet separated them. He could reach out and touch her. She could reach out and touch him. She saw the need in his glazed eyes. He had to be seeing it in hers. She tipped her head back and asked, "Are we playing a game? Who can resist the longest?"

He made a sound that was more of a growl than a chuckle. "We've been playing it for nearly a week."

"I'm not interested in winning," she said.

"I was, but not anymore. Why the hell did you come out here in that nightgown, Laura? Why the hell did you come out here at all?" he asked, stepping toward her. "Do you know how hard it is to be respectful of the fact that you're still engaged to another man when you're traipsing around in the night looking like an angel from heaven?"

His hands planted themselves on her shoulders, massaged them, then moved slowly down her arms. His eyes were dark as the night, but fire sparked in them.

"In my mind I'm no longer engaged to Adrian," she said. "I simply need to make it official."

His hands caught her hips and pulled them to his. Laura gasped, wanting to close her eyes and revel in the wonderful feel of their bodies pressed together. But she also wanted to see the heat of his eyes, wanted to watch his gaze rake over her, devouring her. His hard length pressed against her and sought something she couldn't wait to give.

He wrapped a section of the long length of her hair around one hand, staring into her eyes as he did. "I warned you about wolves once."

"Yes, you did, didn't you? Well, I found one I like very much."

Far off a coyote howled. Caleb let Laura's hair spill from his hand. Then he reached down and took her hand in his. "Come on."

They left the porch and approached the barn, where a lamp dangled from a hook near one of the doors, its wick still burning low. Caleb lifted the lamp and took it into the barn with them. Then he shut the doors. He took several saddle blankets that had been hanging over stall rails and spread them in an open area thickly coated with hay. There Laura joined him.

Shadows cast by the lamplight danced around the barn. In a nearby stall one of the horses nickered. Laura and Caleb sank to their knees. Then Laura drew Caleb's head to her breast. He breathed her name, and his hands went to her thighs. He eased her shift up, massaging her flesh as he did. When the shift reached her breasts, Laura raised her arms and let him slip it from her body.

He caught the hardened tip of one breast in his mouth, and Laura arched to him. Desire spread to every part of her body. Even her fingertips yearned to play, and she let them. They roamed over his powerful shoulders and upper arms, grazed his stiff nipples and delighted in the touch. The hair on his chest was wiry and thick, and Laura ran her fingers through it, loving the feel of it.

She explored the tautness of his stomach, then slid her hands to his back and felt the strength there.

He laid her back on the blankets and stood, slipping from his trousers. Then he eased down above her, his hardened length touching her thigh.

His lips played on her body, kissing every sensitive point until Laura's hands were in his hair and she was whispering his name over and over. He ran his tongue up the inside of one thigh. Laura cried out, her hands grasping his shoulders to urge him to cover her and fill her.

He did. He thrust in and out, bringing her to the point of pleasure, then slowed, torturing her, making every muscle in her body scream for sweet ecstasy. Then his pace sped up again.

And finally . . . the welcomed storm roared over them. Their cries mingled. The flickering light danced around them.

Afterward they lay entwined, talking softly in the dancing shadows. He asked what her life in Bismarck had been like. She told him she had spent a number of years away at school, but during the years and months she was home, Pa always took her to various dinners and parties. Pa had been a very socially conscious man. She told Caleb about the way he and Adrian had subtly maneuvered her into the hurried engagement. Back then she wouldn't have dreamed of disagreeing with them. If Pa hadn't died in February, she would undoubtedly be married to Adrian by now, for wedding plans had been well under way the morning she had gone to the office and found Pa. She told Caleb that since her arrival here, she had begun to realize that her father had had faults as well good points like everyone else. She apologized for Pa's hand in whatever had happened between him and Caleb ten years ago. After much consideration, she now admitted that her father could be manipulative, and since she had learned what an honest, deeply devoted man Caleb was, she had begun to wonder if Pa's business dealings had always been honorable. She still had her memories of Pa as a father—the laughter, the shared times, the picnics beneath that elm overhanging his office. Those were always memories she would cherish, but she had never known the other side of the man. She had never known the businessman, but Caleb had.

Caleb cradled her head against his chest, listening to her soft voice. One hand rubbed up and down her silky upper arm. "You wondered what happened between me and your pa," he said.

She lifted her head and stared at him, her hair spilling over one shoulder. "Don't tell me if you really don't want to."

He touched her lips with a finger to silence her, then pulled her back down to him. Then he talked.

"A year after my pa was killed, Matt Kent hired me as a cattle hand. He went along on a lot of the big cattle drives, made sure everyone got fed well. Most everyone liked him, thought he was real fair. Him, me . . . couple of others were gathered round a big campfire one night near Fargo. Matt said he had a big land deal going if any of us wanted to get in on it. The land would be worth a lot more in a few years. People were starting to grow wheat at the time. Your pa was right when he said the wheat business was about to boom, and when it did, people would crowd into Dakota Territory. He figured the railroad was headed this way, too, someday, and that'd bring people as well. He was right.

"I was twenty years old, itching with land fever. Didn't take me long to take all the money Pa had saved since the day he and Ma got married, some money I'd saved myself, and drop it in Matt's lap. Never signed anything. Went on promises. He wasn't so rich at the time—he made most of his money during the last eight years or so—and on that land deal. Guess he thought I'd just go away after a time like the others did. He was a real upstanding citizen in Bismarck. No one believed any of us when we hollered that we'd been swindled. But I didn't go away. I kept showing up at his house, asking about the land. Finally I told him I wanted my money back. He said, 'What money?' About that time I knew he had me. I was still driving cattle, but the pay wasn't too good, and all the other money was gone. Ma and Stacey spent the winter in a tent near Bismarck. Stacey got real sick and nearly died. I'd told some of the other hands about the swindle, and I think they might have believed me and stormed Matt Kent's house if something else hadn't happened."

He sighed, remembering, and glanced down at Laura's face to see if there was any sign that he was telling her more than he ought to—Matt Kent had been her pa, after all, and she'd never seen his bad side. This all had to be pretty hard for her to swallow.

"Go on," she urged, staring at him with wide eyes.

"Matt knew I'd been talking to the other hands. He told me on the side that I'd better shut my mouth. He knew he couldn't just tell me to leave town. People were starting to listen. Then Matt realized he was missing a lot of money, and one of my saddlebags turned up filled with money. I knew he'd set me up for a hanging. I got away from the sheriff. Decided before I hanged I was at least going to get a little revenge. I rode to Matt's house and caught him alone. He nearly beat me to death. I spent a few days in jail, waiting for the judge to come to town. Then one day the sheriff said he was releasing me. But he said if I didn't get my tail out of town, I'd hang for robbery. I took Ma and Stacey, and we left. I worked for someone else for a time on a big wheat farm southeast of Minot. A man named Owens. He let us stay in a little house on the farm. He paid me good. Part of the pay came in land, the land we're on now. Guess Matt took some of the punch out of me. All I've wanted to do since is work my land and mind my own business."

They lay in silence, Laura running fingers through the hair on his chest and Caleb holding her, enjoying the feel of her body pressed against his. "No wonder you don't want to go back to Bismarck," she said, raising her head. She cupped her jaw in a palm, her elbow resting on the blanket. "You don't want my money, you've told me that, because it's Kent money, but there is more you should consider."

He started to speak and tell her again that he didn't want the money, but she pressed a fingertip to his lips to stop him as he had done to her earlier.

"Isn't it ironic that he took the money from you, yet now you have an opportunity to have all and more that he promised you?" she asked. "All the cattle. All the money. All the *land*. It all belongs to me. *Us,* when we marry. Think of it, Caleb. If what you've told me is true, and I have no reason to doubt you, then some of my money is yours. I can give you more than the amount you lost."

Caleb slid his fingers in and out of her hair. He didn't

know if he'd ever feel right about using Kent money. Right now he knew just the thought of it didn't sit right with him. "I never wanted anything from Matt except what he promised me."

"Exactly. You struggled so hard. Stacey nearly died. You nearly died. You deserve this. You'll have the money and the land and—"

"You. You're all I want, Laura," he said, easing her back down and kissing her lightly. His body stirred, needing her again, and he hungrily caught her mouth with his. Tongues met, hands wandered, and their bodies responded in harmony.

Caleb rolled onto her and buried himself within her velvet heaven. She was hot and wet, and she took him fully, meeting his rhythmic thrusts. His mouth found her breasts again and loved them, kissing the flesh, suckling the sweet nipples. She caught her breath, her body strained beneath his, then her cries of pleasure filled the barn. He watched ecstasy dance on her beautiful features and kissed her eyelids, her nose, her sweet mouth again. He felt his own body teeter on the brink of pleasure, then slip over the edge. Finally he spilled himself in her.

Again they lay together for a time. Then they dressed and slipped out of the barn. The sky had lightened some, but dawn was still a few hours away. Laura had more energy than she had ever had, and even when she slipped under the quilt in her bed, she couldn't sleep. When the purple and pink of dawn began spilling through the thin, gauzy window curtain, she rose, dressed quickly, then went downstairs to make biscuits.

"Thought me and Stacey'd go check on Mrs. Dahl this morning," Ruth said after breakfast.

Laura nodded. "I'll take care of cleaning up. You two go ahead."

Ruth thanked her, then she and Stacey gathered cheese, bread, and milk and went outside. Soon Laura heard the wagon ramble away. She cleared the table, washed the breakfast dishes, and swept the floor in the big room, then stitched more of Amanda's new dress. Amanda played with the quilt blocks and the rag doll, dressing and undressing it.

Later the front door swung open, and Caleb walked in, carrying a wooden bucket filled with coal. He placed it beside the stove, then reached behind the stove for another bucket. It was empty. He opened the stove door and began cleaning it out, using a device that resembled a small shovel. Amanda struggled to her feet from where she sat on the floor and wandered over to watch him.

"Stay back a bit now," Caleb told her. "Don't want to get this in your face."

Amanda scooted back. Laura remembered that she had forgotten to tell Caleb that Amanda had spoken to her. She set her stitching aside and approached Amanda and Caleb, bending down beside Amanda.

"Amanda," she said gently. "Yesterday you said my name. Could you say it again?"

Caleb stopped working and turned, his gaze shifting between Laura and Amanda. Amanda stared at the stove. The rag doll lay in her lap. She made no effort to move her mouth.

"Amanda, can you talk?" Caleb asked. "You don't have to. You can go back to just watching me if you want."

Amanda was silent. Laura was disappointed but wouldn't let her disappointment show. She touched Amanda's arm. "Another time, then."

Caleb turned back to work on the stove again. Laura stood to walk away. She was halfway to the settee when she heard Amanda's little voice speak her name.

Smiling, she returned to the stove to embrace Amanda. "That's wonderful."

Caleb had stopped working again and had twisted around to stare at Amanda and Laura. Grinning, he shook his head.

Then Amanda said his name, her eyes on the rag doll. His grin faded, and his eyebrows shot up. "I'll be damned," he said softly.

Laura gave him a reproachful look from the corner of her eye. "Swearing in the presence of a child, Mr. Main?" she teased.

Chuckling, he took Amanda's little chin in hand and lifted her head so she would look at him. Her eyes were wide. "That's good, Amanda. That's real good."

He went back to work on the stove. Laura went back to stitching. When the creak of a wagon came from outside, both paused and looked up. "Couldn't be Ma and Stacey back already," Caleb said. Laura glanced curiously toward the door. Caleb rose and set the bucket aside, then strode to the door to see who had arrived.

He was two strides away from the door when it opened. Stacey stood there, looking solemn. "Mrs. Dahl. She's dead. Died in her sleep," she said before Caleb or Laura could utter a word.

Caleb shook his head, not looking at all surprised. Laura wasn't surprised, either. They had all known Mrs. Dahl's time was near. Laura was glad Mrs. Dahl had died in the sod house, on the land where her grandchildren and daughter had died. Perhaps Mrs. Dahl was with them in spirit right now. Laura glanced down at her hands and whispered a prayer, asking that Mrs. Dahl's spirit be received.

"Well, let's go bury her," Caleb said. He closed the stove door and brushed past Stacey.

Ruth had stayed at the sod house with Mrs. Dahl's body. Laura helped Stacey gather a basket of food to last the rest of the day. Stacey carried the basket while Laura took Amanda's hand and led her to the wagon waiting near the porch. She lifted Amanda up to the wagon bed, then Caleb was there to lift her and Stacey. He climbed up in the wagon seat, took the reins, and soon the wagon began moving, cutting across the prairie. It passed the creek where Laura had taken the cattle to water with Caleb, and rambled on. The afternoon sun blazed down, and a lone cloud floated gently in the clear sky. Soon the sod house came into view.

Caleb reined the horse, jumped down, and helped everyone down. Laura gathered the basket and followed Stacey and Amanda into the house.

Mrs. Dahl's face was white but seemed less wrinkled than the last time Laura had seen her. Truly she must be at peace.

Ruth had bathed her, combed her hair, and tidied up the little house.

Presently Laura and Amanda went outside and sat on a blanket near the place beside the house where Caleb was digging a grave. He spent most of the afternoon shoveling dirt and tossing it aside.

Once the grave was dug, Caleb set the shovel aside and wiped his brow with his white shirtsleeve. He went inside the house and appeared moments later, cradling Mrs. Dahl's body. Laura whispered another prayer while he lowered the body into the grave.

After shoveling dirt until the hole was filled, Caleb set the shovel aside. Then Ruth, Stacey, Laura, and Amanda gathered near. Finally Caleb spoke the twenty-third Psalm over the grave, grabbed the shovel, and headed toward the wagon.

The ride back to the Main farm was a solemn one. The wagon wheels ground over the prairie as the sun began spilling red and orange. A flock of birds fluttered by. "What will happen to her land?" Laura wondered aloud, thinking of Mrs. Dahl. "Is anyone left to inherit it?"

"Heard she had a son somewhere back East," Stacey said. "We'll ask in town and see if anyone knows, maybe people like Mr. Alman and Mrs. Statum—they've been here since long before Minot even became a town."

"She saw a lot in her lifetime. Both times I met her, I saw years in her eyes."

"She saw too much, if you ask me," Stacey said softly. "Too much. I'm glad her suffering is over."

The next afternoon Caleb was inside the barn cleaning stalls when Sam stirred from where he was lying nearby. Head cocked, Sam trotted to the barn door, then barked to let Caleb know something wasn't right outside. Caleb joined Sam at the door.

A horse and rider aproached the house. The man sat tall in the saddle. His curly blond hair was slightly windblown; his clothes were trimmed with gold thread that shimmered under the afternoon sun, and he held his chin up arrogantly.

Just the way he rode up—as though he'd take what he could and to hell with anyone who stood in his way—didn't sit right with Caleb. Caleb reckoned he didn't need to guess the man's name. Adrian had come anyway, despite Laura's telegraph. Caleb knew if he had been in this man's position, he would have come, too. Laura was too valuable to lose.

Laura shot out of the house. Her hair was loose, hanging to her waist and flowing softly around her face. The image reminded Caleb of the morning he'd gone into the house and her hair had teased his arm. He'd had to fight the desire to sweep her in his arms, and he'd used words to do it, telling her to do something with her hair. Her eyes had widened in shock and confusion. Right now, gazing at the man swinging down from the saddle, they widened with surprise and excitement. Caleb didn't know what to make of that. He knew Laura loved him. Still he couldn't help but wonder if Adrian had just enough charm to convince Laura that she still ought to marry him.

"Adrian!" Laura said.

A heaviness settled on Caleb, and he was sure that the way Laura had said the man's name had something to do with it. He drifted back inside the barn, leaned his forearms on the top rail of a stall, and stared down at his boots. The day he'd been dreading was here. Hell, he'd known it would come. When Laura had sent that telegraph telling Adrian she wanted to stay longer, Caleb had suspected Adrian would come anyway. What man in his right mind wouldn't? Not only was Laura beautiful, but she'd been stranded in a place Montgomery probably knew nothing about. After he'd received her telegraph, Montgomery had probably wondered why the hell any person in her right mind would want to stay in a strange place with strange people.

Sam wandered back into the barn and plopped down near Caleb's feet. Caleb rubbed Sam's head, then went about cleaning a few more stalls. Finally he paused, wiping his shirtsleeve across his sweat-beaded brow. He reckoned he'd better be sociable, otherwise Ma might drift out here, and there'd be hell to pay. Giving himself just a little more time to get used to the idea of meeting Laura's fiancé, he spread hay on the floor of another stall, then brushed his hands off and started for the house. He wasn't any more ready than he had been earlier, but knew he couldn't put off the meeting. He figured he'd go in the house, meet Adrian Montgomery, then go off and do more chores. Laura would want time alone with the man anyway. He just hoped Montgomery would keep his hands off her.

When Caleb opened the door to the house and walked in, Ma and Stacey looked up from where they stood near the stove and stared at him. Ma's look said, "Don't cause trouble." Stacey's was a look of sympathy, and behind the sympathy maybe there was some anger, too.

Caleb knew Stacey wanted Laura to stay, and maybe she was thinking that now that Montgomery had turned up, Laura wouldn't. But even if Laura changed her mind—and he didn't really think she would—the decision was hers. He had to admit he was concerned because he knew Montgomery, like Matt Kent, had always had a strong hold on Laura emotionally. Maybe Montgomery would try to exploit that. Laura needed to find the strength to resist. He and Stacey couldn't send Montgomery away. Laura had to. The time she'd spent away from Montgomery had been good for her, he thought. When someone was getting shot at all the time, she didn't have time to even reload. He reckoned that's what Laura's position had been in Bismarck. Her pa and Montgomery had been coming at her all the time. Caleb hoped Stacey would hold her tongue. He narrowed his eyes and gave her what he hoped was a look of warning, then she turned away and helped Ma set the table for dinner.

Amanda was on the settee. Laura and Montgomery stood nearby, talking low.

"I sent you a telegraph telling you to not come yet," Caleb heard Laura tell Montgomery. "Did you receive it?"

Montgomery picked specks of dirt from his coat. "No. Not that a telegraph would have stopped me. I love you, Laura. I came to take you home."

"Adrian, we have to talk. There's Amanda—"

"Who?" Montgomery asked impatiently.

Laura inclined her head toward Amanda. Montgomery's

eyes shifted to the girl, who was huddled back into one corner of the settee. Her eyes were wide, and she looked a bit afraid of Montgomery. Caleb didn't blame her. He didn't trust Montgomery too much himself. Something told him the man was lying about not getting Laura's telegraph. The man had answered real quick and real smooth.

"Her?" Montgomery laughed in disbelief. "I had no idea you possessed such motherly instincts. Your pa would be pleased. I am. But we'll have our own children someday. She belongs with these people, not you. Anyone here can take care of her. You need to return to Bismarck with me."

Caleb knew Laura's temper. Since she didn't let anyone tell her what to do or where to go too often anymore, he waited, thinking her temper would explode anytime, and Montgomery would go off with his tail between his legs.

But already the hold Montgomery had over Laura showed itself. A little fire sparked in her blue eyes, but her temper didn't explode the way it had with him so many times. "I'm not leaving yet, Adrian," she said softly. "I need to take care of Amanda. I promised that I would."

"These people look capable enough, Laura. I plan to take you with me when I leave tomorrow," Montgomery said, his gaze now fixed on her. He was trying to intimidate her. Caleb had to fight the urge to jump in and protect her.

"I don't want to go. We'll talk later," she responded.

"Be sensible, Laura. That's not really what you want."

Laura's hands nervously gripped the folds of her skirt, and she lowered her lashes. Caleb tensed, watching her. He'd heard and seen enough. He'd meant to mind his own business and introduce himself when Laura and Montgomery finished talking, but he wasn't too sure Montgomery was going to leave her alone about the going-home-tomorrow business. And the man was trying to plant the idea in her head that staying here wasn't really what she wanted. Already Montgomery was manipulating her, trying to weaken her. Despite his vow to not interfere in her business, Caleb decided he had to, just this once.

He fixed a grin on his face and marched over to them, his

hand outstretched. "Caleb Main," he said loud enough so that Montgomery couldn't ignore him.

Turning to assess Caleb with cool gray eyes, Montgomery tipped his head back in a superior way. "You must be the farmer."

"Adrian!" Laura gasped.

Caleb could see Montgomery wasn't about to take his hand. Caleb's hand lashed out, found Montgomery's, and pumped. "That's right. And you're Adrian Montgomery. If you're hungry, we'll set another place at the table and talk over dinner."

It was Dakota hospitality, offered to give Laura a rest from Montgomery's manipulation. Montgomery managed to wrench his hand free of Caleb's strong grasp and put it in a trouser pocket. Caleb knew the man would probably wash the invisible grime off his hand later. Montgomery just glared at him.

Laura latched onto Adrian's coat sleeve. "These people have been very good to me," she said with a plea in her soft voice.

Montgomery gazed down at her, seemed to consider her words for a moment, then nodded. "All right . . . All right, Laura. Mr. Main," he said, his cool eyes fixing on Caleb again. "But later we will talk alone, Laura." There was a threat in his voice, and Caleb itched to set the man straight about how Laura could do what she wanted to do, and if she didn't want to talk alone with him later, she wouldn't. But he could only fight so much of Laura's battle for her.

When Montgomery planted a possessive hand on the small of Laura's back and gave Caleb a smug look of confidence, Caleb nearly jumped out of his skin. The battle might just become his a lot more if Montgomery wasn't careful. Caleb fought the urge to take the man by the scruff of the neck and toss him out of the house. That was exactly the way he would have handled the situation ten years ago. Now, well . . . since that business with Matt Kent he'd changed a bit. He'd learned to face trouble more calmly after a lot of thought and not jump in hot-tempered with his fists up. Course, if Montgomery made too much of a nuisance of himself while he was here, Caleb had Ma, Stacey, and Amanda to think about, and he'd do whatever needed doing. There was always the possibility that, since Montgomery had spent nearly his entire life under Kent's thumb, he might try something like Kent had tried when he'd planted the money in Caleb's saddlebag. What Montgomery didn't realize—and would real fast if he did try anything like that— was that, like Kent had had the people of Bismarck on his side back then, Caleb had the people of the prairie and of Minot on his now. Montgomery would get nowhere out here if he tried anything stupid. Caleb wasn't the least bit scared of the man.

"Washbasin's on the other side of the table," Caleb said, hoping Montgomery would take the hint and leave this side of the room for a bit. In just the few minutes he'd known Adrian Montgomery, he'd already decided there wasn't enough space for him and Montgomery in one room, much less on the same side.

Montgomery hesitated, then moved slowly to the other side of the room to wash his hands. Once his back was to them, Caleb felt Laura step closer to him. "Caleb, please. He's not what you're used to, but please be patient. I'll talk to him, and he'll be on his way by tomorrow."

"I'm not hoping to fight it out with him if that's what you're talking about, Laura. But I'm here if things get too hard for you."

"I need to do this," she said, and he knew she was talking about learning how to handle Adrian. "I know he's difficult to tolerate sometimes, but—"

"Hell, Laura, he's downright hard on the stomach." With that, Caleb laughed in disbelief, then walked off toward the table. Maybe Laura didn't find Montgomery hard on the stomach. Maybe she was feeling sorry for the man, since she'd never meant to fall in love with Caleb. Maybe she was feeling guilty that she had. Whatever she was thinking, she had to sort it all out for herself. He could jump in between Laura and Montgomery if he wanted to, but that wouldn't change Laura's thoughts or feelings.

Best thing he could do was stay back and let her get through this awkward time in her own way.

Laura went upstairs for a few minutes, then came back down. Her hair was braided now, and she looked a little pale. Whenever Caleb tried to catch her eye, she avoided his gaze. She helped Amanda wash at the basin, then the two of them joined the others at the table where another chair had been drawn up for Montgomery.

Ruth served up fresh bread and stewed chicken. Stacey poured milk into the cups. Caleb saw Montgomery look at his cup and frown just the slightest bit—not so everyone would notice, but enough that Caleb did. Caleb guessed the tin cup wasn't good enough for a man who was probably used to crystal. Still, the tin cups had never bothered Laura.

"What do you do in Bismarck, Mr. Montgomery?" Ruth asked when everyone had begun to eat. Even Montgomery was eating, to Caleb's surprise. But then, most everyone liked Ma's cooking.

"Insurance," came the reply.

Ruth nodded slowly in acknowledgment.

"In the past, the insurance was for small businesses that failed. My brother was running things until he decided to go off on another venture, so I've taken over with new policies for larger, more stable businesses that . . ." He shifted and appeared nervous for the first time since his arrival. His eyes darted to each of them, then he laughed, a short, snide sound. "Talking business is habit."

"Sounds like you're a busy man."

"Busy, yes . . . but I will never be too busy for Laura once she marries me."

Caleb fished around in his bowl and found a chunk of chicken. He sure wasn't hungry, but he ate anyway and tried to act as he normally would. Stacey tore apart a piece of bread and looked at him, her lips pursed, her eyes like thunderclouds about to burst. Caleb knew what she was thinking: "Are you just going to keep sitting there, not saying anything?"

"Do you . . . have you set a date yet?" Ruth asked, still

figuring Laura meant to marry Montgomery. Caleb hadn't told her anything different. He wished she'd stop with her infernal conversational questions. Hospitality was one thing, talking about things like that when she'd at least guessed he cared for Laura was another.

"We were supposed to have been married in April," Laura said softly. "But when Pa died in February, I didn't think getting married so soon after his death would be right, so we put the date off."

"*You* put the date off," Montgomery corrected in his smooth way. He looked straight at Laura, trying to intimidate her again, Caleb thought. He knew from his own experience that Laura wasn't easily intimidated, but her usual defiance had faltered long ago under Montgomery's hard stares. "Laura and I have known each other for years. People in Bismarck have always expected us to marry. No one would have been offended if we had gone ahead with our plans."

"It would have been disrespectful, Adrian," Laura responded.

"You must get over those feelings, Laura. Your pa wanted us to marry, you know that." Montgomery sat back in his chair, his cool gaze shifting to each person at the table in turn. "Laura has had a difficult time dealing with her pa's death. I'm certain the coach accident she was involved in has not helped matters any. Then she ended up here. How did you manage that anyway, Laura? The men who brought the bodies of Mr. and Mrs. Trumball and the driver back to Bismarck said the accident was south of here, near some hills."

Laura opened her mouth to respond, but Caleb jumped in: "I found her in the hills and brought her here." He was tired of Montgomery talking to Laura as if she were a child and couldn't make decisions for herself. He understood Laura had had trouble saying no to the man in the past, but now . . . he wanted to shake her. He wanted her to spit fire at the man as she'd spit fire at him so many times. If *he'd* been the one talking to her like that . . . course, he'd never talk to her like that.

Montgomery's gray eyes shifted to him, assessing him again. The room was quiet except for the occasional clink of

forks on plates. Wheels were turning in the man's head—
small nerves around his eyes jerked now and then. Was he
connecting Laura and Caleb? Was he suspecting they'd been
together?

To hell with the man, Caleb thought. *Let him suspect.*

�֍ �֍ ✷
Chapter Fifteen

"I SEE," MONTGOMERY said finally in response to Caleb's explanation that he'd rescued Laura. "And how long did the journey here take?"

"A day," Caleb said.

"Did it not occur to you to take her to a closer place, Mr. Main?"

The man's sharp tone irritated Caleb even more. "Got a closer place in mind out here on the prairie, Mr. Montgomery?" he said, unable to keep the hard edge from his own voice.

Laura jumped in. "There was no other place, Adrian. Caleb did what he could."

Montgomery's gaze went to Laura. "Caleb, is it? You've always been one to conduct yourself in a proper, ladylike way, Laura. That's something your pa and I always found becoming in you."

"She was hurt besides," Stacey snapped. Laura might not be spitting fire at Montgomery, but Caleb saw fire in Stacey's eyes and knew she was about to give Montgomery a setdown. "Caleb couldn't take her anywhere else. Can't very well drag a hurt person miles and miles." Caleb narrowed his eyes at Stacey. She went back to tearing her bread in little pieces.

"And *did* you travel while you were hurt, Laura?" Montgomery asked. "Did you and Mr. Main begin traveling as soon as he found you?"

"We stayed near the hills for a day or so until I had the strength to travel," she answered, lifting her chin in the slightest show of defiance. Something had bent inside her. Finally, thought Caleb. Finally. Maybe she'd tired of Montgomery trying to intimidate her. Caleb watched her closely, trying to measure just how much Montgomery had riled her temper. *Give the man a little of the hell you always give me.*

Montgomery had lifted a brow. "I see. Several days . . ."

"Exactly what are you implying, Adrian?" Laura demanded softly.

He studied her for a time, then shook his head. "Nothing, Laura. Nothing at all."

"I'm glad. Because I wouldn't be alive right now if Mr. Main hadn't pulled me from that wreck."

"You have my deepest thanks, Mr. Main," Montgomery said. But Caleb heard sarcasm in his voice and knew the thanks had taken a lot of effort to impart.

Caleb finished his stew out of respect for Ma and held his tongue out of respect for Laura. She was beginning to show some of the temper he knew was in there somewhere. Maybe she'd do all right where Montgomery was concerned.

Caleb excused himself from the table. He put his bowl and cup beside the washbasin, then went outside and busied himself in the shed, pounding some old nails back into shape. The work made him feel better. Taking his frustration out on the nails was a damn sight better than taking it out on the man inside the house right now.

A while later he paused and leaned over the workbench, bracing himself with his forearms. There was always the chance Montgomery might convince Laura she should return to Bismarck and marry him. Earlier Caleb had felt the whole decision should be Laura's. He'd still like to see her muster strength and say no to Montgomery, but he reckoned he had a little of his own influence over Laura that Montgomery didn't have. Laura damn sure hadn't looked at Montgomery the way she'd look at him so often in the past. And she'd never given herself to Montgomery; Caleb had been her first. That proved something. She loved him.

And because he loved her, he wasn't about to let her be talked into marrying that man simply because there had been an earlier arrangement. Even if she lost her temper with him for interfering, he reckoned that was just a chance he'd have to take. Even if she walked away from him and refused to marry *him*, she'd still be better off married to no one than married to Adrian Montgomery.

He pounded the nails more, glad he'd come to a few decisions in his own mind.

"Where is her mother?" Adrian asked, looking down at Amanda. She sat on the floor near the settee, turning the quilt blocks over in her hands and looking at the different patterns on the material.

"The family lives a few miles from here," Laura said. She didn't like to talk about Amanda in the child's presence. Amanda might have some physical problems, but Laura suspected she had intelligence no one had ever discovered and that she understood more than people thought.

"Why is she here?" Adrian asked.

"I'll help Ruth and Stacey clean up, then we'll go outside and talk," Laura said. "Amanda can stay inside with Stacey."

She went to help clear the table of dishes. Adrian gave her an odd look when she picked up a cloth and began drying dishes after Stacey washed them in the basin. She and Stacey worked in silence, forgoing the conversation they usually had whenever they did various chores together. Ruth took another cloth and wiped the table, then gathered a jug of cream to make the day's butter. She, too, was silent.

While drying the dishes, Laura didn't look to see if Adrian had sat on the settee. She was more than a little irritated with him. She didn't like the way he had been treating the Mains. What she thought of as the pleasant simplicity of this house and the people living in it, he obviously viewed with great distaste. She had not missed his scrutiny of the tin cups they had drank from at dinner. When he first walked into the house, she also hadn't missed his scrutiny of her dress—the one Stacey had spent so much time and love making for her. She cherished it, but Adrian obviously found it too simple. Doubtless, he was greatly annoyed that she was helping Stacey with dishes right now, too. But Laura didn't care.

At one time a gentle reprimand or admonishing look from Adrian would have made her hang her head. But she had begun to lift her head after returning from school and sensing the change in his feelings toward her. She had defied him entirely when she'd told him she was going to Kenmare for the summer. This afternoon her temper had flared when Adrian had provoked Caleb with questions about the accident and the journey, and she had not wavered.

She never would again.

Thoughts of Pa's death still made her chest constrict with pain, and doubtless would for a long time, but she felt stronger inside than she ever had. She had lived under Pa and Adrian's subtle rule for so long that now she felt like a butterfly emerging from a cocoon. The strength spreading through her felt wonderful.

When she and Stacey had finished the dishes, Laura asked her friend, "Would you stay with Amanda for a while?" Stacey nodded, avoiding Laura's gaze. Laura touched Stacey's shoulder. "I'm not going anywhere."

"Maybe not for now."

"When I do return to Bismarck, I don't intend to stay. I need to sort through some of Pa's things and make certain his business matters are being taken care of. Then I'll be back. I'm not going to marry Adrian. I'm going to marry Caleb." Laura said the last slowly to emphasize it.

Stacey's pretty black lashes shot up, and she studied Laura, trying to decide if Laura was serious. She'd sat through supper and had watched Laura shrink under Adrian Montgomery's words. She could hardly believe Laura had made a solid decision, but the proof was there, shimmering in Laura's eyes. Stacey caught Laura in her arms, and Laura returned the embrace. "Go on now," Stacey choked out. "I'll take care of Amanda."

Laura nodded. They separated, Stacey going to sit beside Amanda on the floor and Laura going to the door. As Laura had suspected, Adrian hadn't sat on the settee and made himself comfortable. He stood near the fireplace, looking out a window and rubbing his chin. He probably thought he couldn't possibly make himself comfortable in this farmhouse. Laura had a perfect view of his profile. He was handsome—she would never deny that. His fine blond hair and strong features made him seem almost godlike. His eyes were beautiful, truly they were, and his clothes were elegant. But beneath the refined man, beneath the clothes and handsome face, was a man deeply concerned with only himself. He didn't love her. He didn't even respect her. He didn't care what she wanted, didn't want her happiness even. He wanted only his. She didn't want to be admonished. She didn't want to be treated like a little girl. She didn't want to be ordered about. She didn't want to be *controlled.*

And most of all, she didn't want to marry a man who loved her money more than her. She would marry Caleb, who loved *her.*

Adrian must have felt her gaze; he turned and met it. She motioned to him to join her outside, and he moved across the room to the doorway, then they went outside.

The left side of the porch ended near the shed. Ruth sat there on a little stool, a butter churn in front of her. Laura stepped from the porch and walked toward the open prairie. She didn't know where Caleb was, but she knew she stood less of a chance of him overhearing her and Adrian's conversation if she led Adrian out a ways. Adrian would be angry when she told him what she needed to tell him. And after seeing the anger in Caleb's eyes earlier, when Adrian had pressed her for answers about the accident and the time she had spent in the hills and traveling with Caleb, she didn't want Caleb to hear Adrian raise his voice to her.

"You usually wear your hair in a more elegant fashion," Adrian said as they walked.

Laura breathed the summer-scented prairie air and admired the blue and purple wildflowers scattered just beyond the barn. Farther out, tall sunflowers waved enchantingly with the sweep of tall prairie grass. "Look around you, Adrian. We're not at a ball or a supper party. We're on a farm on the prairie. There's no need to be elegant."

"I'm sure you will be relieved to return to your normal life in Bismarck."

"To the contrary. Life there would seem foreign to me after the time I've spent here."

He caught her hand. She freed it. "Laura, you cannot be serious. You cannot expect me to move to this dreary little

place. My business is in Bismarck, and soon I will have it
built back to what it once was. The house there is perfect for
us. Our position in Bismarck will be—"

"You don't understand, do you, Adrian? I don't care about
position anymore. I'm not sure I ever did," she said, smiling
sadly. She pitied him. He was a man caught up in appear-
ances. Position meant more to him than anything. "What is
there when position is stripped away?" she asked softly.
"What if I weren't Matthew Kent's daughter, Adrian? What
if I hadn't inherited his money? Would you want to marry
me then?"

"Of course I would."

She shook her head. "You answered too quickly, as if you
simply need to give me the answer you think I want to hear."

He stared at her. A breeze swished through the prairie
grass, brushing it against Laura's skirt. The day was hot, but
cool air tempered the heat of the sun. Off to the west, clouds
were gathering. Another storm. Well, at least she, the
Mains, and Amanda were all within range of shelter this
time. There would be no getting pounded with hail. There
would be no runaway horses and a teetering wagon. Laura
shuddered, remembering. Despite the terrifying memory,
she loved this place. She loved the prairie and the people
who lived and worked on it. She loved the farm behind her. It
was home.

Home.

She couldn't remember the precise moment she had begun to think of the farm and the prairie as home, although
she knew she had for some time now. Her heart swelled with
love as she gazed back at the white house, the red barn, shed,
and chicken house.

"What exactly are you saying, Laura?" Adrian demanded.

"That you need money, not me. Unfortunately you
thought the quickest way to get that money was to marry
me."

"I would marry you if you hadn't inherited your pa's
money!"

"Yes, you would. You would marry me because Pa probably promised you money and that part of the agreement

would still stand, despite his death. Such businessmen the two of you were. You probably even put your heads together and drew up some sort of legal paper."

"Do not be foolish, Laura. Every woman of your position has a dowry, if that is what you are wondering about."

"But Pa made mine a bit more appealing than most, I suspect. He picked you for me when I was still a babe. He was such a dominating man—never cruel, never harsh—but dominating in little ways. I never dreamed of saying no when both of you pressed me to become engaged to you. I was worried about what people would think about such a hurried engagement and marriage, but that's far different from arguing the point. I was Pa's only child. He was content with a daughter, but he often mentioned grandsons. And you . . . perhaps you did once love me, Adrian. Perhaps you did, but somewhere along the way you lost sight of me and fell in love with the money."

He didn't respond. They reached a cluster of scraggly trees, and Laura leaned back against one, her heart already feeling lighter. Her head was clearer than it had been in months, and that was a wonderful feeling. She smiled.

Adrian took her hands in his and looked deeply into her eyes. "Laura, you have been away too long. You're not yourself. You're not thinking right. You have never washed dishes or worn a dress like this," he said, his eyes sweeping distastefully over the calico. The goldenrods and black-eyed Susans on the material seemed suited to the prairie and herself. They were wild and free. "Come back to Bismarck with me, Laura. Your gowns are in the wardrobe. The servants are there."

"I don't want to go back."

"We will not marry right away, if that's the way you want it. I will prove to you that I do not want only your money. I want *you*. When I received your telegraph, you do not know how relieved—"

Frowning, she pulled her hands from his. "You received my telegraph? You said you didn't."

Alarm flashed in his eyes. "Laura, you belong in Bismarck, not here. We will go to the house and collect your things. Once you are back in Bismarck and settled again, you will thank me."

"Why did you lie about the telegram?"

He studied her, then blurted, "Because you seemed to have your mind set on staying with that—that decrepit child!"

Laura tensed. "Amanda is not the only reason I don't want to go back."

Adrian skimmed his fingertips up her arm to her shoulder. Then his fingertips pressed into the back of her neck, trying to draw her close to him. "If you want children, I will give you children, Laura," he said thickly.

She lifted a brow. "But you once complained that I was as cold as a winter wind."

A cool, brooding rage passed over his face. A prickle of apprehension eased up Laura's spine.

"You weren't listening. I'm not going back to Bismarck yet, and Amanda is certainly not the only reason I want to stay here. When I do return to Bismarck, I don't intend to marry you. I'll look through Pa's things, take what I want to keep, and sell the house."

With that, she moved away from him and started back toward the house.

She heard his boots brushing through the prairie grass. Then his low voice came from behind her. "If you find me so repulsive, we will sleep in separate bedrooms, Laura. I'll visit your room only as much as necessary to ensure that you conceive. Your pa wanted us to marry, Laura. He wanted grandchildren, and I promised he would get them."

A shiver raced through Laura. She stopped cold and crossed her arms to hug herself. She didn't want to believe what she was thinking. But then, she hadn't wanted to believe Adrian had wanted to marry her only for her money, either, or that Pa had undoubtedly offered Adrian more than what would have normally been included in her dowry.

She turned around and faced Adrian. "Was that part of the agreement? That if I conceived you would get even *more* money? Sort of like a trust?"

Adrian stared at her.

"Answer me," she demanded, trembling. In her heart she already knew the truth, and it was killing her. Pa had loved her so much, yet he had sold her like a piece of property and had made the sale even more appealing by offering Adrian more money if she conceived. Damn Pa's business mind! And damn Adrian for accepting the offer.

"Actually there would have been additional money for every male child produced," Adrian said, as if to drive an invisible blade deeper into her heart.

Laura swallowed hard and fought tears. She and Pa had loved each other so . . . how could he have made Adrian such an offer? The two people she had trusted the most had wounded her deeply. "My," she managed. "You would hardly have slept a night in your room, except during times when I was swollen with child. Your services would have been far too valuable to allow such a thing."

She turned away from him and started for the house again. The shed where Caleb had gone was ahead, and Ruth had disappeared. Laura kept walking, hoping Adrian would simply realize he had lost his hold on her and ride away.

She was a distance of about five feet from the shed when he grabbed her arm and spun her around, the fury in his eyes now unleashed. In all the years she had known him, he had never laid a violent hand on her. Laura's eyes widened with fright.

"Damn you, Laura," he hissed, his fingers digging into her flesh. "I waited years for you. I gave up a lot to have you. When you were away at school that last year, I met and fell in love with someone else! Your pa found out and had the nerve to *reprimand* me. I told him I was going to marry the woman. He offered me money to marry you. Of course, he had to make the offer look very good to convince me. So if you're going to blame someone, Laura, blame him!"

"Adrian, let go. I never said I blamed you entirely," Laura said breathlessly. He was mad. She could see the madness rolling in his eyes, could feel it in his hot breath, in the pounding of his heart as he jerked her against him.

"We could make this work, Laura. Why do you find me so repulsive? Why?"

She struggled to free herself, pushing against him with her other hand and twisting her captured arm. "Let go of me. Adrian, you're hurting me. Let . . . *go!*"

From the corner of her eye, she saw Caleb tear out of the shed. *Dear God,* she thought, *don't let him hurt Adrian too badly.* Only enough to scare him away. She didn't want him to hang for killing Adrian.

Caleb grabbed Adrian, wrenched him away from Laura, and tossed him aside. He landed beside the porch. His head snapped back, thunking against a board. His eyes rolled, then his head and body slumped. Laura put a hand over her mouth to stifle a scream.

Caleb walked over to where Adrian lay and bent down to feel for a pulse. "Go in the house, Laura," he said.

She was frozen. "I . . . is he . . ."

"No. Just out for a while. Go on inside and sit down."

Ruth and Stacey had come outside. Both were frozen on the porch in silence. Stacey stared in horror at Adrian, then Laura and Caleb. Ruth overcame her shock and flew down the porch steps. "Dear Lord, Caleb, what have you done!"

"It's not as bad as it looks, Ma. He grabbed Laura and wouldn't—"

"I don't want to hear about it," she snapped. "All I know is that we have a half-dead man on our property because of you. Help me get him inside."

"He's not going to like our hospitality after what just happened."

"Caleb Main, remember your manners, if you even have any left. Grab his shoulders. I'll get his feet."

Caleb shook his head but did as Ruth asked. "Just hope I don't have to do it again when he wakes up," he said.

Ruth glared at him.

❋❋❋
Chapter Sixteen

MONTGOMERY WASN'T OUT long. He started stirring almost as soon as Caleb hoisted him over his shoulder. Caleb hadn't meant to toss him against the porch—Montgomery had just sort of flown in that direction. All Caleb had been thinking about at the time was getting Montgomery away from Laura.

Caleb had finished hammering the nails back into shape and had been sharpening a knife when he'd heard Laura tell Montgomery to let her go. When Laura had said it a second time, Caleb had heard panic in her voice. He had dropped the knife and gone to the shed door. From there he'd seen Montgomery's tight grip on Laura and the fear in her eyes. Beyond that, Caleb knew he hadn't really been thinking; he'd known Laura was in danger and he'd reacted.

Ruth and Stacey went into the house ahead of Caleb. Laura followed. He wondered if she was angry with him for grabbing Montgomery the way he had. Even if she was angry, he knew he'd do it again if the need arose. He was glad he'd been in the shed. Otherwise, he might not have heard Laura's cries.

Ma twisted her apron, worry wrinkling her brow. Years ago, when Caleb had taken all the money they had saved and handed it to Matt Kent, he'd caused Ma and Stacey some hard years. He would always blame himself for putting many of the lines on his mother's face. She was nearing sixty and looked older than her years. Her mouth was turned down in a frown, and she was pale. The wrinkles around her eyes deepened as she studied Montgomery, trying to measure just how hurt he was.

She stepped back and snatched a quilt from the back of the rocking chair in the sewing corner, a quilt she'd pieced together last year from different scraps of material—dull red, bright blue, and faded pink with little purple flowers. She folded it in a rectangle and propped it near one end of the settee. "Put him here," she told Caleb as she moved aside. "Stacey, go get some water and a cloth."

Stacey sprang into action, moving across the room to the washbasin. Caleb lowered Montgomery onto the settee. Montgomery groaned and tossed his head. He'd have a hell of a headache when he came around all the way, Caleb figured, frowning as he noticed the small trail of blood trickling down the left side of Adrian's head.

"Just get back now," Ma said, irritation and concern edging her voice.

Caleb stepped back and let her bend beside the settee and fuss over Montgomery. "Ma, I only meant to pull him away from Laura. I didn't mean to hurt him."

She sighed. "You're stronger than you know sometimes, Caleb."

Laura stood near the fireplace, arms folded, hands clutching her shoulders. Fear leapt in her wide blue eyes, but Caleb didn't see anger and he was glad. Surely she realized Montgomery, as angry as he'd been, might have hurt her if Caleb hadn't reacted.

Stacey brought her mother a small bowl of water and a cloth, and Ruth washed the trickle of blood from the side of Montgomery's head. There was a long scrape where the trickle had been, and that's all it was—just a scrape. A nail or a rough piece of wood must have caught him on the side of the head as he'd slid down.

Relieved a bit and figuring there wasn't much more he could do here right now, Caleb thought about going outside and leaving Stacey and Ma to take care of Montgomery. But what if he came around soon, saw where he was, and flew off in another bad temper? Caleb decided to stay in the house for now, at least until he was sure Montgomery wasn't going to do anything crazy.

While Ma and Stacey fussed over Montgomery, Caleb drifted to the table and settled himself in one of the chairs he'd carved and pieced together a few years ago.

* * *

As she watched Ruth hover over Adrian, Laura glanced at Caleb and wondered what he was thinking. He was seated at the table, fingering a piece of straw that had worked its way loose from one edge of the egg-gathering basket. Was he thinking that he shouldn't have laid a hand on Adrian? That he should have tried to talk to him instead? She hoped not. She had seen the wild look in Adrian's eyes and had known words wouldn't reach him. Caleb had been forced to do something more drastic, and he shouldn't be feeling guilty. She didn't think he had meant to throw Adrian against the house and deliberately hurt him. He had only wanted to get Adrian away from her.

Since Ruth and Stacey were caring for Adrian, Laura approached the table . . . and Caleb. He looked up as she slid onto the chair next to him. She read concern in his eyes.

"It's all right," she said. "I know you didn't mean to hurt him. Besides, he wouldn't have let me go if you hadn't grabbed him."

Caleb nodded slightly. Laura reached for his hand, covering it with hers.

Adrian stirred more.

Laura heard him grumble something, but she stayed at the table. She was still angry and shocked by what he had revealed during their conversation—that not only had Pa offered him more money than would normally have been included in her dowry, but Pa had set up a provision for Adrian for every male child she and Adrian might produce. Grandsons . . . Pa had wanted grandsons. No matter that they wouldn't carry the Kent name, they would still be males. He hadn't had a son, so he had wanted grandsons. Thoughts of *her* feelings—thoughts of her *happiness*—had obviously not entered his business discussion with Adrian.

First she had learned how Pa had cheated Caleb—and others. Now this.

Adrian groaned, and Laura's attention was drawn to him. He was so different from the man who had once loved her. That man had been considerate, even affectionate at times. He wasn't like that anymore. He was greedy, ambitious, and hungry for power. He was bitter, and he was a stranger to her. Why hadn't she realized that right after returning from school?

She probably hadn't had the strength to acknowledge the truth. She had been frightened of the change in him and had wanted to believe life in Bismarck would pick up right where she had left it before she had gone away for the final year of school. She had wanted to believe . . . well, it didn't matter any longer, did it? It simply didn't matter. She was thankful her life had taken a different direction, that she had found strength, and that she wasn't trapped in a cold marriage to Adrian.

She pitied him. He had allowed Pa to entice him from the woman he really loved. Adrian had lied about the telegraph, but she felt certain he had not lied about falling in love with someone else. That explained his coolness, his anger, his bitterness toward her. Money had so easily led him away from happiness. He hadn't realized that a person needed other things, more fulfilling things. She knew what loving someone was like, and no amount of money would ever tempt her to leave Caleb's side and marry someone else.

"Damn you! Get that away from me!" Adrian blurted, swiping at Ruth's hand.

Ruth stepped back.

Caleb rose and slowly walked over and stood near the settee. Perhaps he wanted to stay within Adrian's line of vision as a silent warning? Laura watched Adrian, hoping he wouldn't do anything else foolish. Caleb had torn Adrian away from her and tossed him aside as easily as she might toss Amanda's rag doll. Surely Adrian would remember that and not think to cause trouble again.

"I should have the sheriff come after you, Main," Adrian growled, glaring at Caleb and pressing a hand to the injured side of his head.

"He won't be too sympathetic when I tell him what happened," Caleb responded.

"To the contrary. I imagine he will be very sympathetic when I tell him I was trying to protect Laura from you."

Laura bolted up from the chair. He was mad! Protect her

from Caleb? "What are you talking about? Caleb was trying—"

"What are you talking about, Montgomery?" Caleb demanded at nearly the same time as Laura. His eyes flashed dangerously. "You're the one Laura needed protection from."

"Laura . . ." Adrian said. "Are you aware that your pa kept diaries?"

Laura hesitated, wondering what scheme was circling in Adrian's head now. "Yes . . . but I never read them. They are part of Pa's private things. Things I haven't been able to make myself look at."

"Your pa wrote some very interesting things in his diaries, things that—"

"You read Pa's diaries?" she demanded, a chill of disbelief crawling up her spine. She moved around the table, stood with her back to it, and stared at Adrian. Pa had always kept some parts of himself very private, and his diaries had definitely been private. As his daughter and only heir, she was the only person who had a right to them. Adrian's or anyone else's perusal would be a horrible invasion of privacy. And how could he have gotten them? He had to have found the key to Pa's desk before he could have read the diaries.

"The diaries are in his desk in the sitting room, Laura," Adrian said.

"I know that. His desk was locked when I left," she said icily. "He always kept it locked. He kept the key in his bedroom. You searched his room for it. How dare you."

Adrian's brow creased, and his jaw shot up, as if . . . as if he felt he had had every right to go into Pa's bedroom, find that key and rummage through Pa's desk—as if she had no right to object.

"You asked me to manage things for a time, Laura. Don't you remember?" he asked. His tone now contained an intimidating, annoying edge. Laura had heard it many times over the years, but she never realized *why* he used it. Now she knew. He was trying to make her feel foolish, as if she had

lost her memory or was going mad. Well, she wouldn't let
him intimidate her anymore.

Anger surged through her, stripping every nerve in her
body raw, and she stepped closer to the settee. She was
aware of Stacey and Ruth backing away as if to give her
room. Caleb stood motionless near the fireplace, watching
her. Amanda had crawled into the rocking chair in the sewing corner. Laura knew she ought to save everything she had
to say until a time when she could speak privately with
Adrian. But she had tried to do so already, hadn't she? And
he had nearly hurt her. No . . . she would rather say the things
that needed to be said right now, spill them and be done with
it, send him away and be done with him.

"I asked you to manage things, yes, but what right did you
have to go into the house and go through Pa's bedroom or
through his private papers in that desk?" she demanded. "*No
right.* The things in his desk there have nothing to do with
his business matters. His business papers are either in his office or with Mr. Trumball's associate. I realize you know the
servants so well that all you had to do was say I had asked
you to look at things and they let you in . . . but that is my
house, and I don't want you in it anymore."

Adrian laughed in disbelief. "Laura . . . listen to yourself!
You're treating me like a stranger, after all the years we
spent together. I was always permitted simply to walk into
the house. You remember that, surely. Your pa wouldn't
want—"

"It's my house now, and you're not welcome there anymore. And don't speak to me in that tone ever again,
Adrian," she said, easing closer. "I'm no longer a little fool
being guided blindlessly about by you."

"I have never treated you like a fool, Laura," he said,
wincing. "I have always treated you with respect. But you
are acting like a fool right now, going on about the desk
and—"

"*Stop.* In one breath you speak of respect. In the next
breath you call me a fool. You never treated me with respect.
When I told you I didn't want to get married so soon after
finishing school, you passed over what I wanted. At supper

one evening you told Pa I had accepted your proposal, and he looked so pleased you knew I wouldn't deny it. Where is your respect for me in that, Adrian? Perhaps we have different opinions of what respect is. But forgive me . . . I forgot . . . you once told me a woman shouldn't have many opinions. I'm tired of being what you want me to be. I'll be what I want to be."

Laura inhaled deeply, trembling with anger, feeling it spill from her, and oh, what a wonderful feeling that was! But there was more, so she hurried on: "Respect . . . respect is valuing an opinion. It's making a person feel as if she has something important to say or do. You never asked my opinion about anything—you always thought and spoke for me. Well, you won't anymore. So don't call me a fool, Adrian. I *was* a fool, but I'm not one now. And don't talk to me about respect!"

There. It was said. She was certain there was more, but this was a wonderful beginning. She felt cleansed for the moment, *exhilarated*.

Adrian studied her as if she *had* gone mad. "You're not right, Laura. I mean . . . you have spent too much time here. It has not been good for you. I'll take you back to Bismarck and—"

Laughing, she shook her head in disbelief, again pitying him. She had said so much, yet her words had flown over him. He was still trying to press his thoughts on her and make them hers. That was the one thing about him that infuriated her the most, and she would never again allow him to do it. "I don't want to go back to what I was. I won't go back to being led around by you. I'm happy here. Right here," she said. "What I want . . . is for you to leave."

His jaw dropped open. Then he clamped it shut and glanced about in confusion. Finally his eyes hardened. "You want to stay here and marry a man who is using you for revenge?" This tone was different from the intimidating one. This tone was also menacing. It sent shivers of dread through Laura because she now realized he was terribly desperate, desperate enough to use the past to try and hurt Caleb. That was why Adrian had mentioned the diaries. Pa

must have recorded the incidents that had involved him and
Caleb long ago.

Had Pa written the truth . . . or a lie? Had he at least been
honest with himself in his diaries? Laura was curious, but
she didn't want the past brought back to life in front of Ruth
and Stacey. They had suffered so much already. She didn't
want them to relive it. Besides, she couldn't be certain
Adrian would tell her the truth.

From the corner of her eye Laura saw Caleb's quick
movement toward the settee. Clearly he had heard enough
and wanted to grab Adrian again. Laura put out an arm to
block Caleb. He stopped. *Respect*, she thought, and kept herself from smiling. Adrian *and* everyone else might think she
had gone mad if she laughed during such a serious moment.
She wasn't mad; she simply felt free.

"I'll toss him again, Laura. Just say the word," Caleb
growled. She knew he didn't want the past brought to life
again in front of Ruth and Stacey either.

"No. Not yet."

"Laura . . . don't listen to him. Let me throw him on his
horse and—"

"Caleb . . . simmer down," Ruth said. She and Stacey had
moved across the room and now stood beside the rocking
chair, watching the scene with wide eyes. Amanda sat in the
sewing corner with her rag doll in her lap, dressing and undressing it; she had apparently retreated to her own little
world.

This is absurd, Laura thought, a drama being played out in
front of an audience. But she didn't want to be caught alone
with Adrian again. She had nothing more to say to him anyway, and he had nothing to say that she wanted to hear. She
could read Pa's diaries for herself when she returned to Bismarck to go through his things. She didn't want to hear about
what Adrian thought was Caleb's big plot to use her for revenge. She had considered that idea long ago. Caleb had assured her that wasn't his intent, and she believed him.

"Leave, Adrian. Leave now," Laura said wearily.

He sat up, still holding the side of his head. Doubtless he
had a terrible headache. She had heard his head thunk

against the porch and had been surprised when he had awakened so soon afterward.

"Five entire pages were devoted to Caleb Main," Adrian persisted.

The diaries . . . he was talking about the diaries again. Laura didn't want Caleb to force him from the house, but Caleb might need to. Adrian didn't seem inclined to stop revealing what he'd discovered.

"Are you aware that Mr. Main robbed your pa? That Mr. Main became very angry when he was accused? He broke into your pa's house, meaning to kill him. Somehow he managed to escape Bismarck with his neck intact, but he was a man with a grudge. Do you think he was not aware of who you were as soon as he heard your last name, Laura? Your pa was kind enough to insist that he be released, but the condition was that he should leave Bismarck. Your pa felt Mr. Main was a dan—"

"Stop it, Adrian," Laura said sharply. "Get out now."

"No, Laura. You need to hear this. Mr. Main knew who you were. When he first telegraphed Bismarck, *he telegraphed your pa.* He was not aware that your father was dead. Have you not realized that perhaps he wants to use you for revenge? Think of it. If he marries you, he gets all of the Kent money . . . all the land . . ."

"That's not why he wants me."

"Ask him. I have been honest with you today. I would like to hear him be as honest."

"You've been honest?" she said incredulously.

Laura heard a click behind her and didn't realize what it was until she heard Caleb whisper, "Ma?"

Laura twisted in time to watch Ruth bring a rifle up to her shoulders and level it at Adrian.

"Get on your feet and get out of this house, Mr. Montgomery," Ruth commanded in a low voice. "I once had to shoot a man who was trying to kill my husband, and I got him right between the eyes. Now, you just get moving. If Laura's decided to stay here, I reckon that's just what she'll do. I won't let you tell her a bunch of lies to try and get her to leave with you. Get out of our home."

At first Adrian stared at her as if he couldn't believe that the woman who had so graciously offered him the comfort of her home—when Laura, Stacey, and Caleb had only wanted him to remount and leave—now held a leveled rifle on him.

Minutes passed. Ruth kept the rifle leveled at him.

Finally Adrian shifted and stood, obviously deciding she would shoot him if he opened his mouth and said anything more. Casting a brief look back at Laura, Adrian walked slowly toward the door, and as he walked, the rifle in Ruth's hands followed him. He opened the door and walked through it. She followed him with the rifle, stopping in the doorway, but aiming the rifle at him long after the thud of his boots on the porch had died. Laura heard the thunder of hooves and knew Adrian had ridden away. She closed her eyes, took a cleansing breath, and smiled. She had stood her ground . . . and he was gone. With help from Ruth, of course.

She wondered what Ruth must be thinking. Was she reliving the years since Caleb had given Pa the money? Ruth and Stacey had barely survived that first winter in a tent outside of Bismarck. . . . Caleb had been accused of stealing money from Pa and had been arrested. . . . Ruth must have lived not knowing whether or not her son would hang. How frightened she must have been—Stacey nearly dying, and Caleb almost losing his life as well. She had as much reason to hate Pa as Caleb did, yet even after she had learned Laura was a Kent, she had spread her arms wide to welcome Laura.

Emotion engulfed Laura, rushing over her in great waves as she stood watching Ruth hold that rifle on Adrian. She wished she could erase all the hurt and terrible moments of fear Ruth must have endured during those years. But she couldn't. They *had* happened. Ruth *had* nearly lost everything to a man named Matthew Kent, a man Laura was only beginning to really know. Laura couldn't erase the memories, but she would try to spread her arms as wide for Ruth as Ruth had spread hers for her. She would try to return the love and the compassion.

Forcing her feet to move, she hurried over to stand behind Ruth.

❄❄❄
Chapter Seventeen

A FEW DAYS later Laura stood with Stacey and Amanda in Alman's Dry Goods store, trading eggs and butter for another six yards of calico decorated with tiny sunflowers. Along with the sugar and cinnamon they had requested, Mr. Alman packed a handful of the hard candy from the counter. Laura frowned playfully at him. "We have a child with us, but that doesn't mean we need candy."

"Course you don't. She does," he said, and his eyes sparkled as he looked at Amanda. Amanda was wearing her gingham dress and clutching a sturdy wooden cane Caleb had carved from a sapling only yesterday.

Caleb and Amanda had spent a great deal of time in the shed. Curious, Laura had gone out to see what they were doing and had found Amanda, her face alight with excitement, watching Caleb smooth the curved end of the cane. Laura had been touched by Caleb's loving gesture. Later, when she and Caleb had sat on the porch steps together, watching the moon and stars, she had kissed him and told him she was thrilled that he had made the cane for Amanda. Caleb had grinned sheepishly, always thinking his thoughtful acts were nothing to fuss about. But surely he knew how much the cane meant to Amanda. She had had it with her every moment since Caleb had finished it. She had even slept with it the night before.

Unable to stop the smile the memory brought to her lips, Laura shook her head at Mr. Alman. "I might be forced to start calling you the candy man if you aren't careful," she teased.

Laughing, Stacey neared the counter. "Might as well not try to stop him, Laura. Ma tried to keep him from giving me so much for a bit. It wasn't long before she realized she couldn't fight something that was meant to be. A hundred years from now Mr. Alman'll be here, handing candy to children who wander in."

Mr. Alman squinted an eye. "Think I'll live that long, do you?"

"You'll live forever."

To the tune of Mr. Alman's laughter, Laura, Stacey, and Amanda left the store. Outside, several men sat in chairs pushed up against the wall along the covered walkway. One man's head had slumped to one side, and he snored loudly. Perhaps he had been lulled to sleep by the lazy summer day and the drone of activity in the dusty street. Wagons rambled along. Horses dipped their heads, waiting patiently at hitching posts. The day was hot, Laura had to admit, and people were moving at a slower pace than usual along the walkways and back and forth across the street, weaving through wagons and around a stage pulled by six horses.

Laura, Stacey, and Amanda neared their own wagon. Stacey lowered the supplies she had carried from the store into the wagon bed and pulled a blanket over them. Laura did the same with the calico she had carried, then wiped perspiration from her brow and took Amanda's hand.

"I want to take Amanda to the schoolhouse," she said suddenly. Actually the thought had occurred to her days ago. Yesterday she had asked Amanda if she would like to go see the schoolhouse, and the girl had said yes very softly.

"Are you sure?" Stacey asked. "Children can be awful mean sometimes."

Laura nodded, as if to say she was sure, and that she understood what Stacey was trying to say without really saying it since Amanda was with them and would hear their words. She didn't need to ask in what manner Stacey felt the children would be mean. She knew. Amanda might be teased about her arm and leg that had been left paralyzed by whatever illness had afflicted her when she had been a babe. She also might be teased because she didn't speak well. What few words Laura had heard her say were usually stuttered. And how many of the schoolchildren had heard about the strange child who had roamed the prairie and sat beneath the willow every Sunday after church? Doubtless many had. Laura didn't intend to leave Amanda at the schoolhouse with the children; she merely wanted to show her what a schoolhouse looked like inside. Someday Amanda might be ready to go to school, and Laura didn't want her to feel petrified when that day arrived.

So the three of them walked toward the schoolhouse.

They found the schoolyard empty, no girls turning jump ropes beneath the many trees that provided shady spots, no boys scurrying about between the trees. Something was different—the few windows were shut tight. On such a hot day?

"I don't think anyone's here," Stacey said.

Laura walked up the steps and reached for the door handle. The door creaked open. Laura peered in.

The benches were empty. A beam of smoky sunlight beaconed across Mrs. Statum's desk where a reader lay open to a spelling page. "You're right," Laura said, baffled. "No one is here. I wonder where everyone is."

"Maybe Mrs. Statum took sick. She has a problem with her stomach from time to time."

"And there is no one in Minot who will teach on days when she is ill?" Laura asked.

"It doesn't really work that way. When she's sick, she just doesn't come to school. The children come, but after a bit they see Mrs. Statum isn't coming, so they just go home. Like Mrs. Statum said, we need a new schoolteacher. She's old and gets sick a lot," Stacey said.

Laura shut the schoolhouse door. Tightening her brow and twisting her lips, she reached a hasty decision: She could teach. She had had plenty of years of schooling, and she had taught children during her last several years at school in Chicago.

Stacey and Amanda walked down the schoolhouse steps. Laura followed. "I'll teach," she said. "Since I'll be staying in Minot, there's no reason why I shouldn't."

Stacey's eyes widened in surprise. "Would you?"

Laura nodded as they walked between the trees. Branches

brushed together overhead, and the sun fought to shine through the many leaves. It managed to scatter pieces of light on the ground in places, pieces of light that moved with the branches. "I'm certainly qualified. Pa saw to my education. He made certain I attended the finest schools."

"Caleb might be a problem," Stacey warned.

"Why do you think that?" Laura asked.

"Because I offered to teach once. He didn't want me riding back and forth to Minot every day—too dangerous, he said. He also said I was too young. Ma agreed."

Laura considered the danger part. There might be some danger, but the children needed a teacher, someone who could be there for them. That was the most important consideration. "Some of the children walk from miles away, through the terrible danger," she said, smiling. "Didn't Caleb think about that?"

Stacey returned the smile. "I don't think he did. You're right."

"If the children are braving the terrible danger, the teacher can too."

"But you're about to be Caleb's wife," Stacey said, suddenly not sounding too certain.

"And why should that make a difference?" Laura demanded.

"Because Caleb might feel that he ought to be able to tell you whether or not you should do it. He won't like it, that's all I'm saying. Yes, the children walk to school, miles sometimes, but that doesn't mean Caleb will want you to."

"I've made the decision to take the position, if Mrs. Statum is really ready to give it up. Caleb knows that for years Pa and Adrian made all my decisions for me. He knows I want to make them for myself now, and he'll respect that."

They walked on in silence, past the train depot, where a train huffed away from the little gray building. Laura didn't think she had convinced Stacey. She suspected she had argued with Caleb about taking the teaching position herself, and the argument must have been a heated one, with Ruth agreeing with Caleb in the end. If it had been Stacey against just Caleb, Stacey might have won, as she did so often when quarreling with Caleb. But with Ruth against her, too, Stacey must have felt that arguing the point further would have been fruitless.

"There'll be trouble," Stacey said.

Laura pursed her lips. "Perhaps. But the children are important, and Caleb will have to try to understand that. I'm going to take the position."

Stacey nodded, but something about the slow nod made Laura think that perhaps Stacey didn't believe a word Laura had said.

They neared Minot's Main Street, dusty and cluttered with wagons, horses, and people. They had just passed the telegraph office when Caleb appeared at Laura's side.

"And where have you been?" she asked, smiling, suspecting she knew. "No, I'll guess. Trying to take poor Mr. Cecil's snuffbox again?"

Caleb grinned a mischievous grin.

"I knew it. That man probably dreads the sight of your face."

"Don't reckon he's ever seen my face. He's always looking at his newspapers. Reckon he reads every one a hundred times or more before he gets another one," he said. He glanced from her to Stacey to Amanda, then back to her. "Where have you three been? To the schoolhouse to see Mrs. Statum? She'll be in the new school in a few weeks. I'll be making the benches. Others will be putting in windows this week. It'll be ready soon."

"Wonderful," Laura said. Caleb seemed to be in a good mood. She had never heard him talk so much at one time, except when he had told her about what had happened between him and Pa so many years ago in Bismarck. In the barn that night, his talking so much had had nothing to do with his mood. There had simply been a lot to tell her. But now, given his mood, this certainly seemed the best time to mention that she intended to take the teaching job.

He began whistling a lively tune. She took a deep breath and blurted what she had to say: "That's wonderful. A new school for the children . . . I'll go visit Mrs. Statum soon and

let her know I'm available if she needs help and that I'm
willing to take over when she's ready for me."

He stopped whistling. She kept walking. He kept walking.
His head turned toward her, and his stare was as cool as a
December wind.

Stacey quickened her steps, hurrying ahead of them, deciding to flee rather than stay for the storm she felt certain
would blow through the valley and Minot any time. Laura
felt the storm brewing and didn't blame Stacey, who had
guessed right. Caleb hadn't said a word, yet Laura already
knew how strongly he opposed her taking the position; his
coolness revealed the way he felt.

But Laura wanted to take the job. The children of Minot
needed a teacher, and she meant to teach them. Even Caleb
couldn't sway her from her decision. She hoped he wouldn't
try. She had told him how she had lived under Pa and Adrian's subtle rule. He wouldn't expect her to live under his
simply because they were going to be married, would he?
Marriage would never work like that between her and Caleb.
He had stirred something within her from the moment she
had met him—a rebellious spirit that had been subdued for
too long.

"Caleb, the children need a teacher," she said. "Try and
understand."

"Didn't know you were available for the job, Laura," he
said in a low voice, still watching her with that stormy expression. "Didn't know you even wanted to teach."

"When Stacey and I went to the school and found it
empty, I decided I was available. The first time I met Mrs.
Statum, she indicated she wanted a new teacher found soon
because she didn't intend to teach for long. Stacey said Mrs.
Statum had stomach problems, and perhaps that's why no
one is at school today. I've already made the decision to stay
and marry you, and I'm certainly qualified to teach the children of Minot. So . . . I see no reason why I shouldn't take
the job," she said breathlessly after rushing to explain.

They walked a little farther. Up ahead, wagons eased
along the dirt street, stirring up dust. Horses tossed their
heads and tails. People clustered in the street and on the

walkways. The sun beat down. Laura wiped perspiration from her brow.

"Maybe I'm a reason, Laura. Did you think about me? Did you think about asking me?" Caleb said.

"Why would I need to ask you, Caleb?" she countered. Amanda was still walking at her side. She sensed the change in Amanda's pace and knew the child must be tiring, so she slowed her steps. Caleb slowed his, too, to stay in step with her.

"You're going to be my wife soon, that's why."

"I don't see why that should make a difference."

"I want you with me at the farm, Laura."

"And I want to teach the children, Caleb. They need me."

He quieted. She heard his soft breathing and the brush of his boots on the dirt. Amanda took Laura's hand, gripping it tightly as if she knew something wasn't quite right between Caleb and Laura. At first Laura wondered if her imagination was playing tricks on her, but she quickly decided it wasn't. Amanda was more sensitive than most children; she would know if something was wrong between two people she loved.

Then Laura felt guilty. Perhaps she should have at least *consulted* Caleb. Perhaps she should have approached the subject more tactfully and not simply blurted her intentions the way she had. Perhaps she owed him an apology. Perhaps she should at least listen to what he had to say. He was certainly being gentle enough. He wasn't trying to order her about.

"All right. I'm sorry," she said, sighing. "I should have discussed this with you. I still want to take the position, but if there are other reasons why you don't want me to, I'll listen and consider what you have to say."

"That doesn't mean you'll change your mind."

"No, it doesn't. I'll listen. And I'll think. But if I don't feel you have a good reason, I'll still take the position."

He sighed heavily. "Then I reckon there's no sense in me wasting words. You're not going to change your mind."

"Perhaps I will if I hear a good reason why I should," she said again.

"I don't see it that way. I know your stubbornness, Laura."

With that, he quickened his steps and caught up with Stacey. Clearly he considered the subject closed. Laura watched his back, and her gaze was so heated that she figured he must feel it.

Stubbornness? *Stubbornness?* He was just as stubborn as she! Laura knew she had two choices: Either she could take the position and hope that by doing so she wouldn't threaten her and Caleb's relationship, or she could not take the position and always wish that she had. She knew if she didn't take it, she would always wonder if the children of Minot were getting their schooling. Caleb wanted her at the farm so they could be together, not necessarily because she was needed there to help with various chores. Ruth and Stacey would be there. If help *was* needed, she could do some evening chores. Besides, what about the long days when Caleb took cattle into Minot to be sold? What about the times when farm work kept him occupied for so long that he didn't have a moment to even glance at her? He was being unfair.

By the time Caleb and Stacey reached the wagon, Laura had considered and discarded a few other reasons Caleb might use to argue why she shouldn't take the teaching position: Perhaps she would be tired in the evenings, too tired to help and talk and be with him later. But she didn't believe she would be. After spending all day away from everyone, she would be excited to see them, especially Caleb. She would be with him every evening. She would sit with him on the porch and watch the prairie sunsets. She would be with him at night, too, in their bed.

What if she found herself with child—a thought that excited her—and she couldn't travel to school every day during and after her pregnancy? If that happened, perhaps Stacey could teach until Laura was able to work again.

Caleb lifted Stacey and Amanda into the wagon bed. When he lifted Laura, she tried to catch his eye and couldn't. He was angry, very angry. She could already feel the strain her decision had put on their relationship, and she regretted that. But she was angry, too. She was needed at the school. She wanted to help. Besides, she and Caleb had worked through bigger problems; surely they could settle this, too. She would try to talk to him again later.

As the wagon started through town, Amanda sat next to Laura, sucking on a piece of the hard candy Mr. Alman had given her. It was ribbon candy, red with white stripes, and the red splotched Amanda's hands. Laura smiled at the sight. Amanda was very slowly becoming more like an average child. Laura was always relieved when she noticed some small improvement, almost as a new mother watched her infant grow and change, she thought.

Laura and Stacey waved at people they knew. Laura looked up just as the wagon passed Warner's Mercantile and caught sight of a familiar face.

Adrian.

He was still in Minot, walking down the walkway. Her eyes followed him past Warner's and past two saloons. Why hadn't he returned to Bismarck yet? Was he planning to cause more trouble? He certainly hadn't been near the Main farm in recent days, or she would have known about it. Minot was too plain a town to suit Adrian's tastes, so she couldn't imagine him staying because he liked the way of life here.

So why was he still in Minot?

❀ ❀ ❀
Chapter Eighteen

CALEB STOPPED IN the plum grove on the way out of the valley. Laura heard the distant chugging of a train and turned, looking back down into the lower part of the valley in time to see a huge engine and a line of rail cars ease to a stop at the Minot depot—so soon after the other train had left. But then the town had grown a bit since Laura first arrived. There were more hastily erected houses nestled along the outskirts of town, more tents, and more businesses along Main Street. She had heard that railroad towns sometimes sprang up overnight, but seeing such growth in only a few weeks was amazing. From what Stacey had told her about Minot, Laura knew the town had been nothing more than a few buildings before the railroad had come through last year. That was difficult to imagine.

Stacey and Amanda went to a nearby tree to pick plums. Laura drifted off some distance and reached up to pluck a fat plum but found she was inches short of reaching it. Suddenly, from behind, strong hands clutched her waist and lifted her so she could reach it.

At first she was shocked. Then she quickly realized the hands belonged to Caleb, and she picked the plum. He gently lowered her, and she twisted in his arms before he had a chance to release her and withdraw. Despite being angry with him about the way he had dropped the argument about the teaching position and walked away, she loved being so close to him.

The smells of leather and horses and the molasses candy he bought and ate every time they went to Minot swirled around her. She smelled the earth on him and his own heady scent. Slight perspiration . . . muskiness . . . Caleb. She

253

found herself spellbound by his dark, intense eyes. Her breath caught in her throat. Her heart pounded erratically. Her gaze fastened on his lips.

She hadn't meant for *this* to happen. She had only wanted to stop him from walking away again. She wanted to talk to him more about . . . about what? About the teaching position—and about the fact that she had seen Adrian in Minot! She shook her head. She could hardly think, much less think *clearly*. All she wanted to do was press her lips and body to Caleb's, touch him and feel his exquisite touch.

She should have known this would happen. Too many times in the past when she neared Caleb, her body had reacted automatically. While she loved being this close to him, she also needed to talk to him. And she couldn't seem to do that, in a reasonable way, without putting distance between them.

She tried to push away from him.

Caleb slid his arms around her waist and pulled her to him. Laura gasped as their hips touched. The coolness she had seen in his eyes during the discussion about the teaching position had fled. His eyes danced and sparkled now.

"Fighting me again, Laura?" he said, and his voice was low and husky.

She narrowed her eyes. "You're being a beast again. I don't know what you mean," she said, pretending innocence.

"Your mind's struggling, that's what I mean. I see it in your eyes."

She battled the smile that wanted to form, and lost. "I won't begin to tell you what I see in *your* eyes."

He chuckled.

"It seems you know me too well, Mr. Main. But Stacey and Amanda are close by and—"

"They wandered off a bit. I made sure of that."

"How?" she asked in surprise.

"When I lifted Stacey out of the wagon, I whispered we'd have Charles over for supper one evening and I'd keep my nose and questions to myself if—"

"If she took Amanda and disappeared for a little while. You are a beast."

Caleb's grin widened. He caressed her waist, then eased his hands around and stroked her buttocks. Laura caught her breath as slivers of delight assaulted her body. She felt him . . . felt his hard length wanting her, seeking her, and she wanted him. But they couldn't . . . not here . . . not now . . .

"Caleb, no. What if they come back?" she managed between quick breaths.

He buried his face in the side of her neck and groaned. "Soon. Soon . . . we'll have to have another barn meeting or something."

She laughed, but her laughter mellowed as she remembered their last barn meeting, reliving every glorious moment of it. How easily they had joined and moved together, as if made for each other. The lantern flame had flickered and danced and the saddle blankets had felt slightly scratchy beneath her. Beneath the saddle blanket the dry hay had crackled, and in nearby stalls, horses had stirred. Caleb's hands had wandered over her, touching every part of her.

"It was wonderful," she whispered, recalling so much, even the shudder of the barn doors as a breeze had whistled through the cracks. She had been aware of everything. But most of all, she had been aware of being held in Caleb's enchanting spell.

"I love you, Laura," he rasped now. "I can't wait till you're my wife and you're in my bed every night."

She stroked his baby-soft hair and said truthfully, "Neither can I."

His lips trailed kisses up one side of her sensitive neck, burning her skin with pleasure. His tongue traced her jaw. Then his lips found hers, and they drank of each other. Laura slid her palms up over his chest. She loved him beyond belief—she wanted him beyond belief.

She caressed his shoulders, felt every tiny movement of the muscles there, and pressed herself against him. Her tongue found his and darted and explored in an instinctive way.

Though she had been the one reluctant to pursue their passion with Stacey and Amanda wandering somewhere nearby, Caleb was the one who broke the embrace and withdrew. Disoriented, Laura was left staring at him, scarcely able to catch her breath. She noticed that the fruit she had picked had slipped from her hand while they had been kissing. How long had they been standing here? Seconds? Moments? She didn't know. Time always slipped away when her body was afire with desire for Caleb.

He bent to retrieve the plum. He brushed it off and handed it to her, grinning devilishly. "Believe you were holding this."

"Yes . . . I was so hungry and—"

"Were you?" he asked, arching a brow slightly. "I've been hungry for days. Now I'm hungrier."

Laura inhaled a sharp breath. "Caleb, please . . . beast . . ."

He chuckled. "All right. Eat your plum, Laura."

She eased away from him, taking the plum with her. She had to put some distance between them in order to catch her breath and slow her heart.

She wove her way between trunks, enjoying the coolness created by a valley breeze and the shade of the plum trees. The branches rustled, and the sun wove shafts of brilliant light between them. The air smelled of sweet fruit and foliage. Laura inhaled deeply, reveling in the beauty of Plum Valley. She had fallen in love with it.

Caleb followed her through the trees. Laura ate her plum as she wandered, lifting her skirt so she wouldn't trip and sometimes speeding up her steps so Caleb couldn't catch her. Sometimes she ran, laughing as she went. She knew he would eventually catch her. With his long strides he could have caught her soon after she had escaped him, but he was playing with her, making her laugh with excitement and catch her breath each time he reached out and pretended to just reach her, but not quite. Then she would burst forward, and the chase would be on again.

She looked back, as she had numerous times now, to see how much he had shortened the distance between them. She wasn't paying attention to what was in front of her; she tripped on something and tumbled head first onto the ground. Caleb growled playfully and pretended to tumble, too. He landed on the ground beside her.

They lay next to each other on their backs, looking up at the patches of sky through the thick branches, struggling to catch their breath.

"Tell me I'll still be doing this foolish business when I'm ninety," Caleb said.

"Ninety?" Laura asked in surprise. "Do you expect to live to ninety?"

"*Hope* to live to ninety. And why shouldn't I live that long? I'm a healthy boy."

She smiled. "Boy? You're hardly a boy. I know."

He turned on his side, supported himself on one elbow, and propped his jaw in his palm. He used the forefinger on his other hand to trace her nose, then her lips. "That so?" he asked softly.

Laura lost her smile as she again felt the force of desire pulse between them and through her veins. It became a tangible thing, something that swirled around them, seizing them in a mighty grasp. "Yes, that's so," she replied.

His head hovered over hers for a moment as he delayed the kiss she knew was inevitable, the kiss her body yearned for. His lips brushed hers finally, and Laura sighed, loving the slight touch but wanting more now, so much more.

She had just brought her hand up to pull his head down closer when she heard Stacey shriek Caleb's name.

The sound echoed through the valley. Panic gripped Laura. Stacey was shrieking . . . something terrible had happened.

Caleb reacted almost immediately, leaping up and tearing off. How did he expect to find Stacey and Amanda? Laura wondered. The valley was such a huge place. The sound could have come from anywhere. Unless Caleb had extremely keen senses, Stacey and Amanda couldn't be easily found.

"Stacey?" Laura heard him thunder after she had lost sight of him. She heard no response. Then she heard a growl. An animal. *Dear God.*

She finally gathered some sense and jumped up. Stacey

and Amanda were in danger. Stacey wouldn't shriek if they weren't. An animal . . . and Caleb didn't even have a rifle with him.

But Laura knew where one was kept anytime the Mains traveled in their wagon—beneath a blanket near the end of the wagon bed.

Only Caleb hadn't gone toward the wagon. In his own state of panic he probably hadn't considered the fact that he might need the rifle.

Laura scrambled in the direction of the wagon. Lifting her skirt to her knees, she darted between the plum trees. Branches beat together. A rabbit rushed out of her way to the safety of a bush. Laura's heart skipped beats. She felt dizzy but forced herself to keep running despite the fear that stretched dark, crooked fingers over her.

Finally, sighting the wagon in the small clearing up ahead, she mustered a burst of speed.

She grabbed the rail nearest the seat and pulled herself up. Then she flung herself into the wagon. Blankets were scattered here and there, but she knew the one she wanted. She crawled to the back, grabbed the blanket, and threw it aside.

The rifle . . . thank God . . . the rifle . . . solid in her hands . . . already loaded.

Another shriek ripped through the valley. Laura cocked her head, listening, trying to discern the direction from which it had come.

East. The direction the wagon faced.

She fought her way back to the seat and grabbed the reins. Her palms were wet, and the reins nearly slipped from her hands, but she held them. She shook them hard and yelled, "Go!" The horses surged forward.

Laura strained to listen for another shriek from Stacey. The valley was filled with heavy silence, then the cry of a bird swooping overhead, then the rustle of a bush nearby. Laura's head twisted around. Only another gray rabbit.

Panic again threatened to stop her heart and breath, but she fought. She knew if she commanded the horses to trot, the creak of the wagon and the thunder of the horses' hooves might drown out cries from Stacey, Caleb, or Amanda. She had to be able to hear. So she somehow held the reins steady with trembling hands, keeping the horses to a steady walk. The rifle lay across her thighs, and she glanced down now and then to make certain it was still there.

Finally it came again—the shriek that had sent slivers of icy fear through Laura. It sent the same slivers through her now. She wanted to freeze on the seat, she was so frightened. Terrified. She was dizzy. Spots of darkness pulsed before her eyes. No . . . if she froze . . . if she blacked out . . . she might never reach the others.

She glanced at the rifle again, then fastened her eyes straight ahead. She had to reach them. Had to . . .

Fear pounded through Caleb. He cut through the trees and bushes, weaving a crooked path. He followed the sound of Stacey's voice and prayed he was headed in the right direction. He darted past a huge elm on his right, saplings and a good-size oak on his left. He shoved a bush aside with a sweep of his hand and tore past it. He leapt over a log and flew between more trees. He heard Stacey yell his name again, close. To the right.

He turned and cut between more trees. He spotted the glitter of the river up ahead. A flash of color, too. Amanda's yellow and white dress?

Then he was at the riverbank, and there was Stacey, in the water up to her waist, her eyes big with fear. But he didn't see Amanda. Questions shot through his head. Why the hell was Stacey in the water? Why the hell had she been screaming for him? What had growled?

"Watch out!" Stacey screamed. "Caleb!"

From the side of his eye Caleb saw something lumbering toward him—a huge mass of brownish-black fur, teeth, and claws. A roar ripped through the trees. Branches cracked. Huge feet vibrated the ground.

Bear. A damn bear was headed right for him, and he didn't have a rifle or even a knife.

An angry bear.

Caleb glanced around for something to use as a weapon. He finally grabbed a thick branch. Not that it would help,

since the bear could easily whisk it right out of his hands and
split it in two, then use it on him. He'd be better off seeing if
the bear would chase him.

"Rifle! Where's your rifle?" Stacey screamed. "Where's
your rifle!"

Caleb waved his arms to make sure the bear had spotted
him. It had. It roared again, baring huge teeth and a dripping
mouth, then thundered toward him. Caleb yelled, then
turned and raced off, still yelling, making damn sure the animal came for him and didn't turn its attention back to
Stacey or Amanda—wherever the hell Amanda was.

He tore through the trees again, not especially wanting to
be caught, but glancing over his shoulder now and then to
make sure the bear followed. It ripped branches, shredded
bark, let loose another ear-splitting roar, put on a burst of
speed. Caleb dodged between trees, hoping the animal
would do the same. Instead it shot straight ahead, shortening
the distance between them.

Caleb cursed. If that bear caught him . . . Fear pumped
through him, scorched his feet so they kept moving, and
tightened every muscle in his body. He never would have believed he could keep going at this pace. It was the fear. And
he'd better keep the fear so that his legs would carry him to
safety.

He knew what would happen if that bear caught him. He'd
hunted a few before, including one with a friend up near Turtle Mountains. He and his friend—Dan was his name—had
gotten separated. Days later he'd found Dan's body, and the
sight hadn't been a pretty one. Then he'd found himself a
bear.

Another roar ripped the air, a roar of pain this time. Caleb
glanced back again, amazed but relieved to see the bear had
stopped running and was stumbling around in a daze. It
growled and swiped at a tree. Slivers of bark peppered the
air. Damn animal must have run blind right into the tree! Caleb thanked whatever luck was with him and raced on, putting more distance between him and the bear and hoping the
animal didn't turn back and go after Stacey again.

He almost ran blind into the wagon, stopped between

trees. *His* wagon. And there was Laura, standing beside the wagon, aiming a rifle in the bear's direction. What the hell—?

"Get in the wagon, Laura!" he yelled between quick breaths. "Get in. Now! Let's go get Stacey!" *And find Amanda*, his mind hollered.

Laura didn't move. With the rifle butt propped on her shoulder, she aimed carefully. *Carefully*, dammit, but what would she hit? What *could* she hit? She might get the bear but not kill it. It was angry now. It would turn white-hot mad if she got it in the shoulder or the leg or the foot. . . .

"Get in the—!"

A shot cracked the air, whizzed by Caleb, and found its mark. There was a whine, a growl, then silence. Caleb glanced back, saw the mass of fur lying still on the ground, and stopped cold in his tracks. "I'll be . . . damned," he said, out of breath.

"What was that, Mr. Main?" Laura teased. But something in her voice . . . a quiver . . . told him she was just pretending she wasn't scared.

Anger gripped him, just like the day they'd ridden through the storm and the horses had run wild. He stomped over to Laura. "What the hell did you think you were doing?" he demanded, yanking the rifle from her hands. He felt the fire of his anger in the gaze he leveled on her. "Damn you, woman! You could've been killed!"

Her eyes flared in shock. "No, *you* could have been killed," she corrected. "*I* prevented that from happening."

"Right. And what if you'd missed that bear? It would've charged again. Would've killed me first, then you! Damn you, Laura, won't you ever do what I tell you to do? You wouldn't jump out of the wagon during the storm when I told you to. Then you go and set your mind on that teaching job. Then you wouldn't get *in* the wagon when I told you to! Damn it to hell anyway!"

At first her jaw dropped open. Then she put her hands on her hips and stared at him, her chest rising and falling with rapid breaths. She was furious now. She had just saved their lives, and he was lecturing her!

They glared at each other, sparks leaping between them.

"I protected Amanda during that storm—I would rather have died than jumped and found out later that any of the rest of you had died. Those children in Minot need someone to teach them. I'm going to do it. And now I didn't do what you told me to do, but I saved your life. If you want a wife who does exactly what you tell her to do every minute, look elsewhere, Caleb Main. You won't find obedience in me!"

He stayed frozen for another minute, then moved past her and put the rifle in the wagon bed. She didn't mean that . . . look elsewhere. No, she didn't mean that. She was just angry.

"Come on," he said. "Let's go get Stacey and try to find Amanda."

"What do you mean—try to find Amanda?" she asked as he lifted her to the wagon seat, a quiver of fear making her voice tremble and her anger dissipate. "Wasn't she with Amanda?"

She settled herself and seemed to wait forever for his answer.

He climbed up on the seat beside her and grabbed the reins. "No. I ran to the river—where Stacey's shouts were coming from. She was in the water. Guess she figured out that bear wouldn't go in after her. She was right. Thought I saw a flash of Amanda's dress between trees, but when I got to the river, I didn't see Amanda, didn't see her at all."

The wagon jolted forward. Laura started praying: *Please let us find Amanda. Let her be safe, untouched. Let me hold her again.*

Trees and bushes passed on either side. Sometimes Caleb had to maneuver the wagon to avoid them. Soon the river and Stacey came into view.

Stacey had just climbed out of the water. Her skirt clung to her legs, dripping water. She looked up, spotted Laura and Caleb coming toward her in the wagon, and yelped with joy. But a second yelp froze in her throat. She didn't see Amanda.

Caleb reined the horses. "Do you know where Amanda is?"

Stacey wrung water from her skirt. "No. One look at that bear and she ran off. I went for the water, hoping it wouldn't follow me. It started to, then changed its mind. I didn't know where Amanda was. That's why I started screaming. I thought it might have gone after her. Don't think it had time between when it left me in the river and you came, but I'm not sure. It was hurt, did you see that? One of its shoulders was bleeding."

"That explains why it attacked the way it did," Caleb said. "Come on. We're going to look for Amanda. And we're going to stay together. If either one of you even thinks about going off by yourself, I'll tan your hide." He glared at Stacey, then turned his glare on Laura, who tipped her head back in a defiant way and glared right back.

Stacey gave him a look of disbelief. Either having that bear go after them the way it had had scared him real bad, or Caleb and Laura had had an argument. She wasn't sure, but she figured the last guess was probably the right one. Considering what he'd said, that made sense. She wondered exactly what had happened after she'd taken Amanda and gone off. Things must not have gone the way Caleb had planned.

"I hear you, Caleb," she said, knowing when she shouldn't argue with him or shoot questions at him. She climbed into the wagon, and it started moving before she even got settled.

Laura knew Stacey was wondering what had happened between her and Caleb. But there was no time to explain. They had to find Amanda. Besides, with Caleb sitting next to her, she wasn't going to try to explain any of what had happened.

She meant what she had told him. She loved him, but she didn't want to argue with him constantly about what she could or couldn't do. The matter of her doing exactly what he told her to do anytime he told her to do it was pushing a wedge between them.

In the wagon they traversed the area near the river for what seemed like an hour, calling Amanda's name and listening for a response—any sort of response. Rustling bushes, cracking twigs . . . anything.

Birds chirped, and branches brushed together. Occasionally a small animal skittered by. Morning turned into afternoon, and the sun blazed down from directly above. Two squirrels scurried up and down a tree, then raced to another tree and scurried up and down it, too.

There was still no sign of Amanda.

Finally Caleb stopped the wagon, jumped down, and said, "Let's go on foot."

Stacey jumped down from the other side. Caleb helped Laura down, and the three of them went off together. Stacey and Caleb called Amanda's name. Laura scanned the trees for any sign of movement. Finally she saw a nearby bush shudder. It sat close to the ground, but perhaps there was enough room for . . . She stooped to look under it.

Wide blue eyes peered at her.

She subdued the urge to cry out in happiness. But, oh, was she happy! She would have searched the land for days, weeks, months, if that had been necessary.

Before Amanda had come to live with them, she must have lived in fear of the wild animals of the prairie and the valley. She must have spent considerable time under bushes like this one. Laura's heart nearly stopped at the thought. But Amanda didn't need to live like this anymore. Ever. Still, the bear had probably scared Amanda so terribly that she had reacted instinctively.

"Hello, Amanda," Laura said, trying to keep her voice from trembling. "You're safe now. You can come out. The bear is dead."

Amanda's wide-eyed look of fear didn't change. She was actually curled around the trunk of the bush. She didn't move.

"Come on, Amanda. We'll go home now."

"You found her?" Stacey asked from behind Laura.

Laura nodded. "Under the bush. But she won't come out."

From behind Stacey, Caleb began whistling. Laura twisted around and stared at him, thinking he had gone mad. He was crouching down, one knee on the ground, the other knee supporting an elbow. He winked at her, and she gave him an incredulous look. He was whistling a merry tune and winking, as if this were some sort of cruel jest! After what they had just gone through? Confronting the bear had been terrifying. Any of them might have been killed. They had searched for Amanda for hours, and now that they had finally found her, Laura had to admit that the thought that they might not have done so had crossed her mind more than a few times during those hours. It had been horrifying and chilling.

And Caleb was whistling and winking!

"What's gotten into you?" Stacey demanded of him. " 'Camptown Races'? You might think that makes the cows let down their milk better, but you can't tell me it'll bring Amanda out from under that bush."

Caleb grinned, then whistled more. Laura stared at him. He had gone mad.

The bush rustled again. Laura glanced at it and saw Amanda crawl out from under it, gripping her cane in her good hand. Her eyes were still wide, but now they fastened on Caleb, and some of the fear left them. They were filled with tears.

"Come here, Amanda," he said softly, then whistled more.

With the aid of her cane Amanda hobbled over to him. She wrapped her good arm around his neck. He wrapped both arms around her, drawing her into a deep embrace. His eyes squeezed shut for a moment, and when they opened, Laura thought they were misted with tears, too. He blinked, and the tears were gone, but they had been there. She had seen them.

Tears of happiness and love sprang to her own eyes as she watched Amanda and Caleb together.

"See now?" he said gently. "Nothing else here to hurt you. The bear's gone. We've got the wagon to take you home. Reckon you and I have a few cows to milk and stalls to clean later this evening, so we'd better get going."

After supper that evening, and long after the events of the morning had been related to Ruth, Laura wandered outside, hoping to find Caleb in the barn or the shed. She wanted to talk to him about the teaching position again and the argument they had had after she had shot the bear. She hadn't had a moment alone with him since their return. She hoped he wasn't avoiding her and wishing their argument would simply go away. She had seen the anger in his eyes when she had told him that he should look elsewhere if he expected complete obedience from a wife. She hadn't really meant that. She had been angry and shocked at the time. But perhaps he thought she really meant that. Perhaps he was so angry with her he was reconsidering whether or not he even wanted to marry her.

He wasn't in the barn or the shed. She even looked in the chicken house, but he wasn't there, either. There were only dozens of clucking hens. She walked back to the house, went inside, and asked Ruth and Stacey if either of them had seen Caleb.

Stacey grinned. "He said something about going back for that bearskin. Then he was gone. He gave up one, after all, some time ago."

"Yes, he did, didn't he?" Laura said thoughtfully, sitting on the settee. "Do you think he regrets that?"

"That he traded a bearskin for you?" Ruth asked in disbelief, leaning over the table, kneading dough for tomorrow's bread. Flour was sprinkled all over the table, and some even powdered the floor. "Now, think about that real hard, Laura."

Restless, needing to talk to Caleb, Laura stood and wandered over to the table. "I don't know . . . we certainly have been clashing lately. Did Stacey tell you that I want to take the teaching position in Minot?"

Ruth stopped kneading and lifted a brow, looking pleasantly surprised. "No . . . but if you want to, I'm sure the folks in Minot would be glad to have you. They've been searching for a teacher for a while now. You should take the position. Stacey wanted to do it once, but she was too young. But you should take it if you want to."

"I wish Caleb was as easy to convince as you," Laura said, sighing. "We've argued a lot lately about things he thinks I should or shouldn't do. I'm capable of thinking for myself. After all, I had enough sense to go for the wagon and the rifle after Caleb went tearing off." She studied her hands so Ruth wouldn't see the tears that had swelled in her eyes. "I love him, but we argue so much. How will we ever be happy like this?"

Ruth was silent for a time. Then she asked, "What do you argue about?"

Laura knew Ruth wouldn't ask if she didn't sense that Laura wanted to talk. Laura did want to talk. She wanted to talk to Caleb, but he didn't seem to be anywhere on the farm.

"During the storm, he told us to jump from the wagon. I didn't. I told him I was going to take the teaching position. He doesn't want me to. When I saw the bear chasing him and I climbed out of the wagon and aimed the rifle, he shouted for me to climb back in and was angry when I didn't. Every time I didn't do what he told me to do, he got angry."

"Sounds like both of you have strong wills and tempers. Course, I could have told you that about Caleb. He's not as bad as he used to be though. Maybe he's just concerned about you, Laura. You spent a lot of time letting Mr. Montgomery tell you what to do and how to act. Maybe that's why you're so riled. Maybe you're comparing the two situations in your mind. They're not the same, Laura."

Laura took an apron from a nearby cabinet, tied it around her waist, and helped Ruth shape bread dough. Ruth was probably right—about jumping from the wagon and climbing back in the wagon. Caleb had been scared for her. He had been trying to protect her. And when she thought about the heated words they had about the teaching position, she recalled that he hadn't actually said, "You can't take it." He had said something more like, "I reckon you've already made up your mind, and I shouldn't waste words."

She was the one allowing the wedge to be pushed between her and Caleb.

She placed one shaped loaf in a bread pan and kneaded another mound of soft dough. "If anything, after what happened today he might be even more against letting me ride into town and back every day to teach," she thought aloud. "He would be right, too. I've even worried about it several times since this afternoon. That bear reminded me of the dangers of the prairie and even of the valley. Traveling back and forth alone every day might not be a very good idea."

"You're right," Stacey said from where she sat in the sewing corner. "He might be more against it. Caleb gets real gruff sometimes, but he doesn't mean any harm, Laura. He's just protective of those he loves."

Laura glanced at Stacey and smiled. She wondered about the tiny pieces of red material in Stacey's hands. Her smile grew as she realized Stacey was sewing another dress for Amanda's doll. Amanda was seated on the settee, undressing and dressing the doll. Laura wondered if Amanda knew what Stacey was doing.

Stacey pulled a thread, clipped it, then made a knot at the end. Finally she held up the tiny dress she had made in the space of a half hour—that's how long she had been in the corner cutting and sewing—and inspected it. "I get mad at Caleb myself, he gets mad at me, and we yell at each other. You've seen us," she said. "Some things we work out, other things we don't. But we still get along most of the time. Two people can't agree on everything."

Laura considered that. Sometimes she thought Stacey was much older than sixteen. Stacey was right about two people not agreeing on everything. She had to admit, the fear had lurked in the back of her mind this afternoon that perhaps she was about to start living her life under the shadow of yet another man. But it wasn't like that with Caleb. He wasn't a shadow lurking over her. He loved her, and she had grown so much since meeting him.

He had been scared for her during the storm when he had told her to jump from the wagon; and he had been scared for her this morning when he had told her to get back in the wagon. She had assumed he was thinking he would jump in the wagon, and they would just race off and find Stacey and Amanda. She hadn't been thinking that he was the one who had lived on the prairie and in the valley for years, not her. Now, of course, when she thought of the way she had carefully aimed that rifle and shot that bear, she trembled with fear. How had she done that? She didn't know, but now that she recalled the entire episode, she understood why Caleb had been so infuriated. She had only learned to shoot weeks ago. Hitting that bear had been lucky. She might not have hit it. The bear could have killed them, Caleb first because he would have been the first one it would have reached, and her second.

All right. The trip back and forth to Minot could be dangerous. Could be. How many times, since she had been staying with the Mains, had they taken uneventful journeys into Minot? There had to be a way to solve her problem—she still wanted to teach those children. They needed her.

An uneasy feeling crept over her as she remembered that, while they had been arguing about the teaching position, Caleb hadn't mentioned not wanting her to travel back and forth alone. Stacey had. *He* had said something about wanting her with him here at the farm.

Laura knew they needed to talk. They needed to talk about several things. The teaching position was only one.

They still needed to talk about the money, too.

❄ ❄ ❄
Chapter Nineteen

CALEB HAD NEVER told Laura whether or not he could accept her money.

She understood that Pa had cheated him. She understood that he, Ruth, and Stacey had suffered because Pa had cheated him. She understood that Caleb despised the thought of using the money because he felt Pa had obtained it by cheating people.

But she wasn't Pa. The money was hers. She had come by it honestly. And as she had told Caleb that night in the barn, wasn't the situation ironic? Pa had taken Caleb's money and had never delivered the land he had promised. Now Caleb had the chance to get back all the money he had given Pa, and more. He had the chance to get the land he wanted, and more.

But Caleb had never responded. She had wanted to give him time to consider everything she had said. She had wanted him to think and reach a decision by himself, so she had said no more about the money.

She also wanted him to realize that she would always be Matthew Kent's daughter, and a part of her would always love Pa, despite the arrangements he had made with Adrian to get him to marry her, and despite what Pa had done to Caleb and Ruth and Stacey. But she wasn't Pa. She was Laura. She was angry with Pa and didn't know if she could ever forgive him for taking nearly everything from the Mains, but that still didn't change the fact that she loved her father.

Nor did it change the fact that she would always have memories of Pa around her, things that were far more valuable to her than the money. She had the locket, and when she returned to Bismarck and went through Pa's possessions, there would be other mementos she would want to keep, things she would want to bring here and have close to her. If Caleb still hated Pa so much, how could he accept the sight of any of Pa's belongings in the Main household? Forget the money—she didn't really care about it. It was such a very small part of what she would bring into a marriage to Caleb. What about pictures of Pa? Pa's diaries? Anything that had been Pa's, anything she couldn't part with?

As she helped Ruth make the bread, her thoughts turned more to Pa and the events that had happened ten years ago. Pa had been a warm, gentle father. She still found the fact that he had been such a ruthless businessman almost impossible to believe. She now knew how Pa had tried to arrange her marriage to Adrian. She had heard Caleb's story from Caleb's mouth. She had witnessed the way Ruth had run Adrian off with the rifle after he had mentioned the business and given Pa's version of it. She believed Caleb and Ruth. She trusted them.

But Adrian had made her curious about those diaries.

She wanted to see them . . . but she didn't want to see them. She wanted to know if Pa had told the truth, at least in the diaries . . . but she didn't want to know. If he had written the truth, she might never forgive him, for that would mean he had known exactly what he had been doing when he had cheated Caleb. If the pages were filled with lies . . . she didn't know how she would feel or what she would think. That might mean he had been a bit mad, that he had blocked out the truth. Part of her still wanted to believe he had not done anything wrong.

So she simply wasn't sure whether or not she wanted to read the diaries. Doubtless she could spend years trying to understand why Pa had done some of the things he had done, and even then she would probably find no answers. Not in the diaries. Not anywhere. The fact was, he had not been the perfect man she had always thought he was. She realized that now and wasn't afraid to think it.

She wasn't afraid to return to Bismarck and face the memories there, either. She might walk into Pa's office and remember the image of him lying on the floor. But she would also remember him sitting on the edge of his desk, smiling at her. And that was what she really wanted to keep with her always.

Deciding to ride into Minot and treat himself to a rare drink of whiskey, Caleb hid the bearskin in a hollowed log and turned Soldier in the direction of town.

Minot was spread below, a mixture of scattered tents and houses and various other buildings. The taller buildings of businesses, many of which had come to Minot just in the last year, flanked Main Street. The reddish-orange glow of the evening sun touched rooftops and the covers of the wooden walkways. From the distance Caleb couldn't read most of the signs hanging above the walkways. He didn't need to, except on the businesses that had come to Minot in just the last week or two, and there were a number of those. They were at the far end of Main Street, so he couldn't even squint and read the signs, even if there were any.

He watched a train roll in, slowing, then grinding to a stop beside the depot. The town seemed brimming with people, but that didn't surprise Caleb. Lately, it was overflowing and a damn nuisance to be in.

He preferred the serene sounds of the open prairie—a howling wolf, a coyote, or a hooting owl, not the laughter and loud voices of people on the streets of Minot or in the saloons or gaming houses. A man could find trouble in those places if he wasn't careful. Caleb reckoned he'd had enough trouble so far in his life to last him the rest of his life. He didn't need the trouble those places offered. He'd rather watch a breeze ripple the green and gold prairie grass and watch the sun bathe the endless horizon. He'd rather watch Sam chase after a prairie dog than watch a fight in a saloon. He preferred peace in his life.

Right now he was thirsty for a drink, so he figured he'd go in, get that drink, then ride out, gather the bearskin, and head home. At home, he'd take care of the skin, then milk the cows. Later he'd sit with Laura a bit. If she'd let him.

He'd been a fool, being so hot about her wanting to take that teaching job. He wanted to marry her, but being her husband didn't give him the right to lock her up at the farm. Wanting to keep her there all the time was selfish of him. Most days he did a lot of chores and never even saw her until supper. He loved her, and he wanted to keep her close to him, but he had to think about what she wanted, too. If Laura wanted to do something on her own after he married her, he didn't have the right to stand in her way.

But her safety . . . that was different. He wouldn't let her ride across the prairie by herself. Laura had learned some important lessons, and she'd learn a lot more—he'd make sure of that, just in case she ever found herself alone—but even so, he wouldn't want her going off alone. He reckoned if she was hell-bent on taking that teaching job, he would take her to the schoolhouse in the mornings and go get her in the afternoons.

She'd want to go to Bismarck someday, too, and he reckoned he'd be taking her there, ghosts or no ghosts. He wasn't about to let anyone else take her, and he wasn't about to put her on a stage and let her go that way. He'd go with her.

He was sure Bismarck had changed a lot, but he knew he wouldn't see the changes. He'd remember the place where he'd had a lifetime of misery and bad luck. Hell . . . he remembered a passel of things now, and cold rushed up his spine.

He remembered Main Street and the sheriff's office and being tossed into jail. He remembered the one deputy who kept coming to the cell, taunting him with comments like "Won't be long. Hee, Hee. Nope, won't be long at all. Judge'll be coming through here. He'll give us the okay, and we'll take you out there and fix you right up."

Days before, Caleb had found the money, had known Matt was setting him up for a hanging, and he'd gone to Matt's house. Standing well over six feet, Matt had met him at the door. . . .

"What do you want, Main?" Matt demanded, filling the doorway. He didn't give Caleb a chance to answer. He said, "Sheriff's looking for you. I hear a pretty good-size bundle of money was found in your saddlebags."

Caleb laughed bitterly, and his clenched fists ached to swing at Matt's jaw. As if the hell he'd already been through—watching Ma and Stacey suffer, knowing he'd failed both of them and Pa—wasn't enough, now he was going to hang. Matt would see to it.

"You put the money there," Caleb accused, "or one of your men did. I don't know which." Everything that happened during the past year was flooding his mind: Matt on the other side of the fire near Fargo, telling about the land deal. Matt taking the money Caleb had eagerly offered. Matt telling him to shut his mouth—people in Bismarck weren't believing him anyway and never would. But they'd started to. Oh, yes, they'd started to.

"Of course," Caleb said now, "anything bad people have started to believe about you will disappear once they hear your missing money was found in my saddlebags. But that's just the way you planned things, isn't it?"

Matt grinned that cocky grin of his.

Standing there facing that grin, Caleb remembered Stacey, huddled on a blanket on the ground in that tent. She was thin, pale, sick ... almost dead. The fact was, with Pa dead a few years or so, he felt responsible for taking care of his mother and sister, and he'd done a hell of a messed-up job of it. With Matt's help, of course.

So he swung at Matt. And Matt hammered him. Right there in the doorway, Kent hammered him. The first blow staggered him backward, then Matt grabbed him by the scruff of the neck, and Caleb felt the crunch of many more blows. He never had a chance to hit Matt once. He thought about it, but too late—he was already sinking into a deep blackness.

Later—how many days, he wasn't sure—he awakened in jail, and that deputy was standing at the bars snickering at him, talking about the judge and how they were going to fix him right up. Caleb gave the deputy a cold stare. He still had a little of his pride left, although Matt had knocked nearly all of it out of him. Yes, he had a little pride . . . and he had a little courage, too, but not enough to raise up and look through the barred window at the gallows he knew awaited him out there. Matt had taken so much out of him that he didn't even want to grab that deputy. He looked at the man, then somehow turned his battered body to the wall.

Caleb rode up to a hitching post in front of one of Minot's saloons. He shuddered, remembering all that Bismarck mess. He'd suffered a lot at the hands of that deputy, and he'd hated Matt for that, too. After being let out of jail, he'd gathered Ma and Stacey and had left Bismarck in a hurry, not caring to ever look back. Matt had finally broken him, and he'd run from the man. Now he knew he needed to go and face everything. He needed to stop running. Yes, he was firmly settled on his farm, not running physically, but in his mind he'd been running for years, from Matt and from Bismarck.

He couldn't hide anymore, not if he wanted to marry Laura. For the sake of his happiness and hers, he had to stop running. He had to face the past, sweat through it, then get on with his life.

Matt was dead, and even if he weren't, Laura wasn't anything like him, except in her pride, and everyone had a bit of that. She still loved her pa. Yes, he'd been a swindler, and yes, he'd tried to force her into marriage with a man who didn't love her. But she had her good childhood memories of her father, as she'd once told Caleb, and she still loved him.

He'd told her he didn't want the money, but she had him thinking about that. He still didn't especially like the idea of taking the money, but he kept telling himself over and over that it was Laura's now, not Matt's. Not that he was actually convinced, but something she'd said to him that night in the barn had a way of creeping into his thoughts now and then: *"Isn't it ironic that he took the money from you, yet now you have an opportunity to have more than he promised you?"*

Well, he couldn't help but be human. He was beginning to think Laura was right about the irony of the situation. Matt did owe him, and since he was still thinking of the money as being Matt's, why not remember that Matt owed him? Maybe he was being paid back for the years he, Ma, and

Stacey had suffered. Laura had hinted at that, and maybe she was right.

Caleb had just stepped away from the hitching post and up onto the walkway when a man stumbled into him, bounced off, then nearly stumbled over a chair. He reached out to steady the man, but his hand was shoved away.

"Just trying to help," Caleb said.

"The last thing I need, Main, is your help."

Caleb knew the man's voice and tried to place it. His slurred words hadn't been easy to understand. The man placed both hands on the back of the chair, steadied himself, and turned around.

Caleb narrowed his eyes. "Montgomery?"

It was Montgomery all right. Only the man in front of Caleb sure as hell didn't look like the Adrian Montgomery he'd had such a hell of a pleasure meeting the other day. This fellow's clothes were crumpled, the gold trim on his jacket looked faded, and his black boots were dull. His hair was a dusty, dirty, tousled mess—something that wasn't a rare sight in this town, but Caleb reckoned it was a rare sight on Adrian Montgomery for sure. Those gray eyes, so piercing and cool the other day, were now dull, glazed, and shot through with bright red veins. And the man reeked of whiskey.

Catching a strong whiff of the sour smell, Caleb drew back and whistled low. "Well, you're a hell of a sight after looking so mighty in the saddle the other day," he couldn't resist observing.

Montgomery let go of the chair back and straightened. He was wobbly, but Caleb shook his head in amazement that the man could even stand that straight, as much as Montgomery had to have been drinking.

"Leave me alone, Main," Montgomery growled.

"You didn't strike me as the kind of man who would tip a bottle too often," Caleb said, thinking he might have to help Montgomery to a boardinghouse or wherever he was staying. He didn't like Montgomery, didn't like him at all, but he'd do the same for him as he'd do for any man. He wouldn't let a man who could barely stand try to dodge horses in the street or climb stairs.

"I wasn't, until the day I rode up to your farm and learned that Laur-Laura had fallen in love with you," Montgomery said, wobbling. He grappled for the chair back and steadied himself.

Shaking his head in amazement, Caleb wondered how Montgomery had handled that mouthful of words when he could barely stand. "Don't try to make me feel guilty, Montgomery. I know you don't love her. You know you don't love her."

"And you do? She's worth quite a lot of money. But you know that. And you hated Matt enough to want to marry her for revenge."

"Did you really read those diaries or did you reach that conclusion by yourself?"

"There are diaries, but I never read them. Matt told me everything over the years, how he had one of the hands plant that money. You just wouldn't leave him alone. Good thing you didn't go back to Bismarck. Matt tolerated one slight. He'd never tolerate a second."

Caleb flinched but quickly reminded himself that the past was the past. He wasn't going to swing a fist at anyone over it ever again. He'd survived it. And he'd outlived Matt Kent, hadn't he? "Matt filled your head with poison, Montgomery. Pity is, you believe it all," he said. "Well, Matt's dead. You'd do well to remember that."

Montgomery tilted his chin up in his arrogant way, as if to say, "How dare you give me advice?" but this time the movement unbalanced him again, and he spilled over the chair. The chair tipped, then Montgomery went crashing to the walkway along with the chair.

Caleb stood there and shook his head. He'd give Montgomery a minute, then he'd try to help him up.

Montgomery sat up and brushed himself off, appearing to be steady enough. But getting to his feet was a trick. He tried twice. Both times he slipped.

"Oh, Montgomery . . . you're a hell of a sight. You're shooting hate at me, but you can't even stay on your feet."

He reached down to grab Montgomery's arm, meaning to hoist him up, although he wasn't too sure how long Montgomery would stay on his feet. Again, Montgomery shoved his hands away.

"I don't . . . do not want your help!" Montgomery snapped.

Caleb withdrew. Montgomery somehow struggled to his feet, stood on those wobbly legs again, and wove his way down the walkway. At the end of the walkway, he toppled off the edge and fell in a heap.

Sighing, Caleb leaned back against the wall, folded his arms, and watched Montgomery get on his feet again. The man wobbled off, then started through the doors of another saloon, shoving another man out of the way in the process. *That* movement was enough to send Montgomery sprawling against the doors, and he was real lucky the man he'd shoved gave him a black look rather than a fist.

Wincing, Caleb went to find the drink he'd ridden into town for.

While he was enjoying it, he kept wondering if Montgomery had shoved the wrong person or was passed out on some table yet. It wasn't his business, he told himself. He didn't even like the man. No, it wasn't his business. But his conscience kept telling him it was. If Montgomery *hadn't* passed out somewhere or hadn't shoved the wrong person by now—him and his damn arrogance—what other sort of trouble might he be getting into?

It's not my business, Caleb told himself again for about the twentieth time.

His conscience still didn't agree.

"Ah, hell," he muttered, pushing the drink aside and wandering back outside. He unhitched Soldier and took him to a nearby livery—just in case he found himself stuck in Minot for hours.

Then he went in search of Montgomery.

He found him, an hour or so later, at a poker table, losing a bundle of money. From his cattle-hand days and nights spent around a fire, Caleb knew how to play a good hand of poker. But he and the other hands had bet things like who would take care of whose horse for the next week and who would take night watch for whom—friendly bets, no money involved. Pa had taught him to play poker, too, but he'd also taught him not to put his money down on tables like this, much less take a seat at one. "It's a waste of hard-earned money," Pa had always said. Maybe years of hearing that was why taking one look at how much Montgomery had lost made Caleb whistle low, then draw back in shock.

From the looks of things Montgomery had lost that insurance company and maybe a lot more.

The game ended. Caleb shook his head, told himself he shouldn't do what his mind was telling him to do. But he took a chair anyway opposite the sharp-eyed man who had just made Montgomery a poor man and picked up the cards he was dealt. Montgomery gave him an odd, bleary-eyed look, managing to lift one brow. He opened his mouth to say something, but Caleb stopped him, growling, "Just put your head down on that table behind you and go to sleep, Montgomery. Don't know why I'm doing this for you, but I am."

Caleb knew he ought to go against everything his conscience said. He shouldn't feel responsible for Montgomery or try to get any of Montgomery's money back for him. He ought to lay down the cards in his hand, say to hell with Montgomery, and get up and walk out. There'd be hell to pay if Ma ever found out he'd sat down at this table—and she would, since he recognized some faces when he glanced around the place. He could get around a passel of trouble by listening to *his* voice, not the voice of his conscience.

All the same, he shifted his hand of cards. . . .

Hours later Caleb dumped Montgomery in a bed at the McLean House, a small boardinghouse on the east side of Minot. He'd had to rouse Hubert and Ardella McLean and pay them twice as much for one night, but at least he'd found a room. He didn't know where Montgomery had been staying and hadn't taken the time to find out. Montgomery had put his head on one of the tables and had fallen asleep. Caleb had lifted him and brought him here, simple as that.

After leaving Montgomery's room, he left a note for

Adrian with Mrs. McLean—something about having a lot of money for Montgomery, money that he had lost but Caleb had won back and still wasn't sure why he had. Then Caleb stepped out into the night and stared up at the moon.

He wondered how Montgomery would see things when he woke up. Either Montgomery would pay another visit to the farm and be angry or a bit humble, or he'd say to hell with the money and ride to Bismarck and never look back. Minot would be *his* nightmare if he did that—the place where he'd had a lot of bad luck. Caleb didn't know what Montgomery would do, and he was too tired to guess. He went to the livery, saddled and mounted Soldier, and stopped only once during the ride home—to grab the bearskin.

Laura turned onto her back and stared up at the ceiling. Through the gauzy, slightly billowing curtain, the moon spilled silver over the room's furnishings. For the hundredth time during all the night hours that had passed, Laura wondered where Caleb was and if he was safe. She slipped from the bed, glancing back at Amanda to make sure she was still sleeping. She was. Then Laura moved silently across the room to the open window.

To her right, some distance away, was the red barn. Nearby was the chicken house, a small but also dark building. Tucked close to the right side of the house so that Laura could only glimpse the corner of its roof, was the shed. She gripped the windowframe and leaned forward slightly, inhaling a deep breath of the cool night air. The moon was nearly full tonight, looking as if someone or something had taken a neat little bite from one side of it. Clouds had formed, and the moon cast a hazy glow on the dark puffs as some huddled together and others drifted away. Laura watched the drifting ones, wondering how she had managed to fall asleep and for how long. She guessed only a few hours remained before dawn. She knew she had slept lightly and would have heard Caleb's boots on the stairs if he had come home yet. She hadn't heard a sound.

Where was he?

Last evening she and Stacey had taken the cattle to water.

After that she had tried to help Stacey milk the cows, but she had never milked a cow before and had only filled the bucket a fourth of the way. Stacey had laughed and said that was good for her first time. Still, Stacey had had to do most of the work.

Then Laura and Stacey had taken the milk inside, Ruth had skimmed the cream off of it after a time, then put the milk and cream away. Laura had finished stitching her calico dress patterned with sunflowers and had sung songs to Amanda. Next she had written letters on the slate and had drawn pictures next to them while Amanda watched.

Amanda was talking more. Actually Laura wasn't sure whether she was learning to talk more or simply getting bolder. She was saying "Stacey" and "Ruth," and Laura suspected she could say other words, too, but wouldn't until she was ready, just as she had done before.

Several times during the evening Stacey had wondered aloud where Caleb might be, then she had left the subject alone. Ruth had said nothing about Caleb, but Laura knew Ruth had sat up later than she normally did, probably waiting for her son. All three of them had worried, but no one had really voiced worry. They had gone about their usual business as if Caleb were with them.

Laura moved away from the window and went back to the bed, refusing to think that anything horrible had happened to Caleb.

Instead she slipped under the quilt and thought back to two days before Pa's death, when she and Pa had saddled horses and raced on the huge spread of land behind the house. She had thought of that day before, but sadness had always settled so heavily on her that she had to shift her thoughts to something else. Now there was still sadness that she and Pa would have no more afternoons together, but the sadness was not nearly as overwhelming as it had been. She'd rather think about the past than conjure images of what might have happened to Caleb.

She thought of other wonderful warm times she and Pa had shared. She didn't know why he had possessed two sides—the kind, gentle side and the ruthless, cold side. She had done much thinking last night and had finally decided to stop puzzling over it. There *were* two sides to him, and there was no answer why. She was still curious about the diaries, but even her curiosity about them had faded some.

When the pink and purple hues of dawn began filtering through the gauzy curtains, Laura rose, dressed quickly in her new dress—the sunflower-patterned calico—and went downstairs. No one else was awake yet. She had just lifted the egg basket from the table and had started toward the front door when she heard a horse whinny outside.

Caleb.

A small cry tore loose from her throat, and she threw open the front door.

In front of the barn Caleb had reined Soldier and was dismounting. Caleb's black hair was tousled, as usual, and his eyelids were heavy. Wherever he had been all night, he certainly had not slept.

But he was safe. Laura was so relieved that dizziness washed over her, and she grappled for the doorframe to steady herself. She had been ignoring her worries and fears so much, pretending they weren't there, and they swept over her now like an overwhelming storm. Minutes passed. By the time she finally managed to conquer the dizziness, she realized Caleb had taken Soldier into the barn.

Lifting her skirt, she raced across the porch and down the steps. She hurried across the distance that separated the house from the barn and slowed her steps inside the barn door. She didn't want to appear as if she had spent hours worrying and was excited and immensely relieved.

She laughed at the absurdity of that thought. She *was* excited and immensely relieved. She *had* spent hours worrying. And she didn't *care* if it showed. The worry had been pushed to the back of her mind, and now it spilled from her in one huge exhalation of relief as she again lifted her skirt, this time rushing to the stall where Caleb was unsaddling Soldier.

She pushed herself between the horse and Caleb and wrapped her arms around Caleb's waist, burying her face in his white shirt. It smelled of perspiration, whiskey, and tobacco smoke, but she didn't care. Beneath the shirt was Caleb, the man she needed to hold, the man she loved.

"My God, I was so worried. I didn't tell anyone, but I was so worried," she said, her voice muffled against his shirt.

"Laura." He breathed deeply, and his arms went around her, pulling her closer, enveloping her in his love and warmth.

They stood there, clinging to each other, Laura with tears in her eyes, Caleb with his hands in her hair. It was unbraided, and she knew he liked taking it in his hands and letting it spill between his fingers as he did now. She lifted her head and pressed a kiss to his neck. He made a throaty sound and let his hand travel slowly down her back to her buttocks. Then he shook his head and withdrew, his dark eyes narrowed on her. "Ma'll be up soon, if she isn't already."

Laura smiled. "Let me help you," she said, easing away from him. She took the reins and bridle off Soldier while Caleb worked on the saddle, uncinching it and lifting it from the horse's back. Laura and Caleb both took brushes. Laura brushed one side of Soldier, Caleb the other.

When they finished, Laura said, "I'll go get the eggs now and meet you inside."

Caleb nodded. Laura left the barn, her head filled with many questions about where Caleb had been and what had kept him. She really had been a lot more frightened than she had realized. The fear had surged forth when she had stood in the doorway of the house, watching Caleb dismount by the barn. In the chicken house she quickly gathered the eggs, then hurried off.

By the time she arrived inside the house, Caleb was already there. He had lit the coals inside the stove and was coaxing heat from them. Laura moved to the table, placed the basket of eggs there, then turned in time to see Caleb start making coffee in the tin pot. She was anxious to ask him where he had been last evening. She listened for creaks of the floorboards above her head and heard none. Ruth and Stacey had apparently not slept well last night, either. Both were still asleep or at least remaining upstairs.

Laura watched Caleb. His eyelids were heavy, and he

moved like a weary man—slow and lethargic. He spilled water, cursed, ground coffee, spilled it, cursed, then shook his head and chuckled. Smiling, Laura walked over and gently took the pot from his fumbling fingers.

"I'll make it," she said.

"And I'll let you," he said, walking off to sit at the table.

"Did you have to fight that bear again?" Laura teased, unable to resist. In the barn she had noticed that he had tossed the bearskin across a stall rail.

He chuckled. "I feel like I've been in another bear fight. Truth is, another bear fight would've been easier."

"What happened?" she asked as she worked.

"Adrian Montgomery."

Laura glanced up, a frown tightening her brow. "Adrian . . . I saw him in town yesterday. Oh, Caleb, he didn't . . ." Suddenly she noticed a small scrape on the back of Caleb's left hand. She hadn't noticed it before now.

"No, no fight. But there was trouble," Caleb said. "All the way home this morning I was trying to figure out why he stayed. He hasn't been back out here, so I reckon he didn't stay to start trouble for us. Only thing I can figure is that he stayed because he felt half ruined already and wanted to ruin himself the rest of the way."

"What?" Laura couldn't imagine why anyone would want to do something like that or how Adrian had tried to do it. She finished the coffee, filled a pottery mug with the steaming drink, and placed it in front of Caleb. "What do you mean by trouble?"

Caleb sipped coffee. "I finished that bear and decided to go on to Minot for a drink," he said, then added hastily: "Something I don't do often."

Smiling, Laura turned and went back to the stove to start frying some eggs and bacon. "I know that, Caleb," she said. "Tell me the rest."

He did. He told her how Adrian had stumbled right into him. How he had tried to help Adrian, but Adrian wouldn't let him. Then how he had found Adrian in one of the saloons later, losing an enormous amount of money. Laura's eyes widened at the latter. "Adrian is not a gambler," she said, turning away from the sizzling bacon. "Why would he do that?"

Caleb shook his head. "Maybe he figured he'd lost nearly everything already. You told me Montgomery Insurance was failing. Maybe after he realized he'd lost you, he figured the business was dead without your money. He got crazy. It's hard to say why. I know what a desperate man feels like. Sometimes he wants to roll over and die."

She glanced at him. He was referring to the things he had endured in Bismarck. "So he threw it all away. That's terrible." The eggs had finished cooking. She used a spatula to put them on a pottery plate, then waited for the bacon to finish.

Once she had put the bacon on the plate beside the eggs, she served Caleb. From a cabinet behind him he reached for the bread Laura had helped Ruth bake late yesterday afternoon. Laura fetched a jar of plum jelly from a cabinet and carried it to the table. Then she sat in a chair beside Caleb.

"Is Adrian still in town?" she asked. "Perhaps I should go talk to him."

"That might only make things worse, Laura," Caleb said. "Besides, he didn't lose all his money."

"I thought you said it looked as if he had lost more than any little insurance company was worth."

"I did."

"Then how do you know he didn't lose it all?"

Caleb took a big bite of bread and spoke in a muffled voice. Laura couldn't understand what he was trying to say. Something about "cards" and "table." She deciphered "Adrian," then pursed her lips and narrowed her eyes in frustration. "Caleb Main, when I first met you, I thought you were the most frustrating man I'd ever met, but at least you had a few manners. Would you please swallow that bread and talk without a full mouth?"

He swallowed, then gulped coffee, his eyes skittering nervously around the table. Laura had never seen him act so odd.

"I sat down at that table, picked up the cards, and won some of his money back. Some," Caleb said. "Pa taught me to play cards, and I learned some while driving cattle, but it's not something I've spent too much time doing. By the time I figured my luck was gone this morning, Montgomery had put his head on the table and was snoring. I packed the money in my saddlebags," he said, jerking his head toward the front door. Laura saw the saddlebags sitting there, and her eyes widened. "After that, I took Montgomery to a boardinghouse. He'll probably sleep all day and wake up wondering how he got there. I left a note with Mrs. McLean, the lady of the house, telling Adrian I had his money—I wasn't going to leave it in the room. I'm not going to give it to him unless I get a promise that he won't go back and put it on the poker table again."

He finished the eggs, bacon, and bread while Laura watched him, her heart swelling with pride. After the way Adrian had treated everyone here, Caleb had won some of his money back for him? Laura wondered what other man would do something as thoughtful—as *crazy*—as that, and quickly decided there simply wasn't one.

Caleb pushed the plate away and sat back in his chair, drawing a hand over his heavy-lidded eyes. He shook his head. "Damn good thing Pa isn't alive. He'd skin me like a prairie dog for even sitting at one of those tables. He used to tell me only a fool picks up a handful of cards and plops money down on one of those tables."

Laura put her hand over his, feeling the roughness, seeing the contrast of his sun-browned skin to her white skin. His hands were huge, the fingers long and thick. She turned the hand over and ran her fingertips over the hard calluses there. Then she smiled, loving all of him. "I can never imagine those hands doing anything wrong."

He studied her. Then he lifted his hand and caressed her jaw. Laura pressed her face into his palm.

"I—uh—I've been trying to figure a way to ask you to marry me. The right way, you know. Only I'm not too good at this sort of thing. I've faced bears and coyotes and was scared when I did. But I'm more scared now."

Laura smiled, fighting the tightness that had formed in her throat. "Why are you scared?"

He lifted a brow. "Well, there's always a chance you might say no. You were pretty angry yesterday."

She brought his hand to her lips, tasting its saltiness and loving it. "I've lain with you twice, Caleb. I wouldn't have if I had harbored any thoughts of saying no. When I stretched my hand out to you beneath the plum tree, I knew I wanted to be with you always. I love you. Teaching the children is something I want to do, but I understand that you're worried about me making the trip back and forth every day. As for me being here all the time, being close to you . . . I know how you watched Stacey and your ma live through such a horrible time in Bismarck, and I know that having the people you love close to you, protecting them . . . is important to you. I—"

He put a finger to her lips to silence her. "I've been thinking. I want you to be happy, that's what I want. If you want to teach, hell . . . that's the way it'll be. I don't want you riding to town by yourself, though, so I'll take you—and you know we'll have a battle if you tell me no again. That argument yesterday wasn't our first and won't be our last."

She leaned over to kiss him. "I won't promise that I'll always do what you tell me to do, Caleb."

He grinned. "Hell, Laura, I know that."

She laughed. He laughed. He pulled her onto his lap and kissed her, leaving her breathless and wanting more. Then he lifted his head and stared into her eyes. "You be thinking about when you want to go to Bismarck. I'll take you. As for the money . . . I reckon you're right about what you said. Matt's dead. He owed us," he said, stroking her hair. "But even without the money, I'll always think of myself as a rich man as long as I have you."

Tears of happiness swelled in Laura's eyes. She embraced him. He held her tightly. Moments later they both heard the creak of floorboards above their heads and separated. Laura returned to the stove to cook breakfast for Ruth, Stacey, and Amanda. Caleb took his plate and mug to the washbasin.

"Reckon we ought to tell everyone soon," he said from across the room.

Laura smiled, wiping away tears. "Reckon we ought to, Mr. Main," she said, mocking him. He narrowed his eyes at her. She laughed again, cracked another egg, and let it spill gently into the skillet.

❋❋❋
Chapter Twenty

LATER CALEB TOOK the bearskin to the shed, stretched it out, and tacked it to a big board which he carried to a place between the house and the shed and left it there so the skin could dry in the sun.

Sam helped him coax the cows to the barn. After milking, Caleb went inside the house to his room, stripped the clothes from his body, and draped himself across the tick and bedstead. He imagined Laura's silky hair in his hands again, then he was asleep.

When he woke, the sun was just beginning to dip in the sky. Sunset was still a few hours away. Light shone into the room, casting a lazy haze on the little table in one corner, the chair in front of it, and the chest of drawers on the other side of the room. Caleb, smelling roast and onions, maybe even plum pudding, rose and dressed. He reckoned he was a sight. He'd wash up as well as he could for supper, and later he'd heat water for a bath.

He was halfway down the stairs when he heard a wagon creak to a stop outside. At first he reckoned maybe Ma or Stacey or even Laura had taken the wagon somewhere and was just coming back. But Ma and Laura were putting bowls on the table, and Stacey was sitting on the floor with Amanda, drawing something on Amanda's slate. Stacey glanced curiously at the door, then at Caleb. He shrugged and strode toward the door.

Before he could even put a hand on it, someone pounded on the other side, and a voice cried, "Mrs. Main? Mrs. Main?"

Caleb pulled the door open.

There stood Charles Duncan, his brown eyes big with

fear. He plucked a twig from his honey-brown hair, tossed it away, and tapped the heel of one boot rapidly on the porch. His dirty, crusty trousers were unhitched and riding his hips. Worst part was, Charles didn't seem to know it.

Caleb, thinking of Stacey's young, innocent eyes, planted himself in the doorway. He growled, "Fix those trousers," just about the time he caught the heavy scent of manure and reeled back. He'd smelled manure a lot—every time he cleaned the barn—but Charles smelled as if he'd taken a bath in the stuff.

Caleb coughed and held a hand over his nose. Flushing, Charles fumbled with his trouser buttons, talking at the same time: "Sorry. S-sorry, Mr. Main. Was in a hurry. Nearly ran the horses to death getting here. Was doing the work—cleaning the barn and after the hogs. That's when my sister LeAnne hollered from the house, 'Get Mrs. Main! Ma's having the baby.' I'd be real thankful if your ma and Stacey could come and help out. LeAnne doesn't know anything about . . . well, you know . . . making sure the baby comes out right and all. Only doctor in Minot's one Ma swears she won't ever let touch her."

An image of Mrs. Duncan flashed in Caleb's mind. A sweet woman, plain-looking with eyes the same color as her boy's and hair about the same, too, but shot through with gray. She was a small woman, and Caleb had heard she'd spent the last few months in bed. Clay Duncan, her husband, was off prospecting somewhere out West, and Charles had been left in charge of the family farm.

"Didn't know it was coming so soon, Mr. Main," Charles said. "Like I said, LeAnne started hollering from the house. I just jumped on the wagon and tore off. Hope this don't hurt my chances with Stacey."

He meant his unhitched trousers. And probably the smell, too. Chuckling, Caleb shook his head. "Come on," he said, drawing Charles into the house. "First thing I'm going to do is find you something else to wear. There's no time for a bath, but I'm not going to have Ma and Stacey riding beside you, thinking they're going to pass out from the smell. Ma!

Stacey! Pack up some things. Seems Mrs. Duncan's baby's decided to be born sometime today."

"Well, praise be," Ma said. "I know she's glad it's time. Poor woman."

Stacey rose from where she'd been sitting on the floor near Amanda. Caleb watched her smile shyly at Charles and was surprised as he'd ever been about anything. Stacey, shy? A blush stained her cheeks, too, as she said a soft, "Hello, Charles." Almost delicate-like. Stacey?

Charles inclined his head and started to stop and talk to her. Caleb gave him a little prod in the back. "Keep moving," he said in a low voice. "Smelling like that, you wouldn't want to stop and talk to a woman."

Caleb assumed Charles agreed—Charles hurried toward the staircase. From the corner of his eye, Caleb saw Ma grab the picnic basket, cut slices of beef, and gather some other things. Laura stood near the stove, looking around, as though she didn't understand the need for the sudden flurry of activity. He, Ma, and Stacey were going about this as if it were something they did every day. Actually, a person never knew what to expect out here and had to be ready for things that did happen, good or bad. They'd buried Mrs. Dahl just a few weeks ago. Now Ma and Stacey would be helping Mrs. Duncan bring a new life to the prairie.

Upstairs, Charles peeled off his trousers and shirt while Caleb gave him some of his own clothes. They were big on Charles, but with the sleeves rolled up and a pair of suspenders hitched to the waist of the trousers, they'd do. Caleb picked up the dirty clothes and carried them downstairs, out the front door, and dumped them in the big wooden washtub over by the shed.

"Let's get you some fresh horses, Charles," he said, eyeing the haggard-looking animals in front of Charles's wagon.

Charles looked doubtful. He hooked his thumbs through the suspenders and shifted from one boot to the other. "Mr. Main . . . Ma . . ."

"If we don't change these horses, you won't get back to your ma. Come on."

Caleb and Charles walked to the barn, then each took a horse and led it out. "Did you bring a rifle?" Caleb asked Charles.

"Yes, sir."

"Know how to shoot?"

"Well, yes, sir. Once shot clear through—"

"Don't let anything happen to Stacey and my ma."

Charles gave him a long look. "I wouldn't, sir. Sometimes I think I love Stacey. Don't know if she's told you that. Don't know what she's told you about me."

Caleb chuckled, remembering the evening Laura had forced him to take the cattle to water and leave Charles and Stacey alone. He remembered how nervous he'd been that maybe Charles wouldn't keep his hands to himself, and that he'd sat at the table earlier that evening and said things that had made Stacey want to hit him.

In just the little bit of time he'd spent with Charles so far this evening, he'd decided he liked Charles Duncan. The young man reminded Caleb of the way he'd been about ten years ago—struggling to take care of a sister and a mother, struggling just to prove he could. All the rumors Caleb had heard about Charles being lazy at the family farm slipped away. Caleb chastised himself for ever listening to those rumors.

"Don't reckon I gave Stacey a chance to say much," Caleb said. "But just a few days ago I told her we'd have you to supper some evening if you're interested."

Charles's eyes widened. "Sure . . . Sure I'm interested!"

"All right. But for now, let's get these horses hitched."

After Ruth, Stacey, and Charles left, the house seemed very quiet to Laura. She had grown accustomed to Stacey's chatter and Ruth's advice. Not ten minutes after the wagon pulled away, she already missed them.

Caleb helped Amanda wash at the washbasin. The roast was already on the table, along with tender onions and thick potatoes. Laura sat near Amanda and across from Caleb. Amanda had learned to use her fork well now, hardly ever spilling a bite on its way to her mouth. She had a healthy appetite, too, and Laura thought she looked as though there was more of her lately. Doubtless, with five mouths to feed and very little food to give them, Blake Kincaid had tossed Amanda the scraps, if there had been any scraps after everyone finished.

Laura realized that for the first time since her own arrival, Ruth and Stacey were absent from the table. They wouldn't be here later, either, to sit with Laura and Caleb on the porch under the stars. Amanda would sit with them for a while, then go to bed. Some evenings she fell asleep on the porch, and Caleb would scoop her up and carry her into the house, probably the same way he had carried Laura inside that night that seemed so long ago. She remembered waking up, wondering if he had lingered over her. Had he perhaps thought about pulling back the quilt and slipping under it with her, the way he had slipped under the blanket with her in those hills after the coach accident? He had been such a stranger to her then, offering warmth, offering an embrace like no other. She had known then that being with him felt right. Oh, she had been uncomfortable the next morning, knowing she had spent the night in the arms of a stranger, but those arms had still felt good around her.

Across the table she caught Caleb's dark, intense gaze and knew he must be thinking some of the same thoughts. Such strangers they had been. She had never dreamed, when she had set out from Bismarck, that she would be taking a journey that would forever change her life.

"A lot of thoughts in that pretty head of yours," Caleb said.

She smiled. "I was remembering the day you found me in those hills."

He lifted a brow. "You remember that day?"

"Parts of it. I remember being trapped and not being able to move. I remember the terrible headache. And I remember the blanket."

"The blank . . . oh, the blanket," he said, grinning, devilish delight suddenly dancing in his eyes. "I was trying to keep you warm."

"Perhaps we should finish this discussion later, Mr.

Main," she teased, shaking her head. She remembered thinking at the time that he was looking at her as if he would like to crawl back under the blanket with her. He had been! The beast.

"Reckon we better do just that, Miss Kent," he said.

Laura's heart quickened. She knew they would find each other later. Already her body tingled in anticipation.

They finished supper, then Laura washed the dishes. Caleb sat on the settee with Amanda on his knee, and Laura watched them from the corner of her eye. He held his hand up with his fingers spread and counted his fingers for Amanda. He caught Laura watching them and narrowed his eyes at her, asking, "What's still cooking on the stove?"

Laura glanced at the stove, and her eyes widened at the sight of the tightly covered kettle. Giving a sudden cry of disappointment, she flew to the stove.

The pudding—how many hours had it been steaming? It was probably rubbery and scorched. Laura started to lift the lid . . . and couldn't. She didn't want to look. After she had learned that plum pudding was Caleb's favorite, she had wanted to cook it, and she had asked Ruth to teach her. Ruth had thoughtfully taken the time. Laura had been so proud. When she had put it in the kettle on the stove, she had thought of how surprised Caleb would be.

Well, she certainly wouldn't present him with scorched pudding, she thought, staring at the kettle.

Caleb walked up behind her, peering over her shoulder at the kettle. "A bit too done? Sam'll eat it," he said in amusement.

Laura stared at the pudding. And the more she stared, the more tears formed in her eyes, blurring her vision. *Sam?* She had wanted to make a delicious plum pudding for Caleb. "I made it for you," was all she could say.

There was silence. Then: "For me?"

She nodded.

"Well, let's get it off the stove, Laura," Caleb said.

He moved away and seconds later returned with two thick cloths. Laura stepped aside to let him take the kettle off the stove. He took it to the table, grabbed another thick cloth, and placed the kettle on it. "I bet it's not so bad," he said.

Shaking her head, Laura turned away. She didn't want to look at it, much less listen to his attempt to make her feel better. "It's terrible. I know it. You know it. Take it out to Sam."

He didn't say anything else about it. He asked if Laura and Amanda wanted to help him take the cattle to water. Laura said yes, and the three of them went outside, saddled horses, and rode through tall prairie grass toward the cattle.

Amanda rode with Caleb. Laura rode to the back and to the left of one side of the small herd; Caleb and Amanda rode to the right. Soon Laura heard Caleb whistling. After a time she was amazed to hear Amanda trying to do the same. Laura had not asked how Caleb had drawn Amanda out from beneath the bush in Plum Valley. The whistling must be something Caleb had started with Amanda before Laura had come along. It seemed to be something that drew them close, so Laura didn't ask how it had gotten started. But she enjoyed listening to them—Caleb whistling, and Amanda trying to create the same sounds. Now and then Caleb would lean over Amanda's little shoulder and say something to her. Amanda would twist her mouth and try another whistle.

The sun began to set. Fiery rivers blended with blue. As the cattle surged toward the creek, Laura, Caleb, and Amanda sat together on the log where Laura and Caleb had sat the evening Laura had managed to pull him away from the farm—and from disturbing Stacey and Charles. She wondered what Caleb thought of Charles now. The young man had ridden five miles to fetch someone to take care of his ma. And if his dirty clothes had been any indication, he had been working in a barn or a pen when he had realized his mother needed help. He didn't appear to be the lazy sort that Caleb had implied he was.

"Pa loved these sunsets," Caleb said, his eyes roaming about the land. "I sure don't remember sunsets like this in Illinois."

The leaves of a scraggly tree rustled nearby, and when Laura looked at the tree, it was a silhouette against breathtaking red, orange, and a very faint deep blue. There was something peaceful about sitting on the log while daylight was dying, listening to the occasional lowing of the cattle, watching them dip their heads toward water and drink. An occasional breeze riffled through the prairie grass, creating the illusion of golden waves. Amanda shifted on the log, and Laura put out a hand to steady her.

"You've been to Illinois?" she asked Caleb, then shook her head. "For some reason I can't imagine you ever being anywhere but Dakota."

"Lived near Springfield until I was seventeen. That's where Ma's family's from. Pa had been in the cavalry a while, going here and there, mostly in Kansas. In seventy-four, he had a chance to settle at Fort Abraham Lincoln near Bismarck. He sent for me, Ma, and Stacey."

"That explains why you stayed in Bismarck."

Caleb nodded. "I remember waving bye to Pa the morning he rode out with General Custer. After we got word of what happened at Little Bighorn, Ma didn't want to leave Dakota. Neither did I, really. We kept thinking land . . . get some land and settle. So we stayed. And you know the land story."

"Yes, I know the land story," Laura said almost in a whisper.

The cattle stirred. Caleb jumped down from the logs and reached for Amanda, lowering her. Then he reached for Laura, and her gaze caught his. A strand of stray hair blew gently across her face, and he tenderly brushed it away, letting his hand linger on her face. His eyes were filled with longing and love. He dipped his head and kissed her. A brush of a kiss . . . but enough to make her want more. Then he moved away.

"Let's go," he said roughly.

He lifted her up to her horse, hoisted Amanda up to his, and swung up behind Amanda. He yelled at the cattle, and the cattle began moving, a mass of dark bodies in the golden prairie grass.

Soon the buildings of the farm came into view. They left the cattle a distance of two or three hundred feet from the barn. Laura heard chickens squawking and jumped when the

crack of a rifle split the air. There was a yelp, then only the
sound of the chickens again. Laura's eyes shot to Caleb at
the precise moment he was lowering his rifle.

"Damn coyote. Same one that's been taking chickens now
and then and making me lose sleep. But this time I got it," he
muttered.

He swung down and lowered Amanda.

After helping Caleb take the horses to the barn and unsaddling them, Laura took Amanda with her to the house. She
suspected Caleb would be outside for a while—tomorrow
there would probably be another skin nailed to another board
and placed in the sun by the bearskin.

Inside the house Laura sat behind Amanda on the floor in
front of the settee. She reached around and put the slate pencil in Amanda's hand. Together they drew numbers, and beside each number they drew objects to equal that number.
Laura knew that if she did this with Amanda enough times,
Amanda would eventually associate the numbers with the
objects. Laura only wrote numbers one through five, and
when Amanda's eyelids looked heavy, Laura put the slate
and pencil aside. Amanda took Laura's hand and pulled her
toward the stairs, something she always did when she
wanted to go to bed. Days ago Laura had learned that
Amanda liked to have Laura help her change for bed, then
she liked Laura to tuck the quilt beneath her chin. Laura had
realized that the feeling of security, especially at night, was
important to Amanda. Since Laura had some idea what the
child's life had been like before she had come here, she understood the need for security and consistency.

Once Amanda was securely tucked in, Laura went to the
little chest of drawers, untied the ribbon binding the tapered
end of her braid, and separated the plaits. After putting the
ribbon in the top drawer, she took the silver-backed brush
she had brought from Bismarck and began brushing her hair.
It was crinkled from the braid, as it always was at night. She
knew Caleb liked to see it this way—in crinkles, flowing
around her shoulders and down her back. She stroked one
last time, put the brush away, and went downstairs.

Caleb was sitting at the table, eating plum pudding.

Scorched plum pudding.

"What are you doing?" Laura asked as she crossed the room. "Eating that pudding?"

He grinned. "*Enjoying* that pudding."

"You're mad. You were supposed to take it to Sam."

"I took him some."

Laura laughed. "Caleb, don't eat the pudding simply to make me feel better about ruining it."

"Wouldn't eat something I didn't like," he said around a bite. Using his fork, he pointed to a spot on the pottery plate where he had pushed aside some thick, discolored pieces. "Rest of it's good."

She shook her head, unable to believe he was eating it. Then she noticed how his eyes fastened on her hair.

"Life's pretty different out here than in the city," he said. "You going to be able to get used to that?"

She smiled. "The first evening I walked into this house, I knew I could stay here if I was ever given the opportunity."

"Because if you don't think you could . . . I mean, I know there's the house in Bismarck where you lived with your pa. There's all his things. I'd understand, Laura. I'd hurt, but I'd understand."

She lost her smile as she stared at him. "That is the sweetest thing anyone has ever said to me," she managed when she finally found her voice. "No, Caleb. I want to be with you, out here, in this house."

"Winters are bad sometimes. Some families just pack up and leave, the weather's so damn bad. Summers, too. We get grasshoppers, bad some years. Last year we didn't have rain all summer. The creek nearly dried up. I thought I'd lose the cattle."

"We'll survive, Caleb," Laura said softly. "Together. As for Pa's things, I don't want to keep very many. I want to find a few letters I wrote to him when I was younger. They're somewhere in the house—he often told me he kept all my letters. The ones I want are ones I wrote to him to ask about my mother. I remember very little about her. I still have the letters he wrote back, long letters telling about her. I want to put my letters and his together. I want his diaries, too. I want the pictures in the house and the portrait of him that's hanging in his private sitting room." She paused. Thinking of Pa and the fact that he was gone was still hard at times.

"I remember when they told me my pa was dead. I didn't believe it at first," Caleb said.

She smiled and brushed a tear away. "I didn't, either. I do now. I need to face everything in Bismarck—the house, the office. Oh, yes, the office. I need to make myself walk in there. I need to sit beneath the elm where we used to picnic. I need to let go of the pain because sometimes it still hurts so bad, and I think the only way to do that is to go there, relive it, believing it, then go on. I want to visit his grave, perhaps ask things I already know I'll never find the answers to. Adrian wouldn't have gotten so caught up in the idea of the money if Pa hadn't dangled it in front of him. I love Pa, and yet I hate what he did to people. I don't imagine the confusion I feel inside about him will ever go away. He was good, yet he was bad. Only he would know the answer to why he was like that, and he *can't* answer.

"In one way I'm like you, Caleb. I want Bismarck behind me. I don't want the house anymore. I don't want all the furnishings and even all of Pa's things, but at least I can look through them now. I've fallen in love with this farm and with you and Stacey and Ruth. I never meant to, but I did. Now I can't imagine being anywhere else. Bismarck will never be home again, and that doesn't make me sad. It's simply the truth."

Caleb reached across the table and squeezed her hand. "I'm scared, you know," he said. "About going back to Bismarck."

Laura knew that for a proud man like Caleb those words were difficult to say. "I know. But I'm glad you can talk to me about your fear. Admitting that is the first step toward forgiveness and healing. By going back, you'll find that nothing there from the past can ever hurt you again. We'll be together, hand in hand."

He nodded but looked doubtful. She knew there was still much hurt inside him.

"I'll be with you," she whispered.

Nodding again, he studied her for a moment, then rose and took the plate to the washbasin. From there he walked to the curtain hiding the bath alcove and pulled it aside. He took two buckets and started for the front door. He stopped at the stove and stirred the coals.

"I'm going to heat water for a bath," he said.

"Should I take the rest of this pudding to Sam?" Laura asked, half-teasing and half-serious.

"I like that pudding. Feed the rest to Sam and you'll have to make me another one just like it."

Laura laughed. "I don't know if I can do that. I mean, I don't know if I remember exactly how long to let it steam to get it scorched like that."

Chuckling, Caleb disappeared through the front door. Laura began washing the dishes and utensils they had used at supper and the plate Caleb had just finished using. She was washing the third plate when he came back through the front door with the bucket and poured water into two large kettles on the stove.

When the water boiled, Caleb carried the kettles to the bathtub and dumped the steaming water. From the well outside, he again filled the bucket and added that water to the boiling water until he had just the right temperature.

Laura had finished washing the dishes. Now she went to the sewing corner to see if there was something there she could stitch while Caleb was taking his bath, something that would keep her mind off of the fact that he would soon be naked just beyond that curtain. She found some pieces of a quilt Ruth had started.

She had just picked up a pair of scissors when Caleb grabbed her around the waist from behind. Startled, she jumped, then laughed.

"I do have a pair of scissors in hand, Mr. Main," she threatened playfully.

He nipped at her neck, and the feel of his warm lips and scratchy beard shot shivers of pleasure through her. She tipped her head to one side to give him better access. He growled low in response, the vibration taunting her sensitive skin.

"Pastor Jacobs. A few weeks," he said.

Breathing swiftly, she wrinkled her brow, at first not understanding what he was talking about. *Pastor Jacobs? A few weeks?*

"I can't stand many more nights of sleeping without you in my arms."

Now she understood completely. He wanted Pastor Jacobs to marry them in a few weeks.

At first she stiffened, gripped by something akin to the odd uneasiness that had overwhelmed her when Adrian had insisted they become engaged and set the wedding date so soon after she returned from school. Then she scolded herself. Caleb was nothing like Adrian, and his motives were certainly nothing like Adrian's. She loved Caleb and wanted to be in his arms every night.

"All right," she agreed breathlessly. "But for now, while things are definitely warm here, your bath is rapidly getting cooler."

"Our bath," he corrected.

Before Laura had a chance to say anything or even twist around in surprise, he scooped her up in his arms. Startled again, she dropped the scissors and hoped they didn't land on his feet. They clattered to the floor. "Caleb, put me down. What if I don't want a bath?" she said, laughing.

He grinned and rubbed his scratchy beard against her cheek. "How can you resist a bath with me?"

Laura managed a stern look, then smiled again. "What if I did?"

"Resist me?" he asked in a tone of great surprise.

"You talk as if that's a terribly difficult thing to do."

"Isn't it?"

She touched his mouth, first with her finger, then her lips. "Oh, yes. Terribly."

Chuckling, Caleb carried her to the tub and put her down beside it. He had lit a lamp and placed it on a high shelf to the left of the tub. The shelf contained other items—cloths, bottles of Stacey's perfume in various shades, and a jar half

filled with the soap Ruth made for baths. Several large towels were draped over a line above and just beyond the foot of
the tub. The towels were actually white, but flames dancing
in the lamp on the shelf cast a glow about the alcove, casting
everything in a soft yellow-orange light.

Caleb began unbuttoning her dress. Laura watched his big
fingers work with the tiny buttons, wondering how he undid
them with such ease. His hands brushed her breasts, and she
inhaled deeply, every nerve in her body leaping. She glanced
up into his eyes. A storm stirred in their blackness, heating,
churning, centering on her. Normally storms frightened her,
but this was one she wanted to lose herself in.

He sank to his knees before her, unfastened her boots, and
slipped them from her feet. Then he stood and began slowly
pushing the bodice from her shoulders. He kissed the hollow
between her neck and shoulder, lingered at it, then eased his
lips over the curve of her shoulder, skimming his tongue
lightly along her arm, following the path of the dress as it
slid down and finally slipped over her hands. Her thoughts
were blurred as she grasped his shoulders, clinging to him.

"If you persist, we may never get into that bath," she said
between little gasps. He was kissing her fingers now, running his tongue up and down each one, tracing them. Then
he kissed her sensitive palm. Laura trembled, and her heart
threatened to pound right out of her chest.

"Oh . . . we'll get to it," he murmured, and the feel of his
lips moving against her wrist as he spoke added to the be-
witching passion that already threatened to explode within
her.

Laura's hands found his baby-soft hair. His head was level
with her waist now, and she watched his eyes flare the tiniest
bit as he pushed the dress down over her hips and thighs, un-
tying and taking her drawers with the dress. He kissed her
bare stomach. His lips continued down. He slipped a hand
between her thighs, parting, seeking, finding, and teasing her
feminine flesh with the soft touch of his fingertips.

Laura gasped again, pressing her hands to his head as he
continued the intimate play, the intimate *torture*. She was
standing—how, she didn't know. Her knees wanted to bend,

give way. Her legs felt soft and shaky. A moment more, and they wouldn't hold her.

Suddenly bursts of pleasure shot through her, and she heard her own voice cry out.

When she recovered somewhat, Caleb had finally lifted his head and stood. She gazed at him in amazement. He had tortured yet pleasured her, and her body yearned for even more. She felt no shame in that, knowing her desire was another part of the beauty she shared with Caleb and only Caleb.

Her camisole found its way to the floor to join her dress and drawers. Caleb grinned a lazy, seductive grin and stepped back, unbuttoning his shirt.

"You look dazed, Laura," he said, and his voice was husky and thick, sensual, slithering around her with the smoothness of black velvet.

She felt naive. She had never known . . . She flushed and lowered her lashes.

Caleb lifted her chin, forcing her to meet his hungry, amused gaze. "We'll share a passel of secrets before our life together's finished."

He kissed her, and she parted her lips. He drank from her. Her hands found his muscled shoulders and pushed the shirt over them and down his strong arms.

He stepped back and removed his boots and trousers. Laura feasted on the sight of his naked body—the flexing muscles of his shoulders and arms, the swirls of black hair on his chest, and the line of hair that ran down his tight stomach and erupted in a crop of curls around the hardened length that made him a man. He was beautiful, and she would never tire of staring at him.

"The bath . . ." he said with a choked voice.

Laura responded boldly: "The last thing I want is a bath."

Chuckling, Caleb took her hand. They stepped into the tub.

Quite a length of time had passed since he had poured the water in the tub. Laura expected to feel cold water, but it was warm, almost hot. Her skin tingled as it massaged her calves.

"You couldn't have added very much cool water to this. It's so warm."

He grinned, taking the jar of soap from the shelf. "I figured we might take a while to get here."

"Devil," she teased as they sat, facing each other. "You planned every moment, didn't you?"

"Every second."

He soaped a cloth, put the jar on the floor beside the tub, and began washing her, starting at her neck and arms and working down. Laura shivered with pleasure when the coarse cloth brushed her erect nipples. Caleb's hand lingered at them, taunting. Then lovingly he ran his fingertips, slippery from the soap, over, around, and under each breast, his gaze following the movements. She was fighting for breath by the time his eyes caught and held hers, and she already knew the answer to the question that spilled from her lips: "Since you admitted to planning every second, what happens after the bath?"

"You spend the night in my bed," he answered without hesitation. "If you want to."

Her lips curved into a smile. She had only known *part* of the answer, it seemed. "An entire night . . ." she whispered.

"If you want to," he said again.

"I do."

He washed her stomach and her legs, and asked her to turn around so he could wash her back. Laura closed her eyes and lost herself in his gentle massage. Every place he touched sparked with a life of its own.

When he stopped, Laura opened her eyes. He was laying back leisurely in the tub, watching her, his eyes narrowed with hunger. His gaze went to her breasts, then slowly traveled down.

Laura caught her breath. He appeared to be savoring the sight of her, and she loved the way his eyes ravished her, but she also found the ravishment unbearable. For a moment she sat still under his searing gaze. Then she reached for the jar of soap, lathered the same cloth he had used on her, and slid forward onto his lap, straddling him.

His hardened length touched her feminine flesh with heat,

and Laura emitted a soft cry of both surprise and pleasure. He sought entrance; her body screamed for her to grant it. Laura couldn't fight the need—she moved her hips against him, wanting him to thrust up inside her.

Caleb put his hands on her hips and held her back. She narrowed her eyes at him and shook her head. "Don't make me wait forever," she whispered breathlessly.

"It just seems like forever," he rasped. "Take the cloth and wash me."

In her moment of profound need, Laura knew she would do whatever he asked. She tipped forward, swirled the cloth over his shoulders, arms, and chest, feeling his powerful muscles contract and relax, contract and relax. His beard glistened with droplets of water, and his lips seemed darker now, more pronounced between his mustache and beard. The hair on his chest was thick and wiry, though softened somewhat by the water. The suds contrasted with the curls, and there were swirls of white and swirls of black until the hair thinned at his tight stomach.

Laura scooted back to soap his stomach. He tipped his head back and shut his eyes. She made little circles with the cloth and watched pleasure flicker across his masculine features. When her hands reached the place where the thin line of black hair erupted into a crop of curls, she hesitated . . . dropped the cloth . . . and touched him.

He tensed and groaned, and Laura withdrew her hands, wondering if she had hurt him. His eyes were open now, but narrowed more than before. Laura felt their heat.

"Laura, sweet Laura," he murmured.

Confident now that she had pleasured him, not hurt him, Laura curled her soaped hands around him, marveling in the thick, hard feel of him. She slid her hands up and down his length. But after only a few strokes, Caleb stopped her. She stared at him, wondering why. Had she done something wrong? Something he hadn't liked?

He sat up, splashed water over her and himself to rinse the soap from their bodies, then stepped from the tub and grabbed one of the towels. He took Laura's hand and urged her to stand and step out of the tub. He wrapped a towel around her, wrapped another around his waist, then took her hand again. "Come on," he said in a thick voice.

He led her to the stairs, the wooden steps creaking beneath their feet, the flat stair rail rough and hard beneath her hand. They left little puddles of water that dwindled to mere droplets with each step they took. Compared to the warmth of the bath, the air was cool, and it touched Laura's skin, making her shiver. Caleb held her hand and led her steadily on.

At the top of the steps they turned right—Laura and Amanda's room was to the left. At the end of the hall, past two more doors, they entered Caleb's room.

Caleb moved across the dark room and lit a lamp. The flickering flame created shadows on the walls but gave the room a soft glow of light.

Laura glanced around. The ceiling sloped slightly to one side, and the walls seemed to huddle together. She wondered how Caleb, as tall as he was, kept from banging his head on the ceiling. Then she noticed there were no furnishings on that side of the room. A chest of drawers and a small table and chair were the only furnishings besides the bedstead in the center of the room. If Caleb slipped from the right side of the bedstead and stood half asleep, she imagined he *would* bump his head. She watched him move easily about the room and was amused that such a large man occupied such a small room.

He closed the door and crossed the room to pull down the patchwork quilt on the bed. Then he held out a hand, beckoning her.

She went to him.

The towels fell away. Bodies touched. Hearts pounded. Laura and Caleb kissed each other deeply. She slid her arms around his neck, let her fingers frolic in his hair, then she lowered her hands to once again marvel at the strength of his shoulders and arms. He whispered her name; she whispered his. He lifted her and lowered her to his bed.

His big hands wandered over her body, making her arch to him, want him, need him. His mouth, hot and wet, seemed to roam everywhere. Their shadows loomed on one wall, and

Laura watched the shadows as she parted her thighs and arched again, inviting Caleb.

He groaned, a deep, almost primitive sound, and covered her.

The first thrust took Laura's breath and shot sweet pleasure to every nerve in her body. The shadows had become one, had merged, and even when Caleb withdrew to thrust into her again, the shadows were still one, mingling and surging in a primal way. Caleb filled her again and again; she cried his name again and again. She wrapped her legs around him and drew him even deeper into her.

They met the explosion together, arching, tensing, crying, loving . . . Ecstasy shattered around them, coloring the room a million different breathtaking, beautiful shades.

Caleb lowered his head to rest on her breast.

❄ ❄ ❄
Chapter Twenty-one

A SOFT NIGHT breeze drifted into the room. Caleb tucked the quilt tightly around Laura's shoulders and molded his body to her back. She was lying on her side, and she'd been sleeping soundly for the last several hours. He hadn't slept at all. He'd gotten stirred up again right after she'd gone to sleep, but he hadn't wanted to wake her. He was a bit exasperated at himself. He wanted her in his bed, but hell . . . he might never *sleep* with her in his bed.

She stirred, moving her head and right arm to shift her position. Her head was even with his chin. He put his arm under the quilt and ran his hand down the side of her body, over the dip of her waist and the hill of her hip. Laura moaned softly, sleepily, and moved her bottom against him. He slid his hand up, back over her hip and waist. She said his name, as if she was scolding him, and he laughed, nuzzling her neck. Finally she turned on her back, and her hands gripped his shoulders. She kissed him and whispered, "Again, Caleb. Again."

He slid into her.

The next morning Laura and Amanda went to gather eggs from the chicken house. One hen was being difficult, pecking at Laura's hand every time she tried to put her hand under it and take the eggs she knew it was sitting on. Laura tried a third time, and the hen actually took a piece of skin this time. Laura snapped her hand back and looked down at the wound. It only oozed a little blood but sure felt worse than a small cut. She pointed a finger at the obstinate hen. "Listen, you, I will get those eggs."

Just then Laura heard the steady thud of a horse's hooves.

At first she thought that perhaps Ruth and Stacey were returning already, but she didn't hear the creak of a wagon and she heard only one horse—she was certain of that.

Caleb was in the barn milking cows, so Laura and Amanda wandered out to see who was riding up to the house.

The man sitting on the horse was tall and lean with reddish hair and a long, thin face. Side whiskers came to a squared abrupt halt and were even with his earlobes on either side. He looked familiar, but Laura couldn't quite place him. Perhaps she had seen him in town several times or at church. She simply wasn't sure.

For the first time since Ruth and Stacey had left, Laura wondered what people would think of her and Caleb staying at the farm alone. She didn't think Ruth or Stacey or even Caleb had had a chance to think about what people might say. She knew she hadn't thought about it. Amanda was here with her and Caleb, but Amanda was only a child, and people would discount her.

Laura hoped for the Mains' sake that whoever this man was, he wouldn't ride to Minot and start wagging his tongue. But that was certainly a possibility. As soon as he left, she would talk to Caleb. She loved him and had been with him in a beautiful way; but not everyone would think of the time they had spent together as beautiful. People who spread rumors had a way of making some situations look ugly, although in her heart what she and Caleb had shared beneath the plum tree, in the barn, and in his bedroom had been extraordinary and would never seem ugly to her.

The man swinging down from the saddle held a rolled-up piece of paper. For some inexplicable reason, Laura's eyes were drawn to that sheet of paper. A feeling of dread fluttered in her stomach. *It's only a simple piece of paper,* she told herself, *rolled up scroll-fashion and gripped in the hand of this man I can't even identify.* She also told herself the man's business could have nothing to do with her.

But her eyes met the man's steady, brown, accusing eyes, and she sensed that that paper had everything to do with her.

He tipped his head in greeting, a greeting she perceived as

being forced. He continued to stare hard at her, as if passing judgment.

"Hello," she said, keeping her voice as steady as possible, though his hard stare unnerved her.

Again he tipped his head. But he said nothing.

"Zeke Taylor," Caleb said from behind Laura.

Laura twisted around to glance at Caleb, knowing that the strange fear that had gripped her about that paper showed in her eyes. Caleb gave her an odd look, then marched forward to grasp and pump Zeke's outstretched hand. "Now, just what is the sheriff of Minot doing riding up to my farm?" he asked. "I know I spent some time in town—"

"Came to talk, Caleb. To you . . . and to Miss Kent there," he said, looking past Caleb to Laura.

Caleb went still. He glanced around at Laura, his eyes filled with wariness and questions. Laura shook her head, trying to tell him she wasn't sure what this was about. His gaze went back to the sheriff, a man who didn't look like a sheriff at all. He wore no badge, not even a gun. He wore a dark brown shirt and simple black trousers with black boots.

"All right, Zeke," Caleb said, dusting his hands off. "Let's go inside. We'll make some coffee and settle around the table for a while."

"That'd be good, Caleb," said Zeke, avoiding Laura's gaze now. "That'd be real good."

Laura made the coffee with trembling hands. Caleb and Zeke sat at the table, talking about the old Minot, how it had once consisted of a small cluster of crude wooden buildings before the Manitoba Railroad had come through. After that no one ever knew how many buildings might be hastily erected overnight. Fortunately the town had drawn good people and honest businesses as well as bad. The sheriff had apparently settled more than one dispute.

"And," he said, sighing heavily, "I'm not looking forward to settling the problem that was dropped in my lap some time ago. Wasn't going to even think about it, either, until someone showed up yelling or something. Figured there was no reason to push good people off good land. There's still no reason. 'Cept once I heard Miss Kent was in town—or close to town—I figured I'd better deal with it."

Laura carried mugs of coffee to the table and placed one before Caleb, the other before Zeke. "Why would my presence here make a difference in whether or not you've decided to take care of something, Sheriff?" she asked him. She felt like a mass of raw nerves, wondering what was written on that blasted piece of paper. "Why would my presence, or anyone else's for that matter, interfere with how you do your job?"

Caleb tilted his head back and studied her with narrowed eyes. "What's wrong, Laura?"

"Nothing," she snapped. "Nothing except the way he rode up here, holding a piece of paper and giving me odd looks. I'm curious, and you're drawing this out, Sheriff. Since it seems to concern me, would you mind telling me what that paper says?"

Zeke calmly sipped his coffee. Her eyes went to the scrolled paper lying on the table now. She had half a mind to simply grab it, unroll it, and read it.

"Oh, you know what it says," he drawled. "You know damn good and well what it says."

Caleb stiffened, and Laura saw irritation flicker in his eyes. He didn't like the way the sheriff was drawing this out any more than she did. "Zeke, what's this about?" he asked.

"Months ago, back in May maybe, a rider brought this," Zeke said, lifting the paper and unrolling it. His eyes never left Laura's, although he spoke to Caleb. "It's a legal thing, telling me to get the squatters off a pretty good chunk of land out here. Seems it's Kent land, and the Kents want to bonanza farm it."

At first Laura was speechless. Then she blurted, "What? In May? That isn't possible!"

Caleb and the sheriff stared at her.

She felt as if this were some sort of joke. Pa was dead. He had died in February. She was the only Kent left, and she certainly had not seen any papers since his death . . . or had she? She remembered Mr. Trumball bringing some papers to her at the house, but . . . She knew what bonanza farming was: Someone bought a huge portion of land and farmed the entire area, employing managers and workers, people to plant, reap, and thresh the wheat. There were many bonanza farmers in Dakota Territory. Pa had other huge pieces of land—she wasn't sure where—and they were bonanza farms. He had talked about buying up more land, but she didn't know where he had been looking or whether or not he had even bought any before his death.

Laura struggled to visualize the papers Mr. Trumball had brought to her that day so long ago. Had any of them entailed the sale of land in this area to Pa? She couldn't remember. The only thing she did remember was that she had signed several of them. She glanced at the sheriff, and a chill raced up and down the length of her spine.

His hard brown eyes bit into her. "Your pa owned the land. He'd written to me a couple of times over the last two, maybe three years. He wasn't threatening nothing legal, so I burned the letters—wasn't gonna bother good people if I didn't need to. Last letter got a little threatening maybe, but I figured, well, let him come on up here and try to do something."

"My pa died in February, Sheriff," Laura said, instinctively feeling the need to defend herself. She was angry, too. She had done nothing wrong, she felt certain, yet here was this man, sitting there looking at her and talking to her as if she had committed a crime. "I don't know when you received those letters exactly, but if there are squatters on the land—"

"What, Laura?" Caleb demanded softly. There was anger in his voice and perhaps shock.

She had said the wrong thing, and she knew it. These people out here were all his neighbors and would be hers soon, too. "Caleb, I—"

"What about the squatters, Laura? They ought to be made to leave?"

She didn't know what to say, so she decided to say nothing. She had opened her mouth to defend herself and had only succeeded in making things worse.

"It has nothing to do with your pa, really. Not a thing,"

said the sheriff. "This is your doing," he said, pointing the paper at her. "It ain't the way we do things here, I'll tell you that. Maybe those folks didn't come by the land honest, but they worked it honest. It's your name here—Laura Kent. Plain as anything. I figure it wipes out the Kincaids, Duncans, Ferans, and Evetts. Now, none of 'em has a whole lot of land. But between the four families, there's a good chunk of land. Land ripe for bonanza farming."

Laura shook her head as he calmly sipped more coffee. "I signed some papers for Pa's attorney right after Pa died, but I don't remember signing anything like that." Actually she couldn't remember *what* she had signed, but at the moment she felt trapped. She couldn't think and she didn't know how to respond. She could deny that she had signed the paper . . . but how could she do that?

The sheriff pushed the paper across the table toward her. It rolled up by itself—a paper that had obviously spent months rolled up and gathering dust on a shelf or a desk. "Look for yourself, missy."

Laura grabbed the paper. It smelled musty and it crackled as she unrolled it. Her eyes skimmed the page. Something about squatters . . . on three hundred acres of land . . . to be removed . . .

It went on, and at the bottom of the page was her signature.

Her signature, as neat as could be: Laura Rose Kent. She couldn't deny that this was her handwriting. She could only stand still, holding the paper, not knowing what to do or say. Zeke was looking at her. Caleb was looking at her. And the look of pain and outrage that wrinkled Caleb's brow and made his eyes glitter killed her inside.

The people of the prairie were his friends and neighbors. The Kincaids and the Duncans . . . she didn't know the last two families—the Ferans and Evetts—but that hardly mattered. They were still people. The sheriff had said the families had worked the land honestly even if they hadn't come by it honestly. Around Minot those four families were obviously not viewed as squatters but as good sincere people.

She was the outsider. Her signature on the paper threatened the lives they had settled into.

What must Caleb be thinking right now? She glanced at him, and he stared at her. She saw the suspicion in his eyes, the pain. Doubtless he was remembering a time when Pa had stripped him of land that was rightfully his. Land he had paid for but had never seen. The difference was he *had* paid for his land. Squatters made a habit of *not* paying for it. But he probably wasn't thinking of that. He was probably thinking: *Here's another Kent taking land.*

"Caleb, I—"

"Be quiet, Laura," he said in a low voice.

All the pain and mistrust she thought they had worked through was back in his eyes, distorting his features.

He thinks I knew exactly what I was doing when I signed this, Laura thought.

During the weeks immediately following Pa's death, when Mr. Trumball had come with the papers, she had not looked at them. Mr. Trumball had talked to her about the management of various transactions, she now remembered. She struggled to remember more. That had been such a terrible time. She had been devastated by the loss of her father. The house had seemed so empty . . . so different. Mr. Trumball had said something about deals her pa had been working on and would want to complete. He had explained how Pa had always insisted on signing everything himself and overseeing most of his business transactions, and since she had inherited everything, approval was now her responsibility. Pa had never taught her how he conducted his business—she wasn't at all certain she would have wanted to learn anyway. He had probably assumed that if anything ever happened to him, she would be safely married to Adrian, and he or Mr. Trumball would take care of matters.

But to tell Caleb all of that . . . now wasn't the time. Besides, she had tried to explain, and Caleb had told her to be quiet. When he finally agreed to listen, would he believe her? Perhaps in his heart he didn't truly believe she had known what the paper said when she had signed it. She had thought they had learned to trust each other. Obviously a thin thread of doubt lingered in Caleb's mind. For him to even suspect that she would strip those people of their homes, take everything from them . . . she would never do that. She would offer them a piece of the land, perhaps hire them to manage part of it.

He was thinking the worst. He had looked at the paper, he had seen her signature, and he simply wasn't looking beyond that.

The sheriff stood, rounded the table, and took the paper from her. "Figure I'll be on my way now. Heard you were here, Miss Kent. Thought I owed you a visit. Figure a lot more people'll owe you a visit before this is over."

Be on his way now? He had ridden up with that piece of paper and possibly destroyed her relationship with Caleb. If Caleb refused to listen to her, if he didn't believe that she hadn't known what she was signing . . . Dear God . . . she could lose him all because of a piece of paper.

Caleb rose and walked out with the sheriff. Laura stood still, too shocked to move. She heard the thudding of the horse's hooves as the sheriff rode away. She heard the clomping of Caleb's boots on the porch.

Then he walked through the door, and she could only stare at him. No words would come, just a stare. What could she say to make this right? What could she do? She finally grappled for words: "Caleb, you can't think . . . I didn't know . . ."

"To hell with it, Laura," he said, his eyes cool and hard and centered on her. Then he turned away, grabbed his rifle from above the door, and left the house. In his mind she was guilty. In his mind, considering his past, this was nearly the worst thing she could have done.

But she hadn't done it. At least she hadn't known what she was doing when she had signed that paper. She had been told to sign, so she had signed. Even if she had known what she was doing, she had not known the Kincaids and the Duncans then. She had not known the struggles of the people here. She had not known about tar-paper houses and the dangers of the prairie. She had always had food, had always had a home unlike anything the prairie people could imagine. She had always been safe.

But, even not knowing the people and their everyday struggles, if she had known what she was signing, she wouldn't have done so without insisting the people on the land be offered *something*. She would never take someone's home. She was hurt that Caleb believed she would.

She wandered around the house for a time. She picked up the pieces of the patchwork quilt she had started to stitch last evening but couldn't concentrate. She sat with Amanda and sang "Pop! Goes the Weasel," but it sounded wrong. The lyrics were clipped. Her voice sounded tight. Her neck hurt. Her head hurt.

Then she became angry.

After all they had shared, could Caleb distance himself from her so easily? He could so easily say "to hell with it"? To hell with *them*? He could so easily walk away from her? Shut a door between them?

She would not let him.

Caleb busied himself, fixing one of the barn doors a stubborn cow had rammed into this morning. He cleaned the chicken house and put down fresh straw for the hens to lay on. He built a bench for the new schoolhouse and started building that new smokehouse he'd had in mind for a while and hadn't gotten to yet. He didn't let himself think. He was scared of what he might think if he got started.

Morning turned into afternoon. The sun blazed down. The day threatened to be a hell of a hot one. He paused several times to wipe sweat from his forehead. Then he worked again, pounding nails, sawing wood, avoiding thoughts. Time went by, which was just what he wanted.

"I brought water," Laura said from behind him, right by his elbow.

"Not thirsty," he said, pounding a nail.

"I brought food, too. Slices of ham and bread. Even boiled potatoes."

"Not hungry."

"All right. Some of the pudding you seem to like so
much?"

"No."

"Then I came to help. There must be something I can do.
I've done everything in the house. I made the beds, washed
the dishes, washed the table, swept the floor, skimmed the
cream, made the bread . . ." She sighed. "Amanda fell
asleep. I can't seem to keep my mind on stitching. Besides, I
pricked my finger with a needle. But I could help you. I want
to be with you."

"No."

"Caleb."

"No."

"I love you, Caleb."

The hammer slipped. It hit his thumb instead of the nail he
couldn't seem to hold steady. Cursing, he dropped the hammer and grabbed his thumb.

"Let me help you," Laura said, trying to pry his fingers
loose from his throbbing thumb.

A breeze caught a wisp of her hair and tormented his face
with it. He could smell her, dammit, and he didn't want to.
Wildflowers . . . The scent tortured him. In his mind images
from last night skittered about—how slick and satiny her
skin had looked while they had bathed together, how smooth
it had felt. She had leaned forward, and her nipples had
grazed his chest. She had smiled and looked seductive without meaning to. . . .

Damn! She was the prettiest woman he'd ever fixed his
eyes on, but he reckoned that didn't matter too much if she
was the kind of person who'd take people's land.

He jerked away from her. Hurt flickered in her eyes, but
he wasn't about to be fooled by that, either. She hadn't de-
nied signing the paper. She'd just stood there, saying nothing, staring at the paper. One look at her face had told him all
he'd needed to know: She'd signed it, damn her. She'd
signed it. She'd said that thing about the squatters, too, and
he reckoned that's the way she really felt inside—no matter
how long the Kincaids, Duncans, Ferans, and Evetts had

been on the land, it was Kent land, and they could just get the hell off.

Something else flashed in his mind, now that all these thoughts were running through it. "Are you scared Blake might want Amanda back someday?" he demanded.

She scowled at him. "What?"

"Answer, Laura."

"Well . . . yes, that has occurred to me several times. But—"

"What better way to get rid of the Kincaids? If you take their land, they've got to move on."

Her eyes grew as big as he'd ever seen them. "That's absurd! I can't believe you would accuse me of trying to do that, Caleb Main! I didn't even know the Kincaids in May. That's when the sheriff said he received that paper. And it had to have been signed months before that."

Tears glistened in her eyes now. He felt a stab of something he thought was shame, but no way in hell would he bend to it. "All right. I'm sorry for that. But that doesn't change anything. That was railroad land, all of it. The Manitoba Railroad sold it to somebody. I didn't know who, not too many people did. Zeke did, I reckon. But nobody said anything, either, when those families settled around there. Everybody knew they were squatters, but like Zeke said, they worked the land. That should count for something."

She stared at him. He shook the pain off his thumb and turned back to his work.

"You believe I knew exactly what I was doing when I signed that paper, don't you?" she demanded softly.

"I don't know what to believe, Laura. I figure I'll work today and maybe sort things out tomorrow."

He hammered more. She stared at him more. Finally she walked away.

Caleb finished building the smokehouse—he'd never built one so fast, at least not one so sturdy. He picked up his rifle, figuring he'd mount Soldier, take Sam, and go roam the prairie for a bit.

Then Adrian Montgomery rode up.

Damn. Montgomery was sure as hell the last person he wanted to see today.

Montgomery tipped his head of curly blond hair at Caleb, who returned the greeting despite his black mood. He wasn't real sure what to say, since he didn't know how Montgomery felt about him winning some of his money back the other night or dumping him in that bed in the boardinghouse. But then, Caleb reckoned he and Montgomery would never get too friendly. Montgomery was the scheming type Caleb had left behind long ago. And Caleb figured *he* was a mite too honest for Montgomery. They just weren't two men who could sit peacefully at the same table for long.

"Good afternoon, Mr. Main," Montgomery said, dismounting. He stayed right by his horse, as though he didn't trust Caleb.

"Afternoon," Caleb returned.

Montgomery shifted from one foot to the other. "I . . . as you probably know, I was feeling quite sorry for myself the other day." He paused, waiting for Caleb to say something.

Caleb nodded.

"I do not usually drink . . . like that. So much, I mean," Montgomery continued. "I do not usually wallow in self-pity, either. Of course, in my life there has not been a lot of pity to wallow in. When I was a boy, there was never time for pity. My parents . . . brother . . ." He twisted his lips and shook his head. Then he laughed in disbelief and looked up at the sky. "This is the hardest thing I have ever done."

Caleb wasn't going to make Montgomery more uncomfortable by waiting for him to go on. "I'll get your money," he said and started for the house.

The door was open a crack. Laura was there, looking through. She opened the door the rest of the way for Caleb. He stepped inside and grabbed the saddlebags filled with coins and bills.

"Is that all he wants?" she asked.

Caleb nodded. "That's all. And maybe to apologize in his own way."

"Apologize?"

"Seems like it."

Caleb went back outside. When he tossed the saddlebags across the horse's back, he spotted Laura standing in the open doorway with her arms crossed, rubbing her shoulders. She was watching cautiously, looking as nervous as he felt and Montgomery acted.

"I did not come merely to collect the money, Mr. Main," Montgomery said. "By all rights, it's yours. You won it. To tell you the truth, I do not even remember your winning it. I came to . . . to say thank you. I probably would have been content to sleep on one of those tables if you hadn't picked me up and carried me out of there. Of course, I am assuming that is what happened. You've humbled me, but you also saved me from total humiliation."

Caleb inclined his head in acceptance of his apology, then stepped back from the horse.

"I will . . ." Montgomery paused, selecting his words. "I will be going back to Bismarck. I stayed in Minot because there seems to be a lot of business springing up. I thought I might find an opportunity. But Minot is not for me. Bismarck is home. I'll return and take my chances with something else there."

He extended his hand then, and Caleb took it without hesitation. Montgomery was more of a man than he'd figured. He'd thought Montgomery would be angry when he came for the money. He wasn't. And he had apologized in his own way, as Caleb had told Laura he thought Adrian was trying to do.

Montgomery twisted around to look at Laura, who still stood in the doorway. He tipped his head to her, and Laura waved goodbye.

Then Adrian swung himself up on the saddle and rode away.

At supper Laura put bowls of ham and potatoes on the table for herself, Amanda, and Caleb while he and Amanda washed at the basin. Laura watched his back, wondering if he was ever going to forgive her for unwittingly signing that paper.

The afternoon had passed uneventfully after Adrian had

left. Caleb had ridden off for a time. When Amanda had awakened, she and Laura had walked through the green and golden prairie grass, close to where the cattle mingled and grazed, and had picked black-eyed Susans—the yellow-petaled flowers with dark purple centers—to put in a cup on the table as a centerpiece.

Laura had thought about the bonanza land situation and had reached a decision. She meant to talk to Caleb about it later, perhaps if she found him sitting on the porch this evening. She wanted to know if he could still trust her and if her father's ghost could stop coming between them.

She placed the last bowl on the table and was just taking her place when she heard the creak of a wagon. Caleb walked over and opened the door. Laura and Amanda followed him.

Charles helped Stacey down from the wagon. Caleb took the porch steps and crossed the space of land between the house and the wagon, which had been stopped near the barn. Laura stood on the porch with Amanda, watching Caleb offer Charles his hand. Charles shook it and shared a few words with Caleb while Stacey lifted her skirt and raced toward Amanda and Laura. She caught Laura in an embrace. Laura laughed and hugged her back.

Laura withdrew to look at her. "My, Stacey Main, your cheeks are glowing," she teased, giving her friend a sly look from the corner of her eye. "The ride here with Charles must have been wonderful."

"It was. Oh, it was," Stacey said almost in a whisper.

"Well, come inside," Laura said, taking Stacey's arm and turning her toward the door. "Tell me about the baby. Then tell me about the ride. Of course, if Charles and Caleb follow, you can tell me about that later. Supper is ready—I managed it by myself. I'm still shocked. Especially after I scorched the pudding we started steaming before you and Ruth left last evening."

"Oh, no." Stacey giggled. "You scorched the pudding?"

Laura nodded. "That's not the funniest part. The funniest part is that Caleb ate almost a fourth of it and plans to eat the rest."

Stacey stopped midstep and stared at her in astonishment. "Caleb hates scorched anything. He must really love you."

Laura inhaled a swift, painful breath. She prayed Stacey was right. She prayed Caleb loved her enough to work through the land problem. He needed to realize, once and for all, that she was not like Pa and never would be.

Charles stayed for supper, and Laura talked softly with Stacey about Mrs. Duncan and the new baby—a strong, healthy boy.

"He started screaming the minute Ma grabbed hold of him," Stacey said, her eyes bright. "It's so amazing, isn't it? I mean . . . he's so tiny, so helpless, so . . . beautiful. Ma will be back in a few weeks. She wanted to stay and help until Mrs. Duncan gets some of her strength back. Maybe we'll hitch up the wagon and take a ride over there after Ma gets back so you can see the baby. He's pretty, Laura."

"I'm sure he is," Laura said. She caught pieces of Caleb and Charles's conversation. They were discussing the wheat crops and the different men in Minot who would thresh, some for part of the crop or part of the money the crop brought instead of for wages.

"Now that the railroad's here, we can ship east. There won't be so much loading of wheat on barges to be shipped up- and downriver. And the rail will be a hell of a lot faster than shipping crops by barge, ship, or wagon," Caleb told Charles.

Charles agreed. "I heard the Manitoba's nearly clear into Montana, too. Pretty soon we'll be shipping west. I'm hoping Pa comes back soon. I have an uncle in Kentucky. A doctor. I want to learn from him."

Caleb lifted a brow. "You want to be a doctor?"

Laura waited, wondering what Caleb was thinking about Charles wanting to do something with his life other than farm.

"Not a doctor," Charles said. His eyes went from Caleb to Stacey to his plate. Clearly he was nervous. "I want to be an apothecary."

Caleb took the last bite of ham and potatoes, chewed and

swallowed, and drew his brows together in a thoughtful way. Laura watched Stacey watch him carefully, and she squeezed Stacey's hand under the table, wanting to say, "Wait. Give him a moment. Caleb will do fine. He likes Charles really."

"An a-poth-e-cary," Caleb said. "That's a mouthful. But I reckon if that's what you want to do, that's what you ought to do."

Stacey gave a cry and jumped from her seat. She raced around the table and wrapped her arms around Caleb's neck. "You're wonderful. You really are!"

Caleb chuckled. Charles grinned—a grin of relief, Laura thought. She smiled at Charles and didn't doubt that Stacey and Charles would marry someday. She watched them exchange a look filled with love, and she glanced down at her plate, not wanting to intrude on their moment.

Stacey returned to her chair and began talking to Laura again. Charles told Caleb about that uncle in Kentucky, and Caleb listened with interest.

Eventually Laura, Stacey, and Amanda began clearing the table and washing the dishes. Amanda took the plates after they had been washed. She placed each one on the table and used a small towel to dry first one side, then the other.

Amanda had dried a third plate when Laura heard her say, "L-laura."

Laura turned. Amanda had placed the plates side by side on the table, and she pointed to each one, showing what she had done.

Then she smiled.

And what a beautiful, beautiful smile it was.

Streaks of red spilled from the crimson sun and painted the sky. Laura sat on the porch steps with Amanda, and together they watched the sunset. Caleb, Stacey, and Charles had gone to take the cattle to water. Caleb had accepted Charles. Laura smiled, thinking Stacey must feel wonderful now.

Laura dipped water from the well and heated it so she could give Amanda a bath. She had just lifted the child into

the tub when she heard laughter and shouts and the pounding
of horses' hooves. Soon Caleb opened the door and walked
in, his rifle in one hand. Kneeling beside the tub, preparing
to wash Amanda's back, Laura caught his gaze. Her hand
froze; her entire body froze. Caleb's eyes were filled with a
silent apology, no longer incrimination and disbelief. He
wasn't looking at her in a wary way, as if she were the
daughter of his enemy. His look said he loved her, that
he *trusted* her.

She wanted to drop the wet, soapy cloth and run to him.
She wanted to wrap her arms around him and hug him. She
wanted to feel his lips on hers. How she loved him!

He tore his gaze from hers and turned to hang his rifle
above the door. With trembling hands, Laura finished
Amanda's bath, then lifted her from the tub and dried her.
She took Amanda upstairs, helped her dress, and tucked her
beneath the quilt in the big bedstead. Then she started downstairs.

Stacey was sitting in the sewing corner stitching. Caleb
sat in the chair across from the settee, an open book on his
lap. He must have heard the creak of the stairs; he glanced
over his shoulder, and again his eyes met Laura's. She
paused on the stairs, one hand clutching the rail. Would any
words they passed back and forth tonight remove, once and
for all, any doubts he had about her character simply because
she was related to Matthew Kent?

Caleb stood, leaving the book in the chair, and walked toward her. He extended a big, callused hand. Laura took it
without hesitation. He led her toward the front door. Hand in
hand, they went outside.

He sat in the chair in the heavy shadows and pulled her
down onto his lap. At the opposite side of the porch a lantern
dangled from the edge of the roof, its light flickering against
the house and on the porch. It was a mere speck of light
when one looked beyond, to the prairie, and glimpsed the
vast darkness. Laura heard a breeze whisper through the
prairie grass and through the field of wheat that would soon
be ready for harvest. Crickets chirped, and an owl hooted

somewhere in the distance. She rested her head against Caleb's chest and listened to the steady drum of his heartbeat.

His hand stroked her back, and he spoke softly: "I love you, Laura, no matter what might ever come between us. I damn sure don't agree with taking the land from those families. They worked it. I think they ought to have some rights where the land's concerned. But the fact is they're squatters when the railroad owned the land and they're squatters now." He sighed. "I did a lot of thinking when we were taking the cattle to water and bringing them back. Zeke was right when he said the paper had nothing to do with your pa. I didn't see that when I looked at that paper. I was thinking about Matt and how he took my land. Hell . . . I never *had* the land. But this is different. It doesn't have anything to do with Matt. The land belongs to you now, and you have rights, too, I reckon. If you want those families off the land, that's your right and I'll try and live with that."

Tears of happiness swelled in her eyes. He had truly separated her from Pa. He was also giving her the right to think for herself, to make decisions for herself. If she wanted to force the families off the land, he would respect her decision. He wouldn't like it, but he would respect it. Not that she ever intended to force the Kincaids, Duncans, Ferans, and Evetts off the land.

"Will you take me to Minot tomorrow?" she asked him. "I need to see the sheriff."

He touched her hair, letting her braid slip slowly through his fingers. "After dinner?"

She nodded. He untied the ribbon at the end of the braid and began separating her hair. She nestled against him. His clothes smelled of horses and leather and the prairie, and those scents mingled with his own heady, masculine scent. She closed her eyes, loving the strength of him and the things about him that made him Caleb . . . his gentleness, his devotion . . . his unselfishness. He was a man who gave completely of himself, and she loved him for that and for many other reasons she couldn't even name.

The night darkened more, if that were possible. They watched the stars for a while—glittering diamonds against black velvet. Presently they rose. Caleb strode across the porch and lifted the lantern from its nail. As he held it next to him, Laura saw hunger narrow his dark eyes.

He offered his hand. She touched her fingertips to his, smiling, teasing, then slid them across his open palm, finally placing her hand in his.

Laura's heart raced as she and Caleb deserted the porch for the barn, where an inviting pile of hay awaited. By the time he hung the lantern on a nail inside the barn and turned, Laura had already unbuttoned half of her bodice buttons.

She caught her breath as Caleb swept her hands aside, unbuttoned the remaining buttons, then slid the dress over her shoulders and let it slip to the ground.

❄ ❄ ❄
Chapter Twenty-two

THE NEXT AFTERNOON Caleb piled three benches for the new school in the back of the wagon, then lifted Laura and Amanda up to the wagon seat. Once they were settled, he climbed up, took the reins, and soon the wagon rattled away from the farm, heading toward Plum Valley and Minot.

"Ever eaten a crab apple, Amanda?" Caleb asked. The horses plod steadily on as the prairie grass dipped and swayed under a bright, shimmering sun.

"No," Amanda said without stuttering. Laura smiled. Amanda's speech was slowly improving. She didn't speak in sentences yet, but at least she was talking, and the simple words she said now and then and the way she said them could certainly be viewed as progress.

"Mmmm . . . crab apples. Haven't had one in years. Use to have them all the time when I was a boy. I had a horse I taught to stand real still. I'd climb on his back, stand up, and pick crab apples. I'd let them drop on the ground, then I'd jump down and me and that horse would share them. I'll have to go back to Illinois someday just to get you some crab apples."

He began humming a song. When they reached Plum Valley, the hum turned into a whistle, the whistle into lyrics. The wagon passed the churchyard and the train depot, where a train was stopped at the platform and people spilled out of the various cars.

"As a-down the moss-grown wood path, where the cattle love to roam . . . From an August evening party . . . I was seeing Nelly home," Caleb boomed as the wagon started past the telegraph office.

Andy Cecil, the telegraph operator, was sitting in a chair

outside the little building. He had a newspaper in front of his face, but Laura didn't miss the way he lowered one corner and grinned at Caleb's back as the wagon eased past. Laura frowned. But Caleb had said Mr. Cecil was deaf . . . and she had gone with Caleb that day to the telegraph office. Caleb had slammed a ledger down on the counter there, and Mr. Cecil hadn't heard it.

As Laura stared at Mr. Cecil, he winked. Suddenly she knew the jest had been on Caleb for however long he had known Andy Cecil and had thought the man was deaf. Andy Cecil *chose* when to hear and when not to hear.

Laura turned and looked straight ahead, trying to arrange her expression so that if Caleb glanced her way, he didn't see that she was amused by something. She would keep this little secret between herself and Mr. Cecil. She wouldn't tell Caleb what she had discovered, since he made a habit of visiting the telegraph office simply to tease Mr. Cecil. But she hoped she would be with Caleb to see his expression the day he discovered that Andy Cecil had simply been ignoring him all this time.

Just past the telegraph office Laura saw Blake Kincaid riding toward them. Amanda edged closer to Laura, who held her hand. Blake was looking at Amanda with an expression of surprise on his face.

Caleb reined the horses, and the wagon slowed. Blake and his horse stopped near Caleb.

"Afternoon," Blake said.

Caleb returned the greeting. Laura hoped the sheriff hadn't said anything to Blake about the land.

Blake shifted. "Amanda looks good, real good."

"She's doing fine, Blake," Caleb said.

"Was just getting some things for the trip," Blake said. "I'm taking the missus and the younguns and going home."

Caleb drew his brows together. "Where's home?"

"Ohio. Got people there. Thought I could come here, get some land, and make something good of it. Ain't working out that way. I'll pull in the crop, sell it for what I can get, then head out."

Laura wondered if Blake meant to take Amanda with

him—she was his daughter after all. But he had never really cared about her. She had been left to fend for herself. He hadn't wanted to take care of her, yet he hadn't wanted anyone else to try to take care of her, either. Surely he didn't think he could step in now, take Amanda back, and assume everything would be fine. No . . . Laura closed her eyes. She wouldn't let him take Amanda. She wouldn't. She opened her eyes and glanced at Caleb, who was studying Blake. "Mr. Kincaid—"

"No, Laura," Caleb said gently. "It takes years to get much back from the land, Blake, you know that."

"Ain't got the patience of most, Caleb. I'm going back. Others have done it. You've seen 'em. They come, try to work the land for a spell, then head out. I've spent two winters out on that prairie. Ain't spending another one."

Caleb inhaled deeply. "I reckon you have to do what you think you need to do."

"That I do. That I do," Blake said, lowering his voice with the last few words. There was silence for a few moments as Blake looked at Amanda again. Laura fought the urge to put an arm around Amanda and pull her close. He couldn't be thinking of taking Amanda. He couldn't—

"Been thinking 'bout Amanda there," he said, and Laura jumped slightly. "Been thinking she ought to stay right here with you, Caleb, if you'll have her, that is. It'd be till she's grown. We never knew what—"

"That would probably be the best thing for Amanda, Blake," Caleb said quickly.

Kincaid nodded. Laura exhaled a breath of relief she hadn't realized she had been holding. Blake gazed off in the direction of the telegraph office and the train station and platform.

"Well . . . reckon I'll be letting you get on."

"Take care of yourself, Blake," Caleb said.

"I'll do that." And with that, Kincaid tapped the sides of his horse and rode on.

Laura, Caleb, and Amanda sat in silence for a few moments. Laura realized she had tears in her eyes, tears of relief and joy. She glanced at Caleb and found his head lowered slightly. When he lifted his head, he grinned, but the color was just coming back into his face.

"You were thinking the same thing I was, weren't you?" she asked.

"I damn sure was."

She squeezed his hand and put her arm around Amanda. "It's fine," she said. "Everything is fine."

The wagon began moving again. It rattled past saloons, Warner's Mercantile, more saloons, and Alman's Dry Goods. Finally it stopped in front of the sheriff's office.

Caleb lifted Amanda, then Laura. He narrowed his eyes at her and asked, "Sure you want to do this?"

She nodded. "In a few days we'll go see the families and arrange to make everything legal. I want them to have part of the land."

Her business in the sheriff's office took only moments. With Caleb at her side Laura stood before the sheriff's desk and asked to see the paper he had brought to the farm only yesterday morning. He furrowed his heavy brows but withdrew the paper from a desk drawer and handed it to her. Laura shredded it and experienced immense satisfaction as shock flickered in the sheriff's eyes. She let the pieces slip through her fingers and scatter on his desk.

"Now, then," she said, dusting her hands, "you and I will rest better, Sheriff."

Then she turned and left the office with Caleb and Amanda.

Once they were outside, Caleb chuckled. "I've never seen Zeke's mouth hang open like that."

"He was certain I meant to deprive those people of their homes and the land some of them have spent years working," Laura said. "Despite what I just did, he'll probably still look at me suspiciously now and then. I'm glad I don't need to convince you that I'm not heartless."

Caleb shook his head. "Out here a person hears stories, Laura, stories that have a lot of truth in them. The Homestead Act is supposed to help settlers get western land, but it's not doing much good. The railroads bought some, big landowners bought some, not just in Dakota, but everywhere. If the landowners don't buy it up, they try to get it in other ways—legal and illegal. Unfortunately Matt was one of those big landowners. When Zeke realized who you were, he probably had some of the same thoughts I did. But he's a fair man. When he came to the farm yesterday, he never thought you'd do something like you just did. He'll wander out in a few days and apologize. And when he learns you want to take that teaching job, I reckon he'll be telling everyone in the valley and on the prairie around here what a good woman you are.

"What a good woman that Caleb Main's gone and married," he said, grinning.

❄ ❄ ❄
Epilogue

Bismarck, Dakota Territory
July 1888

THE DIARIES.

There were five in all, stacked neatly in Matthew Kent's desk drawer. The covers on the older ones were cracked in places, mostly around the edges and on the bindings. Laura removed one of the older diaries from the desk and skimmed her fingertips over the worn leather. She glanced around Pa's sitting room, at the elegant chairs with smooth polished arms, the carpet patterned in squares of green and brown, the huge fireplace, and the leather-upholstered wing-back chair. He had sat there many times, she knew, while reading and perhaps even while writing in these diaries.

She had walked through the entire house, had stood silently in the long hall upstairs, where she had been that day when he had found her, grabbed her hand, and pulled her downstairs and outside to show her the new horse he had bought for her.

She had stood in the huge parlor and cried, remembering how, as a young girl, she had spent many evenings on his lap, and he had told her stories—"Laura stories," he had called them. They were not recorded in books anywhere. He had made them all up, and they were truly her stories. They were in her heart, every detail, and she had already told many of them to Amanda and would tell them again and again over the years to her other children and to her grandchildren.

Her hand rested on one of the diaries she had lifted from the drawer. She tapped it, then put it back in the drawer.

335

She wouldn't read the diaries. Whatever was written in them, good or bad, she didn't want to know, didn't need to know. She had her memories of Pa locked in her heart. She had even managed to forgive him for trying to marry her to Adrian. Dear Pa. He had gone about the arrangements in his usual businesslike fashion. He had loved her, she knew that. He hadn't wanted to hurt her. He had been trying to do what he had thought was best for her. She believed that. She had to believe that.

She didn't know what he had written about Caleb in the diaries, and she didn't care to know. But neither could she destroy them. She would lock them away—she would ask Mr. Trumball's associate to take care of doing that—and her children could have them when they were grown, if they wanted them. But she would ask that they respect her wishes that she not ever know what was written in them.

She closed the drawer and walked out of the sitting room. She moved down the tiled hall to another, smaller hall, one that led outside. And once outside, she followed the path that led to the office.

Bushes still flanked the path, hovering close to the ground. The honeysuckle vine was untouched, curving and stretching to mingle in the bushes. The sweet blooms perfumed the air. Pa's office was a little farther down the path.

The elm draped its well-dressed branches over one corner of the small building. Laura wandered over to touch the huge, rough trunk of the tree. She sat on the shaded grass for a while, taking her time, for now she was truly saying goodbye to Pa. She wasn't sad anymore, not now. She had spilled her tears in the house, and now she truly just needed to say goodbye.

Soon she stood and walked up to the porch steps. There, where she had stopped and turned back so many times before, she mounted the steps, grabbed the doorknob, and pushed the door open.

A thin film of dust covered everything—the desk, the chair behind it, the books lining shelves to the right, even the painting of a proud thoroughbred that hung on the wall to her left. Instead of seeing Pa on the floor as she had found him that morning so long ago, Laura concentrated on remembering the many times Pa had sat on the edge of the desk here and talked to her.

He had more of a presence here than at his grave. She had already been there. She had stood in that bleak cemetery, had stared at the stone that marked his grave. His body might be in the ground there, but his spirit was here. So she spoke to him.

She told him she had decided not to marry Adrian, that she had met and married someone else. She told him about Caleb, that he was a good man and that she was happy with him, joyously happy. That's all Pa had ever wanted for her anyway—happiness. She told him about Amanda and Ruth and Stacey and Minot and Plum Valley and the prairie.

And when she finished, she said goodbye.

Then she walked out of the office and shut the door.

With Laura and Amanda seated next to him, Caleb maneuvered the wagon through the crowd assaulting Bismarck's Main Street. People were drifting out of buildings and homes—ladies in colorful dresses and bonnets, men in white shirts and brown and black coats, some looking important wearing hats and sporting walking sticks. An odd-looking contraption on the other side of the street headed toward the wagon, a contraption with two huge thin wheels on either side, a tiny wheel in front, and an extended bar and a medium-size wheel out back. A man and a woman were sitting between the huge wheels. Strangest thing Caleb had ever seen. He tightened his hold on the reins. "What the hell—?"

"It's a bicycle, Caleb," Laura said in a tone that said, "Calm down now, just calm down."

"How do they even stay on the thing and keep it upright?"

"Practice." Laura laughed, repositioning herself. "They're becoming quite popular."

"I bet it's fun," Amanda said, smiling.

"I'd just as soon ride a horse or a wagon," Caleb said.

Amanda giggled now. "You're just scared of it."

"I am not!" he shot back indignantly.

"You are. Someday I'm going to ride one. Then I'll show you how to ride, Caleb."

"No, you won't."

"I'll ride it with you, then, Amanda," Laura said, drawing her close. Except for her limp and her paralyzed arm, Amanda had made tremendous progress in the past ten months. She only stuttered when nervous or angry. She took great pride in helping with everyday chores around the farm, despite her useless arm, and she was learning at an astounding rate. She had mastered the alphabet, could spell her name and others. She could even cipher some. And of course she whistled a lot, things like "Camptown Races," and "Seein' Sweet Nellie Home." She was so totally different from the little girl who had appeared in the barn one morning so long ago that Laura sometimes shook her head in wonderment.

"Not for a spell, you won't," Caleb warned Laura, talking about the bicycle.

Laura laughed again. Of course, she knew why he was being so protective now. Not only did he love her, but there was more *of* her to love, she thought, touching her slightly protruding stomach. Sometime during November, there would be a new little Main running around the farm. Laura thought of the smile that had lit Amanda's face when she had told her, and the whoop of happiness Stacey had given. Ruth had had tears in her eyes. Caleb . . . well, she and Caleb had been standing on the porch steps, watching the always beautiful crimson Dakota sunset over the prairie. She had told him her news, and he had nearly stumbled down the steps. He had been fussing over her ever since, sometimes bringing her fresh milk, shooing her off to bed long before everyone else, and sometimes . . . sometimes crawling into bed with her and splaying his hand on her belly, trying to feel the new life within.

"Don't worry, Caleb. I'm not quite brave enough to ride a bicycle right now," she told him.

"Just as well," he mumbled.

The crowd stirred, mingling, conversing, shouting, laughing, scurrying, strolling. Excitement was in the air. Awnings on some of the buildings were decorated with ribbons of red, white, and blue. The wagon rattled past a group of outrageously clothed and painted clowns with big red noses and huge floppy shoes. One raised and blasted a gold horn at Caleb, then doubled over in silent laughter and slapped his knee as if he'd just done the funniest thing in his life. Caleb grinned and shook his head. Amanda giggled so hard that Laura thought she might fall off the wagon seat.

"Are you aware, Mr. Main," Laura said, smiling at the clown's antics, too, "that we passed the jail, and you never even glanced at it?"

Caleb's grin faded. He lifted a brow. "I'll be damned. I didn't even see it. Thought I'd be all scared and I didn't even see it. The house didn't bother me too much, either. Guess it doesn't matter anymore, does it?"

She squeezed his arm as people settled on both sides of the street, and the faint sound of music touched her ears. It was a celebration, but there was a much bigger celebration occurring in her heart.

"No . . . I guess it doesn't," she said. "The past really doesn't matter anymore."

Author's Historical Note

Laura's aunt lived in Kenmare approximately six years earlier than settlers began drifting there. But for the sake of this story, we'll pretend Kenmare was already there. As readers, we never actually went there or met Aunt Rebecca, but we can still pretend we did.

Plum Valley. That's what the Indians called the valley Minot lies in. At one time it was filled with plum trees. Not anymore, I'm afraid. But, while writing this story, I closed my eyes many times and saw the valley as the characters saw it. Laura falls in love with it. So if it seems more dressed up than it probably was at the time, that's why.